THE NIGHT ANGEL

This Large Print Book carries the
Seal of Approval of N.A.V.H.

HEIRS OF ACADIA BOOK 4

THE NIGHT ANGEL

T. DAVIS BUNN
ISABELLA BUNN

THORNDIKE PRESS

An imprint of Thomson Gale, a part of The Thomson Corporation

Detroit • New York • San Francisco • New Haven, Conn. • Waterville, Maine • London

THOMSON
GALE

LIBRARY OF CONGRESS CATALOGING-IN-PUBLICATION DATA

Bunn, T. Davis, 1952–
    The night angel / by T. Davis Bunn, Isabella Bunn.
      p. cm. — (Thorndike Press large print Christian historical fiction) (Heirs of Acadia ; 4)
    ISBN-13: 978-0-7862-9589-0 (alk. paper)
    ISBN-10: 0-7862-9589-9 (alk. paper)
    1. Acadians — Fiction. 2. Richmond (Va.) — Fiction. 3. Large type books.
I. Bunn, Isabella. II. Title.
PS3552.U4718N54 2007
813'.54—dc22   2007006090

Published in 2007 by arrangement with Bethany House Publishers.

Printed in the United States of America on permanent paper
10 9 8 7 6 5 4 3 2 1

For my sister,
Bunny Matthews,
who has helped me appreciate
the artist's technique
and spirit

CHAPTER 1

March 1834

John Falconer watched the line of people on the ridge, silhouetted against a leaden sky. When he heard the clank of chains, he knew. He made out a dozen figures locked together. A horseman ambled behind them, reins held loosely in one hand. A leather quirt was tied to the rider's other wrist and rested upon the saddle. The rider wore a low-brim hat that masked his eyes. But Falconer knew the rider watched the chained group with a predator's gaze.

The sun finally managed to pierce the clouds. A golden lance fell upon one of the chained men. His face became illuminated, as though touched by the finger of God.

The chained man turned then. He looked straight at Falconer.

And spoke his name aloud.

Falconer rose from his bed and slipped into

his clothes. The actions gave his hands something to do while his heart resumed a normal pace. Moonlight fell through his window, illuminating a room far too cramped for his massive frame. He lit a candle and watched the sputtering flame for a time, sorting through the dream's images.

For years after coming to faith, Falconer had awoken to dread images and drenching sweats. But this dream had been no nightmare. In fact, as he listened to his breathing steady, he felt something else entirely. Despite how the image linked Falconer to his own tragic past, he felt neither sorrow nor dismay. Instead, he felt exhilarated. What was more, he found himself wondering if perhaps the dream had carried some form of divine message.

Falconer seated himself at the narrow table and read his Bible by candlelight. He had no idea of the hour, though he knew it was very late. The church towers stopped counting the hours at eleven. His eye caught sight of his reflection in the window opposite his little table. The window was filled with his bulk, like a dark-haired beast caught in a narrow cage door. The candlelight flickered, making the scar that ran up the left side of his face writhe like a serpent. He traced the scar with one finger and wished his outsize frame was merely due to the window's uneven glass. In truth, he carried a fighter's look about him. No wonder Alessandro and Bettina Gavi were so alarmed about his affection for their daughter, Serafina.

Falconer folded his hands over the open Book and lowered his head. He presented his midnight prayer, faltering and terse. But Falconer had come to believe firmly in God's ability to look beyond his awkward words and see the heart's message. And his heart was sore indeed.

His first few words were a request for clarity over the dream's image. From there he wandered far. It was difficult for a strong man to face the helpless moment. And Falconer was trapped by his love for Serafina.

When he lifted his head, the candle's glow drew Serafina's image in the window beside Falconer's reflection. Hair the color of winter wheat framed a perfect face, palest lips, and eyes of captured sky. Her father was a Venetian merchant prince, her mother from the Italian Alps. She was rich, she was lovely, and she trusted him so fully he felt crippled by wants and needs he feared she would never share.

He shut his eyes again and rested his forehead upon his hands. Hands made for sword and pike and pistol. Fists so powerful they could punch through a solid oak door, and had done so more than once. Folded now in prayer, turned from violence and wrath by the miracle of salvation. *Father, I am the worst of sinners and the least of all. I have no right to ask you for anything more. Not after you have given me the greatest gift of eternity. Yet ask I must. For I am as power-less as ever I have been. Is there any hope that my love for Serafina might be returned? Flawed and sinful as I am, might I ever know the gift of a wife and family? Give me a sign, Lord. For the days lay empty before me and the nights rest heavy on my heart. Give me a sign.*

Then the knock came upon his door.

Falconer rose slowly. "Who goes there?"

"It is I" came the urgent whisper.

His heart surged. Was this his sign? "One moment." Falconer lifted his eyes to the ceiling close overhead and let his exultation surge in one silent shout. Then he stepped into his boots and opened the door.

Serafina stood before him. Beside her was Mary, the traveling companion from England who had remained as Serafina's maid. Both were dressed in the hurried fashion of having reached for clothes in the dark. Mary appeared terrified, continually throwing glances back down the servants' hallway.

Serafina, however, showed Falconer only steadfast trust. "I saw men. Three of them. With guns."

Falconer moved to his desk and swiftly blew out the candle. He drew the door shut behind them. "Tell me everything," he said, keeping his voice low.

"Something woke me. A sound perhaps. I'm not sure," Serafina began.

"I heard it too," Mary whispered.

"You were fast asleep. I heard you breathing."

"I heard it clear as the nose on my face, miss. I tell you —"

Falconer halted the disagreement with a touch to Mary's arm. "You heard a sound. What then?"

"I moved to the window and saw three men."

"Were you spotted?"

"No. I had crawled across the floor and came up slowly by the glass."

He repressed his smile. "Good girl."

Nonetheless Mary caught his amusement. "How you can find anything humorous in this affair, good sir, is beyond my understanding."

"Tell me about the men."

"Three, as I said. One very tall. The other

11

two thicker and shorter. I saw something in the moonlight. The tall man moved, and I saw he carried a musket. We came to you because they stood between our cottage and my parents' apartment."

The previous summer, when Falconer had brought Serafina to Washington, they had found Alessandro and Bettina Gavi residing in an apartment at the rear of the Austrian legate's manor. The building fronted Pennsylvania Avenue, with six large official chambers stretching along the street. But the apartment assigned to the Gavis contained only three rooms — kitchen, parlor, and cramped bedroom. Serafina and her maid had been assigned a chamber in the manor's rear cottage. Falconer had been given a room in the servants' wing, across the courtyard from the Gavis' apartment. Which meant he was effectively isolated from both Serafina and her parents. This arrangement caused him no end of concern. Especially when the rumors began swirling.

Falconer was treated as just another guest's hired man, only larger and potentially more lethal. Few of the legate's entourage even bothered to learn his name. He slipped about, he scouted, and he listened. That week, Falconer began hearing belowstairs rumors that Alessandro Gavi was marked for destruction.

Falconer repeatedly warned Serafina's father. But Alessandro Gavi was a diplomat by training and by nature, which meant he preferred to take a course of action only when everyone was in accord. Falconer wanted them moved to a private home, where they could be more protected. But when approached, the legate insisted that Alessandro and his family were his honored guests. Alessandro dithered, hoping to move only with his legate's blessing.

Falconer pushed open the servants' exit, motioning for the women to remain well back. The door was at the base of the rear stairs, connected to Serafina's cottage by a narrow brick path. The moon was hidden behind scuttling clouds. The March night was cold and very quiet.

Falconer searched in every direction and saw nothing. But his well-honed senses felt danger lurking close by. He was at full alert as he drew Serafina forward. Quiet as a breeze he whispered, "Where did you spot them?"

She pointed at the likeliest spot for an attack. "There."

Falconer's eyes searched the dark reaches, trying to discern human legs. But it was futile. He backed away and silently shut the door. "We'll go around the front."

Mary protested, "But, sir, I'm forbidden from entering the main rooms."

"As am I. Come along, swiftly now." In fact, Falconer had never entered the formal chambers. They were said to be very grand, not that Falconer cared. He hurried the two ladies down the narrow servants' corridor and through the swinging doors at the end. Down a connecting hall they sped, committed now. Past the kitchens and through another pair of swinging doors, which led into the dining salon. The doors swished softly over the polished marble floor, and one squeaked quietly as it closed. Falconer heard footsteps in the distance, undoubtedly a guard. He hissed softly, "Fly!"

Serafina took the lead. She had been through these chambers often enough, drawn into public view at the legate's insistence. Prince Fritz-Heinrich was a minor prince in the Hapsburg Empire and a tyrant within his own household. He had been known to fly into an uncontrollable rage over a singed roast. The front salons were treated as a distant reflection of the palace in Vienna, and guards were ordered to shoot intruders on sight.

Had they not been in such a scramble, Falconer might have spared a second glance at what they passed. For here on Pennsylvania Avenue stood a sample of royal grandeur. The central hall was a full eighty feet long, the ceiling three stories high and domed. They raced beneath a forest of crystal chandeliers.

"Who goes there!" came a shout behind them.

"Faster," Falconer said.

"Halt!"

Serafina pushed through the connecting doorway to the side passage. Mary's face was stretched tight with terror. No doubt the servants who worked the front rooms regaled their fellows with tales of what awaited those who trespassed. Behind them they heard the clipped sound of leather-clad feet. Then came a sharper sound, one Falconer knew all too well — the metallic click of a percussion rifle being cocked.

Falconer slipped through the hall door and halted just inside. He tensed as the footsteps raced toward them. When the door began to swing inward, Falconer applied all his strength in the opposite direction. The door hammered back, smashing hard against the oncoming guard. Falconer continued straight through, his fists at the ready. But the door had caught the guard square in the forehead and knocked him back a dozen paces. Falconer bent over the supine form, saw he was breathing but unconscious, and relieved the man of his weapon.

He hurried down the side hall and outside to find the two women clutching each other outside the Gavis' apartment door. "Why did you not enter?"

"I left my key in the cottage," Serafina whispered.

Falconer did not want to knock and then bandy about with who goes there and why and all else that others might hear. Instead, he gripped the knob with one fist, readied himself, and heaved.

There was a short sharp crack, and the lock wrenched free of the doorframe. "Inside."

He stepped into the small parlor and fitted the door back into place. Hopefully the damage would be missed in a hurried midnight inspection. "Go wake your parents, lass. Urge them to make haste."

Mary asked, "Shall I light a fire and make tea?"

"There isn't time." Falconer moved to the window. The moon remained shrouded. He could see nothing save light from one window across the courtyard.

Mary pulled the drapes shut and lit one

candle. Falconer shifted one corner of the curtains and kept surveying the courtyard until Serafina returned with her parents.

Alessandro Gavi hurried into the front parlor, wrapping a quilted robe about his frame, his face still rumpled with sleep. His wife followed close behind, looking both confused and frightened.

Falconer silently watched the candlelight waver over the faces of the three Gavis as Serafina continued her explanation of events. Gradually his exultation over Serafina's appearance at his doorway evaporated. In its place was an ache so deep he could hardly breathe. He saw now that his prayerful request for a sign had been answered. Not by Serafina's arrival, as he had first thought. Instead, by the very grave concern he saw in Alessandro and Bettina Gavi's expressions.

The months together with this family had shown him one thing above all else. Serafina would never defy her parents' wishes again. All her early troubles had started through rebellion. She was determined now to honor her family. This she had said over and over.

In this moment Falconer understood why she had repeated the words so often.

As though to emphasize his bewilderment,

Alessandro Gavi finally spoke in English. "I do not understand. You went first to this man and not to me?"

This man. Falconer had saved his daughter's honor. He had sheltered her in a transatlantic voyage. He had reunited her with her parents. Yet here in this moment of danger, he remained *this man.*

Bettina Gavi must have seen Falconer's distress, for she spoke quietly to her husband in Italian. Alessandro tried to recover by adding, "Not that we are ungrateful for your kind assistance, good sir. We remain in your debt. But you must see, after all, I am her father."

"I sought his protection," Serafina replied, her forehead creased in confusion. "Was I wrong?"

"No, daughter." Bettina Gavi gripped her husband's hand and squeezed. "Your father was merely concerned over, how do you say, *decoro?*"

"Decorum," her daughter supplied.

"Exactly. After all, it is — what time is it, Alessandro?"

"My pocket watch is back in the bedroom. But very late." Alessandro Gavi might have been sleepy, but he had a diplomat's smooth ways. "Sir, I of course meant no offense."

Falconer knew he was expected to respond

in kind. But here and now, raw from his desperate nighttime prayer, he saw his answer upon display. The three of them formed a silent tableau, a message as clear as fiery words scripted upon the dawn sky.

Serafina turned not to him, but to her parents. Her parents stood to either side of their daughter, seeking to shield her from the closest present danger. John Falconer, the man they needed, yet feared.

Had Serafina herself shown a desperate love for him, perhaps they might be swayed. Yet she was still recovering from the previous summer's trauma. Her own heart had been sorely wounded. She was truly fond of him, he was sure, and would call him friend all her days. But when her heart healed, her parents would seek another's hand. Someone appropriate for their station. And Serafina would yield to their request.

Falconer felt a burning behind his eyes. He turned back toward the draped window, mentally picturing nothing save a bleak and empty night. He muttered, "I must depart."

"Excuse me, good sir, did you speak?"

Falconer's fists clenched at his sides as he clamped down on a sorrow that writhed and bucked and sought to bring him down. It was a silent struggle, one that no one else noticed. And he won.

He turned to face the four of them. "We must depart. Now."

"What, in the middle of the night? You can't —"

"Think on this, sir. Think carefully. Your daughter saw attackers. Whether they were after you, we can only guess. But I cannot protect you here. Do you understand what I am saying? I cannot protect you or your daughter. You are entrusting the legate with securing your family's safety."

"He is right, Alessandro." Bettina's face was drawn with growing concern. "What if the legate was behind this?"

"He would not dare have me attacked on his own property!"

"Lower your voice, husband." Bettina Gavi took daily instruction from an English tutor. Her abilities were growing steadily, but her accent remained very heavy, particularly now when she was so afraid. "Have you not yourself said the legate seeks to make trouble with the Americans? He could attack us, then accuse the American authorities of being unable to protect their foreign guests even inside their capital."

Rapid action went against the diplomat's nature. "But where would you expect us to go in the middle of the night?"

"A hotel."

Alessandro Gavi wrung his hands. When dressed in his official finery and stationed in the halls of power, he cut a dignified figure. Now, in the depths of a night masked by cloud and fear, his hair a tangle and his movements nervous, he looked frail and aging. "Whatever will the legate think?"

"If you wait and ask permission, he might refuse." Falconer found every word an effort. "If you go and explain on the morrow, it is a deed already done."

Gavi offered Falconer reluctant approval. "You are right. Of course. Very well. We must pack."

"No time." Falconer straightened, as though easing his back. But the internal struggle could only be quashed by motion. "Tomorrow you will send me back with a message for the legate. Mary and I will then fetch your possessions. We must leave now. Before the guard in the formal chambers awakens and raises the alarm."

"I'm sorry, what?"

"Never mind." Falconer motioned toward the door. "Take only what you can carry easily. We leave in five minutes."

"But —"

"Hurry."

CHAPTER 2

Prince Fritz-Heinrich von Hapsburg, nephew of the Austrian emperor, possessed a remarkable example of the royal nose. An uncharitable person might have said that the prince's snout was made for looking down on those around him, and for sniffing his disdain. Both of which the prince did altogether too often.

"Make way there."

Falconer stepped to one side. A liveried attendant in powdered wig and brocaded frock coat led a trio of servants into the grand salon. The doors were opened by two guards, also in full Hapsburg livery. When the doors swung shut behind the small group, Falconer pretended to relax against the back wall.

A man sidled up beside him. Gerald Rivens was the prince's junior coach driver. Gerald had been stepping out with Mary, Serafina's maid. They were often seated in the servants' gallery at the church Falconer attended. A bit of the rough trade was Falconer's initial impression of the man. But Falconer had no problem with those from society's underclass. It was, after all, his own birthright as well.

Gerald asked quietly, "You mind a word?"

Falconer responded by making room for Gerald to join him against the wall. Gerald planted his tricorn hat upon his chest, as though respectfully awaiting a summons. It was a common practice among the prince's servants, adopting positions that suggested they were busy with duties even when idle.

Gerald said, "Mary won't tell me where you've got the family holed up."

Falconer nodded acceptance of the news, well pleased to learn his orders were being carried out.

"Don't blame you," Gerald went on. He pitched his voice low and kept his eyes focused on the closed doors across from them. "I've noticed signs of strangers in the night."

Falconer glanced over. The man was narrow in all the ways that mattered. His face pinched downward to a slit of a nose. His gaze was tight and cautious. Though his frame looked slight, he carried himself with the taut muscles and wariness of one who had survived his share of battles.

Falconer murmured back, "What is your weapon of choice?"

Gerald looked at him and smiled with the knowing grin of one who understood everything that Falconer had left unsaid. "I don't walk those ways anymore."

"I've seen you at church."

"Aye, I came crawling up to the cross a few years back. Accepted my salvation on the only terms that mattered. Empty-handed, broken and needy."

"I like those words," Falconer replied. "Especially when spoken by a man who knows his way about a fight."

"Like I said, I've left the dark paths behind." Gerald turned his attention back to the shut doors with their gilded crests and nodded slowly. "But in a former life, I was partial to the blade."

Falconer nodded also, accepting the smaller man's gift of trust. "You were speaking of attackers?"

"Don't know who they were. But I had a careful look around the day after you slipped away. There were footprints between the cottages and the stable."

"Mary told you where Serafina had seen the figures?"

"That she did. Which was why I went to

have a look for myself. I spied three sets of footprints. And a bit of slow match. You understand?"

"Musket," Falconer replied with another nod. A slow match was a means of firing an old-fashioned weapon. Since the advent of percussion caps, slow matches were used less and less. But the hand-crafted guns of old were still used by marksmen who sought accuracy above all. "Assassin."

Gerald drew his mouth down. "Mary said you had a history of your own."

"I once considered myself a better man than some because I had never played the pirate," Falconer confessed. "Fool that I was."

"I've come to feel the only difference between a strong man and a weak one is the color of the lies he tells himself," Gerald agreed.

Falconer turned to look squarely at the man. "It's a pleasure to make your acquaintance, brother." He offered Gerald his hand and dropped his voice to a whisper. "You'll find Mary at Brown's Indian Queen Hotel for another few days."

Gerald's grip held surprising force for such slender bones. "After that?"

"We've rented a house on Lafayette Square."

Gerald seemed reluctant to let go of Falconer's hand. "Does Master Gavi have his full accompaniment of servants?"

"The Gavis have no need of a full-time carriage driver. But a trusted man who could serve as family guard would be most welcome."

"What of yourself?"

"I am soon to be called away."

The doors across the hall swept open. A royal attendant stepped out, his chin held so far back he could look both up at Falconer and down his nose. "John Falconer, your presence is required."

As Falconer stepped forward, Gerald said softly, "I'm your man."

Serafina stood a pace behind and to one side of her parents. The aristocrats and a few petitioners formed two long arms down either side of the formal chamber. The hall was large, imposing, and very cold. No amount of burning fires or sunlight could warm the atmosphere.

The royal gathering took place each Saturday afternoon, a chance for the titled and near-titled Europeans to gather, play court to one another, and pretend a superiority to the Americans they could only feel when surrounded by their own.

26

Prince Fritz-Heinrich was seated on a raised French chair at the salon's far end. The chair back was as tall as a man and imprinted with the Hapsburg seal in gold leaf. A trio of musicians sat in the far corner, their instruments at the ready, awaiting a sign from the majordomo. The courtiers were mostly European, for not many Americans had the patience to put up with Fritz-Heinrich's associates and their affected ways. That was one of the things Serafina had learned since her arrival in America. Even the most powerful Americans did not care to flaunt their authority. Such mannerisms were seen as shades of the past they had cast off with their Declaration of Independence.

This meant only two types of Americans joined in such formal assemblies. Some were operators, as they were known here. Smelling of hair oil and greed, they weaseled their way in to further their nefarious profit schemes.

Others were there by order of someone more powerful. These diplomats were easy to identify, for they were the only ones all in black, carrying stovepipe hats at their sides. Desperately eager to be gone, they stood in stiff isolation, awaiting their turn before the dais.

Serafina was one of the few ladies in the chamber who did not wear a powdered white wig. Her blond hair was covered with a short white mantilla. From behind her lacy screen, Serafina studied the gathering. Once they had returned to the hotel she intended to work on several drawings of these people and the royal setting. And as ever, Mary would beg for every scrap of detail about what she had observed.

Before crossing the Atlantic with Serafina, Mary had been in service at the household of William Wilberforce. She had used her free Saturdays and Sundays to study in one of the schools Wilberforce had established. He had arranged for space in churches to teach reading, writing, and Bible during times the sanctuaries were not in use. For many of those from Mary's social class, it was their only opportunity for proper schooling. Mary's ambition was to become a private secretary. She had accepted the offer to travel to America as a step toward leaving the restrictive British class system behind.

Serafina's Venetian parents, as warm-hearted and tolerant as they were, couldn't help but be concerned with the casual friendship between Serafina and the woman they viewed as merely their daughter's maid. Serafina did not try to explain that Mary had initially been Serafina's only female companion her own age. Serafina was gradually making new friends at church, but she saw that as no reason to give up someone she had come to call a friend.

Mary responded with a quiet intimacy that revealed many things normally unseen by someone of Serafina's standing. Mary knew that Serafina, in the dark days after discovering her lover was both a scoundrel and a liar, had served as chambermaid in an English Wiltshire manor. The result was that Mary treated Serafina in two distinct manners. In public, she was the demure and silent maid. In private, Mary revealed a wit and intelligence that was hidden to Serafina's parents. Serafina often reflected on these secret times, noting how much was lost by being imprisoned within wealth and social standing.

One of the confidences Mary had shared with Serafina had been the rather obvious fact that Prince Fritz-Heinrich was not well loved among his staff. Quite the contrary.

Serafina looked again around the hall as the line she was in moved forward. Her parents' turn to be presented to the prince was at hand.

Serafina could feel the legate's gaze upon

her. She kept her eyes firmly fastened upon the marble floor at her feet.

Alessandro Gavi was speaking in High German, as the legate required. "Once again, Highness, I apologize for our swift departure. But —"

"I can hardly accept such an apology, Herr Gavi. It was a serious breach of protocol. Particularly as I personally invited you to remain as my guest."

Serafina's father bowed low. "We have faced dire threats, Highness."

The prince used a few of his sniffs as disdainful punctuation marks. "Where, pray tell? Who is the one who dares suggest that an honored guest would not be safe in my home?" He sat forward in his chair to bore holes in the unfortunate Alessandro Gavi.

"M-my personal aide and guard, sire."

"Show him to me. Is he here?"

"In the hall, Highness. But —"

"Bring him forth immediately!" The legate waved a lace-embroidered handkerchief at his hovering aide. "Have him attend me this instant!"

"He is rather rough-edged, Highness," her father warned.

"What else can one expect from this disorderly and loutish nation. How is he known?"

"John Falconer, Highness."

"A common sort of name." The legate sniffed again and dabbed at his nose with the handkerchief. "Your daughter is with you this day, I see."

"Indeed, Highness."

"Step forward, child. Remove your veil. There, that is better. What is your name again? Forgive me, the pressures of this office . . ."

"Serafina, Highness."

"Of course. Such a delightfully Italian name." Another sniff. "You speak German, I take it."

"Yes, Highness."

"Of course you would. Coming from a proper family, as you do." Though Serafina's gaze remained demurely downward, she could feel the stare from the legate. "Tell me, child, are you betrothed?"

She remained silent.

"Your daughter does not know how to properly answer her superiors, Herr Gavi?"

"She is not betrothed, Highness."

"Is that a fact. And such a lovely flower. Speak, Miss Gavi. Your parents tell me you were ill upon your arrival. You are better now, I trust."

Serafina remembered this was the explanation her parents had given for her not attending court. Now that she stood before the legate, there because they had all been so ordered, Serafina understood why her parents had been desperate to keep her out of sight. "Thank you for your concern, Highness."

"Tell me how you occupy your hours."

"My daughter is an artist, Highness," her father inserted.

"Permit her to answer for herself. An artist, forsooth. Do you paint? Sculpt?"

"I currently work mostly with charcoals or pen and ink, sire. But I also use oils and watercolors."

"Then you must attend me," the legate murmured as the doors at the hall's far end swished open. "I should be ever so grateful for a sample of your skills."

Serafina caught the nuance of the words, enough to bring a flush to her cheeks and draw her focus from the floor. She met the legate's gaze as steadily as she could manage and replied, "I should be honored, Highness." She gave a careful pause, then added, "To sketch or paint your wife."

The legate's features turned to stone. "I see your daughter has inherited her father's impudence."

Alessandro Gavi bowed once more. "We count ourselves among the Austrian court's most loyal citizens."

The man quirked an eyebrow at the absence of the proper address. "Vienna's court," he said meaningfully, "and not my own?"

"We are loyal subjects of the king," Alessandro Gavi replied stolidly.

The prince flicked his fingers and sniffed dismissively as Falconer approached. Serafina curtsied with her mother, and together the three of them backed off a pace.

The prince's aide carried a long staff leafed in gold and tipped with a carved crown. He tapped the marble floor three paces away from the throne, signifying that Falconer was to approach no farther. He announced in English, "John Falconer, Your Highness."

"Indeed." The prince waited. Along with the entire gathering. John Falconer planted himself before the legate, removed his hat and held it to his side, stared back at the man upon the gilded throne, and waited.

The aide snapped, "You shall bow before His Highness."

Falconer turned toward the courtier. Whatever he revealed to the white-wigged man was enough to cause the man to falter, and he swallowed noisily.

The prince sniffed, then spoke in accented

English, "Well, it is scarcely a surprise to meet ruffians in this land who have yet to learn the proper courtesies of a European court. From a nation far older and more civilized —"

"All men are equal in our land" came a retort from down the hall.

The prince flushed with rage. "Who said that? Who?" When the room remained silent, he rose to his feet and cried, "The embassy of a recognized country is *not* your land!"

He glared out over the gathering. When no one responded, he subsided into his throne. Like all the other Europeans, including Serafina's father, Prince Fritz-Heinrich wore the clothing of the Austrian court. His pastel long coat had gold buttons, and his powdered wig was almost as ornate as his embroidered vest. His tight pants, tucked into high boots with tassels of spun gold, revealed a potbelly that the waistcoat could not fully enclose.

Prince Fritz-Heinrich demanded of Falconer, "Well? What do you have to say for yourself?"

"You were the one who asked to see me."

The courtier rapped out, "You will address the prince as sire or Highness!"

Falconer glanced over a second time. He

smiled as he added, "Sire."

Serafina found herself seeing Falconer through the eyes of those gathered. It was not merely his size, though he was perhaps half again as tall as the prince and ten times the man in strength. It was his *presence.* The prince might storm and squall all he wished, but Falconer remained untouched. Falconer was unique, and never had the fact been more evident than here, among this gathering of powdered wigs and ceremonial swords. Falconer was powerful both in body and in spirit. He emanated a force that defied them even when he stood as he did now, silent and grave, his internal musings masked.

"So," the prince finally said. "You claim to have seen danger."

"That is correct." The pause was long enough to turn the next word into a slur. "Sire."

"What was it, then? A masked man? An attacking force?" The legate's sneer was undisguised. "Pirates such as yourself?"

Falconer revealed nothing, neither in voice nor face. "Three armed men outside the guest cottage."

The legate's gaze slid over to rest upon Serafina. "We certainly can't permit such lovely guests as these to come under any threat, now, can we? No matter how mythical the claim, or absurd —"

Falconer stepped forward and slightly toward the Gavis, between the legate and Serafina. "Three men," he repeated. "Armed."

"Here now!" The courtier used his staff to tap the floor between Falconer's feet. "Return to your station!"

Falconer lifted one boot and stomped down upon the staff. The power of his thrust was enough to shatter the staff in two.

The entire hall gasped.

Falconer stepped forward until he towered over the chair. The legate crawled farther into his chair and cried, "Get back, you beast!"

"Three men," Falconer repeated, only now his voice had risen to the level of command. It echoed through the chamber like thunder, like the roll of distant cannons. "And if you are as wise as you would like to claim, you will tell these attackers precisely what I say to you now."

"Are you deaf?" The legate motioned furiously to his courtier. "I *command* you to —"

"You will warn them that if anyone ever seeks to harm these people in my protection, I will hunt them down. I have placed myself under oaths. But I fear I might forget them if ever harm were to come to these three."

Falconer leaned forward closer still. "Those few friends I have will come to no harm on my watch."

He now turned to the Gavis, and for a brief instant Serafina saw the man's power unleashed. She shivered from relief that he did not aim his rage at her. As well as from the knowledge that she had herself caused this fury to come forth.

Falconer motioned quietly for their departure.

Alessandro Gavi bowed toward the throne. "Thank you for your time, Highness."

Serafina curtsied with her mother. No sound was made as they departed, shepherded by Falconer.

Near the back of the room, Serafina observed an American diplomat sweep off his hat at Falconer's passing and give an admiring salute. She was sure the gesture was not lost on the prince, and she shivered again.

CHAPTER 3

Falconer stalked ahead of the Gavi family as he led them back to the hotel. The weather was warm for the first week in March, with a wet wind blowing hard down the length of Pennsylvania Avenue. They could have hailed a passing hackney, but the hotel was visible from the front steps of the legate's manor. Serafina's parents followed behind Falconer, speaking in low, terse fragments. She knew they were worried about her. They had remained uncertain about how to treat her ever since she had joined them in Washington. She knew the relationship had changed dramatically and would never go back to the way it had been. Though it pained her immensely to see their attitude toward Falconer, the only way she knew to improve matters was to be a dutiful daughter.

But she was no longer a child. And what was more important, her parents knew this.

They had seen the measure of her willful nature, the lengths to which she could be driven by passion and supposed love. They feared causing her to break away once more. They had yet to understand the profound changes that had come about during her time away from them. The most significant of those was her coming to faith. The second was her gradual recognition of the unselfish love of a good man, though she could not allow herself to accept it.

Brown's Indian Queen Hotel was considered the finest in all Washington. The seven downstairs parlors were all paneled in oiled cherrywood, with fine carpets, velvet drapes, and plush settees. The walls held portraits of twenty-five Indian chiefs who had stayed in the hotel since 1810, there to meet the president and discuss treaty terms with the American government. Many visitors to Washington stopped by the hotel to admire the unusual collection of portraits and to enjoy a fine meal in the restaurant.

The Gavis had taken a two-bedroom suite that overlooked the Center Market. Serafina's parents, in their brocaded finery and powdered wigs, caused a small stir upon entering the hotel. As they started toward the central staircase, Serafina said, "Please, I must have a word with Falconer."

Her parents shared an anxious look. Her father searched for words. "Are you sure that is wise?"

Serafina saw Falconer step away. A small motion, meaningless save to one who knew him and cared for him. Which she did.

"It is not only wise," she replied, "it is vital."

Falconer said, "I went by this morning and spoke to the agent. Your new house should be ready on Wednesday."

Alessandro Gavi sought to express a genuine gratitude. "You have been so very good to aid us in this manner."

Falconer accepted the words with a stiff nod. "You will take advice?"

"From you? Always."

"There is a man who has been courting Mary, Serafina's maid. Gerald Rivens is his name. I have taken his measure and feel here is one we should trust."

"I shall hire him immediately."

Serafina said to Falconer, "Perhaps it would be best if I first accompanied my parents upstairs, but for a moment only. Would you wait, please?"

"Of course."

Serafina did not speak again until they were in the suite's main parlor. She waited as her parents packed away their wigs. Her father took considerable care over his coat, and her mother fiddled with the pins holding her hair. She knew they were searching for a means of finally saying what had been on their minds for so long.

Serafina returned to their native Italian and said, "Please sit down and allow me to make this easier for you."

"Serafina, my darling . . ."

"Let her speak, Alessandro."

Her father dropped into a chair with a sigh.

"You have every right to be fearful about letting my heart rule my head and choosing the wrong man again. I made such a terrible mistake before, how can you trust me to do better now?" She felt a burning at the back of her eyes but used all her might to suppress the tears. She had cried enough. It was time to move beyond tears.

Her mother seemed to sense Serafina's struggle, for she said, "You have apologized and we have accepted. Enough of that."

"Yes." Serafina wished for a handkerchief, anything to occupy her hands. But there was nothing. She clasped her hands and remained standing before her parents. She took a deep breath and declared, "I do not love John Falconer."

The look her parents shared with each

other was etched with a relief as strong as fear. Serafina hurried on. "I deeply care for him as a friend, as a Christian brother. But I do not love him romantically."

"He loves you," her mother now said. "Very much."

"I have known this since before we left Mr. Wilberforce's home in London. I had hoped that with time I might come to share his love. For I am certain he would make a good husband." She raised her hands to still the protest both parents were ready to offer. "But I will not permit this to happen, for I can see that you do not wish for me to wed him."

"He is . . ." Alessandro Gavi restrained his objections with great effort. He was, after all, a diplomat. "Falconer is a strong ally and a trusted one. But he . . . well . . . Daughter, surely you must see . . ."

"He is not appropriate," Bettina Gavi finished. "He does not suit your background, your station, or your family."

"I will not argue such points with you," Serafina quietly responded. She had wondered for weeks how best to approach the subject and found herself relieved that it was now out in the open. "I will not argue with you over the choice of husband at all. I have sought to go my own way. It almost destroyed us all. It will not happen again."

She could see her parents were taken aback by her declaration. Bettina Gavi recovered first. "You sound so . . . so . . . what can I say? So deliberate, so unemotional."

"Which is exactly how I feel. My heart has been cauterized. At night, when I lie awake and consider my future, or at dawn in my prayers, I wonder if ever I shall be able to fully love a man again. Most times I doubt it very much."

Tears sprang to her mother's eyes. "It breaks my heart to hear you speak so."

"I pray I am wrong. The Scriptures speak of God's power to soothe all such wounds of the heart. But even the apostle Paul carried something that pained him deeply all his life. I wonder if perhaps this is my thorn, if my heart will remain so small that I can only know fondness for a man and nothing more."

"Daughter . . ." Once more her father, normally so ebullient and vocal, looked at a loss for words. "It troubles me to hear you speak so intensely of religion."

"It is not religion, Papa. It is faith. It resides in the core of my being."

He opened his mouth to say more but was halted by his wife's hand settling upon his arm. Bettina asked, "You wish for us to select a husband, my dear?"

"In truth, I would prefer never to marry." Serafina raised her voice to stop the protests before they could be expressed. "But I know this is impossible. So I ask you for more time, in hopes that normal emotions will be restored."

"How much time?"

"I would wish for years if you would grant them. Decades. A lifetime. But I will merely ask for as long as you will grant me, and not a day longer." Again the burning behind her eyes threatened to overwhelm her. This time a single tear did manage to escape, for she knew this agreement would further wound a good and trusted friend. "Now if you will excuse me, I must speak with Falconer."

"Serafina . . ."

She was reluctant to turn back, for she feared her resolve would collapse and she would sob away her control. "Yes?"

But her mother merely said, "Be gentle with him."

John Falconer was not pleased with himself, his station, or his future. All was bleak. He could not even say he had served God well this day. He was sitting in the farthest corner of the hotel lobby, his head leaning against his fists.

He was angry with himself for having spoken and acted so brutishly in the legate's chambers. It did not matter that no one else condemned him. Falconer was harsher with himself than he would ever be with another. Today, though, he truly had erred. No matter how foppish and arrogant the prince might have been, no matter what insinuations he might have cast in Serafina's direction, Falconer knew he had acted irresponsibly and recklessly. His ire had little to do with the legate.

"Commander Falconer?" came a voice above him.

Reluctantly he raised his head and found himself looking at the young man who had doffed his hat as they departed the legate's chamber. "I have never held the honor of such status, sir."

"Might I inquire of your proper rank?"

"Captain, but in the merchant navy only. And that was some time ago."

"Would you mind if I joined you, sir?"

Falconer wished only to be alone. But his solitude offered no comfort. He was moored here in this hotel lobby until Serafina returned. Just as he was anchored to this futile state until she bade him depart.

45

"Sir?"

"Of course." Falconer watched as the young man seated himself across the low table from him.

"Nathan Baring at your service, sir. Might I say how deeply impressed I was with your response to the legate this afternoon."

His shame deepened. "I was wrong in what I said and how I said it, and worse still were my actions."

"On the contrary, sir." The man's admiration was clear in his softly spoken words. "Long have I dreamed of confronting Prince Fritz-Heinrich in just such a manner."

When Falconer merely shook his head in reply, Nathan Baring went on. "Your patron's daughter, did I understand that she is an artist?"

Of course. Now the reason for the young man's enthusiasm came to the fore. Falconer examined him more closely. Nathan Baring was tall, slender, clear of eye, fervent of manner and voice. He was dressed in elegant shades of charcoal gray — striped trousers and diplomat's morning coat, gray silk vest, ruffled cravat. Clean-shaven and dark haired, he was a young man of status and means. Falconer felt utterly common in comparison.

"She is indeed a lovely lass," he said now,

keeping his voice as even as possible.

"Yes, I suppose so." Baring clearly noticed Falconer's astonishment at the words. "I mean no offense, sir. But to be frank, my profession has brought me into contact with every manner of loveliness. Yet what Miss Gavi has revealed, if she is the artist I seek, is unique."

"Your profession?"

"I have been in my government's service since I was seventeen, sir. First in the American army, then as a member of our ambassadorial service. Istanbul, Saint Petersburg, and finally London." Baring shifted forward until he was perched upon the edge of the seat. "Tell me, sir, did Miss Gavi do the sketches of your good self and the British court that appeared in the antislavery pamphlet issued by the Powers Press?"

Falconer saw how people in the lobby began turning toward the central staircase. It was always the same when Serafina appeared. He rose to his feet. "Perhaps you'd care to ask her directly."

Serafina stepped into the lobby, her eyes only for him. And in her gaze, Falconer found his answer.

She did not love him.

She displayed the deep affection of a very

dear friend. But it was not romantic love. They had grown to know each other so very well. For eight months, Falconer had spent part of nearly every day in her company. He knew her well enough to know the message she bore before she even opened her mouth.

She was coming to say good-bye.

Oh, it would not be a farewell in the physical sense. They were bound together for life, unless he chose to walk away and never see her again. She would always welcome him. She would keep a room in her home and her life for him. Wherever her future might take her, he would be welcome.

If only he could bear to be with her as a friend. And nothing more.

The young man cleared his throat.

Falconer forced himself to form the words, "Nathan Baring, may I present Serafina Gavi."

She turned to him and said calmly, "Now is not a good time, sir."

"No, of course not." But he did not back away. "Might I ask you one question only?"

"Some other day, perhaps. I would ask that you wait —"

"Serafina," Falconer said quietly.

She acquiesced as he had known she would. She would deny him nothing. Except the one thing Falconer desired above all else.

"Very well, sir," she said. "Your question."

"Did you, that is, were you the artist who drew the Crown's men into the slave vessel? The drawing used in the Powers' antislavery pamphlet?"

"Yes, I was."

"Oh, I say."

Something in the man's voice caused Falconer to look beyond his own pain. He saw a young man who genuinely seemed affected not by Serafina's beauty but by her *character.*

"I understand the Powers remained with William Wilberforce during that period. Did you happen to speak with the gentleman?"

"I had that honor," Falconer replied.

"Oh, sir." The man clasped his hands in front of him. "Might I ask, what was he like? William Wilberforce?"

Serafina responded, "That is three questions, sir. Not one." But her voice held no acrimony.

"Of course, ma'am. You are quite right."

"William Wilberforce was a man already connected to heaven," Falconer said. "He was the best part of blind. He did not have the strength to hold a glass to his own lips. Yet . . ."

Nathan Baring held himself with the eagerness of a young lad. "Yes?"

"He was the most powerful figure of a man I have ever met. He spoke to me, and it seemed as though I heard a voice speaking with heaven's authority. Time held little meaning while I was in his presence. And after, I felt as though I walked away a better man."

Nathan fumbled with his hands and his words both. "This means more than I can say. When I learned that I had been assigned to London, I wrote a dozen letters begging to meet with Wilberforce. My father admired him above all others."

Serafina asked, "Your father was an antislaver?"

"Indeed, Miss Gavi. And his father before him. They were merchants. I lost my father last year."

"I'm so sorry."

"Thank you, ma'am. I wanted to go into the ministry, but my father wanted one son to become a diplomat and perhaps a politician. The other, my younger brother, has taken over the business."

"Do you know the Langstons?" Falconer asked, naming their closest allies in the Washington area. Reginald and Lillian Langston ran a Georgetown emporium and owned a fleet of merchant ships, one of which had carried Falconer and Serafina across the Atlantic.

Nathan Baring replied, "I count the Langstons among some of the finest people God has ever created."

Serafina seemed drawn to speak by the young man's clear-eyed enthusiasm. "They have asked Falconer to join them. We met with them just last week, and they asked him again."

"Oh, sir, but you must. The Langstons are goodly people, known to treat their staff as family."

"I am first held to aid the Gavis with an urgent matter of their own."

"Of course. I certainly understand duty's call. Well, I shall not keep you longer." He offered them each a card. "If there is any way I can be of service, you must please not hesitate to call upon me." He bowed to them both, then said in a lower voice, "Might I say, if you are interested in finding others opposed to the slave trade, we meet after Sabbath services at Saint John's Church on Lafayette Square."

As the young man departed, Falconer reflected on how Baring had noticed Serafina's beauty yet counted it as insignificant. Falconer tried to recall another young man responding in such a way, as though utterly immune to her appeal.

Serafina said, "I had hoped to have a private word."

Falconer turned back to her. She kept her hair covered by the lace mantilla. Her dress was modest, a long-sleeved formal gown of linsey-woolsey. The color was blue and the weave was as soft as sea-foam. Unlike the other women Falconer had seen at the legate's gathering, she wore no jewelry. He swallowed hard. "There is no need."

"Yes, Falconer. I must —"

"Serafina." How he loved to speak her name. "I do understand."

She studied his face with the calm resolve of one who trusted him utterly. Open-eyed, taking her time, giving little notice to the scar that frightened so many. Discounting the shadows of past crimes. "How could you not," she said quietly. "You know me so very well. Will you sit with me?"

He followed her lead, moving to a pair of high-backed chairs set slightly behind the central staircase, hidden from the view of most people in the lobby. Falconer kept his back to the wall and the stairs so he might continue to scout the passing faces. There was no danger in such a public place, but such habits died hard.

"I know what you wish for, John Falconer," Serafina told him. "I have wished that I could give it to you."

"You do not love me." The words dropped from his mouth with the dull weight of frozen stones.

"There are two issues, and both stand against us. The first is my affection, which is great for you. As great as for any I have ever known since Luca." She stopped then. "Luca. How I screamed and cried that name aloud and in my heart. How can so much poison be held within so few letters?"

"At least he made it possible for us to meet." Falconer's voice was so low she leaned forward slightly.

Her gaze was calm, deep. A woman's gaze, to match the loving concern within her voice. "What an awful price to pay for coming to know my dearest friend. I never thought I could thank God for such agony. But the Bible says He will sift out the gold from all our dross. And He has. Even here."

"You said there were two problems."

"Yes, dear Falconer. Even if I cared for you . . ."

"Romantically."

"Even then, there would still be my parents. With God's help, I shall never go against their will a second time. And they

. . . well, you see how they are."

"I am not suitable."

Serafina remained silent in a woman's fashion, allowing her stillness to answer for her. Then, "A part of me had hoped they would change with the passage of these weeks and months."

"As had I."

"But they have not. I shall honor them, John Falconer, in my choice of husband. After all the suffering I have caused them, I must. You see this, do you not?"

He had so many things he wished to say. Confessions of love, yearnings for what was being denied him. All his vast strength was useless here. He felt like a hulking brute brought by some vast error of fate into an alien world. And here before him sat all that he could never claim as his own. Of course he saw. Yet just then his throat was caught in a vise grip of regret, and he could say nothing.

Falconer rose to his feet. He opened his mouth, but the words would not come. He bowed to her, bidding farewell to all his futile dreams. Then he did the hardest thing of a hard and brutal life.

He turned and walked away.

CHAPTER 4

The Gavis' move to their new quarters was delayed a week by a late snowstorm. Washington was an odd sort of place when it came to weather. One day seemed firmly wedded to the southern states, particularly the fiercely hot summers when the wet air clung like damp blankets to the skin. In the depths of winter a south wind could blow in several days of piercing blue sky and temperatures that had people speaking of spring in January. The next day, however, a gale could arrive from Connecticut. The wind would slice through the thickest coats. The poor of Washington suffered hard on such days. The missions were packed, and famished children flocked to the back roads where the constables did not patrol, begging for pennies.

That week a blizzard cut Washington off from the rest of the nation. The turnpikes both north and south were shut. A ship ar-

riving from Charleston carried the astonishing news that even the ports of Savannah
and Jacksonville had been blanketed by
snow. Food was growing scarce. Then suddenly the sun emerged, and within two days
the snow was a memory. The city roads that
were not bricked turned to bogs. Streams
ran down the center of some avenues. All of
Virginia's and Maryland's rivers broke their
banks. But the sun remained strong. By
week's end some of the most hardy dogwoods were beginning to show the first buds
of spring.

The Gavis' house stood four down from
one formerly owned by Dolley Madison.
Their new home, the smallest on Lafayette
Square, had been erected to fit into a very
narrow lot, one of the square's last free
spaces. But the stone and brick edifice held
a warm artistry, a place of charm rather
than grandeur. The windows were tall and
the interior filled with light. Directly across
from them was the manor of Martin Van
Buren, and beyond that rose the bare-
limbed forest that backed onto the White
House. Although placed in the very center
of Washington, Lafayette Square was broad
enough to hold almost a country air. Falconer had taken to walking either here or
along the Potomac, seeking momentary

freedom from the city's confines, which was how he had chanced to learn the house had suddenly come available.

Falconer worked alongside the Gavis but remained at an inner distance from everyone, even himself. He observed the family taking in the home and its well-portioned rooms, talking excitedly as they decided where everything was going to go and which rooms would be for what purpose. They were a family facing problems together. Three of them, loving one another through the good times and the bad. Falconer slowly walked down the front stairs. He stood removed from where the two wagons from Langston's Emporium were being unloaded. He had been alone all his life. But he had never felt it so clearly as now.

Even here, however, he was not to find solitude. For soon enough Lillian and Reginald Langston arrived in a carriage followed by two more wagonloads of goods. Reginald hailed him with "Did the first items arrive safely?"

"I doubt there will be enough room inside for everything, sir."

"There, you see?" Reginald addressed his wife as he helped her down from the carriage. "Did I not say you were burdening them with too much?"

Lillian Langston, wife of the emporium's owner, was a British lady aging with beauty and grace. There were tales that she had relinquished a title and vast holdings, but even her staff were uncertain of the truth. For Lillian Langston preferred to speak only of her life here in Washington and of the husband she loved so dearly. "And I told you, my dear, to allow the women to decide what should be required."

"Hmph." Reginald Langston doffed his hat to Falconer. "I am seeing far too little of you, my friend."

"The snows," Falconer said awkwardly. "My work guarding the family."

Lillian stepped up alongside her husband. "Are they still in danger?"

"Hard to say, ma'am. The legate was certainly displeased over their departure from his manor. But if Serafina says there were men with guns, we had all best believe her."

"I am so looking forward to seeing them again. And the house."

As if on cue, the three Gavis came rushing down the front stairs, crying aloud with that odd Italian mixture of joy and astonishment and protest. Lillian and Reginald were hugged by them all. The Langstons smiled and stood as the Gavi family ran around the wagons, peering under wraps and exclaiming to one another. Then there were more hugs and laughter as Bettina lost her English entirely. Her husband then discovered the walnut desk with the gilt-edged leather top that was meant for his study. His cries were loud enough to attract attention from people across the square. Which only caused the others to laugh. Falconer remained upon the sidewalk, five paces removed from the exuberant celebration. The Gavis almost sang their joy, speaking English with such gusto that even a simple word was enough to have the Langstons laughing and all the busy workers smiling and chattering in reply. Everyone was swept up in the joy of entering a new home. Everyone, that is, except John Falconer.

Alessandro Gavi could not stop his exclamations. "The desk! The chair!"

"The carpets!" Bettina whispered to her daughter, then seeking an English word, added, "the chandelier!"

Mother and daughter hurried inside to tell the workers where to deliver the next load, which was a set of six high-backed chairs with carved arms. But midway up the stairs Bettina rushed back to embrace Lillian Langston in a childish flurry of excitement. Everyone was so happy they

59

managed to ignore the fact that Falconer was the only one who did not join in. He was, after all, a stern man by nature.

"Grazie, di cuore. Grazie mille." Bettina pulled Lillian toward the house. *"Vieni. Presto, vieni!"*

"She says you must come with us now," Serafina called over. "Mama, where does this go?"

"Cos' è?"

"A table, I think. With drawers."

"It is called a sideboard," Lillian explained.

"Oh! What wood! *Che grande!*" Bettina would not let go of Lillian's hand.

The three women disappeared inside the house, chattering in a pair of languages, not really caring now that little was being translated. Reginald Langston observed, "I do believe they have become the best of friends."

"Sir, Mr. Langston." Alessandro extended his hand over the stream of items and workers proceeding into his house. "I am speechless."

"First of all, you must call me Reginald."

"Reginald. I am Alessandro." The man's eyes shone with astonished delight. "One moment we are homeless and wondering whether we shall even have clothes for the

60

morrow. The next, we have a home and all the furnishings."

"First of all, the home was Falconer's doing."

"Yes, yes, of course." A trace of the stiff formality returned as Alessandro bowed to Falconer. But not much. "We are ever in the gentleman's debt."

"As for me, sir, I must tell you, we are here because we expect something in return."

"Ah." Alessandro wished to become the skilled merchant and negotiator. But the day was too much. "Anything, good sir. If it is in my power, it is yours."

"Not your power at all, sir, but Falconer's. We seek him to join our firm."

"But . . . but, Mr. Falconer has agreed to help me."

"As he has explained. We shall wait because we must. But Falconer has agreed to join us." Reginald did not even attempt to hide his vast satisfaction. "Finally."

Langston's Emporium in Georgetown was but one segment of the merchant empire. Reginald Langston and his partners controlled a fleet of merchant ships and had established trading stations in such far-flung spots as Philadelphia, Wheeling, London, Paris, and Amsterdam. Falconer saw no need to explain to Alessandro Gavi that he had agreed to Reginald's request with just one condition. That his work in the company require that he be sent far away.

"Surely, sir, there must be something I can do for you as well," Alessandro offered. "The Gavis are known far and wide as merchants of quality."

"I thank you, and I look forward to seeing how and where our interests mesh," Reginald replied evenly.

Even Falconer noticed the sudden shift.

"But there is something more I can do for you, yes?" Alessandro asked.

"Falconer has told me in no uncertain terms that he will only join my establishment once he has concluded his work for you. But he will not tell me what this work is, nor how long it will take."

Alessandro bit his lip, his former good humor gone. "It must remain a secret, good sir, only because it is dangerous."

"If you do not trust those you can, how can you be sure that you will succeed?"

"True, true." Alessandro Gavi searched about him, ensuring that the square remained empty. He cast a glance at Falconer. "I must thank you for being so guarded with my confidences."

"It is your secret," Falconer replied. "Not mine."

"But you feel I should trust him, yes?"

"If it were my decision, I would have confided in him long ago."

"Bene." Alessandro turned to Reginald. "I represent a council of Venetian merchants. As payment for a debt, we have been given ownership of a gold mine."

"Whereabouts does it lie?"

"Two days ride from Charlotte in the Carolinas," Falconer answered for Alessandro, very glad to have it out. "In the Appalachian foothills, or so I am told."

"Don't know it; don't have business there. Our trade has all been north and west. But I could make inquiries."

"No, please, I must respectfully ask that you not share this information," Alessandro inserted quickly. "My lawyers here, they have sought to determine what they can. It has been slow, so very slow. The country is wild, the people not welcome to outsiders."

"But the mine exists?"

"There is a mine. That much we know. How profitable, how large a holding, I cannot say. Apparently there are no . . . I am sorry, I do not know the proper term . . ."

"Assayers," Falconer supplied. "Mining engineers."

"Yes. Assayers who are not already committed to other mines. It is all so very primitive, you see. And very closed to outsiders."

"So why not just take cash and be done with the matter?"

"Because the gold, sir. The gold!" Alessandro's hands began to weave in a distinctly Italian fashion. "All the Venetian jewelers and Murano crystal makers, we must pay a levy to the Vienna court for all our gold. Why? Because either the shippers or the mines themselves are controlled by members of the emperor's court. Now, suddenly, a source has been offered to us, one that we may own!"

Reginald Langston understood the problem immediately. "So you want Falconer to travel down and take the measure of this mine."

"And return with our first share of the gold. Only when we have something in our hands can we truly believe this to be real." The hand gestures grew more dramatic still. "But negotiations have taken forever, good sir. Our lawyers here in Washington have claimed it is faster to deal with London than this provincial town of Charlotte."

Reginald was already looking ahead to the next problem. "The Austrian ambassador, how is he known?"

"The legate, Prince Fritz-Heinrich."

"I don't suppose he's all too happy with the development."

Alessandro repressed a shudder. "He must not know."

"But if he does?"

"Even if he suspects, my life and that of my family are in grave danger. Very grave."

"And Falconer? What of him on the road?"

"I can take care of myself," Falconer said. "And move easier if I remain alone."

Reginald started to argue, then thought better of it. He said to Alessandro, "You need people here with your family that you can trust. Especially once Falconer sets off on his mission."

"Good sir, you have already done so much, I could not possibly ask anything more of you."

Reginald gave no sign that he had heard. "Three men should be enough. One who can behave as a proper manservant. Two for the outside."

"I have located one good man already," Falconer offered. "A carriage driver and jack-of-all-trades. He's the one you see there, carting in the crystalware."

"Which means you require one man within the house and one outside." Reginald nodded. "I'll see to it this very day."

Alessandro began, "I could not possibly repay —"

"A date," Reginald responded firmly. "A date when Falconer will be done with this and ready to begin duties with our firm."

Falconer listened to the exchange, knowing he was being offered not just new employment but a new life. One which by his own request would take him far away from Serafina.

If only the future might hold some shred of hope.

Falconer berthed in the small two-story cottage at the back of the long and narrow lot. His room was on the ground floor and faced the main residence. Gerald Rivens had taken the chamber across from his. The two men being sent over from the Langstons would reside upstairs. Mary lodged in the main house's top floor, a long room that stretched beneath the eaves.

Falconer's little table was situated by the window, from where he could scout the rather unkempt grounds and the house. There was a high stone wall to either side and a gated fence behind the servants' cottage. The residence's front windows all had stout oak shutters, which were now closed and locked. He had seen to that himself.

The others had remained behind for the evening meal, but Falconer had carried back portions of bread and cheese and fruit, which now sat untouched beside his Bible. The Good Book remained untouched as well.

The sky was gunmetal gray, the air so cold he could see frost forming in the corners of the glass. Though the evening was just waning, he was very tired, and not merely from the day's work. Falconer was not sleeping well. His bed had become a narrow prison of regret and recrimination, mostly at himself.

He picked up an apple and used his knife to carve off a slice. But he held it, untasted, in his hand. He lifted his gaze and stared at the shutters over Serafina's window.

The only task he had ever been good for was facing danger. Guarding this family was child's play compared to previous responsibilities. He yearned for action — anything to temper the aching hunger. Something to still his hopeless pain.

Falconer bit the apple but tasted only dust. So many of his actions over the past weeks had been wrong. And his attitude had been worse. He had bulled through situations that required silence and stealth. He was circled by people who cared for him and wished him only well. Yet all he could give in return was a severe remoteness.

He would prefer facing the enemy and holding fast. Taking aim at the goal and giving it his all. Anything but more days of staring at what would never be his.

He rose from his little table and walked out behind the cottage. The rainwater cistern was covered with a thin skim of ice. He cracked it with a knuckle, drank deep, then washed his face and hands. Gasping, he returned to his chamber. The light was dimming. He fumbled for the tinderbox, then set it back down. He would merely light the candle and watch it flicker, his gaze slipping over the Good Book, the words unread.

Falconer lowered himself to his knees. He bowed his head and crouched upon the floor in pain, all muscle and drive and blindness. And mute. All he could say was, "Father . . ."

He could not have said how long he knelt thus when a change came into his small chamber.

Falconer heaved himself to his feet and stood in the center of his darkened room, his chest pumping in and out. He strained to detect what was now gone.

For once his disappointment was vanquished. A fresh wind had blown through. One strong enough to clear away the smoke and the charred ashes from his heart.

Falconer tasted the air with all his senses on full alert. The air remained as highly charged as if a lightning bolt had blasted into the room.

He had heard a voice.

He was in no doubt whatsoever of this. A few words, spoken so clearly they might as well have been whispered into his physical ear.

Wait upon the Lord.

CHAPTER 5

Serafina woke to a March dawn, the room dark and beyond her shuttered window only night. Still, she rose and washed her face, shivering as she dressed. Ever since her time in service at Harrow Hall, she found herself unable to sleep beyond the first hour before morning, which was very odd for a young lady who two years earlier could lie abed until almost noon.

She lit a candle and trod carefully along the upstairs hallway and down the home's only staircase. Everything was of course very new. The windows did not have proper drapes yet, just the closed shutters. All the rooms had a rather unfinished look. The furniture seemed as artificial in their station as plants just settled into the garden. Serafina walked down the hallway separating the living and dining rooms from her father's office. She entered the kitchen and gasped at the sight of a figure shrouded in shadows.

The form shifted and turned from the window. "It's only me, lass."

"F-Falconer?"

"I'm sorry to have startled you."

She held up her candle, her heart slowing its pounding. "Why are you standing in the dark?"

"I was praying. Here. Let me make some more light." He moved to the corner where a modern galvanized stove was situated. He used tongs hanging from the wall to open two lids. Instantly the room was bathed in a warm glow. "Would you take tea?"

"That would be nice. Thank you."

She watched Falconer draw two mugs from a packing crate. He set a pot onto the stove lid that was still closed. While the water boiled, he opened a sack and put a heaping spoonful of tea into a mug, followed by a good dollop of honey. Serafina remarked, "Sailor's tea."

"You remember."

"I'll never forget." She accepted the mug with a smile of thanks. "Will you join me?"

"Yes, if you wish."

She studied him more carefully as he poured himself a cup. "Something is different. You've changed. What is it? You seem calmer, more at peace. Yes. That's it."

Falconer said nothing. He lowered himself

into a chair at the end of the table and took a cautious sip.

"Are things to be better between us now?"

Falconer seemed to taste his response with the tea. The stove's glow reflected on his face, and she could see the pensive cast to his eyes. "Has God ever spoken to you?"

Serafina heard more than the question. For the first time in weeks she heard again the voice of one who had become her dearest friend. The man she had trusted with her honor and her life. The brother who had helped her to trust in God.

His dark eyes looked almost copper in the light. "Has He?"

"Of course." She found herself recalling the first time they had spoken like this. How astonished she had been to meet a man who treated God as the unseen presence within every room, every moment. "He speaks to me through His Word. He speaks to me in church. He speaks to me through a sunrise. Through the lessons I have learned in my mistakes. Through my family. And through my friends."

"No. I mean . . ." Falconer fumbled with the words. "Has God ever spoken to you in a voice that you could hear?"

"I don't understand," she said with a small shake of her head. "What difference is there between one voice and another? If I have indeed heard Him, it is all the same. Is that not so?"

He nodded slowly. "You have grown in wisdom, Serafina."

A shiver went down her back. Not at the words, but the way he said her name. With ease. Again. Finally. At long last. "Have I?"

"Very much. Do you know, this is the first time I have asked your advice about faith."

"All I can offer you, John Falconer . . ." She sipped from her mug to ease the restriction in her throat. "Whatever I have learned, it is because you were there when I most needed a friend."

He had such a strong face. Fierce even in repose. Fierce and yet gentle. Equal amounts of strength and sorrow. She wanted to trace that scar with her fingers, but of course she would not. Yes, the sorrow was still there, and it wounded her to know that his unanswered love was the cause. Yet there was a new calm to the moment. A sense that God was there with them — a healing balm, even now. Falconer said, "Friends."

"Oh yes," she said and smiled. Though the man at the table's other end was rimmed by tears that could be held back no longer.

That night Falconer slept a full eleven

hours. He fell into bed at dusk and slept until the church bells woke him. He rose too swiftly and had to grab the wall for balance, he was so groggy. He stumbled while drawing on his pants, then stumbled again over the doorstep and would have sprawled flat had Gerald Rivens not caught him. "Steady on, friend."

Falconer walked barefoot across the almost frozen ground. He dunked his entire head into the rain cistern. Bits of ice laced his skin before he came up blowing like a whale.

He walked back around and hurried inside, for he saw now that Gerald was seated on a narrow bench beneath the cottage window next to Mary, and both were dressed for the Sabbath. Falconer tugged on boots and donned a formal high-collared shirt. He combed his hair and tied it back, then returned outside and demanded, "Why did you not wake me for my watch?"

Gerald made wide eyes. "Was that you? I thought a bear had crawled inside your lair, eaten you whole, and suffered from indigestion."

Mary hid a giggle behind one hand.

"I suppose I did need the rest," Falconer allowed.

"Yes. I reckoned as much."

As Falconer started for the kitchen, he said over his shoulder, "I will spell you tonight."

"Don't forget the new man is here to help share duties," Gerald called after him. "What's more, you don't owe me a thing, John Falconer."

The house held an empty silence. Falconer assumed the family had already left for church. But there were signs of early activity. Every surface in the kitchen was covered with dishes. A vast iron pot simmered on the stove, filling the air with fragrances of tomatoes and fresh herbs. Someone had thoughtfully left a jug of apple cider, along with bread and cheese on the windowsill. Falconer took his breakfast along as he wandered around the new house. Through the front windows he spotted a flock of dark-cloaked figures headed for the church at the square's farthest corner. He recalled the young man and his invitation and went back to the cottage for his coat.

Saint John's was a quiet place, one that embraced all believers in whitewashed wood and simple lines. Falconer arrived just as the last stragglers were being sent upstairs to the loft, as the downstairs was packed. Just as at the Langstons' church in Georgetown, most of the congregants were dressed in dark colors. The men wore frock coats and stiff-collared shirts, the women gray or black cloaks and stiff little hats tied under their chins. Falconer slipped into a pew by the loft's back wall just as the pastor began his welcome. The man's first words caught him unaware.

"Some of us come in joy," the minister told the gathering. "Others in sadness. In the Lord's eyes, what matters most is that you have come at all. Is your heart troubled? Come. Is your world fraught with peril? Come. Are you filled with joy and triumph and a sense of accomplishment? Come. Have your prayers been answered? Come. Is there pain, anguish, an unraveling of the mortal coil? Come and find welcome in the name of our risen Savior."

Falconer had been impacted by many Sabbath services. Never, however, had the words felt so keenly directed to him as this day. God was speaking through the pastor. To him. The force blew aside Falconer's ability to question. He was struck by a divine cannonade that began with the opening welcome and continued to the benediction.

He listened to the pastor read a passage from the thirty-seventh chapter of Ezekiel.

A valley of bones, the pastor intoned, a place of death and loss and mortal despair. Without hope or future, the man explained, without any sense of life. And God asked His prophet, can these bones ever walk with life and purpose again?

"Yes." Falconer was astonished to find he had spoken aloud. Yet the power flooding through him would not be denied. "Yes!"

"Indeed so." The pastor found nothing untoward with a response from the balcony. Nor, clearly, did the others. There were murmurs and nods throughout the congregation as the pastor went on. "The day of renewed hope that the Lord spoke about is certain to come. Those, my brethren, are His own words. Wait upon Him. He will call His divine winds to course through your dark valley and draw forth life. Will you remain heartsick, alone, even sad? Perhaps. Even the apostle Paul was commanded to bear his thorn. But God will knit together your bones and from your despair bring forth reason."

Falconer slipped off the pew and onto his knees. A few glanced over, but attention soon turned away. He covered his face with battle-scarred hands and offered a warrior's prayer, as direct and well-aimed as a stabbing sword. *Give me your purpose, Lord.*

Make gold of my dross. I am your man, and I am ready. Amen.

Falconer spotted Nathan Baring as he exited the church. The young man made his way through the black-frocked crowd. "Falconer, how good of you to join us," he said in his genial way.

He saw Nathan scout about and saved him the trouble of asking about Serafina. "She is not here."

"Pardon?"

"Miss Gavi. She accompanied her parents to mass."

To Falconer's surprise, the young man did not seem that interested. Nor did he halt his perusal of the crowd. "Ah. The Gavis are papists, are they?"

"Actually, on Wednesday evenings Miss Gavi worships with the Methodists in Georgetown. She attends Sunday mass out of respect for her parents."

"How extraordinary." The young man's attention was now riveted upon Falconer. "You mean to say she is genuinely devout?"

"She is."

"Forgive me, sir. It was an impudent question. But one so lovely as Miss Gavi, particularly a European from a titled family . . . well . . . Never mind."

Despite his own initial hostility, Falconer found himself liking the gentleman. "I understand perfectly."

"Yes, a gentleman of the world like yourself, I should imagine you do." He went back to searching the crowd. "There was someone I wished for you to meet, though I fear he did not wish to be seen with us."

Falconer remained caught up in all he had experienced within the church. "Might I ask you a question?"

"By all means."

"Have you ever heard God speak to you?"

"What, you mean audibly?" His focus came back once more, calm and penetrating. "What a remarkable question."

"I take that as a no."

"In a sense. My father, God rest his soul, knew I wished to become a pastor. I took aim at the pulpit when I was just thirteen. All my young life I wanted nothing else. But the morning after my seventeenth birthday, my father brought me into his study and announced that God had spoken to him in the night. I should enter government service, and my brother would be going into the family business. My father asked me to trust him and trust God. But if I refused, he would not object."

Nathan Baring turned to let an approaching woman pass, closing the gap between them so they would not be interrupted. "Because I loved him, Mr. Falconer, I could not refuse my father's request. Though it left me heartsore and wretched."

At this close range, Falconer could see the shadow still in the man's smoky green eyes. "Was your father right?"

"Upon his deathbed, my father asked me the very same thing. Had he been correct in speaking as he had? I could not lie, not then. I told him I did not yet know. Though eight years had passed since that morning, still God had not revealed to me a purpose I could not also have accomplished through the ministry. Or so it seemed to me. My father said merely, 'Everything in God's time.' Those were his last words, Mr. Falconer. I hope and pray he was right."

Falconer felt a sudden bond with the gentleman. "I am not as patient a man as you, Mr. Baring."

"I would ask that you call me Nathan."

"My friends know me simply as Falconer." He paused and looked into the face near his. "I could not endure eight years of waiting."

Nathan had a diplomat's manner of saying nothing with great volume. He asked, "What did God say to you, Falconer?"

"To wait." Falconer shuddered. *Eight years.*

"Will you take advice?"

"Gladly."

"Three things. First, God will not send to you more than you can endure. Second, you will learn immense lessons in your fallow time."

"That much I can already attest to. And third?"

"Thirdly, yes. I should encourage you to not wait in solitude. Speak of your hardship and your need. Pray with others. Find comfort in the company of believers."

Falconer offered his hand. "God brought me here this morning with a purpose, Nathan. I am grateful for your advice."

"Your words do me great honor." Nathan Baring did not release his hand. "I apologize for speaking of such matters here on hallowed ground. But the gentleman who has vanished, he carried with him a warning. Of danger and peril."

"Against the Gavis," Falconer said. "Yes. Thank you. I already know of this."

"Not the Gavis," Nathan corrected. "Against you."

Serafina returned from church with plenty to accomplish. Other than Mary, they had no female help around the house. Finding a suitable cook was going to be very difficult. Lillian Langston knew no one who had even the slightest idea of Italian cooking. And like most Italian men, Serafina's father was very particular about his food. So Bettina said she would cook and teach her daughter at the same time. That evening they were playing host to Reginald and Lillian Langston. No proper Italian could say thanks without spreading a feast.

Serafina found great pleasure in the shopping and the preparations. The previous evening Serafina and her mother had spent hours making long sheets of pasta. The fresh dough was featherlight as they rolled it flat. Serafina had laid out streams of finely milled flour before her mother's rolling pin, and the table upon which they had worked was covered with a wet cheesecloth, such that the pasta would adhere to the cloth and not peel or tear. Overnight the pasta and the cloth had dried together. Now Bettina peeled it away from the cloth and sliced the hardened pasta, rolling it gently so it would not break, as Serafina ladled in the fresh tomato sauce they had made that morning. They would then add spinach cooked with fresh basil and some cheese. The *reggiano* and *mozzarella* they would have used in Venice were not available. But they had bought an aged cheese made from cows' milk by a German dairy farmer. They could only hope it would prove adequate.

Serafina loved the work and the closeness to her mother. It was a return to her happiest recollections. She recalled other such times, the two of them making pastries in the kitchen fronting the Venetian street or setting the table while gondoliers sang their way through sunlit waters in the canal beyond their dining room window. They laughed over such memories, as though the interim tragedy had never happened. They tasted sauces and kneaded dough for *panini.* Eventually her mother asked how she had fared in England. The question came naturally, two friends wishing to catch up on each other's lives. Finally managing to speak of the lost weeks and months.

Serafina's tale about Aunt Agatha and Harrow Hall took them through the rolling of the veal in ground pepper and sage and setting it in the oven to roast. She cleaned potatoes while her mother sliced carrots, and Serafina described the young lord's attack and how Falconer had saved her. How he had taken her to church. How he had reintroduced her to hope.

Together they set the table as Serafina

described Gareth and Erica Powers and their mission to abolish slavery on both sides of the Atlantic. Bettina Gavi made coffee as Serafina scrubbed the kitchen table and related their travels to the home of William Wilberforce and her two drawings for the pamphlet — the one of Falconer and the one politicizing the slave trade. She and her mother dipped *biscotti* into their demitasse cups as Serafina told of the pamphlet's impact, the passage of the bill eradicating slavery within the British Empire.

When she finally stopped, the kitchen was filled with the fragrances of roasting meat and fresh spices. Her mother toyed with her tiny spoon and avoided her daughter's eyes. "Stories upon stories," she murmured.

"I did not mean to disturb you, Mama. Perhaps I should not have spoken so." Serafina saw anew the fresh lines of age and worry in her mother's lovely features and blinked back tears over being the cause. "If only I could change all the mistakes I have made."

"Daughter, if I could wind back the hands of time, I would have done so long ago. We do not regret the past mistakes. We move on." The way her mother spoke left Serafina in no doubt that she had often repeated the words to herself. Bettina met her daughter's gaze. "I was just thinking on how you have grown in these past few months."

Serafina could not help but release tears. "Never did I imagine that the world could hold such sorrow."

"Or joy," her mother admonished. "Never forget that."

"No, Mama. You are right. Or *joy.*"

Serafina was startled to hear her father say, "The Vienna royals are involved in the slave trade."

"Papa, I did not know you were there."

Bettina obviously did not share her daughter's surprise, for she merely said, "Would you care for coffee, husband?"

"Half a cup, perhaps."

She rose to fetch a cup and saucer. "Join us, dear."

"Thank you." He seated himself at the head of the table. "I did not want to disturb your conversation, but I could not help but listen."

"I have no secrets from you, Papa." The contrast her simple statement made to the previous summer, when she had lived for a secret love, one that tore their family apart, almost reduced her to tears.

"There, there. None of that. We are here, we are together, and as your mother has said, you have indeed grown." Alessandro patted his daughter's hand, then continued to the two women, "The Hapsburgs have no direct holdings in Africa. But they are partnered with their Belgian cousins."

"And the Portuguese," her mother added, pouring her husband a cup of coffee. "In Africa and Brazil both."

A thought struck her. "The legate, Prince Fritz-Heinrich?"

"His family partners with others whose empire is based upon sugar and slaves. He accepted this posting so as to keep an eye on their American buyers," Alessandro said, stirring in sugar. "As vile a business as ever there was."

Serafina recalled the confrontation with the legate. "I meant no harm to your concerns, Father."

"Slavery has never been a concern of mine, nor of any on the merchant council. I have made sure of that." He sipped his coffee. "I am proud of you, daughter."

Her mother asked, "Are you bored here, Serafina?"

"How could I be, Mama? I am here with you!"

"It is a valid question," Alessandro said. "You have played a role in mighty deeds. You have traveled and you have matured. Yet here in Washington you have remained hidden away in the back rooms of the legate's manor."

"I have used the time to sketch and draw," Serafina said. She heard more than the question. She heard the tone in which they spoke to her. As a beloved daughter, yes. But also as an adult. She gave the question the attention it deserved. Serafina had no idea what she wanted or did not want, which was very odd, for previously she had been a headstrong and independent young lady. Just now, she was content to remain at her parents' side. "All I have thought of up to now is being with you both again. And healing. And restoring our family."

Bettina gripped her daughter's hands with both of hers, sharing a long look with her husband. But before she could speak, the front door crashed back and they heard Mary cry, "Miss Gavi!"

"In the kitchen."

The young maid who had accompanied her from London came rushing back, followed by Gerald Rivens. Her eyes were as wild as her hair. "I have terrible news!"

CHAPTER 6

They were still deep in worry and discussion when Falconer returned. That is, Serafina's father and mother were talking. Serafina had little to say. Gerald Rivens was naturally silent. Alessandro Gavi paced while his wife alternated between checking on the meal and wringing her hands in a most Italian fashion. Mary stood by the back window alongside Rivens while she took tentative sips from her cup.

Her parents were clearly displeased when Falconer appeared with a stranger in tow. It took Serafina a moment to recognize the newcomer as the young man from the hotel lobby. After Falconer had introduced him as Nathan Baring, her father gave a perfunctory bow and said, "You must forgive us, sir, but now is not at all a good time. We have urgent matters to discuss with Falconer."

Falconer inspected each face in turn.

"You've heard, then."

"Heard?"

"About the legate's new threat."

Alessandro sank down into a chair. "How . . ."

Nathan Baring held his dark hat with the black silk stripe in both hands. "You will not remember me, sir, but I was in attendance at the legate's court last Saturday."

Her father's gaze tightened. "I don't understand. You are a courtier?"

"Diplomat, sir," Baring corrected. "My present duties require that I attend the legate on occasion."

"Nathan has friends in court," Falconer added.

"Allies," Baring said. "I would hardly call them friends."

"You mean spies," Alessandro interpreted.

Baring's only response was to twist the rim of his hat in his hands.

Serafina offered, "Mary gave us the warning."

Falconer noticed the young woman's nervousness in this company. He gestured Nathan into a chair, then pulled another near Mary. He slipped off his coat and pulled in close. "I'd be most grateful if you'd tell me what you heard."

"I already told them everything I know, sir."

"I'm not a sir, lass. You know that full well, don't you? I'm just a man trying to do his duty to the Gavis and to God, just as you." His gentle tone and his sheer presence shut out the others in the room. "It would help me a great deal if I could hear it straight from you."

Gerald Rivens patted the young woman's arm. "Go on, Mary. We're among friends here."

"Well, sir. I made friends belowstairs at the legate's. Not many, mind. Just two. One works in the kitchen. The other is maid to the princess."

"She and the legate do not see much of one another," Falconer commented.

"That they do not, sir. It was an arranged marriage, so it was. And the legate, well, he's not what you might call a gentleman." She blushed and twisted her fingers together.

Falconer nodded encouragement. "So you heard something from the upstairs maid."

"She attends the same church as us, sir. She came to me today with the most dreadful news." She cast a nervous glance at Nathan Baring.

Falconer understood perfectly. "I trust this

gentleman, Mary. I suggest you do the same. He will not say a word that might endanger anyone."

"I will speak of this to no one," Nathan promised.

"Well, sir. She told me of a conversation. One the princess heard. Between the legate and another man. The prince, sir, he has a man on his staff. A man the others don't care to talk about. He chills the blood, so they say."

"His name?"

"My friend doesn't know, sir. I asked her the very same thing. She said it was best not to know too much about this man."

"So the legate has a frightening man who does his bidding," Falconer repeated, his voice low and very assuring. "This is most helpful, Mary. I am ever so grateful to you for this information. Did your friend happen to say anything about the man's appearance?"

"Tall, he is. Tall and slender. He wears a hooded dark cloak when he comes. And he only comes at night. That's all she said."

"He's a mercenary," Gerald Rivens put in. "His name is Vladimir."

Mary shivered at the way Gerald said the name.

"You've seen him?" Falconer asked.

"Never had the chance," Gerald replied. "Never sought one either."

Gerald Rivens was so spare Serafina would not have imagined it possible for his features to tighten further. But she observed his face become even more taut and pale. Serafina was struck by the impression that these two men, Falconer and Rivens, held a common quality. It was not in physical appearance, for Rivens was as slight as Falconer was massive. Yet they understood each other so well a subtle communication passed between the two men at a level far below words.

"A ghost, is he," Falconer said.

"By training and preference," Rivens confirmed. "I've heard tell he was on the king's staff back in Vienna. He came from somewhere else. He did the king's bidding, and afterward he had to flee."

"An act so vile not even a king could protect him," Falconer mused. "Vladimir must be an evil man indeed."

"You know how people belowstairs are given to talk," Rivens said. "They'll make dervishes of anything they don't understand."

"But you don't think that's the case here. Do you."

Rivens gave Mary a glance, then looked

back to Falconer, saying in gesture more clearly than words what he thought. "I saw his horse once. Biggest steed I've ever come across. Must have been all of twenty-one hands. Black as night. Saddle to match. Long-bore musket holster. Carried three blades. A saber in a special scabbard, one that tied to his girdle so as not to flap about. Two small knives hidden in the saddle itself."

"Throwing blades?"

"That would be my guess."

Falconer nodded once, then turned back to Mary. "We know what comes next, lass. So you mustn't be worried over what you have to say."

But the conversation between Falconer and Rivens had left the young woman so rattled she clung to Serafina's hand and said nothing. Falconer nodded, as though he both understood and accepted. He said softly, "The legate and this strange man, they talked about doing someone harm, didn't they." He waited through a time, then continued at slightly more than a whisper. "And it wasn't the Gavis they were discussing. Was it."

She shook her head in a slow sweep back and forth.

"Who did the prince tell his man to go

after, Mary?"

She whispered, "You."

The difference between her parents and Falconer was brought into sharpest contrast during the next hour. Alessandro Gavi and Nathan Baring talked the language of diplomacy, working through what the discussions meant. How the words might have been misinterpreted. What the legate was after. How they might proceed. Falconer said nothing, not even to respond when asked a direct question. Instead, he leaned forward and had a very quiet word with Gerald Rivens. The man nodded, then drew Mary from her seat and together they left the kitchen. When Alessandro demanded to know where they were going, Falconer replied simply, "They'll be back shortly."

Serafina rose to help her mother with the meal. Bettina Gavi was so distracted she accomplished very little save get in the way. Her clearest impression from the discussion was that Nathan Baring was a remarkable gentleman. He was handsome, yes, but Serafina had met so many handsome men the physical aspects had come to mean very little to her. The young lord at Harrow Hall had been attractive in a coarse and loutish way. As had her lying paramour in Venice.

Luca. She shivered at the recollection of that man.

"I do not know what your secret mission may be," Nathan Baring was saying. "Nor do I ask. I might suggest, however, how the legate could fit in to this."

"By all means," Alessandro Gavi replied.

"I do not know where your own sentiments lie, sir. And I mean no offense. I must tell you, though, straight out, that I stand in lifelong opposition to the slave trade. Were I called, I would offer my own life in sacrifice to this cause."

The meal's preparations were almost complete. Serafina slipped the rosemary-flecked panini into the oven, just as her mother had taught her during the months since she had joined them in Washington. Back in Venice she had done no kitchen work at all. In fact, she would have been hard put to boil water. Serafina smiled wryly as she checked the fire grate to ensure the coals were cooked down to a steady heat. She adjusted the bread tray and slid it in beside the high-edged pan of *cannelloni alla primavera* that she and her mother had prepared that morning. And she listened.

"The Gavis are opposed to slavery," Alessandro stated gravely. "Now, in the past, and for all our days to come."

"I am most heartened, sir. Falconer had assured me of it, but still I am very glad to hear this from your own lips. For I must tell you, the legate is deeply involved."

"We know of this."

"Of course you do. What you may not realize, sir, is that the issue has become a dividing line among the nations we call allies." Nathan Baring's tone hardened to the sound of stone striking stone. "Mark my words, sir. A war is coming."

Serafina felt a shiver down her spine at the dire prediction.

"I can only hope you are wrong," her father responded.

"I offer my own prayers every night that this is the case. But the southern states have come to rely on this source of cheap labor and easy profit. We men of conscience cannot abide this poison within the body of our good nation. The slave owners say they will never relinquish this power. And we say they must."

"War," Alessandro sighed, shaking his head.

"Allies are being sought by both sides. Lines are being drawn in the sand. It will not come this year, or next. Perhaps not for a decade. But come it will."

Serafina used the soft towel to lift the coffee pot from the stove's warming corner. She moved around the table, filling the demitasses. She used the opportunity to study this young gentleman. Nathan Baring had the intent focus she had come to associate with others who had influenced her past — Falconer, Gareth and Erica Powers, and many of those who had worked among the Wilberforce community. He spoke with the determination of a man who was committed heart and soul. A man who knew his calling, and obeyed. She shivered again and this time did not understand why.

"Our current mission must remain confidential, sir," her father was saying. "I must tell you, though, that it is not tied to the slave issue. Not at all."

As she turned away, Serafina felt eyes upon her. She looked over and saw that Falconer had observed her studying Nathan Baring. His dark gaze held a multitude of emotions and silent communications. How well he could read her. And she him.

Nathan Baring countered, "If your mission has anything to do with money or power, the legate will judge you as either friend or foe. Are you an ally or an adversary, sir? That is the simple question before the legate."

"Venice has been a part of the Austrian

Empire for a hundred years," Alessandro Gavi replied. "Napoleon conquered us, and when the Hapsburg king swore allegiance, Napoleon gave us back. That is the simple answer."

"It is a diplomat's answer," Baring stated, then rose to his feet. He set a calling card before Falconer. "Mr. Falconer, if there is anything I can do, you must please call upon me. My private address is on the back. Day or night, sir. Day or night."

Alessandro rose with his guest. "Might I ask what draws such allegiance from you for our household, sir? We are, after all, complete strangers."

"I feel I have known of Falconer and your daughter since last summer's triumph, sir."

"Excuse me, my daughter?"

"The pamphlet drawings," Bettina Gavi said. "The acts of the British Parliament to abolish slavery."

"Just so. The impact of your daughter's artwork and Falconer's testimony before Parliament could not be overestimated." He bowed. "Falconer, Miss Gavi, I am your servant. Good day, all."

There was a long moment of silence after Alessandro Gavi saw their guest out of the house. He returned to the kitchen table and studied his hands. Serafina walked over and seated herself beside him. All eyes were upon the older gentleman when he said, "Wheels within wheels, threats from all sides." He looked at Falconer and demanded, "What do you make of this?"

"They have decided you are too protected. I am the natural target."

"Natural," Bettina repeated softly, shaking her head. "Oh, this is so disturbing."

Falconer was unperturbed. "They want to stop this threat to their profitable gold trade. They also know the Venice merchants oppose their slave ventures. They want to halt any such opposition. They assume I am here to help you. Clearly I am not simply a guard. Plus, if Nathan knows of my actions in England, so will others."

Serafina could tell her father was deeply torn between the danger and the need. She asked for them all, "What will you do?"

"That is simple enough," Falconer said. "I shall leave tonight."

There was a general cry of protest from those at the table. Finally Alessandro said, "They have *threatened* you!"

"Sir," Falconer replied calmly. "This is what I do."

Alessandro Gavi leaned back in his seat. "What of my lawyer's struggle?"

"Give me the documents. I will carry

them with me to that town you mentioned."

"Charlotte."

"Let me see what I can discover. That is what we want above all, is it not? Answers. Answers and gold."

Serafina could not recall seeing her father so distressed as he replied, "We pile one debt upon another. And now we put your life in peril."

CHAPTER 7

As the result of a note from Falconer, Reginald and Lillian Langston arrived early that evening. Bettina Gavi's worry over Falconer was tangled with concerns that her first dinner party in her new home was to be disrupted. Other than Serafina, however, it was doubtful that anyone else noticed. Their guests were accompanied by a doctor named Rutherford, a stern-looking gentleman with a silver handlebar moustache and the reddest cheeks Serafina had ever seen. He took one look at Falconer and declared, "I do believe the Lord God gave you a double measure of substance, sir."

"If only it had been of wisdom and faith," Falconer replied.

Though the doctor held himself with military rigidity, he permitted himself a small smile. "I see the gentleman is as you described, Reginald."

"Rutherford is a trusted ally," Reginald

explained to the group.

"If Mr. Langston vouches for you, sir," Falconer said, "I could ask for no more."

"Forgive me," Alessandro Gavi said. "I don't understand. Is someone ill?"

"I am about to become so," Falconer said. "At least, as far as the rest of Washington is concerned."

Bettina Gavi exclaimed, "No, no, this won't do! I won't have my first guests in our new home arrive and launch into . . ." She turned to her daughter and spoke in Italian.

Serafina translated, "Plans of worry and woe."

"Please," her mother continued. "You will all be seated. Alessandro, no, at the crown."

"The word in English is head of the table, my dear."

"Lessons later. Now we are to eat, yes?" She gave Serafina swift instructions in Italian, then bustled away, calling out more as she left.

The doctor said in genuine admiration, "I can only assume the Italian tongue has an extra muscle which our poor American mouths lack."

"Please, good doctor," Serafina translated for her mother. "You will sit beside Mrs. Langston, and then Falconer, my mother, then Reginald, then me. Papa, would you please bring in another chair?" She hurried to set another place as her mother had instructed, then followed her back to the kitchen.

Mary had returned with Gerald Rivens. Gerald was set to carving first bread and then meat. Mary helped carry plates and hid a smile at the sight of her suitor in a frilly apron, but not for long. She might not have understood Bettina Gavi's rapid-fire Italian, but she most certainly caught the tone.

The guests were swiftly served steaming plates of cannelloni alla primavera, rolled pasta filled with curds and grated cheese and steamed vegetables, topped with a spicy tomato sauce and fresh basil leaves. This was followed by slices of roast veal with potatoes that had been first boiled, then hand-coated in olive oil, rolled in fresh rosemary, and baked. Bettina played the true Italian hostess; she and her daughter remained seated for seconds only, continually refilling serving bowls and anticipating their guests' every wish before they even spoke.

Over dessert of fresh-made *tiramisu*, the doctor declared, "Madam, I have been transported to a land of nectar and heavenly manna. I now see why the Renaissance painters had so many smiling cherubs. They had just eaten at your ancestor's table."

Bettina Gavi blushed yet replied as a proper Italian hostess would. "You cannot possibly mean it, sir. You have hardly touched a thing."

"On the contrary." The doctor worked open the lowest button of his vest. "I have eaten so much I have rearranged the order of my internal organs."

She turned her attention to Reginald Langston and implored, "Surely you can manage one more small slice of *dolce*."

Reginald made great round eyes, ignored his wife's frown, and allowed, "As we have a doctor on hand, perhaps just a small one."

"Reginald, you are making a spectacle of yourself," Lillian murmured with a knowing look.

"It is only proper," Alessandro Gavi insisted as his wife hurried away with Reginald's plate. "Nothing pleases an Italian hostess more than a guest who overindulges."

Lillian shook her head as she smiled. "Then my husband has no doubt sent your dear wife into raptures of delight."

They took coffee in the parlor, and for the first time Serafina had the impression of being in a place she could call home. When Gerald Rivens, at Falconer's instructions, moved about closing the shutters to the gathering dusk, the sense of familiar comfort only increased. Falconer helped Mary set a fire and tossed in a double handful of cedar chips.

The doctor took a deep breath and declared, "A perfect spice to finish a wonderful repast, madam. I commend you on your ability to make such a delightful home, one that contains the best of both our worlds."

Lillian Langston interjected, "The Gavis have been in this home only a few days."

"Impossible!"

"We have become so comfortable only with the help of the Langstons," Alessandro said. "Our gratitude to them knows no bounds."

"It was Falconer who found the home," Serafina reminded them.

"And Falconer who brought us together," Reginald added.

The doctor set his coffee cup aside. "Which brings us to the matter at hand, does it not?"

Bettina rose from her chair. "Perhaps I should begin with the cleaning up. Serafina, would you join me?"

"Mama, if you don't mind, I would very

much like to hear this."

Bettina looked quizzically at her husband, who nodded once. Reluctantly Bettina resumed her seat, casting uncertain glances at her daughter.

"Perhaps you should tell us your plan," Alessandro said to Falconer.

"I leave tonight. The time of delay is ended." Falconer turned to the doctor. "I asked Reginald to bring you in hopes that you might spread word among the diplomatic community that I have been taken seriously ill. And that you were worried enough to quarantine the entire family."

"I am loath to tell an outright lie, no matter how justified the cause." Thoughtfully the doctor stroked the ends of his moustache. "Would you happen to suffer from any symptoms?"

"I do sense a considerable tightening around my middle."

"Cholera," the doctor said decisively. "You know, there was an outbreak just this past summer. One never can be too careful. Anything else?"

Falconer kept his gaze firmly upon the doctor. "I have suffered recently from severe pains in the region of my heart."

"Scarlet fever. Or perhaps both. Oh my, yes, we must seal this family away immediately."

"I shall dispatch two more trusted men to ensure the quarantine is not broken," Reginald declared. "And to see to any outside contact you might require."

"We are to be locked up?" Bettina demanded. "For how long?"

All eyes turned toward Falconer.

"It is unlikely the ruse can last more than a week."

"Seven days should be more than enough time to ensure the public's safety," the doctor agreed, rising to his feet. "I shall send my man within the hour to tack the quarantine notice to your door."

When the doctor had taken his leave, Falconer turned to Reginald. "Would you have any reason to send a carriage south at short notice?"

Reginald did not need to ponder. "There is a lawyer in Richmond waiting my response over a land sale issue. I could order my attorney's aide off this very night, with instructions that papers be delivered the instant the Richmond office opens."

Falconer rose and offered Reginald his hand. "It seems that I shall be even more in your debt."

"Debt?" Alessandro bounded to his feet. "You speak of debt? You protect my daughter, my family, my own life, you give us a home, you bring us new friends where we have none, you help me with my quest, you accept threats upon your life and limb?" He almost choked over his need to express the impossible. "You *dare* speak of debt?"

Serafina watched how Falconer studied her father. Time crystallized as she realized what he was thinking. His feelings were etched upon his features, clear as ink upon fresh parchment. She knew her father's response. At this point in time, Falconer knew Alessandro Gavi would refuse him nothing.

She heard her mother's breath catch in her throat. Serafina sensed her mother had just realized the same thing. Mother and daughter shared a long look.

Lillian Langston must have noticed the change in the room's atmosphere, for she rose to her feet and said, "Come, Reginald. We must be off."

"But, my dear, what of the plans to be made?"

Falconer's focus did not move from Alessandro's face as he said, "Have your carriage readied the hour before midnight. I will slip out the back and make my way to your stables. Tell the attorney's apprentice that I am one of your servants, sent upon an urgent errand. Nothing more."

"But what —"

"Reginald," Lillian said, gripping her husband's arm. "We are off."

Comprehension finally struck Alessandro Gavi hard. The blood drained from his features.

Their farewells were perfunctory. Reginald Langston looked from one face to the other and swiftly followed his wife into the gathering dusk.

When the door shut behind the Langstons, Falconer said simply, "We must speak."

Alessandro Gavi studied Falconer, as did Serafina, as did her mother. The three of them faced a man of unworldly determination. Never had Serafina seen such force unveiled. The man appeared made of steel, of stone, of some fire-hardened substance beyond the ken of mortal man.

Alessandro looked at his wife. A silent communication passed between them. Bettina had the wide-eyed look of an animal fearing unseen talons. Alessandro sighed and led them back into the dining room. He seated himself at the head of the table, pushing aside the dessert dishes. When his wife reached to gather them, he raised one hand and then pointed her into the seat next to his own. Another hand signal, and Serafina was directed into the chair next to her mother. Alessandro watched Falconer round the table, his features resigned.

Each click of the mantel clock seemed spaced hours apart. Serafina had ample time to examine her own heart. And the truth was, one simple thought filled her entire being. She would not disobey her parents again.

Falconer did not seat himself. He gripped the back of the chair across from Bettina and asked, "You have the legal documents related to this mine business here in the house?"

"Upstairs." Her father's voice was so hoarse it sounded like a different man.

"How much gold do you have at hand?"

"How much . . ." Alessandro struggled to make sense of the unexpected question. "Four hundred ducats. Perhaps five."

"Keep a hundred for yourself. I ask that you entrust me with the remainder. There is no telling what I will face upon the road. Gold may help to pave my way."

"Y-yes. Of course, whatever . . ." Alessandro's voice failed him entirely.

Falconer's grip upon the chair back tightened. Serafina watched the knuckles bunch and whiten. She could see the pressure stretch the muscles of his forearms. The wood creaked beneath his grip.

Yet when he spoke, his voice was soft as the rain now pelting the window. "Nathan Baring."

"W-what?" Alessandro stared at Falconer in bewilderment.

"The young man who was here earlier." The wood of the chair back groaned louder. Serafina's mother winced at the sound and the sight of so much raw power. Still Falconer's voice remained almost sibilant in its quiet. "The diplomat. The Christian."

"Yes. Of course. Your friend."

Falconer stared across the table at Serafina, and his dark eyes trapped and held her. She met his gaze because she had to. Why, she could not say. Though she did not understand what was occurring here, she knew one thing with unfailing certainty. Falconer would never harm her. *I will obey.*

Falconer's eyes were the first to drop, and his hold on the chair loosened. Serafina watched as he took a breath and struggled to speak.

"I feel God's hand upon this encounter," Falconer finally said, his voice muffled by his emotion. "He comes from a merchant family. He is well educated. He is commit-

ted to his faith and his cause. I can say nothing more, because it is all I know. I feel he
is someone who is well suited. . . ."

Falconer turned and stumbled toward the
rear of the house.

"Wait!" Alessandro had to grasp the chair
arms to force himself to his feet. "What of
you?"

Falconer had his hand on the doorjamb
leading to the kitchen. But he did not turn
back. "I am a man called to walk the path
of peril so that others may live in safety."

Serafina found herself standing beside her
father and crying. She wept without understanding, without regret, without joy. As
though her tears were required simply to
mark the end of one moment and the beginning of another.

Alessandro's own features struggled with
confusion and relief and a desire to reach
beyond himself and touch this man he did
not understand. "What . . . what of payment?"

Falconer opened the door and trod
through the kitchen. "Whatever is fair."

"A fifth of the mine's value! No, wait. A
fourth!"

The kitchen door had already closed shut
behind him.

Serafina hurried to the rear window. Her

parents rushed to join her. Together they watched Falconer cross the back garden, his massive shoulders slumped inward and his footsteps faltering.

Serafina traced one finger down the length of a raindrop upon the glass. She knew she had never observed a stronger man.

CHAPTER 8

An hour later Serafina had dried her face and decided she would be able to face Falconer without breaking down entirely. She wanted to be strong — especially now when he was leaving. She stepped to the small rear cottage and knocked on the door. A voice invited her in, and she found Gerald Rivens seated upon the stairs leading to the second floor.

Gerald removed the small clay pipe from his mouth. "I'll be going with him far as the first Richmond bridge, ma'am. See to it he gets off in safety and secret. The Langstons' men have just arrived. They're scouting around the perimeter now, getting a feel for the place. They'll be taking the upstairs chamber here for themselves. One of us will be on duty at all times. Tell your parents that. You folks will be safe enough."

"Thank you, Gerald. Your words offer me great comfort."

"Thought they might." He pointed at the closed door. "That man yonder, he's a singular sort of fellow."

Serafina swallowed hard. All her determination seemed less than smoke in a storm. "Yes, he is."

If Gerald noticed her distress, he gave no sign. "Falconer calls me to live the Word without opening his mouth. Leaves me wishing I was a better man."

"You are very good indeed." Her voice had turned so husky she scarcely recognized it. "A rare man, and a friend."

His pale eyes glimmered. "He'll come home to us safe and sound, ma'am. Don't you worry."

She wiped her eyes, tried hard for a smile, and asked Gerald if he could tell Falconer she was there. Gerald immediately rose to do her bidding.

"Mama and I made you provisions," she said when Falconer appeared in the doorway.

"Then I shall feast indeed. Please give her my sincere thanks." He bowed his head slightly in her direction but did not meet her gaze before turning back into his room. Serafina could see the satchel he was packing on the bed.

"Papa has the papers and the gold ready

for you in the front room," she said, raising her voice and keeping it as steady as she could.

"Gerald!" he called.

"Here."

"Go fetch them, if you would. And then it's probably time to leave for the Langstons."

The slender man left without another word.

Serafina set the food beside his satchel. "What you said back there . . ."

"Lass."

"Yes?"

"We are friends, are we not?"

"Yes." Her heart wrenched with the bittersweet truth.

"Then there is no need for you to say anything further. Is there?"

Her voice emerged hoarse and low. "Promise me you will come home."

Falconer finally turned to look at her. And smiled. "Home. What a nice thing to say to a man who has wandered all his life long."

"Wherever you are, however far you travel, you must always remember that. Our home is yours, John Falconer. A room is always here for you, a place at the table, a . . ."

They shared a long look. Two friends with a world of memories and caring between them. Then he went back to packing his belongings. He looked to be carrying just one satchel. In went the Book. A single change of clothes. The food. A brace of pistols. Powder and shells. She pointed at the small metal box he put in next. "What is that?"

"Percussion caps. For priming the pistols." His movements were as easy as his speech. "New-fangled invention. But they speed up the loading process, so I suppose they might prove useful."

"Were you ever afraid of anything?"

"What a question. Of course."

"I don't believe it for a moment."

"I face fears every day."

He was silent for a long moment, and something in the downward cast to his shoulders left Serafina certain he was thinking of her. Which only left her more helpless and worried. "What was the first thing you were frightened of?"

"The dark."

She laughed. "Just like any child."

"No, not really." He straightened after fastening the satchel. "I told you once of my early days. How I was apprenticed to a ratter. When the rage was on him, he'd send me into cellars alone. I hated those times. Eight years old was too young to be sent into a cold, dark place, my hands too full of cages to even carry a light."

"Stop, please," she whispered. "It is too terrible."

His gaze refocused upon her. "I have God now, you see. God and good friends. They see me through so much. Even this sad day of farewells and wishes I shall never share with another."

She was weeping so hard now she could hardly speak. "I'm so sorry."

"Shah, lass." Hearing the soft word from him, so full of affection, only caused her to weep the more. She could see his hand reach for her, then fall back to his side. "Shall I tell you a secret?"

She took a long moment to reply, "Only if it is a nice one."

"That it is, lass." He leaned closer, and she could smell his masculine scent. "God spoke to me about you."

She wiped her face with both hands, knowing she looked a mess and not really caring. Only wanting to see him clearly, her dear friend. "What did He say?"

"That you are right in what you have decided about us."

"Oh, Falconer."

"Shah, now. Is that not grand? How often do you face the darkness of doubt and know that God has blessed you with wisdom?"

"Please, Falconer, you must return. Please. I shall need your friendship all my days."

"There is one thing I have learned in my walk along God's ways, lass. Those whom the Lord has brought together are bound for all eternity." He touched her then, a single finger upon her face, capturing one tear, clenching it up tightly. "Stay in peace, little one."

She wanted to tell him to go in peace also. But the words would not come.

Falconer sat at the desk in his bedroom and checked his pocket watch again. His satchel sat ready by the door, his light saber strapped to the top. Alessandro's four suede sacks of gold were stowed inside, along with the leather oilskin of papers. Gerald Rivens had already slipped away to check on the Langston carriage and make certain all was ready. He had promised to leave Falconer a horse tethered in a nearby alley.

Across the rain-swept garden, the main house was dark and silent. But Falconer doubted anyone slept easy that night. He spotted one of the two guards leaning against the side wall, using the eaves to protect him from the downpour. The doctor had been good to his word. A yellow placard was nailed to the front doorpost, warning all the city to stay well clear. After the previous summer's cholera scare, the alert would indeed be heeded.

The watch's slow ticks taunted him. It was always thus before launching into a new adventure. Yet he felt oddly at peace.

The chair creaked dangerously as he leaned back, laced his hands across his belly, and listed his problems upon the ceiling overhead. He carried enough gold to attract every thief and cutthroat east of the Mississippi. He did not know where he was going. He had no idea what he would find when he got there. From the outskirts of Richmond he would travel alone. A foreign assassin had been set upon his trail. He had all but suggested to the woman he loved that she would be better off with another man.

And it was raining cats and dogs.

Falconer lowered his head and caught sight of his reflection in the dark windowpane. He had no reason to be smiling. None whatsoever.

He checked his watch once more and decided it was time. Even if it wasn't, it was close enough. The night was so miserably cold and wet he would gain nothing by waiting longer.

The only thing left to do was pray.

Falconer planted his elbows upon the table and knotted his hands together. He studied the hands as though they belonged to another man. In a sense they did, as the scars had been created by a past he no longer wished to claim. Where his left thumb joined with his wrist, three jagged white lines formed cicatrices, the script of action and foul deeds. When a pirate had whipped a razor-edged chain at his neck, Falconer's broadsword had been broken in two from the force, and the trailing edge had caught his hand. Farther up that same arm were scars from when his own musket barrel had once erupted. He had been so caught by the heat of battle he had been unaware of the wound. His right hand was laced with a multitude of rope burns that merged into one giant blemish across his palm. He bore sword cuts on his wrist, forearm, shoulder. Another wound beneath his left shoulder blade. His left thigh. And, of course, there was the most visible mark of all there upon his cheek.

In the candlelit window, Falconer studied the way his scar moved with his facial muscles. To think he dared hope that Serafina's parents would ever welcome such a one as this.

Slowly, back and forth, he shook his head. Denying his futile yearning with the finality of a decision he would never revoke. His destiny was the road, the danger, the quest. Alone.

He bowed his head.

The thought came to him, not in an exclamation, as he might have expected. Nor in a blast of power. Not even a whisper of sound.

Falconer lifted his head, his eyes wide open now. He listened to his breathing, for there was no other sound in the room.

Even so, he was certain he was no longer alone.

The thought that had come to him was too foreign to be his own. Not for an instant did he doubt he had been visited by a heavenly messenger. In the space of a single solitary heartbeat, an image had been planted. Complete, unquestionable.

Falconer rose to his feet, his hands still clasped. He brought them forward until they struck his chest. He lifted his face to the ceiling once more and spoke aloud. He spoke not to a distant God. Rather he addressed the God with him in his room.

"Thank you, Father. I am ready."

He dropped his hands and his head. He

blew out the candle, reached for his cloak, buttoned it into place about his shoulders, and planted the slouch hat upon his head. He reached for the satchel and opened the door to his room, took a last look at a darkened window in the main house, and then turned away.

The quest was on.

CHAPTER 9

The carriage jounced and rattled as it crossed the final bridge before Burroughs Crossing. The Chickahominy River flowed quickly in the high spring tide. The entire bridge shivered with the waters pushing hard against the timber supports. John Falconer heard the horses whinny in fear. The carriage driver called sharply in response and cracked his whip. Then they were across, and the sleeping city of Richmond lay ahead. Dawn was scarcely a glimmer upon the eastern hills, but Falconer had been awake for hours. Awake and awaiting this moment.

The carriage slowed, the high polished wheels caught in the riverbank's viscous mud. Falconer remained as he had throughout the night's final hours, slumped in the corner of the carriage with his cloak wrapped about him, feigning sleep. The carriage's only other passenger, an attorney's aide ordered to Richmond to disguise Falconer's journey, was sprawled across the opposite seat, snoring gently. The aide assumed Falconer was a house servant and had not spoken a word to him since setting off. Falconer, who had spent a lifetime more comfortable with blade and pike than words, welcomed the silence.

Gerald Rivens, the carriage driver, lightly thumped his fist against the carriage roof. Falconer reached for his satchel stowed beneath his seat. His sword's scabbard clanked softly against the satchel's latch. Falconer checked the aide's face, but the young man continued snoring. Falconer opened the carriage door, tossed his belongings to the driver, and clambered quietly up beside him.

"Burroughs Crossing is half a mile ahead," Rivens said in greeting. He pointed at the musket propped against the seat beside him. "I want you to take that."

The Whitney musket was worth a year's salary. "The sword and pistols are protection enough."

"If not for protection, then take it for food." Rivens was small and hard and tempered by a past not far from Falconer's own. "I'd rest easier knowing you traveled with it by your side."

The Whitney was one of the new versions, fitted for percussion caps, which did away with the need to prime the trigger. Falconer hefted the musket. "Thank you, Gerald. You are a friend."

"Your turning's just ahead." Gerald tugged on the reins. "We'll be praying for you."

Falconer patted his friend's shoulder, slipped the musket on top of his satchel, and used his free hand to climb over the carriage side. As Falconer slipped downward, Gerald waved a silent farewell. It was enough. All the words had already been spoken.

As the carriage slowed even further for the bend, Falconer dropped to the road. He took two running strides and was swallowed by the forest. He stood and listened to the carriage disappear into the distance. Falconer unstrapped his sword belt, fitted it about his waist, jammed in the pistols, hefted his satchel, and started back toward the road.

Falconer looked carefully around, then turned toward Richmond. Away from the dawn and into danger.

The city of Richmond had begun paving its main streets in oyster shell and fire-hardened brick. Or so Falconer had heard, for he had never been this way before. Though he was much traveled, it had always been by sea. He was now the farthest inland he had ever been in his adult life. He longed for a horizon of white-capped waves, one rimmed by gulls and salt-laced wind. But Falconer held to his present course.

Richmond's sophistication did not reach this far out. The Washington Turnpike was graded gravel and crushed rock, but recent rains had coated everything with a sheen of sticky mud. The road broadened where villagers had cut away the underbrush, opening the space so temporary pens could be erected. A pair of goats bleated nervously as Falconer approached. He slipped into the trees beyond the corrals and settled upon a log. He opened his satchel and took out a bundle wrapped in white linen. He lifted the linen to his face and breathed deeply. There beneath the smell of fresh bread and damp cheese he caught a faint hint of Serafina's perfume.

By the time Falconer finished his breakfast and folded away the linen, the light had strengthened to full day. In the distance the small village outside the town began to awaken. Falconer drank his fill from a nearby stream. He washed his face and hands, then swept back his hair so tightly he could feel his eyes pulled into the squint he had worn for years. He tied it with a black silk ribbon. He checked the satchel's three purses of gold and made sure the waxed coins would not clink. He slipped a fourth purse into his pocket beneath the pistol at his back. He checked the priming on his pistols and settled one on top of the purses. The day was warming, so he tied his black oilskin cloak to the satchel with the Whitney rifle. The knife's scabbard was by his right hand, his sword worn at his left. It was a pirate's manner of dress, such that Falconer could cross his arms and draw both weapons to parry and strike all in one lightning motion.

The clearing was dappled now with sunlight and buttercups. Falconer knelt there by the log he had used as a stool. He prayed long and hard. He prayed for safety. He prayed for success. He prayed for wisdom. He prayed for everything except the one thing his heart wanted most.

He rose to his feet, hefted his satchel, and headed out. Walking the boggy road toward Richmond's outlying town, he no longer headed into one quest, but two.

Richmond lay due west of the drovers' village known as Burroughs Crossing. To the south rose a pair of hills marking the borderlands of the James River, a twisting and cantankerous body of water that had flooded six times in as many years. The plantations atop those two hills were safe, of course. But here in the lowlands the signs of flooding were everywhere. The village's outermost cottages had water stains high as Falconer's waist. Where the villagers had stopped clearing, rubbish was banked up against the far trees, swept there by the latest heavy surges. Although the day was dawning bright, the ground glistened and puddles were everywhere.

The main buildings of Burroughs Crossing consisted of a tavern connected to a general store. The tavern was bordered on its other side by a large chicken run and a barn. An even larger corral opened into a meadow where ten horses gamboled, clearly enjoying the first warm and dry day in several weeks. Four drovers sat at a table by the tavern's front stoop, hunched over tin plates and steaming mugs.

A young boy gathering eggs was the first to notice Falconer's approach. He raced into the barn where a woman milked a lowing cow. "Mama! Look there!"

The woman needed only one glance to declare, "Run for your father. Hurry now."

"Papa! Papa!" The boy raced for the tavern on muddy bare feet. His cries alerted the drovers. Two of them pushed away from the table. Falconer kept his hands in clear view as he approached.

A big-boned man filled the tavern doorway. He wiped his hands on a stained leather apron and said to his son, "Go fetch Old Joe."

The boy did not need to be told twice.

The woman had risen from her milking stool and stood watching Falconer with arms crossed at her middle. The forgotten cow lowed mournfully. A pair of jays called their harsh warning. Otherwise the day was silent.

The innkeeper reached inside the doorway and came up with a long-bore musket. He cocked the piece with the same easy motion that brought it partway to his shoulder. "That's far enough."

"I'm after fresh food and supplies," Falconer announced.

"Then you'll be dropping your hardware in the dust at your feet."

Falconer motioned to the drovers. "They're still armed."

"Them I be knowing, stranger. You do what I say or else keep on down that road."

The boy came racing back with a narrow-faced black man in tow. The man might have stood taller than Falconer, if only he were to walk upright. But he remained somewhat bent, as though burdened by a massive weight.

Falconer drew out sword and scabbard, then his knife, then the pistols. The innkeeper said, "Joseph, gather up them pieces and stow them in the pantry. Son, get yourself on back and help your ma."

"I want to watch, Pa."

"You heard me." When the stooped man had gathered up Falconer's weapons and disappeared, the innkeeper warned, "I don't do nothing on credit 'cept maybe offer you a drink from my well."

"I will pay in good coin."

The innkeeper studied Falconer a long moment, then allowed, "You'll be after grub, I suppose." At a hand signal from the innkeeper, the drovers settled back to their table and fare, though all four men kept a steady eye upon Falconer. The innkeeper uncocked the gun and set it back behind the door. "Joseph will see to you. Come find me when you're done eating. I got chores that can't wait."

The house was called a drovers' tavern in these parts, or a tippling inn farther north. Such places sprouted by the side of busy

131

turnpikes like mushrooms in boggy soil. They served as gathering spots for the sort of folk not welcome closer into town. Men who bore the stench of animals, or the stain of danger. Wayfarers and wastrels and ne'er-do-wells. No wonder the drovers kept their weapons close at hand.

Falconer chose the bench that ran down by the horse trough, as far from the four drovers as he could manage. He set his satchel where it rested against one leg, leaned his back against the wall, and closed his eyes. The sun felt good on his bones. After a night without sleep, it would have been far too easy to doze off. But his quest was only beginning. Narrow heart, he reminded himself.

The black man came back bearing a tin plate and a cup of coffee. Falconer started to thank him as he set the items down on the bench. But he was already turning away. Joseph wore a slave's cast-offs. The pants could have held two of him. Hemp rope cinched the trousers about his middle, and the ragged hems ended midway up his calves. The shirt was threadbare. Joseph's face was tainted by a pain so deep it cut cavelike furrows across his forehead and cheeks. Falconer watched him shuffle away and felt himself convicted of all the silent

132

crimes embedded in that man's face and stooped walk.

Falconer finished his breakfast of beans and corn bread and fatback, washed down the last of his coffee, then rose from the bench. He carried his utensils in one hand and his satchel in the other as he entered the kitchen. "Thank you, Joseph. That was fine fare."

"Suh." The word was little more than a quiet cough.

"Could I trouble you for another cup of coffee?"

Wordlessly Joseph used the broom to indicate the pot settled by the fire.

Falconer used a singed rag to protect his hand as he filled his tin mug. "Where might I find the innkeeper?"

"Mas' Burroughs is over opening the store, I 'spect." The man did not lift his gaze. He had clearly come to know safety only through seeing nothing, acknowledging no one.

The dry-goods store was housed in what had once been a barn attached to the inn's north side. The innkeeper scooped nails into a barrel. He said without looking up, "Breakfast is two bits."

Falconer set his satchel and the coffee mug on the counter. He drew a leather pouch from his pocket and unknotted the drawstring. He pulled out one coin. And waited.

The innkeeper finally looked over, saw what Falconer was holding, and dropped his ladle with a clatter.

Falconer turned the coin so that it reflected the sunlight. "I told you I could pay."

"Let me see that coin."

"It's real enough."

"I said, let me see it." The innkeeper moved swiftly for such a big man. Falconer let him take the coin. He watched as the innkeeper slipped it between thumb and forefinger, feeling the waxed surface. Falconer knew what the innkeeper was thinking. Highwaymen often used waxed coins, for the wax kept the money from clinking. The innkeeper's features stretched tight with a smile that did not reach his eyes. "You aim on paying for a two-bit meal with a twenty-five dollar gold piece?"

"I'm after a horse, two donkeys, and supplies for the road."

The innkeeper made the coin disappear. "I can do that."

Falconer added, "And your man."

"Eh, what's that?"

"Your man Joseph. I've taken a liking to him."

The innkeeper was shaking his head before Falconer finished speaking. "Can't do it. Old Joe's part of the family."

"Sell me a good fast horse, two mules, some grub and gear, and Joseph," Falconer said. "I'll give you a hundred fifty dollars in gold coin."

Falconer knew such costs well. During his work against the Caribbean slave trade, he had run a chandlery, an emporium for merchant ships and island colonials. His clients liked nothing better than to compare the prices of man and horseflesh from South America to the southern United States. These days, a slave fetched anywhere from two to three hundred dollars, if the buyer paid in bank paper. A good horse started at fifty dollars, again using paper money. Payment in gold dropped the price by more than two-thirds.

"Show me the coin," the innkeeper said.

"When you've shown me the horse and mules and we've shaken hands on the deal."

The innkeeper tried for a laugh, but the sound came out a squeak. "You're too low by half, stranger."

"This is a take-it-or-leave-it offer," Falconer replied.

"And what if I say no? You think a highwayman on foot is gonna get anywhere down Richmond way? Why, they'll string you up in a Yankee minute."

Falconer held out his hand. "Give me back the gold."

The innkeeper realized he was losing out on a deal. "Now, you just hold on, stranger. There ain't no harm in dickering."

"Not if you have time to waste, which I don't. Here's the only dickering I'll offer." Falconer made his face go stone hard. "Do me wrong by this, and I'll come back again."

The innkeeper backed up as fast as a horse fleeing an open flame. He came up hard against the nail barrel. "There ain't no reason to talk to me like that."

"Either show me the wares or give me back that coin." Falconer hated the sound of his own voice. "I won't be asking you again."

Falconer started back up the same road that had brought him to Burroughs Crossing. He rode a dappled gray mare with a broad back and a mane one shade off white. The innkeeper's boy had wept aloud as Falconer had started off, for the mare had been his charge. Falconer had kept his face hard, though the boy's sorrowful wails had pierced deep.

Joseph rode one of the mules and held the

tether for the other one. He carried all his worldly possessions in a checkered cloth knotted to his saddle horn. His long legs almost scraped the ground as the mule trotted along. He had said nothing over his own sale. Just followed Falconer's terse orders and kept his face clamped down tight.

Falconer rode along until there were two long bends between them and the settlement. He slowed and inspected the road in both directions. He could hear cows lowing off to the north, the creak of wheels rumbling across the bridge up ahead. But he saw no one. He turned off the road and took a path headed into the woodlands.

"Suh, there ain't but one way 'cross that river," Joseph called out, "and it's straight on up ahead."

"We're going this way."

Joseph shrugged, clucked, and said, "Come on, mule."

The path was little more than a game trail. Branches closed in so tight on both sides Falconer finally dropped from the horse and led by the reins. The mules disliked the confined forest and brayed loudly. Joseph gripped the reins and tugged them along, saying nothing more.

As Falconer had hoped, the trail led to a meadow bordered on its north side by the swollen river. Others had clearly camped here, for there were several fire rings set with flat river-stones. Falconer tied his horse to a neighboring tree limb and loosened the saddle. He knew Joseph was watching him nervously. Falconer hated the man's fear but knew there was nothing he could do about it except keep his motions slow and deliberate. "Tie up those mules and come over here, please."

Falconer dropped his bedroll and satchel to the ground. He did not look up as Joseph approached cautiously. From his satchel he drew out the black-bound volume and held it out. "Do you know what this is?"

Joseph's eyes flickered over, then away. Not once had he actually looked at Falconer's face. "I 'spect it's the Good Book, suh."

"It is. Can you read?"

"Not even my name."

"Are you a believer?"

This answer was far slower in coming. "I was, suh. Once."

Falconer took hold of the Bible in both hands. "I stand before you at the beginning of a quest. I feel God has put it in my heart to make some small retribution for my sins. Not that I can atone for them. Only the

Savior can do that." Falconer paused long enough that Joseph finally raised his eyes, but he still would not look into Falconer's face. "I was first mate and then captain of a slave vessel. The one voyage I made on that vessel brought me to the Lord's saving grace. We carried four hundred and nineteen wretched souls. I do not know their names. I doubt I even saw one of their faces."

Falconer knew the man probably did not understand one word in five. And those Joseph understood, he probably did not believe. Falconer went on, "My quest is to free a slave for every one of those I carried into bondage. You are the first."

Falconer drew out Joseph's bill of sale and knelt on the ground. From his satchel he pulled out a quill and a bottle of ink. He unstopped the bottle, dipped the quill, and wrote out the words. He offered Joseph the paper without rising. "This is yours. I offer it with my abject apology. Nothing I can do will ever wash away my sins. That was the gift of Jesus. This I do simply as a symbol of my repentance."

Joseph made no move to accept the paper. His entire body trembled. "What you want from me?"

Falconer returned the cork to the inkwell and weighted the paper to the satchel with the bottle. He rose to his feet, keeping his motions slow. Even so, Joseph backed up a good half-dozen paces. His eyes scattered fear and incomprehension all over the sunlit meadow. Falconer showed him open palms, though he knew his actions meant less than nothing.

"You can leave now. Maryland is a day's hard push along the turnpike. I will give you money. Or you can stay."

Falconer repeated the words a second time. Then a third. Finally the man's violent trembling began to subside.

"You jes' be letting me go?" he asked.

"If you want."

"If I *want?* Whatever in this whole world is about what I *want?*"

Falconer shut his eyes and prayed, not so much a prayer of words as a silent plea for help. He held to this with as strong a grip as he knew how. But all he felt was weary.

When he opened his eyes once more, Joseph was looking at him for the very first time. "I walk that road north, don't matter what no paper says 'bout words I can't read. I'd be picked up and sold 'fore sunset."

"Then you can come with me. Only as a free man, though. I have work to the south. When it's done, I'll take you north myself."

"You'll take me far as the free states?"

"And give you money to start you on your way."

Joseph kept his head cocked to one side, his neck twisted as unnaturally as his body. He blinked slowly. "I asked you afore. What you want from me?"

"I need help." Falconer knew he should be saying it all better. But he had not slept a decent hour for a week now. Fatigue coated his thoughts and his tongue like tar. "You know what they do to people who free slaves?"

"Every slave knows that," Joseph replied. "They brand 'em and lash 'em and then they hang 'em. The man who frees 'em and the slaves both. Put a sign 'round the man's neck saying let this be a warning." He was watching intently now. "Hang 'em high."

"Four hundred and nineteen souls," Falconer repeated. "I need help finding them, and I need help buying them, and I need a way to get them north. So this is what I want. Give me something I can do to win your trust. You don't have any reason to believe a word I'm saying. But if you can think of anything that might make you accept what I'm saying as the simple truth, then I'll do it."

Falconer turned and headed for his bedroll. He was so tired he stumbled. His quest was started, and all he could think of was where to lay his head. His last thought was of how he was failing yet again.

CHAPTER 10

Falconer awoke to the comforting smells of campfire, coffee, and hot food. He tossed aside his blanket and rose to his feet, feeling rested after a few hours of sleep. The sun was lowering into its afternoon slant. Midway across the meadow, set where the afternoon light warmed and dried the surrounding earth, Joseph had built a strong fire, then let it burn down to a heap of coals. The fire was banked around a pair of flat river stones. On one sizzled cuts of fatback from Falconer's recently acquired stores. Nestled in the grease were six lumps of cornmeal frying into crisp griddle cakes. On the other stone simmered a pot that emitted the fragrance of brewing coffee.

Falconer walked to the stream, washed his face, and combed his hair with his fingers before retying his ribbon and returning to the campsite. "I half expected to find you long gone."

Joseph's only response was to use his shirttail to lift the pot and pour Falconer a tin cup full of coffee.

Falconer walked to where his saddlebags were slung over a tree limb and extracted a cloth sack containing squares of brown sugar. He squatted beside the other man and dropped five cubes into the tin cup. Joseph watched this carefully. Falconer offered him the sack. Joseph hesitated long, then carefully extracted one square. He slipped it into his mouth, sucked, and shut his eyes with pleasure.

Falconer took his time over the mug. It was a true campfire brew, as strong as tar and cooked long enough for the grounds to settle. Joseph forked the fatback and corn fritters onto two plates. He watched Falconer bow his head over his food, then slowly did the same. The two men ate in silence. Falconer set down his plate and held out his cup for a refill. "I have forgotten just how good food can taste when cooked over an open fire."

Joseph still said nothing as he poured the coffee. Falconer dropped in another five sugar lumps, offered Joseph the sack, watched the man take a single lump, and put the sack on the ground between them.

Then he waited.

Joseph took his time sucking on the brown sugar. Finally he squinted into the waning sun and said, "Seem mighty strange how a man come walkin' into Burroughs Crossing. Buys himself a fine horse, two mules, a man."

"I told you the truth about this quest."

"This man don't have nothin' to his name 'cept a purse of gold," Joseph went on, gazing toward the setting sun. "Don't even have tin plates for his supper. Gotta buy everything, right down to the sugar he's wasting in his coffee."

"It's a seaman's weakness, the use of sugar." Falconer felt his pulse quicken as he sensed the testing in the man's voice. "I have been given an impossible task. A second quest, besides the freeing of slaves. This other quest is one I do for another man. One that must remain secret until I am certain you're with me. It has meant I've had to depart by stealth. I traveled far as the bridge with others. I slipped away under the cover of night, leaving everything but this gold behind. For now, even my name must remain a secret."

Joseph weighed Falconer's words. In the lowering sunlight the deep seams in his features seemed carved by a wicked blade. "Hour before dawn a carriage come by, heading fast and hard for Richmond. Fancy a rig as ever I seen."

Falconer used his own shirt to lift the coffee pot, though he had little desire for more. What he wanted most was to move. He could feel his muscles quiver with the hunger he had not permitted himself to feel before now. How much he needed a new ally, someone he could trust when he needed to shut his eyes and forget the unattainable mission he had set for himself. "You notice a very great deal."

"Slave wants to stay alive, he gots to stay awares."

"You're not a slave anymore."

Falconer's words hung in the warm air. Their meadow was ringed by tall pines and birdsong. Joseph remained immobile long enough for sunset's border to rise up his shoulders and move across his chin. The stream chuckled a soft note to Falconer's right. He sipped from his cup to give his hands something to do.

Finally Joseph spoke. "You asked was there something needed doin'. Something to make me believe what you been saying."

"Just tell me what it is."

Joseph's entire body clenched with the emotion. "I had me a woman," he said, his voice raw.

"Your wife?"

"We never stood before no preacher. But she was mine just the same."

"And children?"

"Two boys. Nine and thirteen." Joseph wiped his face with a shaking hand. "We was owned by a gamblin' man. Bet against Burroughs in a horse race. The man lost the race and turned me over to him as payment. I worked the man's fields since before he was born. He just signed the papers and walked away."

Falconer tossed out the dregs of his cup. "Where is he?"

Joseph reached over and gripped Falconer's wrist, his motion lightning swift. He looked at Falconer, his face holding a feverish gleam. "Don't you be messing with Joseph. I ain't got nothing. I ain't never trusted no man. Don't you be saying this and crushing me just 'cause you can."

Falconer held the man's gaze. "Where is this man's farm?"

Joseph waited a long moment, then said, "Moss Plantation, down Petersburg way."

"Can you find it in the dark?"

Joseph released his grip. " 'Spect so. I done lived there all my life."

Falconer rose to his feet. "Then let's move out."

■ ■ ■ ■

They held to game trails until they had bypassed Burroughs Crossing. The gathering dark slowed them until they emerged from the forest. They faced a city aglow with firelight and lanterns. Richmond was built upon hills ringing the James River. The higher slopes contained the wealthier homes, and the deepening twilight revealed lights glimmering from a host of manors. Brick lanes shone like gold ribbons.

Falconer and Joseph chose a route that took them through Richmond's darker south side. They paused only to ask directions from taciturn wagon masters. Toward midnight they joined the well-traveled Fredericksburg Turnpike. As soon as they left Richmond's city lights behind, Falconer saw the stars were gone, the sky wrapped in yet more clouds. Thankfully there was no rain. They passed teams of oxen lashed eight to a wagon, and the occasional horse-drawn cart. They kept to the middle course and made good time.

Toward dawn they slipped off the road, then moved farther into the woods until they came upon a likely meadow. This one they shared with other travelers, most of whom were asleep. The sort of wayfarers who could not afford an inn were not likely to notice a lone man traveling with a servant, or so Falconer hoped. They shared another campfire meal while the horse and mules chomped oats in their feedbags. Falconer watered them at the neighboring stream and returned to find Joseph packed and ready to move out. A single glance at the man's fevered expression kept Falconer from asking if he needed rest.

Morning was a feeble affair. They trekked up and down a series of steep-sided hills, every crest revealing an endless sky of bluish-gray hues, peaks and valleys and whorls that might have been beautiful were Falconer not so weary. The land through which they traveled was sharp in unattractive contrast. The constant rains had delayed the onset of spring. Hardwood trees were still bare. The tilled fields were brown and empty. The only humanity Falconer saw was there upon the turnpike. Now and then he glanced over at Joseph. The man sat well upon the mule, upright and strong, too intent upon what lay ahead to pay his body's exhaustion any mind.

Suddenly Joseph raised up and squinted into the gray distance.

"What is it?"

In response, Joseph kicked the mule's sides. The two beasts, roped together as they were, began cantering away. The mules had a curious gait — not a gallop like a horse, yet surprisingly fast. Falconer let Joseph take the lead. The turnpike was forty feet wide as it swooped down the hillside. The bottomland was flanked by a broad stream. Where the road narrowed to cross the plank bridge, two wagons approaching from opposite directions had become tangled. The drovers were shouting and the oxen lowing. Joseph did not even slow as he twisted the mule's reins and led the beast away from the impassable bridge, down the slope, and into the stream.

At the stream's central point, the water rose and wet Falconer's boots in a chilling rush. The mare was surefooted and rock steady, which was fortunate, since Falconer had little experience at riding. After a night in the saddle, his back ached and his thighs burned. He could not imagine how Joseph felt, nor what drove the man forward with such urgency.

The mules were lathered and snorting hard by the time they crested the next ridgeline. Joseph pulled up sharp, squinting into the distance. "Oh Lawd, no, no," he cried, "it's more than a body can stand."

Falconer had a seafarer's eye, trained by studying distant horizons. Yet all he could see was a line of people walking upon the next hill. A dozen of them, silhouetted against the murky sky. A horseman appeared to lead while another followed the group.

When he realized what he saw, a cold wash of dread swept over him. "You recognize them?"

"My boys." Joseph's words were a groan.

"You're certain?"

"Solomon's walking third in that devil line. Isaac is fifth. Sure as my heart is breaking."

"You hold to a steady pace. We can't blow the mules." It was Falconer's turn to dig in his heels. "Hyah!"

The mare was bigger and stronger than the mules. Even so, by the time Falconer crested the next ridge, the horse's chest was heaving and its sides were lathered. The hill's southern slope was far more gentle, leading not into yet another valley but rather sliding gently through well-tended farms. Smoke rose in steady plumes from beyond the next line of hills, marking the turnpike's approach to Petersburg. Falconer spotted the human train less than a quarter mile ahead and slowed to a walk.

The horsemen fore and aft kept their charges tight against the roadside, allowing the swifter wagon traffic to pass unheeded. Falconer knew he should be planning what he was about to say, but his mind was locked down tight by the spectacle.

The rear horseman rode a speckled gelding and held to a pace that was easy on his horse. His charges were bent with fear and fatigue. Falconer's hands gripped the reins so tight the horse whinnied and skittered nervously. An approaching drover cracked his whip and cried, "Guard yer course, there!"

The two horsemen turned at that. The rear guard carried a leather quirt strapped to his right wrist and resting upon his pommel, which would make it difficult for him to pull the pistol from his belt. The lead rider had no such problem. He swiveled his steed about and drew a bead with his musket.

Falconer forced his hands to unlock, though there was nothing he could do about the rage scalding his face and throat. "Hold hard there."

"I ain't in the habit of taking orders from strangers creeping up on me." The lead rider shifted the muzzle a fraction. "You best cross over to the other side and keep on going."

"I'm after doing business with you."

"And I ain't asking you again." The lead man cocked his weapon. "Now git."

Falconer kept coming. "I'll pay in gold."

The man lowered his weapon a notch. "Talk is cheap, stranger."

"I need to reach into my saddlebag."

"Use your left hand. Keep the other up high there, 'less you aim on eating lead for breakfast. Ain't much chance of me missing at this range."

Falconer fumbled with the buckle, for he was reaching across the saddle while holding his horse steady with the wrong hand. Finally he managed to unknot the tie and draw out a leather pouch. He used his teeth to pull the drawstring and let two of the coins slip free.

"Cody, you keep a sharp eye on this feller."

The other man slung his quirt on the saddlehorn and drew his pistol. "I got him covered."

The lead rider lowered his weapon, then leaned over his pommel to eject a long stream of tobacco juice. He wiped his mouth with a stained sleeve. "Which ones you after?"

"All of them."

"Is that gold eating a hole in your pocket?"

The lead rider's sweat-stained hat was pulled down low over his forehead. "Mister, you ain't even checked 'em out."

Falconer knew he was expected to get off his horse and make a slow procession down the line. But he feared the inner fury such an action might unleash. Falconer had sworn an oath never to take another life, not even if it meant giving up his own. Yet he found it nigh on impossible to keep his hands where they were. He dared not even look at the people in that line. "I've seen enough."

"We gonna sit here chawing or are you gonna —"

Falconer said the first thing that came into his mind. "I'm taking charge of a mine down Gastonia way."

At that, three of the older people in line, a man and two women, began wailing. It was a wordless cry, a dirge so hopeless it caused the passing oxen to low in fear. Falconer's heart felt wrenched from his chest.

The lead rider, however, grinned broadly enough for yellowed teeth to appear within the tobacco-stained mouth. He flipped back his hat so it hung from the leather strap around his neck. His eyes were as empty as his grin. "Well, why didn't you say so? I knew you for a hard man first time I laid eyes on you. Which mine you overseeing?"

"That's not your concern."

"Naw, guess not." The lead rider pointed a thumb toward the south. "We got us a dandy auction right down there in Petersburg. First in nigh on a year. Hear tell they's gonna be all sorts of folks looking for good stock. Don't see how I could take less than top dollar from you."

"How many will be offering you gold?"

"Yeah, you got a point there, I can't deny it." The lead rider shot out another brown stream. "I'll take twelve hundred dollars for the lot."

"Too much."

"All right. All right. You're a hard man, didn't I say it? Nine hundred for all twelve. That's my last and final price."

Falconer knew he was overpaying. Knew also he was expected to dicker. But his hands were itching to pound this pair into the earth. Rage made his entire body stiffen as he counted out the coins and turned his voice to a growl. "Make out the papers."

The people in line were all wailing now, caught up in the fear of those who understood what it meant to work the mines. The two riders paid them no attention.

The lead man passed the musket to his fellow and counted aloud as he let the coins

155

fall through his fingers. "Don't believe I caught your name, stranger."

The misery chained in that line left Falconer feeling as though eternal darkness seeped from the earth, rising up to blind him. "John," he murmured, scarcely aware he had spoken at all.

"Nothing else?"

"John will do."

The slaver dropped to the ground, pulled a sheaf of papers from his saddlebags, and signed them with broad strokes. "There's your titles, free and clear, Mr. John. I'll even throw in the chains and a pair of canteens to show there's no hard feelings. You'll be needing these keys. Now then. You aim on taking this load south all on your lonesome?"

Falconer found himself unable to look the rider straight in the eye. "My man's leading mules off behind."

"They's good 'uns, you'll see. I deal strictly in quality merchandise." He offered Falconer his hand. "The name's Jeb Saunders. This here's my brother Cody. You be wanting more of the same, I work mostly out of Rock Hill."

Falconer pulled the horse's reins away from the man's hand. "I'll be in touch."

"You do that, Mr. John." The slaver let his

hand drop with another barren grin. "Always a pleasure dealing with a man who pays in gold."

CHAPTER 11

The empty-handed slavers headed south, casting a few glances over their shoulders. They soon left the straggling band far behind. The older one, Jeb, kept his horse reined in tight to his brother Cody's side, their legs almost touching as they entered Petersburg.

Jeb Saunders scarcely seemed to notice the city or take heed of where he was going, Cody noted. This was most unlike his brother. Most times, Jeb would crow for hours over taking a man like he just did back there on the road. Cody shook his head and shrugged.

Jeb kept just enough grip on the reins to head his horse for the lone tavern fronting the slave docks. Petersburg was a strange sort of town — neither this nor that. The families with power put on airs like they were as good as folk up Richmond way. The town itself was as old as any. But where

Richmond and Williamsburg had grown and prospered, Petersburg had festered. It did not expand so much as sprawl. Cody had heard it described as all mouth and dark underbelly. Which was why it contained one of only two permanent slave docks in all Virginia, the other being by the port of Norfolk and almost never used these days.

The tavern was just the sort of place they liked — dark and quietly welcome. Tipplin' hours meant nothing to a place like this. Cody started to climb down from the saddle. His brother remained where he was. "You aim on sittin' there all day?" Cody demanded. "My throat's bone dry with road dust."

Jeb continued to stare at nothing. "I knowed that horse."

"What you goin' on about now?"

"The one that feller was riding." Jeb slapped the reins on his leg. "I seen it before."

"Don't mean nothing to me." But Cody was watching his brother more carefully now. He and Jeb made a good team because they both knew and accepted the others' strengths. Cody was the doer, Jeb the thinker. Cody walked the line, kept things under control. Jeb plotted and dickered and traded. "But one thing I know for certain.

He didn't ride like no trail hand."

The saddle creaked as Jeb eyed his brother. "Say that again."

"You saw it same as me. That feller sat on his horse like a lump of cold meal."

"Cody, you done put your finger right on it. Here I been, worrying it like a dog with an old bone. Who said you were dumb?"

"Nobody in shooting range, that's for sure."

But Jeb Saunders was off again, staring at the distance. "Feller said he was rounding up hands for a mine."

"So?"

"So whoever heard of a mine overseer that couldn't ride worth a hoot?" His fist struck the pommel. "Old man Burroughs."

"Now you done lost me."

"The merchant up Richmond way. That was his horse."

Cody pondered on that. "Now you mention it, I do believe I recall seeing a white-maned mare in his pasture."

"You know what I think? I don't think there's any mine at all."

"What difference does it make? We're the ones sitting here with the fool's money in our pocket."

"Which is why we can afford to ask around. See if this feller is up to something."

Jeb Saunders pointed back up the north road. "Why don't you mosey up to Burroughs Crossing. Ask that innkeeper what he knows about this feller John."

"First I'm gonna wet my whistle, eat me some good home-cooked grub, and get me some shut-eye." Cody leaned over and punched his partner's saddlebag. "But not before I watch you count out my share of the gold."

Jeb's grin was almost lost beneath his scraggly beard. "I didn't know you was such a cautious one."

"Don't normally come upon a feller willing to pay double what the goods is worth. And do it in waxed gold coin."

The grin vanished. "Which is exactly why we needs to be checking on John. If he's a do-gooder, we know what to do next."

Falconer sighed and settled his back against a longleaf pine. Overhead the clouds were giving way grudgingly, plucked aside by a rising wind. The trees whispered in a soft musical rush. He yawned and scratched his back against the tree trunk. He was as tired as he could ever recall. But he was too joyful to sleep. Falconer was not a man to apply such a word to himself. Yet joy was the only word to describe how he felt.

His charges were sprawled about the field, full with Joseph's simple camp fare. The chains were heaped at the forest edge. The folks slept where they had fallen, so exhausted none even moved. Joseph slept with one arm wrapped around each of his boys. Their reunion had been a wonder to behold.

Falconer knew he and his kind had certainly contributed to this tragedy. Yet he could not keep lashing himself with guilt. He had done wrong in the past. He had come to the Cross. He had felt a call to this quest. He was doing all he could. Falconer yawned again, pleased with the morning's accomplishments.

He must have dozed off, because the next thing he was aware of was the fragrance of fresh-brewed coffee. Joseph must have seen him stirring and brought over a cup and the sack of sugar. He squatted on the earth next to Falconer with the customary silence. Even so, Falconer sensed a change. Joseph held himself more erect. His burdens were lighter. Falconer sipped the steaming brew. Then he said, "Tell me about this man Moss."

"A gamblin' fool," Joseph quickly replied, clearly having expected the question. "I 'spect his daddy must be rollin' in his grave."

Falconer rose to his feet. Instantly the dusty gathering began to shift. They looked about with dull eyes, expecting nothing save another helping of sorrow. None would meet his gaze save Joseph. Yet this one change Falconer counted as a blessing and reward both.

"You are all free," Falconer told the group. As with Joseph, the words simply did not register. "Free. I have bought you to repay an old sin of my own making. You can leave if you wish. Or you can stay and I will do my best to deliver you to a place of safety."

He repeated it all once more. None moved nor looked his way. But several turned to watch Joseph. Falconer asked him, "How far to the Moss homestead?"

"Five, maybe six miles."

Falconer said to the others, "Joseph and I must go away for a time." He glanced at his pocket watch, then realized the hour meant nothing to them. "I will return by nightfall."

"You just aim on leaving them here?" Joseph asked.

"Look at them. They're half starved and worn out."

"They's also free. Or so you say."

"We could go and come back in five hours, maybe less."

"And them night riders could swoop down

in five minutes."

One of the women began to wail at the thought.

"We'd be back long before sunset," Falconer said.

"Them night riders, they carry their own dark everywhere they go," Joseph said.

"All right," Falconer said to the group. "Those who want to come with me, let's move."

The Moss homestead occupied the southern slant of a long low hill, some hundred and twenty acres in all, according to Joseph, who had worked the soil since the age of five. The house was located on the pinnacle. The bottom acres were bordered by a creek almost broad enough to be called a river. The middle slope was given over to tobacco, the tall stalks stripped bare save for the last meager leaves. Joseph huffed in disgust at what he saw. The fields should have already been plowed under and prepared for spring planting, he told Falconer. Joseph pointed angrily at an orchard where fruit littered the ground. Falconer understood little save the man's lifelong attachment to land that was not his.

The whole group except for one youth came with them. The young man had vanished somewhere along the road. Joseph had clicked his tongue and shook his head in worried disagreement but said nothing.

Falconer directed his motley band into the final line of forest, then walked the last part of the drive accompanied only by Joseph. The home looked impressive enough from a distance. Then the long drive entered a grove of poplars, and when it emerged, the house revealed its shabby state. Paint flaked and scattered gray petals over the front lawn. Two holes in the roof had been poorly repaired. A front step was rotted through, a window boarded over.

Falconer stopped by the final poplars, holding to shadows. "Will you be safe going off alone?"

"I know this land better'n my tongue knows my teeth," Joseph replied. "Won't nobody see me if'n I don't want 'em to."

"Go find your wife. See if she's up to the journey."

Joseph did not show any eagerness to move. "Journey to where?"

"I don't know." Falconer saw no reason to give false hope. "Events have moved faster than I expected. I had planned first to find a proper route to freedom. But you see what has happened."

Joseph studied him openly now. The eyes

held a yellowish tint; the face was still bladed into deep caverns. Yet the man had been revealing a keen intelligence and a hunter's intensity. "All you done told me, it's the truth?"

"Every word."

"You aim on buying a passel of slaves and setting 'em free?"

"Four hundred and nineteen."

He shook his head. The man was evidently working on a decision. Falconer saw no reason to rush him. "You better have a pot of gold somewheres, the way you be spending it."

Falconer said nothing.

Joseph nodded slowly, as though Falconer's answer was what he had sought. "I'll be back soon enough."

He returned like a soft breeze, a quiet puff of sound, and suddenly Joseph was squatting on the earth beside Falconer. "She can move easy enough. She's had a wet chest every winter since she was a child. But she's a good woman, and strong."

"Her name?"

"Geraldine." The depth of his feeling was not revealed until that moment. For when Joseph spoke the name, his voice broke. Falconer did the decent thing and stared at the plantation home.

"My own name is John Falconer."

Joseph gave that a moment's respectful silence, then went on. "She says things is the same 'round here, only worse."

"Moss is still gambling?"

"Had some of his wretched lot up to the house for a day and a night of sinnin'. Already lost what he got from selling my two boys." Joseph tossed a stone. "When he ain't gambling, he's drowning in the bottle."

"How many others are left?" Falconer asked.

"Slaves?" Joseph's face tightened. "I ain't much with numbers."

"Try."

"They's two in the kitchen. Maybe fifteen in the fields. Two workin' the big house. And old Mammy, she don't do nothin' no more 'cept sit in the sun and suck on her corncob pipe."

Falconer opened his satchel. He plucked out his final full pouch and slipped it into the pocket holding the other, which was almost empty. Not enough. Not enough by half. But he could not see himself leaving a single solitary soul in this dismal place. "You wait here."

"What you be doing?"

He did not know was the answer. Falconer

walked toward the house in silence, offering up a prayer of guidance, a swift plea for he knew not what. His concentration was interrupted by the sight of a figure flitting before an open window. There and gone in an instant. The sort of motion made by an enemy. Or maybe someone constantly living in fear.

Falconer stepped across the broken stair, crossed the veranda, and knocked loudly on the door. There was no reply. He pounded this time. His fist caused a booming echo through the downstairs rooms.

A woman, black face rather pinched, looked at him through a crack between door and jamb. "The house ain't open to visitors."

"I'm here on business."

"Massuh Moss, he ain't well."

Falconer saw the tremor to her features. He knew what she thought. Here was yet another man coming to barter in human souls. "Ma'am, I mean you no harm."

The words were meaningless. "You best be comin' back another day."

Falconer used the flat of his hand to keep her from shutting the door in his face. He spoke scarcely above a whisper, "Joseph is here with me."

She held off a fraction. "Joseph been sold."

"He is here. But please don't tell anyone." When he was certain she would no longer lock him out, Falconer dropped his hand. "May I ask your name?"

She squinted at the kindness in his tone. "Maybelle."

"Miss Maybelle, I have urgent business with Mr. Moss. Business that will serve you and all the house well. I ask that you trust me on this."

"Massuh Moss, he still layin' abed."

He spoke in the soft cadence he might use to calm a frightened child. "Please go tell him he has a visitor. One who has brought gold with him." Falconer drew out the smaller pouch and extracted a coin. "Show him this."

The trembling returned. "You gonna be after buying more of us, sure to goodness."

"Ma'am, I am a servant of the Most High God. I speak to you as one who would never own another human being for fear of forfeiting his rightful place in heaven." Falconer saw she was not taking in his words. "For all our sakes, I ask that you trust me."

"What you said about Joseph, you wasn't jesting?"

Falconer walked to the edge of the veranda, where he stood in full sunlight. The poplar grove looked empty. He waved his arm back and forth over his head. And waited.

A man stepped from the shadows. Falconer pointed and asked, "Do you see him there?"

From the doorway, the woman clasped her hands to her chest and murmured, "Never in all my born days."

Falconer motioned again, and the man disappeared. "Do you think your master will speak with me?"

"For gold, Massuh Moss, he'd rise from the grave." She turned back toward the inside, then said, "You be wantin' to come inside, suh?"

Even standing in the doorway was enough to hint at the foul odors inside. "I'll stay where I am."

"I'll have the girl bring you a pitcher of spring water and some biscuits." She left the door open and shuffled away.

Falconer tested a high-backed porch chair before easing down. Truth be told, he was as weary as from a night of hard fighting. He was not made for a horse's back, and the trek from Richmond had tired him mightily. He pulled the chair forward to where he could prop his feet on the railing. In three minutes he had fallen asleep.

"Who wants to talk with me about gold?"

a voice demanded.

Falconer dropped his feet with a thump. It was unlike him to give way so easily to slumber, especially when in unknown surroundings. He rose to his feet. "My name is Mr. John, at your service."

"John? Uncommon strange last name." Moss was a pudding-faced man, lumpish with fat and foul ways. His hair was a scraggly mess and so pale as to be translucent. His eyes held a greedy tightness. "You're not from around these ways."

"No, sir. I hail from Washington now, but I have spent the past decade on the island of Grenada."

"Is that a fact." The man's interest faded. He turned to the woman hovering in the doorway. "Where's that coffee?"

"Done put it on to brew, suh."

"Well, be quick about it." He turned back. "You'll be wanting a drop of something stronger than that well water is my guess."

"The water will do me fine."

"Hmph." Moss frowned his opinion of a man who did not drink. "Well, I'm a busy man, Mr. John. The girl said you wanted to talk some business."

"Indeed, sir. I wish to buy your slaves."

"Which one?"

"All of them."

Moss laughed until he coughed. "All? That's absurd, man. How would I live?"

"I'll answer that," Falconer replied, "after you hand over my gold coin."

Moss started to object, but something he must have recognized in Falconer's face kept him silent. Even so, his hand only hovered over his watch pocket. Finally he pulled it out and dropped it into Falconer's hand. The act left him angry. "I asked you a simple enough question."

"And I shall answer in kind. You will not require your slaves, sir, because I wish to buy your plantation as well." Falconer held up his hand to halt the protest. "I will pay in gold."

The eyes tightened further. "This land has been in my family for five generations."

Falconer said nothing. He merely glanced down at the broken front step.

Moss flushed but held his anger in check. "A place this fine, I'd expect top dollar."

"Which I will pay."

The negotiations took the better part of two hours. They would have taken far longer if Falconer had not been impatient to be off. He could feel the homestead's misery like a stain in his heart. Finally Moss brought out the yellowed deeds and land surveys and signed a covenant agreeing to sell Falconer the land, buildings, and slaves. "I'll be taking your remaining farm workers with me now."

Moss's hands itched for the gold still in Falconer's fist. "Now, why would you be thinking I'd agree to any such thing?"

"Because they're the ones you would most likely sell again before I return."

Moss started to protest, but something in Falconer's gaze halted the words unformed. "You ain't taking my house women. I ain't keeping my own table for the three weeks you got to return with the rest of my payment." He reached out. "Now give me my gold!"

Falconer handed over his remaining coins. He had twenty-one days to return with the remaining sum. He had fought hard for more time. But Moss had burned with resentment over needing to sell the farm at all. The tight timing was his prized bargaining chip, the only reason Falconer was able to leave with any of his slaves. "You can keep one house servant, long as it is not Geraldine. She comes with me."

"Eh, what's that?" Moss was so intent upon counting his money he took a long moment to look up. "How'd you come about knowing the name of one of my women?"

Falconer gave the answer he had just formulated. "I acquired Joseph from the Burroughs innkeeper. I intend to make him my overseer."

"Here on the farm?"

"No. At a mine down in Carolina. I find my men work better if their families are intact."

Moss pondered that a while, then waved his hand in dismissal. "Take her. And good riddance to the both of them."

Falconer rose, for to stay a moment longer would have risked him breaking his vow. He folded the deed of sale, stowed it in the now-empty pocket, and said, "I shall see you in three weeks or less."

"You don't, the gold you done left here is mine, we clear on that?" Moss pitched his voice loud enough to chase after Falconer. "Come dawn on that twenty-second day, you done lost yourself a passel of coin."

CHAPTER 12

In the end, they took the old woman they called Mammy along with them as well. Joseph claimed Moss wouldn't notice the loss, as he had never come down to the quarters since his father's demise. And Geraldine was loath to leave the old woman. Nobody else looked after her. So she came. There were twenty in all, less the young man who had vanished into the forest, and not counting Joseph. They were aged from nine to years beyond count. Mammy had no idea how old she was. She rarely spoke at all. Geraldine rode the mare and Mammy was on one mule, while the second mule toted their gear. They held to a slow pace and made only a few miles before they stopped for the night.

Geraldine was by then too weary to help her husband cook up their remaining provisions, so Falconer joined Joseph by the campfire. The three sacks of cornmeal and side of fatback were swiftly cooked and consumed. But no one would take it from Falconer's hand. They might have been starving, yet none would meet his eye or take his food. So Falconer tended the fire while Joseph set his two children to gathering up large leaves on which to serve the meal. The others accepted their fare and ate without once looking Falconer's way. They all sipped from Joseph's one cup, refusing to touch Falconer's, though he left it on the rock by the pot. Joseph shared his plate with Geraldine and the boys. Falconer took his own provisions to one side and ate alone, knowing it was wrong to feel ashamed, yet feeling it just the same.

Most of the group curled up and slept, long trained to take rest when and where they could. Joseph's two boys nestled up to either side of their mother. Falconer heard a few soft words from the trio, then nothing. From the surrounding forest he heard one lark. Or perhaps a mockingbird. From farther still came the faint rumblings from the Petersburg Turnpike. But they were alone here in their small clearing. Which was a good thing, because Falconer needed time to plan.

Joseph refilled Falconer's cup and used it as an excuse to approach. Falconer took

that as a gift of trust and returned it, saying, "I need to discuss something with you.
Ask your advice."

Joseph remained standing to one side.
"Don't recall ever hearing a white man say
those words to me before."

"We have twenty souls in need of safety.
Twenty-one, counting yourself."

"Twenty-two," Joseph corrected.

"I didn't count myself."

"I wasn't neither." Joseph motioned with
his chin toward the forest. "The boy's been
back since you started frying up that meat."

"The one who ran?"

"The very same." Joseph raised his voice
slightly. "You don't come on out now,
Aaron, I'll eat this food myself."

The shadows among the trees were still a
moment longer, and then a youth of perhaps
sixteen stepped into view. He stood at the
outskirts of the circle, his eyes glittering in
the firelight. Joseph kept his voice low
enough not to disturb the others. "You see
where the vittles is at. Go on now. Eat up
and get some rest."

The boy moved like a frightened animal,
keeping the fire between himself and the
two men, hunching over and taking the food
in fierce gulps. He retreated back to the
edge of the woods and, to Falconer's eye,

simply vanished.

"Is he gone?"

"Gone to sleep." Joseph obviously saw what Falconer could not. "He's smarter'n I reckoned. He'll be with us from now on."

"I haven't seen him before now."

"Aaron's half wild. But he's a fine worker when he sets his mind to the chore. And he can hit a turkey on the wing with a slingshot. Surest eye I ever did see."

"Can he shoot?"

Joseph looked down at where Falconer sat. "You truly don't know nothing, do you."

"I take that as a no."

"I reckon the boy could shoot the eye from a piney wood at five hundred paces if'n somebody trusted him with a gun."

Falconer nodded slowly over all that comment contained. "We are out of money and out of provisions. Slow as we'll be moving, I can't see us making safety in less than a week."

Joseph hunkered down beside him. He pitched his voice lower still. "Where you aim on heading?"

"That's the problem. The map in my saddlebag shows the territories west of Virginia to be closer. But the mountains look formidable, and the roads are sketched out. Like they might be there, or they might not. Maryland is no help. They're neither fish nor fowl on the slave issue. Back in Washington a black man walking on his own is as good as sold. Pennsylvania is our other choice, but that would be quite a trek."

"Did your map show you where the night riders is at?"

"I don't understand."

"Night riders and bounty hunters both. Any Negro north of Richmond is fair game. You know what they do to a white man caught helping a Negro leave the slave states?"

"We've spoken of this already."

"They brand 'em. They lash 'em. And they hang 'em." Joseph shook his head. "Don't head north."

"Then where?"

Joseph picked up a stick and carved in the dust at his feet. The firelight revealed a man in the throes of hard choices.

Finally he spoke. "You hear talk 'bout places that'll help any slave that makes it to their land."

"Can you be certain about them?"

"Ain't never met no slave who's got free and come back to talk." Joseph continued writing in the dust. "There is one name. I heard about it since I was just a little child. Often enough and from enough different people, I reckon this might be real."

"Where is it?"

"South," Joseph replied. "Four days hard walkin'. Down the Catawba Trail."

Dawn found them well beyond Petersburg. They continued on the main route, headed now for a town with the unlikely name of Roanoke Rapids. The turnpike was home to every manner of folk, from wagonloads of settlers to dandy carriages and fast-moving postal riders. Falconer kept his people to the drovers' trail that ran alongside the turnpike. That was how he thought of them now. His people. They did not trust him, and none save Joseph would either meet his gaze or speak his way. Which was not altogether bad. Already he was gathering the wrong sort of attention by being the only white slaver he'd seen on foot.

The morning after he and Joseph spoke, Falconer had entered Petersburg with his mare and the two mules and returned on foot, leading mules piled high with provisions. Whether it would be enough to feed his people for five more days, Falconer had no idea. But it was all the merchant had been willing to offer for the gray mare, and also all the animals could carry. Falconer had not been sorry to see the last of that horse, at least initially. But the miles stretched far longer on foot, and by the time he arrived back at camp, he bitterly regretted both the decision and the need.

The day remained overcast and close. Falconer distributed the sacks of goods among his people so that Mammy could ride one mule and Geraldine the other. The wagoners they passed frowned at the sight of a white man walking while his servants rode. The drovers spat his way. But Falconer soon grew too tired to notice.

Their progress was slow, painfully slow. The people were bone weary in a manner that no single night's rest could vanquish. The children in particular suffered. The fact that they did so in silence granted Falconer no peace. He kept his impatience to himself and urged them forward only in prayer.

At Five Forks they halted for a cold midday meal. Aaron slipped away into the forest and once again was gone. Falconer glanced at Joseph, who shrugged a silent reply. The boy would return.

Falconer walked alone into town. He traded his dagger, a fine instrument of damask steel with a hilt chased in gold cord, for two sacks of coffee, a round of cheese, and a bushel of pears. Even more than provisions, though, Falconer needed information.

While the cheese was being wrapped and tied to the bushel, Falconer said, "I'm told I need to take a route called the Catawba Trail."

The merchant was clean-shaven and tall, which only accented the potbelly that was framed by his suspenders. "What on earth for?"

"I'm after work in the mines."

The merchant humphed his opinion. "Well, for one thing, it ain't called the Catawba Trail no more. It's the Colonial Trading Route. Been that since my pappy started this here drygoods store."

Falconer smiled in the direction of the woman bundling the coffee sacks together with twine. She was big boned where her husband was thin. She grew unsettled by his attention and bustled after a child crawling on the floor. Falconer asked the merchant, "Where did the original name come from?"

"Catawba Injuns, I reckon. They's still some down Carolina way. Used to be good trappin' territory. Folks say Davy Crockett hisself carved out that road. Ain't hardly used no more."

"Why is that?"

Falconer was the only customer that overcast day, and the merchant appeared glad for the excuse to talk. "You know what they say about that region. God made the Carolina Piedmont last, and the good stuff was already done used up on Virginia."

Falconer waited through the merchant laughing at his own joke. "So how do I find this Colonial Trading Route?"

"Ride west out of town. Can't miss the trailhead 'cause there ain't but one right-hand turning. Nowadays it ain't hardly a road at all. You got wagons?"

"Just mules."

"That's good. On account of it being a ferocious bad route. Things get better once you make Burkeville and head south. Not a lot better, but some." He slid Falconer's knife from its scabbard, twisting and turning it so the blade caught the light. "This here's some fine work."

"It was made in Africa, or so I was told."

The merchant caught Falconer's wistful regret over losing the knife and made the weapon disappear under his counter. "So you're after minin' yourself some gold, are you?"

"If I can."

"Well, you know what they say about a fool and his money. I was you, I'd stick to the turnpike far as Roanoke Rapids, then head west."

Falconer chose his words carefully. "I have friends along the Catawba Trail."

"Must be lonely folk is all I can say. Ain't a town of any size between here and the state line." He pushed Falconer's purchases across the counter. "Keep a good watch at night. You carrying a musket?"

"A Whitney."

"That should do ye. Tie them mules up tight. If the Injuns don't get 'em, the bears will."

CHAPTER 13

For Serafina, their voluntary quarantine became a time of remarkable contrasts. The weather closed down once more, as it had so often during that long winter. The downstairs front windows remained shuttered, while rain formed liquid bars upon the upstairs windows. Serafina was unable even to see the square's opposite side at high noon. The street outside their home became a stone-bottomed river. There was little need for the Langstons' three guards to warn anyone away. The downpour kept passersby to a minimum.

She found the days almost comforting. The outside world was reduced to a distant worry. Each dawn she met with Mary and Gerald for a Bible study. Gerald had confessed to reading with difficulty, and Mary enjoyed this quiet communion together. Serafina found great peace in starting her day helping others to become closer to the Word.

The study was halted each day when the Langstons' carriage pulled up to their doorstep. An employee ran up the stairs and deposited two hampers outside the door. One was filled with the day's provisions, and the other contained mail collected at the local post office, along with journals and an assortment of pamphlets. Alessandro Gavi spent hours pouring over the news. Their confinement weighed most heavily upon him. The fact that they were well cared for and were restrained by choice did not keep him from fretting.

Together Serafina and Mary prepared a breakfast for themselves and the guards who had been on duty all night. Then Mary began her morning duties while Serafina prepared breakfast for her parents. It was another activity that gave her great comfort, one she insisted upon doing alone.

The fourth morning after Falconer's departure, Alessandro entered the kitchen as Serafina was unpacking the hamper of news and letters. He was dressed as usual in a smartly ironed dress shirt, cravat, vest, and street pants. He carried himself with a distracted air.

Serafina kissed the top of his head as she

set a cup of coffee topped with frothy hot milk in front of him. "Good morning, Papa. Would you like your morning papers?"

He might have said yes, or it might merely have been a sigh. She set the hamper of papers on the floor beside his chair. "The Langstons have included the new pamphlet from the Powers Press," she told him. "You remember my telling you of Gareth and Erica Powers, don't you, Papa?"

He made no move for either the papers or his coffee. "Never would I have imagined being sealed inside such comfortable surroundings could be so distressing."

She settled into the chair beside him. "You are a man of action."

"A man of the world," he responded. "A diplomat. A man who yearns for people and trade and deeds and deals!"

"You feel helpless," Serafina said.

Her tone as much as her words caused her father to focus beyond himself. "You worry for Falconer as well."

"Yes, Papa."

"And yet you seem so cheerful. So —" he searched for the proper word — "so peaceful."

Serafina was slow in shaping her response. "I have never before found prayer such a comfort. Nor has it come as easily as now."

187

"Prayer," he repeated.

"I pray for Falconer with almost every breath, it seems. I thank God for having brought us together. I pray for his safety and his success. And I find myself almost walking the path alongside him. Wherever he is . . ."

"I think of him also." Alessandro sipped from his cup. "I thought I knew all manner of men. But never have I had an exchange as the night of his departure."

"Will you take something to eat, Papa? There is some lovely marmalade and fresh-churned butter in today's hamper."

"Not now." His pat on his daughter's hand urged her to remain where she was. "Explain to me his response to my offer of the mine's ownership. We did not shake hands on it, nor did he ask for anything in writing. Does he trust me so, a man he has known only for a few months?"

"It is partly trust. In truth, though, Falconer cares little for money. He has been rich before. He mentions it with a deep shame. I have never asked for details because of the pain it causes him. He lives for God now."

"*God.* The word comes so easily to your lips."

"Yes, Papa. It does."

He sipped from his cup, then set it back in the saucer and toyed with the little spoon. "This other thing he mentioned. About the young diplomat."

Serafina leaned back in her chair. "Nathan Baring."

"Did Falconer speak of this with you before?"

"No. Not a word."

"I thought . . ." He retreated into his cup, then said, "I thought Falconer was going to ask for your hand."

"So did I."

"He loves you."

Serafina fought down the burning in her eyes. "Yes, I believe that is so."

"And yet he seemed to suggest that we allow another man to pay court."

She swallowed hard. "Falconer is the strongest man I have ever met."

He studied his daughter. "You are not speaking of his physical size. Are you?"

"No, Papa. I mean his faith in God."

To their surprise, Bettina Gavi asked from the doorway, "Do you wish to take holy orders and enter a convent, daughter?"

Serafina rose to her feet. "Good morning, Mama. I did not see you. Would you like coffee?"

Bettina walked over and kissed her husband. Her hand upon Alessandro's shoulder, she said, "I would ask that you answer my question, Serafina."

"No, Mama. I have no interest in joining a convent."

"Why not? You speak of God with such ease. Does this not seem the proper step?"

"Not that we wish to lose you," Alessandro hurried to add. "But lately we have wondered about this, your mother and I."

"I have too much of my father's nature." Serafina studied her parents. The strain of this discussion was evident on both their features. "I carry my Lord's peace with me. I wish to take this out into the world, not retreat away from it."

No matter how welcome and pleasant such conversations might be, they were unable to halt her father's restlessness for very long. That afternoon, Serafina and her mother made dinner while Mary set the table and Gerald repaired a section of the roof where the rain had found an opening. All the while, she heard her father pacing back and forth through the front rooms. The parlor and study were by far the home's nicest chambers. Yet being on the ground floor and fronting the square, they were also permanently shuttered. It was the common practice whenever a house was placed under quarantine, so that communication with someone on the street could only take place from an upstairs window, thus halting the spread of disease.

Back and forth her father paced, his leather heels clipping across the polished wood floor, then becoming muffled as they touched the parlor's carpet, then back to crisp sounds when they struck wood on the carpet's other side. Twice Bettina started to say something, but she refrained only by compressing her lips into a thin line. The pacing worried Serafina. She feared her father would find the waiting interminable and break off the quarantine too early. Serafina wanted them to give Falconer as long as they possibly could.

Finally she could bear no more. She set down her ladle, washed her hands in the basin of water, and dried them on her apron. Watched by her mother, Serafina stepped from the kitchen and followed the footsteps into the parlor, arriving in time to watch Alessandro approach the fireplace, plant a fist upon the mantel, and rest his forehead there. He looked ill with the strain.

"Papa, won't you come back and keep us company?"

He lifted his head, stared at the fire, and

said nothing.

"Papa?"

"Perhaps I could do Falconer more good if I were out tracking down his attacker." He turned to his daughter, seeking her permission. "Perhaps this Vladimir might even be stopped before he leaves town. Is that not worth considering?"

Serafina knew to argue would only add fuel to his distress. "Reginald Langston is already hunting this man, Papa. His contacts are even better than yours. And Nathan Baring offered his assistance. Remember?"

"Surely they could use my help as well."

She cast about for something to say or do, something that would keep him engaged and content. If not content, then at least willingly occupied.

An idea struck her. "Papa, let me paint a portrait of you and Mama."

He did not even bother to glance her way. "You would add to my confinement by pinning me to a chair?"

"You could stand." The idea grew wings, lifting her own heart with new enthusiasm. "I could place you behind Mama. She could be seated and you on your feet."

Footsteps hurried down the hall from the kitchen. "Alessandro, what a lovely idea!"

"You know how much I detest the idea of

being made to stay in place for days and weeks on end."

It was true, her father had never been willing to sit for a portrait. "I shall do it in watercolors."

He grunted, unconvinced. "This would make a difference?"

"Of course it would. You know this as well as I. Watercolors take no time at all." She began thinking out loud. "I would place you opposite the dining room window, with Mama seated in your chair and you behind her. I would draw you both in pencil, then use a pastel wash."

"How long would this chore require?"

"Chore," his wife scolded. "What a way to describe your own daughter's wonderful offer. Shame on you."

"How long, daughter?"

"Three days," she promised. "And not a moment more."

The next day Serafina took her time over a few initial sketches. She had only a small portable sketch pad, and the last pages were quickly used. She then took sheets of her father's best parchment and two of his finest quills. He grumbled a bit until she took down the paintings hanging in the dining room and replaced them with her initial drawings. She knew her parents were astounded by the likenesses, but she was utterly dissatisfied. Although she had done some sketches in the legate's house, she hadn't done any serious artwork since leaving Venice. Her work looked clumsy to her eyes.

Gradually she slipped back into the artist's frame of mind. The world retreated. Her entire universe became defined by light and line and shade. Her parents became images upon the page.

"Have you not heard a word I have said, Serafina?"

"Please don't move, Mama."

"Daughter," she repeated, louder this time. "The guard says there is someone outside our front door."

"Mary can see to it. Lift your chin a bit please, Papa."

Bettina rose from her chair. "Mary is the one calling to you."

Her father asked, "Is this better?"

"Yes, thank you."

"What difference does the angle of my chin make?"

"Don't speak, please, Papa. I want to straighten the line of your neck. And this new angle accents the power of your jaw. No, Papa, don't thrust your mouth forward, it looks unnatural. Yes, hold it there, please. I'm almost done."

Bettina appeared in the doorway leading to the kitchen. "A young gentleman wishes to have a word."

Alessandro asked, "Which young gentleman would that be?"

"Papa, please."

"Nathan Baring," her mother replied. "And he wishes to speak with our daughter, not you."

Serafina wiped the quill's nub on a bit of rag and set it down on the scrap of wood she was using as an ink palette. She wiped her hands. Carefully she studied the two sheets of parchment. One sketch was of her mother, the other her father. She had angled the faces so they looked across the divide of space to inspect each other. She was making progress. She could see that. But something was still missing.

"Daughter!"

"Yes, Mama?"

"You are making the young gentleman stand in the rain!"

"Very well."

Serafina rose and left the dining room. She climbed the stairs and entered her parents' bedroom. She crossed to the front window. Only when she reached to pull up the shade did she realize she still carried her ink-stained rag.

The rain had changed to a heavy gray mist which shifted in roving bands about the square. The air was so still she could hear a hawker's cry from the market three blocks away.

Nathan Baring stood in a dark overcoat glistening with rain. He held his hat before his chest with both hands. Serafina opened the window and called down, "Put your hat back where it belongs, sir, before you catch your death of cold."

He grinned as he settled the hat back into place. "You sound like my mother, Miss Gavi."

"Then she must be a very sensible woman indeed."

This only made him smile more broadly. "I came to ask how you and the family were faring."

"That is most kind of you, sir. I am doing well. You heard about the quarantine?"

"The Langstons kindly explained the reason for it."

"The hours bear heavy upon my father," Serafina said.

"I can understand that. A man of affairs, a merchant who has traveled the globe." He nodded. "The confinement would be a double burden. He feels imprisoned, and he is kept from putting his hand to the wheel."

Her parents' bedroom and her mother's dressing room ran the entire length of the house. A plush chair had been drawn up by the front window, for it was from here that all communications with the outside world transpired. Only the doctor was permitted to enter and leave their home, and only once every three days. All the rules had been set into place during the previous summer's cholera outbreak. Serafina settled into the chair and replied, "He completes all his correspondence by noon. Afterwards he paces. Or he did."

"And now?"

"Now I am painting a portrait of him and Mama. That is, I am trying."

He caught her tone. "You are not satisfied?"

"It is functional." She rested her chin upon an ink-stained hand, seeing anew the two latest drawings in her mind's eye. "The lines are there. But not . . ."

"The emotion," he finished for her.

Her head turned quickly toward him. "What did you say? Pardon me, but what do you mean?"

"It seems natural enough," Nathan reasoned. "You are confined. Your emotions are penned up inside you, a reflection of your external state. There must be an enormous wealth of sentiments you harbor toward your parents and all you have experienced together."

Serafina nodded and said slowly, "Mr. Baring, you have no idea."

The silence took hold then. The gray mist was a perfect companion, a soft wash that stripped away all color from the world beyond her window. The square was an ethereal backdrop. Other pedestrians stepped to the far side of the street, avoiding proximity to the quarantined house. Even with the cholera outbreak six months gone, a conversation between someone standing in the lane and another nestled in an upstairs window, with a yellow-rimmed paper barring the distance between them, drew little notice. An occasional carriage clip-clopped into view and then swiftly disappeared into the mist. The only thing Serafina could see with any clarity was Nathan Baring.

"I would ask a favor of you," she said.

"Anything, Miss Gavi."

"Do you know the printers' shops on Connecticut Avenue?"

"Certainly."

"They stock art supplies. Would you

purchase for me a full set of watercolors, six brushes, two of each size. . . ." She thought aloud. "A broad quill for drawing. A box of charcoals. A dozen of their best sketching pencils. A pack of Arches finest drawing paper. This is most important. Can you remember all this?"

"I am a diplomat, Miss Gavi. I am trained to keep long conversation clearly to mind, as very often I am unable to write for hours at a time."

At some other point she would have found that fascinating. Now, however, her mind was already continuing to form further needs. "The paper should be their largest size. Ask them for cold press linen and silk weave. A half dozen backing boards for watercolor paintings. They will know what I require. And three of the largest easels they have. Are you sure this is not too much trouble?"

"It would be an honor to help you in this way." He opened his coat and pulled the watch from his vest pocket. "I must hurry, Miss Gavi. The store closes in less than an hour."

"Oh my, where has the day gone?"

"The clock struck five as I was arriving here."

"Let me ask Papa for payment —"

"No need for that. Actually, I prefer to ask a favor of my own instead of payment."

She was instantly on guard. "Yes?"

"Two things. First, that you paint a portrait of my mother. I have long wanted to have this done."

"I must warn you, sir. It has been far too long since I have last held a brush. I shall be painting my parents using watercolors."

He waved that aside. "Whatever medium you choose, Miss Gavi, I am certain it will be beautiful."

She felt warmed by his kind words. "You said there were two things?"

"Indeed. A group of friends meet one evening each week. We study Scripture. We talk. I would ask you to join us."

"I should be honored," she replied, and to her surprise she found she meant it. "Soon as this official confinement is behind us."

"Then I shall keep you no longer." He bowed toward her. "Good evening, Miss Gavi."

Serafina watched him walk quickly down the lane. Long after the swirling gray mist had hidden away his figure, she stared out at the deepening twilight.

She returned thoughtfully to the dining room to find her parents standing over her most recent sketches. Her father inspected her a long moment, then said, "Daughter, these are magnificent."

"I had no idea," Bettina quietly agreed.

"I have always known you held talent. These, however . . ." Alessandro returned his attention to the drawings. "You have matured in more than one way, I must say."

She walked around the table to stand beside her parents. She viewed the sketches with a clearer sense of distance now. They were indeed fine in terms of quality and refinement and accuracy. She whispered, "Emotion."

"What was that, daughter?"

Strange that a man with whom she had exchanged words only twice before could see the need so accurately. She knew exactly what was required now. Nathan's observation sparked an image she knew she could follow and achieve her aim.

She looked at her parents and declared, "I shall paint you tomorrow."

CHAPTER 14

Morning on the sixth day of their confinement brought a clear blue sky. Sunlight bathed the bedroom as Serafina got dressed.

"Now, you both must get ready for your final sitting," Serafina told her parents a half hour later as they finished their breakfast. Her father groaned good-naturedly and wondered if he couldn't just wear his dressing gown. The three shared a laugh, and Serafina said, "No, Papa, you must dress to look as good as Mama."

"That is an impossibility, my dear," he said, rising from his chair and leaning over to give his wife a kiss.

Serafina hurried to the dining room to set up for the painting session. When her father entered the room, tugging on his vest, he asked, "You are certain this is the proper garb?"

"You look fine, Papa." The dining room was transformed. Sheets covered the floor

202

beneath her easel. Clay jars of water stood upon a covered side table. The wall to her right was adorned with the seven sketches. The dining table was covered with several layers of cloth and held a sharp knife for quill trimming, a block of India ink, ink-well, more water pots, two palettes, charcoal, and her new watercolors. "Where is Mama?"

"Changing gowns for the third time." He stepped behind a chair and assumed a dignified pose. "I had thought I would rest one hand upon the chair, like so."

Serafina walked around the table and pulled two chairs close together. "Papa, I want you to sit down."

"But yesterday you wanted me to stand."

"I know I did, and that has been part of the problem. We are not after dignity here."

"Are we not?"

"No, Papa. We want to picture what makes you and Mama so special. We want your love for each other."

"Can we not have both affection and dignity together?"

She resisted the urge to explain that she already had in her mind a precise vision of how the image would take shape. Because she had never attempted something like this, she wanted to make sure she could accomplish the transformation from mental impression to canvas. "Papa, whatever you do, however you stand, your natural dignity will show through."

He clearly liked that comment very much. "So then. I shall stand, yes?"

"No, Papa. Sit."

"But —"

"I want you to trust me." She looked up as Bettina entered the room. "Mama, would you please sit here?"

"Do you think this gown catches a proper light?"

Serafina gazed lovingly at her mother's face, then at the emerald-green gown of silk taffeta. "Yes, Mama, it is *almost* as beautiful as you are."

Bettina allowed herself to be guided into the chair. "Can you make me appear younger?"

"You are truly lovely, Mama. That is what I will show." She stepped around to the table's other side. The two faces stared directly at her, both looking a bit nervous and tense. "Look at each other, please. No, Papa, don't tilt your head so. You are looking down your nose at Mama."

"Isn't this the pose you told me to take yesterday?"

"I will hold the angle of your chin from

the drawing. Now I want to affect a proper balance."

She worked on their angles and posture for almost an hour. Gradually they stopped arguing and accepted their role as models. It proved harder for her mother, which was a surprise. Her father was a diplomat, she realized, accustomed to rearranging himself to fit the vagaries of court.

Finally Serafina said, "Mama, do you trust me?"

"What a question. How can you ask me, your mother, such a thing?"

"Then I want you to please stop quarreling with me."

"I am not —"

"Mama. Please. Trust, remember? Be silent and do what I say. Lean forward just a bit. No, straighten your shoulders. Good. Now angle your face a bit to the right. No, not like that." Serafina moved around the table so that she stood midway between the easel and her father. "Turn your face so that you are looking straight at me. Good! Now look at Papa. No, Mama. Don't move your face. Just your eyes. Turn back to me again. Now look at Papa. Fine, yes, excellent."

She moved back to the easel. Finally the positions from her nighttime imaginings were realized.

"Please, the both of you, take careful stock. This is precisely the position I want you to maintain. Whenever we take a break, please come back to exactly here. Look at how close your faces are. Feel the position of your bodies, how your shoulders are angled. Can you do this?"

Her father grumbled, "It feels most unnatural."

She selected the lightest of her drawing pencils and sketched hastily. Their eyes. She would begin of course with the eyes. But as she traced the first lines, she stopped.

"Daughter?" her mother intoned.

"Of course," she whispered. She took a step back. No longer was she seeing a blank canvas. Instead, the drawing was complete in her mind's eye. The drawing, the pattern of shade and color, the paints. Everything.

She did not need to have them reveal their true natures. She had a lifetime's experience to draw on.

"Did you hear me, my dear?"

"Please remain still." Serafina drew in swift, confident strokes. What she had required was the physical balance alone. That was accomplished. She could see how the light played upon the planes and surfaces. The emotional quality she would add from the reservoir within herself.

As Serafina worked, other things began to take shape, her mental image racing a few strokes ahead of the images upon the canvas. She would not fill the entire canvas with color. Instead, it would be a layering. She had seen such images by the few Renaissance painters who had worked with pencil and watercolor. Serafina traced the lines all the way to the borders of her paper. But it would only be the pencil. The coloration would not progress that far.

She dropped the pencil and with her broadest brush began the outermost border, a pale wash, scarcely one shade from ivory.

Her parents spoke to her again. First one, then the other. She heard them, and yet the sounds came from a very far distance. She was only dimly aware of movement when one of them would leave the room, then the other. Somehow, though, they seemed to be able to return to just the right positions they had left.

The closer she moved to faces, the more brilliant became the colors. She wanted to have the chance to see each face anew and redo the coloring if she was not satisfied. Most especially she wanted to rework the eyes. The eyes were the key. Weren't they?

"Daughter."

"Yes, Papa, please, one moment longer."

"Serafina, no. We must finish now."

She winced at the sudden pain in her shoulders. Where had the hours flown?

That evening she ate because Mary set a plate in front of her and Bettina ordered her to eat. But there upon the kitchen table alongside her plate was the same uncertainty. She knew the eyes were crucial. They were the windows to the soul. What else was there? The worry that she was missing something gnawed at her worse than hunger, worse even than the stiffness in her neck and shoulders.

After she had eaten, Serafina looked wearily at her parents. "I know I told you one day of sitting, but —"

"Yes, we know, dear," her mother said quickly. "We'll be ready in the morning. However, we all need to get some rest now."

Serafina returned to her room and collapsed upon the bed. She awoke four hours later, according to the clock on her mantel, just long enough to slip into her nightdress and drink three cups of water. She tried to think further on the mystery, but her mind and her body retreated into sleep.

She awoke later than usual and heard people moving around downstairs. She entered the kitchen and accepted her parents' greetings. She took her breakfast into the dining room and ate while staring at her canvas. The previous day's work was acceptable. Even more than that. She could see hints of the final structure everywhere. The eyes were fine. She could see that the choices of materials and colors would work well. Her focus returned time and again to the middle section of the canvas. What else could it be?

Her parents entered unbidden and resumed their positions. Serafina corrected the hold of their shoulders. She moved them slightly closer together. And she began once again to paint.

She completed the faces and did the final work on the clothing just before the church tower rang the noon bell. She dismissed them, declining their invitation to join them for lunch. When her mother returned with a plate, Bettina did as Serafina had requested and refrained from coming around to where she could see the painting. Bettina looked closely at her daughter, started to speak, then silently left the room.

Serafina ate out of a confused sense of duty. She knew her parents would worry if she did not. But the food tasted only of watercolor paint and her eyes scarcely left the canvas. The remaining small damp spots of color offered a special grace to the lines, fading and smoothing them in unexpected places. The result was a sense of humanness and timelessness. The sharp lines of youth were no more. Yet in this imperfect touch was a singular beauty. She did not think this as much as felt it. Serafina pushed her plate aside and picked up her finest brush. She extended the lines out around the edges of the clothes, drawing them out into a soft melding with the borders. The figures flowed into the pastel border and on into the mystery of unfinished lives.

Mystery. Serafina picked up her lightest pencil, cut the nib to a delicate point, and focused anew upon the eyes. The paint here at the center was so dry the paper crackled softly as she drew. She made mere suggestions of angles and further precision. Too little and the watercolors would appear weak. Too much and the lines would overshadow the color.

She stepped back and used the stained rag to clean her quill. And saw the answer.

The chair creaked as she seated herself. She dropped her pencil to the floor.

"Serafina?"

Her mother entered the room. She inspected her daughter, then came around to look at the canvas. She drew in a sharp breath.

The canvas shone with what was not painted at all. Balanced between the two faces and two sets of eyes was their shared love.

"Bettina?" her father called. "Is she ready for us again?"

Serafina could hear her mother swallow hard. "Come see."

Her father stepped into the dining room, and she could hear his own quick intake of breath.

Serafina understood. It was finally clear. The issue had not been only the eyes but the balance between the two figures. They had to express an identical message, one that became the fulcrum upon which the two could be balanced. This was the purpose behind the exact tilting of heads, the shading, and the subtle blurring of lines.

She looked up at her parents. What did they see? A pleasing portrait? Probably a little more than that. Yet it did not matter. She studied the canvas again. Was this what it meant to create good art? Would she be required with each canvas to find a mystery that would only be answered when the work was complete?

Her father said, "My darling daughter, this is astounding."

"Magnificent," her mother added.

"Thank you, Mama. Papa." She had to try twice to push herself from the chair. "Please excuse me. I am very weary."

As she prepared for bed, she felt as though someone else was asking questions of her. What happened if the mystery remained unresolved? What if she painted a canvas and at the end felt the hidden mystery was not clear, not even to herself? What then? Would she destroy the work? Would she confess her failure? Serafina thought these things, and yet they drifted in and left just as easily. All she could say at the moment was, this time the mystery had been resolved. Everything upon the canvas drew the focus toward what could not be seen, only felt. Love.

CHAPTER 15

They saw no Indians. But the bears were plentiful. As were wild boar and feral dogs. Even cougars. At least that is what Aaron told them. All Falconer knew was that some beast made a howling racket their second night on the trail, tracking around their perimeter and terrifying the women into wide-eyed panic. Only Joseph's sharp voice kept them from bolting. The mules shrilled louder than the women and fought against their hobbles. Joseph and Aaron wrapped empty provision sacks around the mules' eyes and tied their traces to logs. They could drag the logs but neither snap the traces nor escape, Joseph explained.

The progress of the group remained painfully slow. They would have starved long before reaching the state line had it not been for Aaron. The boy vanished at first light, slipping into the forest and melding with the natural cover. Come sunset he found them again, a variety of wild game hanging from his belt. He handed his catch to the women and retreated to the camp's perimeter. He never spoke, at least to Falconer.

But Falconer was not satisfied to let things remain as they were. He saw a good deal of himself in the wild young man. Where Falconer had escaped to the sea, the young man used the forest. But the half-savage way of dealing with a cold and uncaring world was the same.

On the third afternoon since leaving the turnpike, they finished the pears. Three people ate from each fruit, save for Falconer. He did not bother to try and share his portion, for still no one took food from his hand. He watched Aaron from across the campfire. The boy crouched like an untamed animal with a good eye for cover. The waning sunset turned his taut features into sharp planes of fear.

Falconer rose slowly, hating how the entire group tensed when he moved. They watched without turning their heads as he picked up the musket and crossed the clearing. When he arrived near to where Aaron gnawed on the pear's core, he settled on a rock, the musket lying across his knees. The lad was a half inch from bolting.

Falconer addressed Joseph, who was

seated by the fire, watching intently. He said quietly, "Would you join us for a moment?"

When Joseph approached, Falconer asked the young man, "Have you ever handled a musket?"

The lad said nothing, nor did he look straight at Falconer. His keen interest, though, was clear enough.

Falconer carefully lifted the weapon from his lap. He explained each of the components in turn. Explained how to cock and fire. How to aim. How to load. Knowing the lad would need to hear such things several times more. Taking it as a prize that the lad watched his hands straight on and remained crouched there beside him. Which was all he had been after.

So he went through the entire explanation a second time. Trying to reveal through his tone of voice that he could be trusted. Then he asked, "Would you like to fire it?"

The lad made no sign he had even heard. But his eyes never left the musket.

Falconer did not wait for an answer he knew would not come. Instead, he asked Joseph to tell the group that he and Aaron would be stepping into the woods for a bit of target practice. "Don't anyone become frightened," Joseph finished.

Rays from the departing sun spread like a

215

fan above the western hills. They were camped upon a ridgeline with nothing save forest and advancing shadows in every direction. Falconer motioned to Joseph and Aaron and walked to where the ridge path spread out over a rocky outcropping. He knelt beside the lad, such that the young man was now taller. He nestled the musket into his own shoulder, explaining how important it was to maintain a proper stance. He explained the way to take a sighting. Then he handed Aaron the weapon. And touched the lad for the very first time.

He could feel the young man's flesh quiver beneath his fingers. The tension radiated up through Falconer's hand, taking hold of his own gut. Falconer fought to keep his voice calm. He showed how to jam the musket into the muscle. How to aim down the sights at a tree trunk. How to balance the long barrel. How to fire.

The gun's bark echoed over the empty hills. Falconer walked them over to where the trunk remained unscathed. He showed where the ball had plowed a furrow from the earth less than a handsbreadth from the trunk. He explained that this was a remarkable first shot.

He helped the lad reload. And fire again. He gave Joseph the pistol, mainly so the older man would feel included. But Joseph fired with both eyes tightly shut. He also assumed the harder he pulled the trigger, the straighter the pistol would fire. His arm clenched from forearm to neck with the effort to fire straight. Falconer did not correct him.

They returned to camp when it grew too dark to see the target. As they reentered the firelight, Falconer said to Aaron, "Why don't you keep the weapon, see what you can bring down tomorrow."

He walked away without a backward glance. He unfurled his bedroll and sighed his way down. He lay for a moment looking at the stars. For once the cloud covering was gone and the night clear. He cast a quick glance across the camp. Aaron stood cradling the musket, staring across at where Falconer lay. Falconer closed his eyes and counted the day a success.

Up close a musket gave off a solid bang. At a distance of more than fifty paces, particularly when the sound was muffled by vegetation, it was more like a harsh cough. The next day, their little band heard an occasional cough from the surrounding forest. By the time they halted for the midday rest, the sound had grown more distant, and no one paid it any further mind. Not, at least, until Aaron returned at sunset. The lad was so weary he walked bowed over the musket. He stank of burnt sulfur at twenty paces. His clothes and face were charcoal stained. One eyebrow was burnt halfway off. His game pouch was completely empty.

He stumbled over to where Falconer chopped kindling. "I cain't hit nuthin' with this thing."

Falconer pretended not to notice that everyone was watching. "Did you strike the first animal you went after with your sling-shot?"

Aaron swiped at his sweat-beaded face, streaking the soot. "I's wasted a passel of shot and powder, suh."

"You haven't wasted a thing, Aaron."

Aaron made a feeble effort to hand back the musket. "But, suh —"

"Give it a few more days. Let's see what happens." Either Aaron would bring home heavier game than he could bring down with the slingshot or they would soon go hungry. But Falconer did not say it, deciding there was nothing to be gained by adding to the lad's sense of anxiety and guilt.

Falconer was not naturally a patient man. He was most comfortable with testing bodies to the limit — both his own and those under his command. But here he was dealing with the infirm, the aged, the weak. None of the band had shoes except for himself. The trail was rocky and steep and long disused. At times he and Joseph had to use the sword to chop back the undergrowth. Falconer could not press them harder. So they rested long at midday and they halted before sunset. And their supplies continued to dwindle.

Which made his internal state uncommon strange.

Falconer was not given to inner reflection. He was born to action and molded by hard days and worse nights. Yet here he was, chained to a snail's pace by his charges, all of them facing starvation around the next bend. Yet he felt as happy as he had ever been in his entire life.

Not even Serafina's absence could taint the glory he felt rising in his heart. He went to bed replete and slept deep. The nightmares that had plagued him for years were now so distant they might as well have happened to a different man. Which, in a sense, Falconer suspected they had.

When they halted, Falconer applied himself to whatever chore needed doing. As soon as the food was shared and the others were resting, he opened his satchel and pulled out the Bible. He used a dogwood leaf to mark his place. It went as flat as the pages to either side. Falconer pulled it out that evening and held it so the firelight shone through its translucent surface. Even a fragile leaf held heart-stopping beauty.

A scrabbling sound caused him to drop the leaf back onto the page before him. Joseph approached and said, "My Geraldine, she wants to ask you something."

"Of course."

The woman was handsome even in illness. Her ailment was no worse than when they had first set off, but not much better either. Afternoons found her wearied to where she could no longer hide her rough breathing. Falconer used her hacking cough as the signal to halt for the day. Geraldine fiddled with her threadbare dress and spoke to the ground at her feet. "Suh, I was wonderin'. Would you be reading from the Good Book?"

"I am. Would you like to read with me?"

"Can't hardly make out my own name, suh." She pointed at the pages, a shy and fearful gesture. "Would you mind readin' a word to us now and then?"

The gift of trust was so great he felt his throat clutch tight. Falconer dragged his hand across his mouth, a slow motion intended to grant him time to regain control. "I would be honored. Is there any particular passage you would like to hear?"

"Don' hardly matter, suh. Long as it's the Word."

He rose to his feet and approached the fire, moved almost to tears by the sight of so many of his band drawing in close. "In that case," Falconer said, "I will start at the beginning."

Aaron appeared an hour after dark. The lad was so weary and burdened down he could scarcely hold to his feet. Across his shoulders he carried the body of a young deer.

Everyone was up and jabbering and trying to help take the load. When the animal was lifted from his shoulders, Aaron collapsed onto the ground. A cup was held to his lips. He drank too swiftly and choked. Another cup was brought, and a cold griddle cake. He devoured it with trembling hands. Then he tried to push himself upright. "I gots to be going."

"Rest," Falconer said.

"Suh, I left the musket back there in them woods."

"You can find it in the morning." Falconer stood over him until the lad's eyelids stuttered and closed. Then he turned to the deer. He lifted the rear haunch. The animal weighed almost as much as Aaron.

Joseph and the old woman were already busy. His sons were sent off for more firewood. Within minutes the flames rose as high as Falconer's shoulder. They roasted a haunch while others built a drying stand. After the days of short rations, the smell was maddeningly inviting. The younger folk danced in anticipation around the fire. They had to shake Aaron very hard to award him with the first slices. The lad ate and collapsed once more.

All night two of the group took turns remaining awake to stoke the fire and keep the coals burning steady. By morning the meat on the drying racks was done. They stowed the venison jerky in the empty provisions sacks, breakfasting on the last of the fresh meat.

Soon after they started off, it began to rain. The accompanying breeze was light but carried a hard wintry edge. Falconer unstrapped his cloak from the mule's saddle and handed it to Geraldine. "Wear this high so it will keep your head dry."

"Suh, it ain't proper."

"Do as he says," Joseph instructed, stepping up beside Falconer. "Thank you, suh."

"You'll need to rope it around her waist

to keep it in place," Falconer replied. He stripped off his long black coat and carried it to the second mule. "I hope you're not going to argue with me too, Mammy."

"No, suh." She draped the coat over her head and let him button it into place. "God bless you, suh."

Such little things had never affected him before. The thanks of a woman who had nothing, the wash of rain upon his face. He moved to the front of the line, taking pleasure even in the bite of wet cold through his shirt. The surrounding forest was alive with the sound of pattering water. High overhead the breeze whispered through the pine boughs. One of the children laughed. The music of angels could not have sounded any finer.

By midday, however, they were all cold and shivering. They needed shelter, but Falconer could find none. When they stopped for a meal of jerky and rainwater, Falconer sidled up next to Joseph. "How much farther do you reckon we are from safety?"

"Can't hardly say, suh." Joseph swiped at the water streaming down his face. "It's already farther than I thought."

"What are we looking for?"

It was a conversation they'd had several times before. Joseph repeated the same words. "Hold fast to the Catawba Trail. You make it to where it opens up, folks'll be there to spirit you away."

"They didn't give you any name?"

Joseph shook his head. "Body can't tell what he don't know."

Falconer glanced around. The trail held to the side of a steep valley. A swollen stream rushed down below. He looked up. "I suppose I could climb the ridge again."

"Won't see any more than before. Forest is too thick."

"I think we should keep going," Falconer decided. "Resting in this weather is impossible. If we stay here, we could all come down with the croup."

In response, Joseph rose and began drawing the others into a semblance of order. For once, Falconer was glad their provisions were almost gone, for it meant they carried almost nothing and their hands were free. The trail was little more than a yard wide and slick with mud. The rain did not strengthen, nor did it ease. It also remained bitingly cold.

By midafternoon Falconer was shivering with the others. He moved to where Aaron walked, so weary his mouth hung slack. Joseph walked alongside him, carrying the musket and pistol both. The old man was showing his age.

"I know you're bone tired," Falconer said to Aaron, "but I need your help."

The words were enough to straighten the lad's shoulders. "Suh."

"Scout about. We've got to find cover for these folks before nightfall. A cave, a lean-to, anything so long as it's dry."

Aaron stepped off the trail and in two paces was lost from sight.

Falconer started toward the front, when he noticed how Joseph's younger boy was limping. Falconer stepped up alongside Isaac and asked, "Is something the matter?"

The child was shivering so hard he mangled the words. Falconer squatted in the mud and lifted the boy's ankle. A gash ran down the ball of his foot. "How long ago did this happen?"

The child assumed he had done something wrong and whimpered softly.

Falconer swept the boy up in his arms. "What a strong, brave lad you are."

He moved to the front of the line, taking fierce comfort from the trembling form. At every turn in the road he scouted in every direction. They raced the dimming light now. They must find shelter.

And that was when Aaron found them. He came trotting down the trail toward them. "They's a barn up ahead, suh!"

Falconer breathed a silent prayer. He lifted his voice. "I know you're tired," he called down the line. "But we've got shelter up ahead. We need to move while there's still light to see our way. Joseph!"

The voice came from far behind. "Suh!"

"Keep the stragglers moving. Hurry, everyone!"

The dark came upon them far too swiftly. Branches leaned out to swipe at them and slow them down. Finally they rounded another bend, just one more kink in the trail, and the forest was behind them. Aaron moved down the line to tell the others and came back carrying the firearms, for now Joseph carried another child.

The wind caught them here, and the rain, both biting deep. Up ahead Falconer could just make out the dark silhouette of a barn. He could not recall anything ever looking quite so fine.

They stumbled and slid their way inside. The barn contained six tethered goats and two cows. But the beasts were welcome company, for they warmed the interior considerably. The roof leaked in a half dozen places. There was no door. But there was room for them all to lie down, and straw to cushion the plank floor. Falconer tethered the cow against the rear wall so it could not step upon a sleeping child. He eased Isaac down and covered him with a bit of burlap. The child was already asleep. Falconer threw himself down beside the lad and was gone.

CHAPTER 16

Three carriages halted together beneath a sullen morning sky. Nathan Baring alighted from one, the doctor from another, and Reginald and Lillian Langston from the third. The doctor was there to formally remove the quarantine, the others to rejoice in the Gavis' freedom. Such celebrations had become a tradition among churchgoers during the previous year's cholera epidemic — a time to give thanks for the passage of fear and dread. And the visitors' presence also removed the stigma attached to a house flagged with the dreaded yellow seal.

From her place in the dining room, Serafina heard her father shut the door and then declare, "Never did I imagine simply opening my own front door and shutters could carry such exhilaration."

"And you were not even ill," the doctor reminded him as he followed Alessandro into the house. "In your prayers this night, I ask you to think of those for whom a quarantine carries a far heavier burden."

Reginald shook Alessandro's hand with both of his own as his wife embraced Bettina Gavi. "We have brought provisions and news."

"I am far more famished for word of the outside world than another meal," Alessandro said. "Though I and my family are deeply grateful for both. You have literally saved our lives and our minds with your regular provisions."

"It has been a privilege to help with such an endeavor," Lillian quickly responded. "One larger in importance than we might even imagine."

Serafina continued her work at her easel. She had requested that her parents delay showing their portrait to others, for there were further refinements she wished to add. They would not hear of it. So she hurriedly inspected the painting and made what alterations she could.

She heard Nathan Baring say, "The young woman from the legate's household whom your Mary befriended has become a trusted ally. She reports that the dark-suited henchman came and went once more. There were angry exchanges. The man has not been

229

seen again."

"They suspect Falconer has departed," Alessandro Gavi surmised. "Their man is no doubt pursuing Falconer."

"I fear that is the case," Nathan agreed. "Hopefully we have bought Falconer some time."

"May it be enough," Alessandro declared fervently. "If only we could have convinced Falconer to take along others to aid and protect him."

"With respect, sir, I disagree," Reginald stated. "I have worked with men like Falconer before. We cannot presume to know his requirements for action."

Lillian Langston added, "The best thing we can do for him now is pray."

"Amen," Reginald agreed. "Let us join hands and beseech heaven for Falconer's safety."

Serafina hastily laid aside her brush and palette. "Wait, please, I am coming!"

"There you are!" Lillian Langston stepped forward to embrace her, but a wet stain upon Serafina's blouse halted the motion. "Whatever have you been doing?"

"Working." She rubbed her hands upon a rag so stained now it contained its own pastel rainbow. "Perhaps it would be best if you did not touch my hands."

"You really must see —" Alessandro began.

"Please, Papa, that can wait," Serafina interrupted. "And this cannot. Let us pray."

Against her objections, Serafina's hands were taken by Lillian on one side and Reginald on the other. She saw her parents hesitate, and Serafina realized it was the first time they had ever joined hands with strangers for prayer. If Reginald noticed the Gavis' discomfort, he gave no sign. He took his time, a strong and fervent man beseeching God. He gave thanks for friends, for health, for guidance. He asked for protection and wisdom to be bestowed upon their dear friend and brother John Falconer. Serafina found her heart blooming in pain and the hot rush of tears flooding her eyes. By the time Reginald stopped speaking, her cheeks were wet.

Bettina's face was tear-streaked as well. Lillian Langston was graceful even when wiping her own eyes. Alessandro stared thoughtfully at the carpet by his feet.

The doctor was the first to speak. "I was, as some of you know, a military man. I have known men of Falconer's caliber. Not many. A very few, actually. Though I have not known him for long, I gauge him a singular sort of gentleman."

"Unique," Bettina agreed, wiping her face with a handkerchief.

"I do not know what venture you have sent him on, or what risk he faces," the doctor continued. "I am certain, however, you could have found no finer ally to your cause."

There was a moment's silence, then Lillian repeated her earlier question. "What have you done to your hands, child? Why, you even have pigments in your hair."

Alessandro Gavi was remarkably subdued as he drew his guests forward toward the dining room. "Come and see."

They stood about the easel in silence. Lillian Langston stood next to Bettina, then Reginald and Nathan and the doctor, and finally her father. Serafina remained to one side, such that she could see only an angle of the painting. The portions she had recently touched up glistened damply. She wanted mostly to study the faces of the observers.

"Most remarkable," the doctor murmured.

Bettina said, "I have looked at it for hours and still I am amazed."

"I'm waiting for them to speak to one another," Lillian said.

Nathan was the first to look toward Serafina. "You will not forget our agreement?"

"What agreement is this?" Alessandro asked.

"I purchased supplies in exchange for Serafina's promising to paint a portrait of my mother."

"A splendid idea," Reginald said. "How is the dear lady?"

"Not well, I'm afraid. She has never managed to regain her strength."

"Then there is no time to lose."

Serafina was surprised to find it was her father who had said those words.

Bettina objected quietly, "Our daughter must be exhausted from this endeavor, husband."

"And these are friends who have aided us in our own hour of need." Alessandro addressed his daughter. "When do you think you might begin, Serafina?"

Serafina found herself filled with an eagerness to step into the world. Return to a life beyond the confines of the small house in Washington. She smiled at Nathan for the very first time. "If the rest of you will excuse me, now would be fine."

"Are you a believer?"

They were seated in the Barings' sunlit

front parlor. Eleanor Baring rested upon a daybed with a quilted robe tucked in tightly to her chin. A small lap blanket covered her legs. The woman looked very ill. Her complexion was pale as chalk. The skin of her face was slack, as though both flesh and life had been drawn out. Only her eyes were alight. They were pale brown, almost fawn colored, and very clear.

Nathan Baring was seated beneath the parlor's central window. He held a book and seemed to be reading. Now and then he raised his gaze but looked only at his mother. Serafina had started to object when Nathan had said he wished to remain in the room. She did not take to the idea of being observed while she worked. Yet Nathan had evidently sensed this before she had spoken. He had positioned his chair so he faced his mother and could not see Serafina or her easel without twisting around.

"This is not a difficult question, my dear," the woman said mildly. "Do you live with faith in our Lord Jesus in your heart and mind?"

Serafina had never been required to speak while painting. She found the demand to respond more than irksome. It drew her away from the effort required to join the image she was seeing before her to the one in her head and then to the paper. "Yes, madam," she managed, concentrating on a particularly intricate area of the painting.

"I find that quite remarkable. You are beautiful, wealthy, and gifted. Such a combination would suggest a person too confident in her own strengths to make room for God."

Serafina studied the image on the canvas. She had the form correct, and the drawing was good. But once again she confronted an unanswered mystery.

She lifted her head to face Mrs. Baring. "Madam, I can speak to you about our Lord and other matters, or I can paint. If I try to do both I shall do neither well." She heard her own voice and knew the snippish tone came from her frustration over the unresolved mystery, not this woman. "I suggest you permit me to complete the purpose that brought me here."

To her surprise, the woman smiled. "And spirited as well. How very remarkable indeed."

Serafina scarcely heard her comment. For in her smile, the woman had revealed what Serafina had sought, the unseen connection that would bring the canvas to life. Mrs. Baring's smile contained the secret portion of the woman's character. The older woman was transformed from mere human flesh to a true person. There before Serafina was a brief and rare glimpse of Mrs. Baring's soul.

Serafina set down her brush and said softly, "The spirit of the person."

"Indeed. I find it vital to comprehend someone's internal nature. How do they stand in their relationship with God. Is it healthy? Do they know His strength in the dark times that come to us all? Can they rely upon Him when all else fails?"

She looked at the woman upon the bed and compared this to her drawing. It was a correct rendition, and that was the problem.

Serafina rose to her feet. "Madam, I would ask that your son be allowed to show me one of your favorite dresses. I need something other than the robe as the surrounding color."

Eleanor Baring's voice was as pale and ghostlike as her skin. "How very remarkable."

"Something light blue, perhaps. Or rose," she decided, trying to envisage a color that could return life and strength to that wasted face. "A shade that will accent and not overwhelm."

"I fear it should no longer fit me."

"You won't need to wear it, madam. If I may only see it against you."

"Nathan, be a dear and show the young lady my wardrobe."

"Of course, Mother."

Only when they arrived at the top of the stairs and entered the woman's bedroom did Serafina understand just how serious matters were. The room had the untouched look of not having been in use for quite a long time. "Oh my."

Nathan spoke in a matter-of-fact tone that showed a hint of sorrow beneath his briskness. "My mother became ill last summer. She has not recovered." He expelled a heavy breath. "The doctors do not give her long."

"I am so very sorry, Mr. Baring."

"Thank you. Her dresses are in this armoire."

She made a pretense of studying the clothes, but her attention was primarily upon the son. "What was she like, your mother? I mean, before —"

"A source of light and joy to everyone she met," Nathan said, and his sorrow slipped closer to the surface. "My father was a difficult man. Not a bad man, mind you. Not by any means. Just stern and commanding. My mother was the reason our home remained happy."

" 'Blessed are the peacemakers,' " Serafina said almost without thinking. She stroked the sleeve of a day dress the color of pale amber. This would do nicely. Then she saw the well of grief upon Nathan's features. "I'm so sorry. I did not mean —"

"You are quite correct." But he seemed to draw no joy from the words. "She was indeed a peacemaker. She loved us and she soothed us. I do not know how I shall go on without either of my parents."

"You are very strong."

"I'm not, you know. I am weak and I am confused. I pray and I taste dust in my mouth from the emptiness of my spirit. I look for answers and find no hope, no reason to proceed."

"In dark times, it is easy to question everything," she replied in heartfelt sympathy. "Even the things that are with us always."

He did not seem to hear her. "The doctors say she could go any day. My brother is in Boston, and I am alone."

"You have friends. You are trusted. You are a good man who is valued by many."

He stared at the sleeve held in Serafina's grasp. "How will I manage to live without her?"

"By finding the strength you need in God. By being patient through the dark hours. By growing stronger still."

He looked at her then. And she inwardly remarked upon the same point she had found in their earlier contacts. He did not discount her attractiveness so much as look beyond it. He was not looking at her because she was lovely. He did not seek to draw closer to her physical form. Instead, he seemed to be searching in her gaze for an inner spirit.

"How is it," he asked, "that a woman as young as you speaks with such wisdom and experience?"

"Because I am not as good a person as you," she said, astonished at her own honesty. "Because I fashioned my own sorrow and am only just recovering. Thanks to God."

Serafina did not know how she was going to proceed until she returned to the front parlor and draped the day dress over the back of the lounge on which Mrs. Baring rested.

Eleanor Baring smiled. "That was one of my favorites."

"It is a lovely dress, ma'am."

"Please, won't you take it when it has served its purpose here? I think you and I were once of a size. I should very much like to think someone else finds delight in it."

Serafina was about to object when she saw the way Mrs. Baring stared at the dress. She was not looking at the cut of the cloth nor the lovely design. She said to her son, "Your father brought that back from his trip to Europe. Do you remember, Nathan?"

Nathan nodded as he too examined the dress. "Father watched you open the box. He took such delight in your reaction."

Serafina settled herself behind her easel. "Mr. Baring, would you be so kind as to move closer and take your mother's hand?"

"If you wish." He put his book on the windowsill and drew his chair closer. "Am I in your light?"

He was, and now a shadow was cast upon his mother's features. But no matter. "You are fine just as you are."

The two of them gazed at one another. And in the look they shared was a hint of what was now gone from this earth. The joy and pride of a young mother. The affection of a caring son. The timeless quality of a love-filled life. Serafina rubbed out the eyes and sketched again. As she did, she decided aloud, "Now."

"What, my dear?"

"Nothing, madam." She was ready. The time for sketching was over. She would use a wash for thick borders, perhaps umber and tan. She would focus solely upon the face. She would apply the shadows as a means of capturing the woman's youth once more.

The moment ended for the two of them. His mother faltered, her strength ebbed, and the light dimmed in her eyes. Nathan straightened and became the polite son once more. He said something Serafina did not hear and moved his chair back to the window. The diplomat was again in place. The mother was once more a sick old woman. It did not matter. Serafina held to the image. And the moment's power still enclosed the room.

CHAPTER 17

Falconer awoke and rolled over, groaning loudly. He heard singing. His wet and exhausted body had stiffened while he slept. The straw was no longer a comfortable cushion, and the lumps and the boards beneath felt like spikes against his bruised frame. Falconer struggled to sit up and groaned again.

The singing continued. Through the open doorway, Falconer spotted a young boy with hair like autumn flax approaching the barn. His voice was bell-like and pure as he swung a milking pail as far as his arm would extend, forward and back, in time to the hymn. When he stepped into the structure and his eyes adjusted to the gloom, the singing chopped off and the pail clattered to the floor at his bare feet.

"We mean no harm, lad," Falconer said.

The boy turned and catapulted out the door, falling and tumbling. When he regained his feet he came up running. "Uncle Joshua! Uncle Joshua! There's Injuns in the barn!"

Falconer rose slowly to his feet. Twenty-two pairs of dark eyes watched him as he stretched and rubbed the sorest points on his frame. He searched out Joseph and said, "Let's put the pail to good use. Who knows how to milk a cow?"

"Every last one of us here."

"Except for me." Falconer motioned to the goats. "Milk them as well. Feed the sick and young people first. And hand out some jerky."

Falconer stepped into the light. The previous day's weather conditions were erased completely. The vista looked sweet as heaven's foreground. Rolling hills were squared into emerald fields. The pastures were framed by hedgerows and wooden fences. A trio of homes nestled together on the far ridge. Six barns marched down the gently sloping face. Clouds wandered overhead, like fat lazy beasts feeding upon endless blue acres.

With Joseph's help, Falconer drew the others outside. He understood their fear but refused to allow them to hide indoors. The barn's floor was damp from the water that had pooled off their rain-soaked bodies. The new day was almost summertime warm, and the increasing sunlight was strong enough to ease his very bones. He waited until they were all squatted about the barn's entrance, then drew the Bible from his satchel and began to read aloud. He saw no reason to suspend a personal tradition that had helped to define his days.

He kept reading, halting only to drink from the frothy pail when his turn came. Finally Joseph rose to his feet and pointed behind Falconer. "They's comin', suh."

Falconer turned to see eight men round the side of the central house. Sunlight flickered upon metal, and Falconer knew all were armed with long-bore muskets. "Aaron."

"Suh."

"Go fetch the musket and sword."

The lad scampered into the barn. Swiftly he returned and handed Falconer the two weapons. "Go back and sit down. All of you, stay down. You too, Joseph."

Falconer started walking across the field. The running men slowed and spread out at his approach. Falconer heard the click of cocked muskets. He saw two of them slip a hand into a pocket and fit something onto the gun. A percussion cap, Falconer guessed. Which meant the men were armed with the most advanced weapons available.

Falconer stretched his arms out as far as they could go. One held the musket and sword. The other his Book. He kept walking forward.

All of the men were dressed the same, almost like a farmer's uniform. Black trousers and dark suspenders, white collarless shirts, round dark hats. All the men wore beards. The central figure had a gray beard as square as a shovel blade. He called out, "Here, now, what's this?"

In reply, Falconer bent over and placed his musket and sword on the grass. He took two steps away from his weapons. He kept his hands in plain view. "I won't be needing those, will I."

"That depends, stranger." At a hand signal from the central man, the others halted and lowered their muskets a notch. The man kept coming toward Falconer alone. "Slavers aren't welcome in these parts. We stand against them and their godless trade."

"I am not a slaver."

"That so." The man appeared to be in his sixties. But he was erect and barrel-chested, and the eyes shadowed by his broad-brimmed hat were crystal clear. "Then who be those folks stretched out beside my barn?"

245

Falconer slowly let his arms drop to his sides. "My friends."

The farmers said nothing more until they had marched Falconer back to where his charges were slowly coming to their feet.

"Who be you folk?" their spokesman called over.

None spoke, nor looked their way. One of the other farmers, a young man taller than their spokesman, said, "Look at their wrists, Joshua."

"I see them." The old man was fierce once more. He re-aimed his musket at Falconer. "You think taking off their chains will make you safe?"

"Joseph," Falconer said.

"Suh."

"Tell them, please."

Joseph hesitated so long Falconer feared he would not speak at all. Finally he said, "The man here's done bought us to set us free."

"He pay you to say that?"

"No, suh."

"What makes you think he's a man of his word?"

To Falconer's surprise, it was Geraldine who replied. "He sold his horse to keep us fed."

Then Mammy spoke to the ground at her

feet. "He done made me ride that mule there, and he walked the whole way from Richmond. When it rained he give me his own coat and walked hisself through the bone cold with nothin' 'cept the shirt on his back."

Another soft voice, one of the men. "Sold his knife too."

Joseph's son. "I cut my foot, suh. He carried me."

Aaron added his own voice. "He taught me to shoot."

There was another long silence, interrupted by one of the farmers behind Falconer. "Well, I'll be."

Finally Joseph looked at Falconer. Straight at him. And he said, "He reads the Book to us every morning. I thought God was lost to me 'til I heard that man speak."

Falconer lifted his gaze to the lazy clouds overhead. There had perhaps been a time that his heart had felt fuller. But just then he could not recall it.

The old farmer asked, quietly this time, "What is your name, stranger?"

"John. John Falconer."

"Gather your charges and come with us, John Falconer."

"There are ill and injured among us."

"We won't be going far. Come along now."

They were clearly not the first of their kind to arrive at this particular farmstead. By the time they reached the swept clearing that fronted the three homes, the womenfolk had built a fire and set a massive caldron on to boil. One of the barns had a long roof that stretched over the clearing like a tongue. Falconer's charges were settled down upon benches and the surrounding earth. Food was brought, good fare of biscuits and stewed beef and pickled radishes and beans. Falconer ate with the others, so hungry he felt his stomach distend painfully. Afterward he sat with his back against the barn wall and tried to keep his eyes open. Most of the others dozed in the warm morning, fed and safe. Falconer wanted to join them. But he forced himself to sit and watch where the farmers clustered, talking among themselves. He feared nothing. The muskets were stacked like cordwood against the central home's rear porch. The men ate the same food as their guests. Falconer had the feeling they were waiting for something to happen. So he stayed awake and waited with them.

Their dress was somewhat odd to Falconer's eye. Very clean, for one thing. The few farmers Falconer had known were content to go about their daily toil in mud-caked garb. These folk were dressed in clothes boiled so clean they sparkled in the sunlight. The men were all bearded, but their hair was well trimmed. The women were somewhat formal in their actions. Two of them worked their way through Falconer's charges now, applying salve to suppurating wounds caused by the chains. Another used a boiled rag to clean Isaac's foot. They wore hats too narrow to be proper sunbonnets, small affairs that covered their hair and were tied with white ribbons. They spoke with comforting voices. They watched Falconer with gazes that were both clear and cautious. He nodded whenever their eyes met but said nothing.

This was altogether a different land from what they had encountered upon the trail. The hills were gentle and set far apart, the land well tilled. Forest bordered the distant perimeter, but the vista from where Falconer sat was one of civilized prosperity. A neat little village was nestled in the broad valley, perhaps two miles distant. The winding road connecting the farms to the hamlet was lined with paddocks and pastures. Barns and houses looked all built to the same stalwart design. The fields were bordered by split-pine fencing. A flock of children stood on the adults' other side, some eating from tin plates and the others watching the newcomers with solemn eyes. But there was no fear among them. Even the cows looked fat and contented.

A pair of farm dogs approached. Falconer took them for a mother and an almost-weaned pup. The mother held back, but the pup was a curious sort. Falconer offered the last bit of meat from his plate and watched as the pup licked his fingers. He stroked the soft puppy fur and smiled as the pup nuzzled his palm. The mother came over and gave Falconer's other hand a good sniff. He dipped his fingers in the remaining sauce on his plate and let her lick that away. As he did, the towheaded lad who had dropped his pail peeked around the side of the barn, watching.

Falconer kept his voice low so as not to frighten the lad. "Are these your dogs?"

"Just the little one, sir. The mother belongs to Uncle Joshua. This here is my uncle's farm."

"And a lovely place it is too. Where do you live, then?"

"In town, sir."

"The one I see in the distance there?"

"Aye, sir." Gradually the lad emerged into view.

"As pretty a town as ever I've seen." The

adults clustered on the yard's opposite end watched cautiously but did not order the boy away. "What is it called?"

"Salem, sir."

"You're a polite and well-brought-up lad. And when I saw you this morning, you were helping your uncle with chores. Your parents must be very proud."

"My pa's in heaven, sir."

"I'm sorry to hear that." Falconer lifted the pup and settled it into his lap. The mother whined softly but made no move against him. "I lost my own father when I was very young. I can't really remember him."

"I remember Pa." The boy walked over and settled into the dirt beside Falconer. He stroked the mother dog with one hand and the pup with the other. "I fear I might forget him. But my ma says he will stay with me all my life long."

"Your mother sounds like a very wise woman."

Up close the lad smelled of soap and the animals. He was dressed in a child's version of the adults' clothing — collarless shirt, dark trousers, suspenders. Only his head and feet were bare. Falconer saw that all the buttons on his pants and shirt were cloth.

"I like working the farm," the boy said.

251

"My uncle says I was born to the land."

The gray-bearded man called softly, "Matt. Come over here, lad."

The boy rose, such that he stood at almost eye level to Falconer. His eyes held a green translucence, like sunlight seen through an emerald. "The men fear you are a highwayman, sir. Is that so?"

"Matt!"

"Best do as your uncle says, lad."

Matt grinned, as fearless as he was handsome. "My aunt says you are a danger to none, no matter what scar you carry. I think she is right."

Falconer watched the lad run off. Though he had little experience with young boys, he reckoned that one to be very fine.

He was alerted to coming change by how the lad cried out and pointed at the road. Falconer searched and saw a small dot where the road emerged from the village. Matt declared it was his mother, and Falconer nodded his approval of eyes as sharp as a bird of prey. The uncle and his mates turned to watch the arrival. Falconer rose to his feet, aware that his boots were scarred and muddy. His pants were ripped and filthy. His shirt was little more than a rag. Mammy slept upon his coat.

The speck became a horse and two-wheeled rig. The rider became a woman in a dove-gray dress and small white bonnet. She handled horse and cart very well. The horse cantered into the yard and halted at a single sharp tug on the reins. Two of the younger farmers walked over to help her down. Falconer could well understand their eagerness, for she was lovely indeed.

The lad took hold of the horse's bridle, and the horse swung him off his feet with a simple shake of its head. The child laughed delightedly, in the manner of one long accustomed to this play. The woman smiled and spoke softly. Falconer heard the music in her tone, and the love.

Then she turned Falconer's way and all levity vanished.

The gray-bearded man gave her a solemn welcome and spoke too softly for Falconer to follow. Joseph rose to his feet and came over to stand beside Falconer. "I done heard of these people," he said, his voice low.

Falconer turned to the squinting man. "What did you hear?"

"The gray lady. I thought mebbe it was a legend. 'Bout how a gray lady waits at the end of the trail." Joseph nodded once. "Reckon this one tale is true, sure enough."

The woman walked over, accompanied by Matt and three of the men. Up close she was even more lovely. Her hair was almost too dark to be called auburn, save for the copper tint where the sun touched. Her eyes held the same emerald illumination as her son's. "What do they call you, sir?"

"John Falconer, ma'am. I apologize for my appearance —"

"God's greetings to you, John Falconer. I have seen before what the trail can do to a man." She turned to Joseph. "And you, sir. Your name, if you please."

"I's called Joseph, missus."

"I am Ada Hart." She looked over the other folk, then turned her gaze back to Joseph. "Sir, I ask you to give me one good reason why you would trust this white man's word."

"He bought me, took me into the forest, and wrote I was free on the papers they give him."

"Do you have those documents?"

"I do," Falconer said. "In my satchel."

"Fetch them, if you please." As Falconer stepped to his almost-empty sack, she asked Joseph, "What makes you believe this man will do as he says?"

"He's used up every cent he carries to buy us. Tha's my family over there. My two boys, they was takin' them away."

"Who was? Slavers?"

"Yes'm. This man, he bought the whole line. I watched his face, missus. It tore him up to see these people in chains. Tore him up somethin' awful."

"Thank you, Joseph." She watched Falconer approach with a sheaf of papers in his hands. "What are those?"

"The bills of sale for all those you see gathered here."

"You are just giving them to me?"

"I hope and pray for your trust, and that of the people here," Falconer replied. "How could I offer you anything less in return?"

She gave the pages careful inspection. By the time she finished, all the farmers were gathered around her, including two young women and a lad just old enough to have a bit of fluff on his chin. "Just exactly who are you, John Falconer?" Ada Hart asked.

"My story is perhaps not one for these young folks to hear, ma'am."

She held him with a gaze both steady and timeless. "They may as well hear of the world's woes while sheltered within our clan. Speak."

He took a very hard breath. "I am a seafaring man. I worked mostly on merchant ships. But one journey I skippered a slaver."

A quiet moan flitted through the gathering, a sound of sorrow on what was otherwise a pristine day. Falconer forged ahead. "The evil I did stained me, true enough. It also brought me to my knees. I stand here today saved by the blood of our Savior, Jesus Christ."

"Amen," said one of the other farming women, and it was echoed by several others in the group.

Ada Hart, however, continued to watch him carefully. "Please continue, John Falconer."

So he told them all of it. Or nearly all. How he had most recently been hired by a cautious Venetian merchant prince to determine whether a gold mine truly existed. And given four purses of gold, supposedly to pay for his travel and his safety. The farmers grew round-eyed at Falconer's account. Their children crept in close, as if they were hearing fanciful tales by an evening fire. The tow-headed boy held onto his mother's skirt, so entranced by Falconer's tale he ignored the pup toying with his dusty feet.

Ada Hart, however, was made of sterner stuff. She heard him out in watchful silence, then observed, "You have made no mention of why you chose to buy and free these slaves."

This breath was harder still. "I feel that God has spoken to me, ma'am."

"He has called you to buy slaves and free them?"

"The slave ship I skippered held a manifest for four hundred and nineteen poor souls. They are lost to me. But I seek to free at least that number of their brethren."

Even Ada was stunned, and the group murmured among themselves. "Four hundred and nineteen slaves will cost you a king's ransom, John Falconer," she said. "You had best hope your mine proves of enormous value."

"I will spend what I have, Mrs. Hart. I can do no more."

The gray-bearded farmer said softly, "Ada."

She turned from her inspection of the man before her. "Yes, Brother Joshua?"

"Enough." The man spoke with gentle authority. "It is too long, this questioning."

"There is still more I wish to know."

"As do I. We can speak further when he is bathed and properly rested. The man speaks truthfully and shares our cause."

"You are persuaded of this, Brother Joshua?"

"Standing here in the sun any longer is not proper. The man is exhausted, along with his little band. More questions will not bring us any closer to certainty.

That I do know."

Ada pursed her lips in deep indecision. She gave Falconer a final inspection. Then she nodded cautiously. "Very well. But your charges must leave you here, John Falconer. You cannot know where they go. Nor can you ask."

"I deliver them into your care," Falconer solemnly agreed. "Were I in your position, I would require exactly the same."

Yet his words seemed to do nothing to erase the anxiety creasing Ada Hart's features. Approaching footsteps turned them both about. Joseph shuffled over, nervous at drawing near yet determined. "Y'all is gonna put us on the ghost train to freedom?"

Ada's gaze shifted away from Falconer. "Your name is Joseph, is that not correct?"

"Yes'm."

"Joseph, there are some things of which it is best never to speak. Do you understand me?"

"Yes'm." Though the man's face remained tense and deeply lined, he held his ground. "Reason I'm askin', missus, I wants to stay with Mistuh John here."

Falconer saw Geraldine rise to her feet. He quietly protested, "But your family, Joseph."

"They's gonna be safe on account of you and what you's done, suh. I knows that for a fact."

"We will do our best to bring you to freedom," Ada said.

"Ain't nobody never done nothin' for me before this man." He managed a single glance straight into Falconer's eyes. "And when he reads to us from the Book, missus, I hear my heart singin'. Ain't never heard that before. Not my whole life long."

Geraldine came over to stand beside her man. She gripped her husband's arm and looked Falconer full in the face. "They's gonna be a new tale told now. Folks who ain't got nothing, too scared to dream, they's gonna hear about this. 'Bout a man who travels hard roads for the King. Big man with an angel's heart. Strong man. Ain't afraid of the night or nothing else." Her head moved up and down slowly. "They's gonna hear. They's gonna hope."

The gray-bearded farmer settled a hand upon Ada Hart's shoulder and spoke more firmly this time. "We have heard enough, Ada."

CHAPTER 18

His name was Cody Saunders and he was Jeb's younger brother. The Saunders brothers had a reputation that stretched from Fredericksburg all the way to Atlanta. Cody Saunders took pride in being who he was and the fear people showed when they heard his name.

He was grinning with pleasure now as the tavern keeper at Burroughs Crossing reached inside the doorway for his musket. Cody said, "Get your hands out where I can see 'em, old man."

"I know who you are, Cody Saunders." The man drew his hand back into view. Along with it came the musket, which he cocked and brought to his shoulder. "And I'd as soon plug you with lead as offer the time of day."

"And I'm telling you to lay down your piece." Cody Saunders twisted in the saddle, causing the leather to creak. He was no more concerned about the merchant than he was the drovers who clustered by the first corral. "You take aim at me again, my brother'll burn your place to the ground. But not before he hangs your whole family from the rafters. And you know I'm talking truth."

"What do you want?"

The saddle creaked once more as Cody Saunders worked the knot from his shoulders. It had been a long hard slog through rain and muck, and he was tired. "I ain't telling you again, old man."

Reluctantly old man Burroughs set the musket down by the doorstep. "I asked you a simple question."

"Now that we're jawing polite, I'll tell you. I'm after information. Give me what I want and I'll ride on." He pointed his leather quirt at the drovers. "Y'all stop playin' all restless with them pistols. Else somebody's gonna be breathing their last."

"Do as he says," the merchant ordered. When one of the drovers started to make a move, Burroughs raised his voice. "Don't you know nothin'? This here's Cody Saunders. Only man I'd worse like to squabble with is his brother Jeb."

When the drover let his mates pull him back, old man Burroughs said, "What information might that be?"

"You owned a gray mare? White-maned with leggings on its forefeet?"

A voice piped up from within the inn, "They's talking about my mare, Pa!"

"You just pipe down and let me handle this. And stay back there like I told you." The merchant squinted at the dirty rider. "I mighta had a horse like that. What's it to ya?"

"What can you tell me 'bout the man what bought it from you?"

"Not a solitary thing. Don't even know his name."

"He just waltzed in here outta nowhere?"

"Pretty much. Walked down that road there, plunked down good gold coin, bought supplies and my horse, then headed south."

"And Joseph, Pa," the lad cried. "You forgot Joseph."

"I ain't tellin' you again, boy." He turned to glare into the dark room behind him.

Cody Saunders slipped from his horse. "Who's this Joseph, now?"

"Slave I bought me a while back. There's too much work needed doing round this place for me and my clan."

"So this feller John comes up outta nowhere. He plunks down waxed gold coin, buys a horse and supplies and a slave. And heads south without a by-your-leave."

The merchant was eyeing him tightly. "I didn't say nothing about them coins of his being waxed."

Cody bit down on his retort. This was why he hated dealing with the outside world without his brother by his side. "I knowed it anyway."

"And I didn't say his name was John. On account of how I didn't know it myself."

"So how did you sign the papers selling him your man?"

"I didn't. He took the bill of sale and left. Same as I'm asking you to do."

"He bought a slave and didn't have you fill in his name? That means the slave is still yours to claim." Cody tried to get his tired mind to work faster. "Don't sound like any slave owner I've ever met before."

The merchant chewed on his beard, clearly conflicted. "If'n you find Joseph, will you bring him back to me?"

"What else do you know, old man?"

"First you tell me what I want to hear."

"Yeah, all right. We find your slave, we'll deliver him back. Now tell me what it is you're chewing on there."

"Maybe it ain't nothing," the merchant said. "But I took Joseph off the Moss Plantation. For gambling debts."

"You said Moss?"

The merchant was sharp enough to have survived years dealing with the kind of folk who had no business in downtown Richmond. "You know him," he observed.

"Yeah, I mighta met him somewheres before."

"Joseph was born on the place. He had himself a common-law wife and two boys. He pined something awful for his family."

Cody Saunders knew he was being given the pieces to a puzzle. Only his brain wasn't made for fitting facts together like his brother could. He walked over to the horse trough and dunked his head. He came up gasping. "Bring me a plate of that fatback and beans I'm smelling. And some fresh-baked corn pone."

The merchant was back on familiar territory. "That'll cost you four bits."

Cody Saunders wasn't in the habit of paying for his vittles. But something told him his brother might want him to visit with this merchant another time, so he fished a coin out of his vest pocket and tossed it over. "You got any fresh coffee?"

The man caught the coin. "You'll eat and be gone, and next time I see you will be to return me my slave. That right?"

"Sure thing, old man," Cody lied. "Now

bring me my grub."

Falconer rose from his bed long before daybreak. Dawn was little more than a faint stain upon the deep blue sky. Out west the stars were still clear, the moon a fingernail's sliver. He walked to the well in the inn's forecourt and took his time washing. As the light gradually strengthened, a mockingbird challenged his claim to the morning.

Ada Hart ran Salem's only guesthouse, what her son had called the Strangers' Inn. It stood on Main Street, about midway between the central church and the outlying paddocks. The home was large, with a full three stories framed in stout red brick. The downstairs rooms were floored in heart of pine, waxed and aged until it shone like frozen honey. Falconer took his Bible to a bench placed by the inn's eastern wall. He prayed silently until the light became strong enough for him to see the words on the page. He turned to the verse he had been reading to his charges when the armed farmers had arrived. Falconer found himself missing this group of people. So he prayed for each of them in turn and asked for a swift passage to a safe haven, one that would welcome and succor and offer them a future. And he tried not to let his own loneliness taint the silent words.

The sun rose to where the eastern hills became golden waves. The distant trees wore their spring green like delicate mantles. Ribbons of chimney-smoke rose into the cloudless sky. Falconer closed his Bible and gazed around him, feeling the sense of reward the dawn held. He had started his quest. He had delivered his first charges to safety. By noon he would be filled with restless hunger, for he was not the sort of man to remain sated for long. A doer, a man of action, and God's entry into his life had not changed that. Only the direction and how he got to the goal.

Falconer heard the young lad before he came into view. He rounded the corner singing another hymn and swinging another pail. He beamed at Falconer and cried, "I told Mama you were up with the Good Book for company. But she shushed me and said I was to let you sleep."

"Where are you off to this morning?" He could see the boy looking at his scar, and he turned slightly so the sun was shining on his good side.

"We keep one milk cow in yonder barn. Mama says it's too far out to the farm and back every morning, and our tenants deserve fresh cream with their porridge."

266

"Your mother sounds like a wonderful innkeeper." Falconer rose to his feet and followed the boy. "And you strike me as a great help to all your family. But I see no barn."

"It's hidden beyond the trees and God's Acre there."

"I beg your pardon, beyond what?"

"God's Acre," the boy repeated. "Right there before you."

"I only see a cemetery."

"Which is God's own resting place," the boy said, grinning up at him. "God's Acre. That's our name for it."

"Who is it doing the naming?"

"Moravians, sir. Do you not even know where you be this fair morn?"

Falconer laughed aloud. Not at the question, but rather at the boy's odd mixture of childishness and adult speech. "I confess I was so tired I probably heard and then forgot before the words took shape."

"How can someone forget the place they labored so hard to reach?"

Falconer followed Matt around the cemetery and along a path through the stand of hickory and dogwood. Falconer heard a cow lowing from the lean-to up ahead. "The trail was very hard for us."

"I've heard some of the brethren speak of

it. But I've never been beyond Bethabara."
He set a milking stool beside the cow and
sat down. "Is it ever so exciting?"

"Sometimes," Falconer allowed. "Mostly
it is hard. Some days, however, can be very
exciting indeed."

A woman's voice spoke up from beyond
the barn's shadows. "I shall thank you, sir,
not to be filling my son's head with idle
chatter."

"He wasn't, Mama. Honest. I just asked
him about the trail, is all."

Because of the growing light, Falconer saw
only the woman's silhouette. But he recognized the voice and the woman's erect
stance. "A very good morning to you, Mrs.
Hart."

The woman stood in silence for a moment
longer. Her shadow cut a very womanly
silhouette. With a slender neck and a fine
figure, even her petite stature carried its own
presence. "I do not hear anything touching
your pail, Matt."

The milk began rattling into the bucket.
"I'll be just a few minutes, Mama."

"Hurry, now. I'm about to call our guests
to the table." She turned around. "John Falconer, a word, if you please."

"Of course, ma'am." He followed her into
the sunlight. "I can't thank you enough for

your hospitality, Mrs. Hart. As I explained last night, I have no more money with me. I'm good for the debt, though, I assure —"

"How long did you intend to stay, John Falconer?"

"To tell the truth, ma'am, I had no plans beyond seeing these first ones brought to safety. A few days — long enough to gather some provisions and perhaps find a horse. That is, if I'm able to arrange a loan."

"One of your charges, as you put it, is waiting for you by the front door. The man known as Joseph. He seeks a word."

"Thank you, ma'am. If you'll excuse me, I'll go —"

"That is not what I wished to speak with you about, sir." She led him back through the grove and directed him to a bench beside the cemetery. "Would you be so kind as to sit with me a moment?"

"Certainly, Mrs. Hart."

When they were seated, she did not speak. Instead, the woman pulled a handkerchief from her sleeve and knotted it, bunching it tightly between her hands. "I would ask that you speak to me again of your plans, John Falconer."

He realized with a start that the woman did not like him. Or perhaps merely distrusted him. Whatever the cause, the tension radiated off her in waves. "There is little more I can tell you, ma'am. It is all so new and unshaped in my head, I can scarcely find the proper words."

"Do the best you can," she replied tersely. "It is the most we can ask of any man."

So he repeated all he had said the previous day. Of his sense of being called to free the same number of slaves as he had transported into captivity. Of the gold mine. Of his plans for the money.

She stared over the graves as he spoke. Her expression was taut. Falconer had no idea of her age, but he guessed it as somewhere around his own thirty years. When he finished talking, he continued to watch her. He sensed something deeper beneath the surface. A dark stain, a sorrow perhaps. Or an illness. Something that she most likely thought was hidden from the world.

When she finally spoke, it was to the rising day and not to Falconer directly. "You did not mention having acquired the plantation."

"Did I not?" Falconer tried to recall. "It was an omission due to weariness, Mrs. Hart. I do not seek to hide anything from you."

For some reason the words only pinched her face up tighter still. "What do you seek to do with the farm, John Falconer?"

"To be honest, ma'am, it was arranged on an impulse." He felt foolish even speaking of it. More than that. Her rigid inspection of the horizon left him feeling that he had done something wrong. "I have no use for land, Mrs. Hart. I just thought . . ."

"Yes?"

"I thought if I had all these freedmen passing through, it might be good to have a place to let them rest up. Maybe find a more regular channel from there to safety." He hesitated, then asked, "Have I done something ill-advised?"

She started to respond, then clamped down hard on her words. "I ask that you attend the morning church with us, John Falconer. There are several matters which must be addressed."

He took that as a dismissal and rose to his feet. "I have no money, Mrs. Hart. But I will repay what I will owe you."

She waved that aside, as though of no consequence. "Go and speak with Joseph, sir. Breakfast will be on the table when you are done. Church begins at nine sharp. You will be called by the ringing of the bell."

"Thank you, ma'am." He could use the second set of clothes he carried in his satchel. He crossed the rear yard and started around the tavern, wishing he knew what he'd done to upset the good woman so.

Joseph was seated by the tavern's front door. He gazed out to the north, his face so intent it seemed to Falconer that every furrow was realigned so as to magnify the aim. Falconer came over and seated himself on the bench. The more he came to know this man, the more he respected him. "You wanted to see me?"

Joseph shook his head at the rising sun. "Never thought I'd hear a white man talk to me like that."

Falconer eased himself back to rest against the tavern wall. "Like what?"

Joseph turned then, drawing the furrowed intensity around to where it aimed straight at Falconer. "Like I was his equal."

"God says all men are brethren."

"There you go again, sayin' them words. Like you was taught a different language. One that sounds the same but ain't."

Falconer felt the testing behind the speech and the look both. As with the woman he had just left, he sensed an undercurrent he could not identify. "Perhaps you have to sink as low as I have fallen. Descend into the depths where the gates of hell are a mouth waiting to swallow men whole. Only then can you truly recognize how little difference there is between one man and another. How the color of skin does not distinguish the soul. How we have all fallen short and can claim salvation only through God's eternal grace."

"Them words you say, they might as well be comin' from a dream." Joseph shook his head very slowly. Back and forth. But the dark and flint-hard gaze did not stray. "Geraldine and I talked away the night. I still wasn't sure what to do when I got up this morning. Now I know."

"Joseph, you are not beholden to me."

"Now I know," Joseph repeated. "If you're called to the road, then so am I."

"We covered this ground yesterday. Ada Hart will —"

"I told you the first day we was together. You don't know nothing. You need a strong arm and a steady eye and somebody who'll talk to folks who'd run at the sight of you."

"What about your family?"

He turned his attention back to the northern horizon. "West of the road we come in on is another village. They call it Bethabara. My Geraldine, she calls it heaven on earth. They's more of us there."

"Freed slaves?"

"Some of 'em. Others born free. We's all

welcome there. They don't hold to slaves in this place. Mostly they send folks north and west, along the Underground Railroad. You heard of that?"

"Yes."

"Them folks, they's already heard 'bout what you're doing. They told me my family'll be taken in and cared for so's I can go off to watch your back."

Falconer mulled that over. "So people know about me."

"Don't you worry none. These folks, they know how to guard a word." Joseph rose to his feet. "When do we leave?"

"Tomorrow or the next day."

"I'll be ready." Joseph started away, then turned back to add, "The others we come with, they's callin' you their Night Angel. Reckon it's their way of saying thanks."

Ada Hart sat and stared at the gravesites. Her son passed by, tilted sideways by the weight of the full pail. He spoke to her. But Ada Hart could not make sense of the words. Matt followed the direction of her focus. Matt was an intelligent and sensitive lad. He had seen her seated in this place often enough before, lost to the earthly realm. Matt's face creased in a sadness far too old for his years.

When she spoke, it was to say, "I do not want you growing over close to this stranger, my son."

"All the folk say he is doing God's work, Mama."

She started to disagree but could not. For she knew the truth of this as well. "The stranger will be leaving us soon."

"I do like him, Mama."

"Do as I say." She watched him take a two-fisted grip on the pail and stagger toward the inn. Ada wished she had found better words to explain. In truth, though, she was in such tumult she had no idea what to say, even to herself.

The grave closest to the bench was more than three years old. Rain was just beginning to darken its façade with the paint of time. Moravians believed all were equal in both life and death, so the tombstones were all the same, rounded headstones with the names and dates and nothing more. But Ada had sat on this bench and written reams of words. About how no lad should lose his father or a young wife lose her man.

Ada Hart had any number of possible suitors. For she was not only beautiful, she was wealthy by Moravian standards. She had a share in her family's farm, in the manner of fields she leased back to her brothers.

Her husband had been an only child, a rarity in Moravian culture. His own parents were gone. The Strangers' Inn was hers now. In the dangerous world of the Carolina Piedmont, many travelers sought safety within the Moravian enclave. They paid well for Ada's comfort and hearty fare. She could have her pick of any man in the five villages.

The problem was, she cared for none of them.

Her husband had been a genuine individual in a society that rewarded sameness. A firm believer, yet a rebel in his own gentle way. A man who loved joy and singing and wind and adventure. He had spent hours seated at the inn's tables, listening with glistening eyes as strangers described the world beyond the Wachau borders, the Moravian name for their settlement. It also was the name of the Austrian estate of their German patron, Count Zinzendorf. Salem was the largest of the five Wachau villages. The Strangers' Inn anchored the village to the road and the world beyond.

Ada felt the sun on her face and knew she should be inside, calling the stragglers downstairs for breakfast and preparing herself and Matt for church. But she remained where she was, trapped by all she had lost when they had laid her husband in the ground.

Three years of solitude was a very long time. It was especially long for a young woman who still felt the fire of life singing in her veins.

Ada Hart sighed and plucked at her dress. The gray weave was, she feared, the color of her future. She would wed soon enough. The community had been patient, but she knew people had begun talking. A young woman with a young son needed a husband. They would bring her before the elders, and they would select a man if she did not choose one for herself. She had seen it done twice in the years since her husband's accident. She dreaded the day and hated the helplessness with which she saw it approach.

Her mother had been against the man Ada had chosen. Both Ada's parents came from farming families, wedded to the land for seven generations. Ada's mother had not cared about how this innkeeper had ignited the flame in Ada's heart. Her mother had spoken of pasture and cattle and people who understood the earth. But Ada's father had seen the joy in his only daughter's face and had offered them his blessing. And they had wed. For six years and three months they had been blissfully happy. Until that fateful night when a bolting horse had thrown her husband, crushed him, and laid him down forever. The burial shroud had been sewn about her life as well as his.

Ada rose to her feet. She moved like an old woman, bowed down by the thousand identical days she had yet to live. She would wed a man from the area. She would move to his farm and bake and mend and clean house and tend his needs. He would be a good man, conservative and steady and content with Wachau life. And never again would she sit before a roaring fire and listen to tales from beyond the boundaries of her safe little world.

She raised her face to the sun and whispered words no one would ever hear. "Why did you come here, John Falconer?"

CHAPTER 19

Cody Saunders could not have said why he took the cut leading west off the turnpike. Surely he had no business with Moss, nor did he much care for the dice cup. His brother, now, that was a different story entirely. Jeb Saunders plied Moss as he would a well, drawing out a fistful of gambling gold every now and then. Jeb never won so much as to be unwelcome, of course. Cody debated going down to Danville and returning with his brother. But he was saddlesore and disliked the thought of another full day of riding for what Jeb would probably say he should have handled on his own.

Truth be told, Cody Saunders did not even know what he should be asking of Moss. Jeb was the thinker for the both of them. Even so, he rode down the winding tree-lined lane and started up the final rise. He slowed as he approached the main house and gave the surrounding farmland more careful inspection.

The Saunders brothers had been raised on a hardscrabble farm down east, a half day's ride outside Edenton. When Jeb had been fourteen and Cody ten, they had slipped away and never looked back. Only occasionally did he and Jeb speak of the family they had left behind. They wondered about their nine brothers and sisters, many of whose names neither of them could remember. But they did recall the chores. Especially at tobacco harvest time, when they walked the long rows, dragging the burlap sacks tied to their shoulders and plucking the broad ripe leaves. By the end of the rows the sacks were so heavy the twine cut into their flesh. The heat was maddening, as were the flies. The biggest flies Cody had ever seen, and they bit. Worse even than the flies was the stench. The tobacco gave off an odor Cody still smelled in his sleep. The tar turned his fingers black and seeped through his skin into his blood. By the end of the day he was sweating tobacco juice, his head thundering and his gut churning. No, Cody did not miss the farm.

But he knew the cycle of farming seasons.

And what he saw did not make any sense at all.

When they had come through last, Cody had stayed with their string of slaves bought from a handler outside Richmond. Jeb had gone to the house alone. No sense in showing Moss what they were after, was the way Jeb explained it. Cody had resented waiting in the muck and the rain with their ragtag chain gang. Jeb had returned leading six more slaves, only one of which he had paid for. The other five he had won in a two-day dice match. Which meant Cody was now seeing the farm for the first time that season.

A voice behind him said, "Makes you plumb want to weep, don't it?"

Cody's saddle creaked as he shifted his weight. He recognized the overseer. "Where's Moss?"

"Done taken himself off to Richmond." The overseer was rail thin and hard faced, as were most of his kind. A good overseer drove himself as hard as he did his charges. The man's current idleness did not sit at all well. "The gold was just a-burnin' a hole in his pocket."

"Mind if I draw water for me and my horse?"

"Help yourself."

Cody slid down and led his horse to the

281

well. He plied the bucket and filled the trough, then drank long and slow. Only then did he speak. "Moss won himself some gold, did he?"

The overseer laughed until he bent over in a coughing fit. He straightened and said, "That man ain't never won nothing except trouble."

Cody took his time. It was something he'd often seen Jeb do. A man who wanted to talk would often give up information without being asked, if only the questioner waited him out. So he filled the ladle and drank again. As he did he inspected the plantation. The main house looked dilapidated. The fields were in even worse shape. Fences were down. The last season's crop might have been harvested, but the stubble still stood. A good farmer would have plowed it under, giving the earth a chance to renew itself with this natural fertilizer. Beyond the pastures stood an orchard of apple and cherry and pear. He could smell the rotting fruit from where he stood.

The overseer shifted impatiently. "Had a feller come in not long after your brother was here. Offered to buy the whole spread."

"That a fact."

"Wouldn't be saying it if it wasn't." The overseer spit a stream of tobacco juice. "The fool agreed to Moss's price, plunked down his money, and rode off. Craziest thing I ever did see."

"So Moss has sold out?"

"If the stranger shows up with the rest of his money, Moss is gone. I asked the stranger if I had a job. The man didn't even give me a by-your-leave."

"What'd this stranger look like?"

"Right big feller. Looks like he could handle himself in a fight. Wore the cross blades like a highwayman."

"Black hair? Got a scar running from jaw to eye?"

The overseer squinted at Cody. "Where you been seeing him?"

"Don't rightly recall." Cody hoisted himself back into the saddle. "You catch the man's name?"

"I heard Moss say it was Mr. John."

"Yeah, that's our man." Cody adjusted the brim of his hat. "Guess I'll be off, then."

The overseer called after him, "You see that feller again, you tell him he won't find a better man than me to work his crew."

Falconer was coming out of the inn when he heard the noise. At first he thought it was a small beast, a calf perhaps or a baby goat. The sound was more like an animal's keening than a child. But when he rounded the corner, he spied a crop of blond hair atop a huddled form, crimped into the corner where the brick chimney met the inn's foundations. Next to him was the pup, who whined in time to the boy's quiet sobs.

Falconer neither thought nor hesitated. He reached down and lifted the boy, holding him around his shoulders, and stepped back into the sunlight. "Shah now, lad. You're safe now. What's happened? Who did this to you?"

The boy tensed in his embrace, then relaxed a trifle. "I-I'm all right, sir."

"Of course you are. You're as brave and fine a lad as any I've ever met." The boy's puppy gamboled about Falconer's feet, coming close to tripping him up. "What is your dog's name?"

"M-my mother won't let me name him, sir. She says dogs and strangers don't mix, and . . . and we must give him away."

"Well, I'm sure your mother is wise as they come. She loves you very much and wants only the best for her strong lad." Falconer spoke mostly to let the boy hear the sound of comfort. "But my guess is you've given the dog a name in secret, haven't you."

The lad moved away from Falconer's shoulder and dragged his sleeve across his face. "Rusty."

"And what a grand name that is." Falconer looked down at the pup. "Move back, Rusty, before I step on you."

The lad added his own voice. "Down, Rusty."

"Look there, he minds you and not me." The lad smelled of ash soap and sunlight and animals and youth. "Did someone hurt you, lad?"

"No, sir."

"You can tell me. It will be our secret. I'm good at keeping secrets, you know."

"No one has harmed me, sir."

The boy's frank gaze and tone did not seem capable of lies. Falconer led him over to the bench and eased himself down. The lad made himself comfortable on the seat next to Falconer, his body set firmly against the big man. The pup played about his feet and gnawed on Falconer's boot.

Falconer did not have any experience with young boys. But his heart went out to this likely lad. "Do you want to tell me what left you feeling so sad? Is it something more than wanting to keep the dog?"

The boy gnawed on his lip.

"Well, never you mind. I have known many a day when sadness was my only companion, or so it seemed. And I was never one to go sharing my troubles with others. Except God, of course. I have always found God to be a good listener."

The boy began picking a splinter from the side of the bench. "I talked to God a lot after my pa died. I wished He would speak back to me. But He never did. At least I couldn't hear Him."

Falconer caught the old sorrow in the lad's words. He sensed Matt was sharing a secret with him, one he had perhaps not told to anyone else. "You may be surprised to find in later days that God spoke to you just the same, lad. At a level far deeper than words. Down where your soul heard and where your heart was calmed."

The boy looked at him. "Have you lost a loved one, sir?"

"Aye." Falconer leaned his head against the wall. He saw Serafina's face in the sunlight. Heard her voice, with the accent so fresh and remarkable it turned a simple greeting into song. "Aye. I have."

"Did God speak to you?"

"In a way."

"What did He say?"

"He sent me off on this quest." Falconer looked down at the boy. In the sunlight his eyes were almost transparent, as though Falconer peered directly into the lad's soul. It left him wanting to confess what he had said to no man. "My greatest fear is not having heard the Lord correctly."

The young boy tilted his head, such that his hair became a golden wave in the sunlight, almost touching his shoulder. "If God speaks, how can you not hear Him?"

"Because I am not as good nor as innocent as you. I have done many ill deeds. They stained my soul until I was washed in the Savior's blood. Even so, I still feel their shadow at times. I fear they cast a veil about my spirit, such that I do not hear the Lord correctly. I can only pray that I do His bidding. Pray and hope. And pray some more."

The boy had clearly never been spoken to in such a way by an adult before. His tears forgotten, he asked, "Are you a highwayman like they say?"

"My world is the sea, lad. Or it was. Upon the open waters they would be termed pirates. And I never was one. But I was other things."

"A slaver. I heard you say that to my mother and Uncle Joshua." He scrambled off the bench, almost tripping over the puppy. "Have you been to many lands, sir?"

"Aye." Falconer could not help but touch the lad's shining hair. "Many times many."

"Will you tell me of one?"

"If you like."

"Sir, I should like it ever so much. Where —" His words were cut short by the ringing of a distant bell. Matt's eyes grew wide. "Church! I forgot about church! Sir, are you coming?"

"I'm right behind you."

Matt leaped away. "We must hurry!"

The church was built of the same red brick and oak beams as the rest of the village. The entire community, as uniform as the surrounding buildings, streamed toward the central structure. There was a quiet joy to the day, an orderliness won from a grudging and reluctant world. The men were stout and strong, with hands and faces hardened by endless work. The women looked like gray doves, with traces of white at their heads and wrists. The men wore dark coats and hats, their boots scraped clean of the red earth. Falconer's first impression was how the children appeared as eager as their parents to enter the sanctuary.

One of the younger men Falconer had last seen at the farm greeted Falconer with a handshake. His grip was firm, his skin as callused as tree bark. He directed Falconer upstairs, to what in other churches might be the choir loft.

He found himself seated among others

who were clearly strangers to this world. There were traders and travelers and several black families. Falconer chose a place by the front railing so he might observe the community. He saw Ada Hart enter with her son. The woman moved with an erect grace. Matt turned and craned upward as they walked the central aisle. When he spied Falconer he grinned hugely and waved his free hand high over his head. Ada Hart turned to see what was attracting her son's attention. Her face creased and her step faltered when she spotted Falconer. He raised his right hand in an unobtrusive greeting to them both, wondering anew what he might have done to offend this good woman.

Ada directed her son into a pew occupied mostly by older women. She did not follow Matt, however. Instead she stepped to another pew, where a stout man rose to accept her greeting. Ada spoke briefly. The man nodded twice, then turned at her direction and looked up at Falconer. The man standing beside Ada nodded agreement to whatever she said and bowed as she turned and walked to where her son was seated.

The congregation appeared shaped of curious groupings. The left front pews were all young men. The right, where Ada and

Matt were seated, were mostly older women. There were a few children near young ladies, but not many. All were dressed the same, in the gray dresses and the starched white caps. The men were hatless now, their faces sunburnt where the hat's protection ended. Some talked quietly among themselves. Most, however, sat in the peaceful calm of people content simply to be where they were.

The seat next to Falconer was taken by a scrawny man whose breath smelled of plug tobacco. He leaned upon the railing and murmured, "Makes for a pretty sight, don't it."

"Indeed."

"Name's Johanson. Wagoneer. Make the run from Columbia to Danville twice a month. Always try to stop off here for the Sabbath. Got a special feel, this place does."

He paused then, and Falconer knew he was looking for a response. But Falconer had no interest in offering his own name. "This is my first time in the area."

"Them Moravians, they's a closed lot. They welcome my trade, but I ain't never been inside a home. And I been making this run for almost five years." He pointed with his chin to the congregation below. "They's got a special way of sitting together, don't they. Called choirs. Up front is the bachelors' choir. There to the right is the widows' choir."

"Of course," Falconer murmured.

"Married folk are all in the back. I hear tell them choirs ain't just for singing. It's how they manage life. I'm told they share all they have — a third to the church and a third to the choir. 'Course, since nobody gets inside the homes, it's hard to tell what's truth and what's fable."

A voice spoke from behind them. "John Falconer."

"Yes?" He turned to see the young farmer who had greeted him in the vestibule.

The farmer murmured, "Come with me."

Falconer followed the farmer out of the loft and down the rear stairs. The farmer pointed him toward a man encircled by a half-dozen graybeards. All eyes turned at Falconer's approach. Some were cautious, others seemingly hostile.

The central figure wore a pastor's white cloak. "You are John Falconer?"

"I am, Reverend."

"Joachim Schmidt." He was not as tall as Falconer, nor as robust. Yet he commanded respect with a presence that shone from his features. His gaze was brown and piercing, his hair long and silver-white. He took his time inspecting Falconer, giving no indication whatsoever that the entire village waited for him inside the nave. "Where did you gain that scar, John Falconer?"

"On the foredeck of a slaver, I'm sorry to say, Your Reverence."

He nodded, as though approving of the answer. "The entire village is speaking of little else besides your act of generosity."

"I do not see it as a generous act myself, sir."

"No? How would you describe it?"

"Penance, Your Reverence. For the woes and sorrows I have wreaked upon the innocent."

Again there was the fractional nod in response. "I am told you felt God's voice leading you, John Falconer."

"Sir, my greatest fear is that I am so tainted I may have misheard His direction."

The pastor turned to one elder who bore a hostile expression. "What say you, Brother Rupert?"

"We close ourselves off for a purpose, Pastor Joachim." But there was uncertainty now in his voice.

"I will not insist, Brother. Nevertheless, I do ask this of you."

The older man sighed. "I do not stand against this, Pastor."

"Very well." The pastor turned to Falconer and continued. "I would ask that you take the second reading today, sir."

A bolt from heaven could hardly have surprised him more. "You want . . . ?"

"You shall enter with us and stand where directed. Upon my signal, approach the altar. Your reading is from the fifth chapter of James, the first eight verses." Before Falconer could shape a response, the pastor said to the others, "Brothers, I wish you a blessed morning service."

At the murmured response, the pastor turned and led his elders into the church.

A wave of quiet astonishment followed Falconer's appearance up the aisle. He kept his focus on the men before him, looking neither to the left nor the right as he proceeded toward the altar. He felt eyes upon him from every side, but only one voice carried clear to his ear. He heard Matt say, "Mama, *look!*"

He took his appointed spot by the front left window. From this position he could angle himself so that he watched the altar instead of the congregation. He could do nothing, however, about the eyes he felt boring into him with questions and uncertainty. The pastor came to the podium, offered a Sabbath blessing, and spoke a few words.

Then the singing began.

Falconer was transported beyond his self-conscious concerns. For these voices did not merely sing. They flowed together in beautiful harmony. They called with a joy that would not be denied. To begin, a woman hummed a single note. This was taken up by the congregation at large, and this then was transformed into words and song. And what song. Three hundred voices and more, from the graybeards to the youngest child, all singing with the heartfelt power of those who *lived* for such moments.

When the song ended, they began another. And a third. A fourth. When they finished, the chamber echoed for a long moment, then fell silent. Falconer breathed out slowly. No matter where he went, how far he traveled, he would carry the memory of that time of worship in song with him all his days.

The singing left him so euphoric he forgot to be nervous, even when the pastor turned and motioned him forward. As soon as he saw the passage opened on the pulpit, he understood the pastor's choice. He read in a clear, strong voice, powered by the truth displayed before him:

"Go to now, ye rich men, weep and howl

for your miseries that shall come upon you. Your riches are corrupted, and your garments are motheaten. Your gold and silver is cankered; and the rust of them shall be a witness against you, and shall eat your flesh as it were fire. Ye have heaped treasure together for the last days. Behold, the hire of the labourers who have reaped down your fields, which is of you kept back by fraud, crieth: and the cries of them which have reaped are entered into the ears of the Lord of sabaoth."

Falconer paused a moment, his hands gripping the sides of the podium. Then he raised his voice on the last verses.

"Ye have lived in pleasure on the earth, and been wanton; ye have nourished your hearts, as in a day of slaughter. Ye have condemned and killed the just; and he doth not resist you. Be patient therefore, brethren, unto the coming of the Lord. Behold, the husbandman waiteth for the precious fruit of the earth, and hath long patience for it, until he receive the early and latter rain. Be ye also patient; stablish your hearts: for the coming of the Lord draweth nigh."

Falconer stepped down from the dais and

felt the village's eyes follow him down the central aisle. His footsteps sounded upon the wooden stairs as he climbed back to the loft. Several dozen astonished faces greeted his arrival, none more surprised than the wagoneer. Falconer slipped back into his seat and looked forward, only to discover that the pastor still watched him from the front of the sanctuary. The gray-bearded man nodded once, very slowly, then continued with the service.

"Well, well, there's no question as to who you might be. No sir, not a hint of question." The speaker was the gentleman Ada Hart had approached at the beginning of the service. He stood now to one side of the square fronting the church, somewhat removed from the chattering throng. He offered Falconer his hand. "Paul Grobbe at your service, sir."

"An honor, Mr. Grobbe."

"I don't suppose you have the slightest idea who I am, now, do you?"

"Only that I saw Ada Hart speak with you, sir."

The man was portly and red-cheeked and spoke with a boisterous, cheery air. But his eyes were the color of tempered steel, and just as hard. "I understand you are in need of assistance, sir."

"Truly so, sir, and in so many directions, I scarcely even know what to ask for."

"Come, then, let us sit ourselves down upon this bench here." The largest oak fronting the square was encircled by a wooden bench. Their progress was slowed by many wanting to speak with Paul Grobbe, or so it seemed to Falconer. Yet no one approached once they were seated, though glances were continually cast their way. "Now take your good time, sir. The Sabbath is the one day where hurrying is truly ill-advised. Tell me what it is you are looking for."

Falconer's thoughts remained somewhat scattered by the experience within the church. Each time he began, he found himself hearing the singing anew. But he managed to press his way forward with the task at hand. "I am utterly broke, sir. I need funds — a loan — sufficient to buy supplies and horses. I also require the expertise of someone who knows his way around a gold mine. Someone I can trust. And contacts in the area, if you have any. People I might turn to in a time of dire need."

When he finished, the portly gentleman stroked his beard for a moment, then said, "I run a bank, sir, by the name of Wachovia.

That is, my brother and I run it, in care for this entire community. Wachovia is a rendition of Wachau, the estate where our greatest benefactor once lived. But never mind. My brother operates our branch in Charlotte, which is the trading center closest to the Carolina gold mines. I shall write a letter which you must present to him."

"Sir, I am most —"

"Now then. As to your other needs." The man clearly had no interest in Falconer's gratitude. "If I have your good word that you shall endeavor to pay what you owe, I am willing to loan you whatever sum you care to name."

Falconer leaned back until he came up square upon the tree trunk. "I do not know what to say."

Grobbe rose to his feet. "The reverend said something very interesting after the morning service, John Falconer. He called you a righteous man. In our community, it is a term used only for one of the brethren. I cannot recall it ever being said about a stranger before." He nodded his approval. "I will give further thought about someone to assist you with your gold-mine survey. I bid you good-day."

CHAPTER 20

"This is Meyer's glass and pottery shop," the boy was saying. "He does the fancy stuff. There's a lantern and window store down the street there. Meyer does real pretty things, and folks come from all over for his pressed glass."

"His wife is an artist." Ada Hart spoke so quietly that Falconer had to lean over to hear her. He had the feeling that she was participating against her will. Which was very strange. For she had offered to join them as soon as her son had suggested he take Falconer on a tour of their village. "She paints their pottery and ceramics with lovely designs. They also make etched glass, which she adorns with gold."

"He has his very own kiln out back." In contrast, Matt constantly seemed ready to either laugh or sing. "Folks call it the groundhog kiln because of all the little friends he has in the ground through the winter months. Guess they like the heat."

"Last winter Mr. Meyer put Matt to work stoking the kiln," Ada mentioned, looking to the ground at her feet. "Then he came down with a chest croup that kept him in bed for a month."

The boy could not skip because the dog kept pulling on the leash, tugging in one direction or another. He cheerfully waved at everybody, gathering smiles as if he were harvesting a midmorning crop. "I had to stoke the kiln every half hour. I was freezing by the woodpile and sweating by the kiln. It's the only work I didn't like even a little bit. Well, I don't like mucking out the barn all that much either."

They were walking down the tree-lined main street of Salem, a nicely established little town with a uniformity that reminded Falconer of far older British villages. Most shops had bow windows to either side of the front door, their names announced by way of gilded signs hanging from wrought-iron poles. The oldest homes had thick plaster walls strengthened with woven branches. Most, however, were stout brick affairs with whole trees used for corner posts. Almost all of the village lanes were bricked, which not even the nation's capital could claim.

"This is the doctor's place," the boy declared. "He's the only one from Charlotte to Danville. We get lots of ladyfolk staying in the women's choir. It's on account of them wanting a doctor on their day."

His mother's cheeks grew pink, and she quickly changed the subject. "Our people came originally from Mecklenburg. It's a state in Germany up by the Baltic Sea. First they moved to Pennsylvania. Then in the middle of the last century they bought these three valleys and planted Salem village at the center point."

"The Germans, they didn't like us on account of what we believed," Matt explained, eyes bright with knowledge. "We didn't want to be part of any state church, and we wanted to own our land and live free. Isn't that right, Mama?"

"Yes, son."

"I remember Daddy telling me that. They taxed us something awful, Mr. Falconer. They even taxed our closets!" His clear voice drew smiles from those who shared the road. "They said closets were rooms too and they taxed them! That's why every room in our home has its own closet, sometimes even two, just so we're reminded what it means to be free!"

The men they passed doffed their hats at

Ada. And everyone gave Falconer a curious, sometimes guarded look. The pastor might have offered a blessing upon the man and his mission, but these people, in the heart of their village, let him know just how much he did not belong.

Falconer decided this was why Ada kept her eyes downcast and her voice subdued, regretting her decision to come at all. He asked, "Shall we turn back?"

The boy exclaimed, "But we're not halfway done yet! And there's so much more to see, Mr. Falconer."

She glanced at her son with an affectionate smile, the first Falconer had seen on this outing. "Perhaps the gentleman has had enough of your antics."

Falconer replied quietly, "If ever I was blessed with a family of my own, ma'am, I would hope and pray to have a lad as fine as yours."

She stopped so suddenly the people behind them almost collided with her. But Ada seemed unaware of how others on the street stared openly at them. "Why do you not have a family, sir?"

He felt defeated by the goodness that shone from these two faces. "Like I told you, ma'am, I have been many things."

"But now," she pressed. An uncommon

urgency entered her speech. "Why have you not settled down since your conversion?"

He struggled with several answers, most of which began and ended with Serafina. For reasons he could not explain, though, her name did not seem to fit at the moment. "Since coming to know our Savior's blessing, Mrs. Hart . . ."

"Yes?"

"I have pressed forward with the task of fighting slavery."

The boy had tugged the pup back so he could stand next to his mother. "Papa was doing that too, wasn't he, Mama?"

"Shah, child. Let the man speak. You were saying, Mr. Falconer?"

So he recounted a bit of his story. Of the pastor Felix and their crusade to end slavery and the vile trade in the Caribbean. Of his travels to England. Of the pamphlet. Of Parliament.

The young lad's eyes grew round. "You've seen the whole wide world, sir!"

"No, my young friend. There are a great many places I've never been."

Ada took a long breath. "I have underestimated you, sir. I thought . . . well, that is . . ."

Falconer understood all too well. "I shouldn't worry about it, ma'am. If I were to see me walking down a street, I'd be thinking the very same things."

She smiled again, just the slightest movement at the corners of her mouth. Yet a light gleamed in her eyes, and Falconer felt as though he had gained some ground in her estimation.

"What is it, Mama?"

She looked down at her son, the same light still in her features. "You wanted to show the gentleman our town, yes? So let's finish the tour, shall we?"

"Come, Mr. Falconer, sir!" The lad attempted to take hold of Falconer's hand, but his smaller grasp could only encircle two of Falconer's fingers. "Look down this lane here, sir. That was the first well of Salem, and beside it is the common kitchen. Most folks do their cooking here. But Papa built us our own because of the take-ins."

"Your paying guests," Falconer interpreted with a nod.

"That's it, sir. Our home, it's called the *Fremdehaus.* That's German for strangers' home. We're the only place in all of Wachau where strangers are made welcome. Excepting the women here to see the doctor."

The pup, disliking the lad's pause, pulled even harder on the leash. Falconer slipped it off the boy's hand. The puppy looked up at Falconer and must have decided here was a man too strong for him to drag forward. He settled into a big-pawed lope at Falconer's left leg.

The lad went on, his free hand waving expressively, "Papa built up our kitchen so Mama wouldn't have to stoop. Lots of home kitchens are lean-tos with a door out to the dug well. Papa said Mama was such a beautiful lady she never ought to stoop for anything and anybody save God."

"Matt, that's enough."

"It's true, Mama. I remember him saying that."

"Perhaps Mr. Falconer would prefer not to hear such a complete account of our home life."

"I find it fascinating, ma'am," Falconer said truthfully.

"Please do not encourage him," she warned, but there was a twinkle in her eye.

"I so appreciate hearing the lad talk."

They proceeded on past the schoolhouse, sweetshop, wheelwright, blacksmith, lantern and glass maker, and finally the village smokehouse. Gradually the town gave way to country. An orchard in early spring bloom formed a fragrant border to the landscape. Here Matt took back the puppy's leash and let the dog free. The dog barked for the first time that day and raced after a pair of ringneck doves. The boy's laughter lifted behind him as he took off after his dog.

Falconer watched the two of them disappear into the blossoms. "He is perhaps the most engaging young man I have ever met."

"He is a good lad."

"From what I have seen, he works hard and cheerfully. He takes his responsibilities with a good and willing heart. I also note how much he loves you." Falconer noticed she was biting her lip. "Forgive me, Mrs. Hart. I have said too much."

She lowered her head and the bonnet hid her face. "If it had not been for Matt, I do not think I could have survived these past years."

Falconer heard the sorrow and counted it an honor that she would speak to him of this. They walked down the road in the vague direction of a barking dog and a laughing boy, the silence between them very comfortable now. The wind was strong enough to pull strands of his hair free from its ribbon. He untied the dark ribbon, pulled his hair tight, and retied it. When he dropped his hands, he found Ada Hart watching him again, that newly open look to her gaze. He spoke the first thing that came to his mind. "The wind mocks me here."

"I hear your words, sir, but I do not understand them."

Another couple appeared beyond the smokehouse, headed their way. The woman still wore her dark churchgoing cloak, and her companion was bearded and very upright. Falconer had the sudden notion that they were here to keep watch over Ada Hart and her strange companion.

Falconer placed another half step between him and Ada and pointed at the distant hilltop. "See the top limbs there? They reach so high they appear ready to grip the sky. They are unable to, of course, so they make do by snagging the wind. They take hold with green talons and try to wrest it from its course."

"You have a poet's heart, John Falconer. You see God's glory where others see just another early spring day." Ada nodded a greeting to the pair as they passed, their expressions meaningful in their grimness.

"I feel caged as the wind here," Falconer began. "And threatened. Yours is a prison of beauty and charm, Mrs. Hart. Salem has grace and green forest for bars. I could fall asleep here and forget what the blue world has ever meant to a seagoing man like myself."

To his astonishment, she rewarded him with the most open smile she had yet revealed. "Fall asleep, John Falconer, or wake up to a new vision of God's creation? Become imprisoned, or adapt to a new realm?"

He studied her in silence, as baffled by her words as by his own admission.

She waved a hand lightly. "You do not offend me, John Falconer. On the contrary, it is good to hear the reflections of a man from beyond our small green world."

Ada Hart worked in the kitchen her husband had built and equipped for her. Her husband, also named Matt, had been silent in the way of most Moravian men, sparse with his words and speaking loud with his deeds. He had clearly expressed his love in the design and furnishings of this kitchen. Where most cooking areas were dark and airless, Matt had given special time and attention to making this a happy and light-filled space. The cooking range stretched the entire width of the rear wall, a full sixteen feet. The fire chamber was split into three segments by movable panels of solid metal plate. There was a long open range with an adjustable spit. Beside this was a covered iron stove with six round holes of various sizes. Then a full-sized baker's oven. The kitchen was nearly twenty feet long with windows on both side walls. Beneath these were worktables fitted with iron basins. Their well fed directly into the house, a rarity.

Ada and her husband had spent many happy hours poring through store catalogs, trying to decide what they should order next. It was an extravagance criticized by many of the more conservative folk in their community, but Matt had claimed it was simply necessary for hosting as many strangers as they did. In truth, he mostly did it for her. One-third of everything they earned went to the church, another third to the married-choir community. Even so, between their farm animals and the paying guests, there was always money left over. The Moravians did not permit the wearing of jewelry or fine clothing. So they indulged in kitchen implements and in fine porcelain for the Fremdehaus parlor.

The shelves above and beneath the workbenches held three ball-shaped coffee roasters, four waffle irons, a variety of stewpots, candle molds, cake pans, two-handed sieves, hand-carved butter boxes, ice-cream churns, skillets, special irons hollowed out to hold hot coals, even a pair of cone makers that came all the way from France. Almost half of her implements were loaned out to neighbors. Sometimes Ada would reach for a utensil and feel her heart clenched by memories and loss.

She now bent over a low-rimmed skimming bowl, one of the last items Matt had purchased for her. The bowl was as broad as her largest skillet and had come all the way from Holland, from a ceramics company called Delft. The skimming bowl held milk her son had brought in that morning. The cream now had risen to the top, and Ada skimmed it off and ladled it into a butter box. The nicest boxes were carved on the inside as well as the outer surfaces. When the whey was pressed out, the butter indented with the box's carvings. This one held images of biblical prosperity — wheat sheaves and laden donkeys and ripe grapes.

Through the open door leading to the inn's front room, she could hear John Falconer speaking with Paul Grobbe, the banker. Though her eyes never left the bowl, she listened to the conversation, surprised at the refined timbre of Falconer's voice and vocabulary when compared with the recounting of his rather rough life on the high seas.

Goody Sample, who lived three doors down from the Fremdehaus, worked in Ada's kitchen when there were several paying guests. A woman from beyond the Moravian world, Goody had been born to a merchant family in Wilmington and had met her husband when he had brought a wagonload of produce to the shipping docks. The Carolina Moravians permitted their men to marry outside the community so long as these new wives understood the role they were to assume. Though Goody had lived in Salem for thirty-three of her forty-eight years, some folks still treated her as an outsider. But Goody was Ada's closest friend.

Goody spoke from where she was turning a lamb shank on the spit. "Now, there's a mountain of a man."

"Yes, Goody?"

The woman glanced over her shoulder at Ada, then turned back to ladle sauce and herbs over the meat. "Straight up and down is what they'd say back east where I come from. A hurricane in human form." The spit squeaked as she rotated the meat, and the drippings caused flames to rise and lick the roast. "Is he of good faith like they say?"

"I know little of him, Goody."

"Most likely he's got a strong bone of godliness, since the pastor had him do the reading. I thought he read like he meant it."

"Yes, it seemed rich and full of emotion," Ada noted. "He *felt* the words."

"And he likes your boy. I heard folks talking of how the two of them were together this afternoon."

"Like they've known one another for years," Ada quietly agreed.

"And he's opposed to slavery."

"Yes. I heard him describe his calling from God, and it was clear this lies at the very core of his being."

Goody wiped the perspiration from her brow, the spit moving slow and steady beneath her other hand. "I wonder if he would like to stay around these parts and help . . ."

Ada didn't ask Goody to explain further.

Goody knew her well enough to read meaning from Ada's silence. "There are folks here who'd treat him the same as they treated me. If he's happy in his calling, though, it wouldn't hardly matter to such a man as that one."

Ada turned and looked at the open door. "But he's leaving, Goody," she replied, saying the words mainly to remind her own heart. "And soon."

Falconer's talk with Paul Grobbe was of crucial importance, both to his mission for the Gavi family and his own personal quest. He worked at paying attention as voices drifted from the kitchen along with the savory aroma of roasting lamb. He heard the young lad singing as he set the dining room table and felt surrounded by appealing impressions.

Paul Grobbe finished his perusal of Alessandro Gavi's documents and set them on the table between them. He said gravely, "I am grateful for this gift of trust, John Falconer."

"You are providing me both money and contacts on nothing save my word," Falconer replied. "I am the one who must thank you for trusting me, sir."

"How many people know of your reasons for traveling south?"

"None save the folks in this community. I did tell a pair of slavers I was headed to the mines, but they do not know which one, nor my purpose."

Grobbe frowned. "These were the men from whom you bought the people you just freed?"

"Yes." Falconer saw the concern. "I had

to give them some reason for taking on so many new hands."

"Indeed, indeed."

"You seem concerned."

"The one thing slavers hate most in this world are those who wish to set their charges free. The region from Richmond north is full of the worst kinds. They hunt white and black alike, sir, and they're paid well for those they capture." Grobbe leaned forward so as to hide his words from the kitchen. "Dead or alive."

Falconer lowered his voice as well. "I appreciate both your warning and your unease, but I repeat what I said before. I feel that God has set me a task. I intend to give freedom to four hundred and nineteen indentured slaves, and when that is completed He may call me to do the same again."

Grobbe studied him intently. Falconer met his gaze and waited. The grandfather clock in the Fremdehaus's front hall counted out the long seconds. Finally Grobbe nodded and said, "John Falconer, a banker is charged with the duty to keep safe the finances of other people. He is paid to be cautious. However, I must tell you, sir, I feel God's hand upon this moment and upon your quest. I would count it an honor to serve as your supporter as well as your financier."

"I cannot explain how much it means to hear a man such as yourself grant me such sanction, sir."

Grobbe rose from his chair. "Would you take a turn with me?"

"As long as I can be back in time for dinner. Those heady scents have stirred my appetite."

"Aye, the Hart house has been long known for the quality of its table." Grobbe walked to the kitchen doorway and said, "Mrs. Hart, may I borrow one of your guests for a half hour?"

Ada appeared, rubbing her hands on her apron. "No longer than that, Mr. Grobbe. I will not have you threatening my roast with overcooking."

"I will make certain we are back on time, ma'am. Your roast smells fine as heaven's manna," Grobbe said as he settled his hat into place and touched the rim. "Mrs. Hart. Miss Goody. Come, John Falconer."

They turned off the main street into a side lane shaded by elms. The early spring leaves formed a green veil through which shone the sunset. Grobbe said, "When Ada Hart was younger, folks said her eyes could laugh as engagingly as her voice. But she has not

315

had much to laugh about in recent years," he finished somberly.

"I wish Mrs. Hart and her son only the very best, sir."

"Precisely the answer I'd have expected you to give."

The banker headed first to the village stables, where he instructed the livery owner to supply Falconer from his best and send the bills to the bank. After Falconer had chosen horses and pack animals, Grobbe continued down the lane to a long single-story building with a tall cross bricked in above the double front doors. "This is the single man's choir. You may already know that choirs are our way of segmenting our community. This is also the residence for any visitor to Salem from our outlying villages, and for unmarried men who work here in the town."

"You wish for me to move out of the inn?"

Grobbe chose his words carefully. "We are a close-knit community, sir. So long as you were just another *Fremde,* the house run by Ada Hart was the place for you to stay. However, the whole community is aware of your walk with her to the edge of town." The banker's small smile took any accusation from his statement.

Falconer studied his internal response, an

unusual course for him. How could he stand in the gathering dusk and speak about a woman he had known for such a short time? Serafina's long distance away, as much in emotion as miles, continued to leave a hollowness within. And yet . . .

"I mean no offense, John Falconer," Grobbe interjected into Falconer's thoughts, obviously taking his silence for irritation.

"A friend's task is to offer wisdom," Falconer replied. "Would you advise that I take my evening meal elsewhere?"

"I would not think of depriving you of that excellent lamb I smelled." Grobbe clapped Falconer on the shoulder, clearly pleased with his response. "But before we go, I want you to meet someone who is living here with the other unmarried men."

Grobbe pushed open the door and called, "Theo!"

"Ich komme."

A rawboned young man appeared in darned socks, a frontiersman's canvas pants, and a well-washed collarless shirt. The simple movement of adjusting his suspenders revealed whipcord muscles.

Grobbe said, "Theo Henning, John Falconer. Theo is my guard for any shipment of valuables, be it money or documents. He is not much for talking, is Theo. But I've trusted him with my life on a number of occasions."

Everything about Theo Henning proclaimed his German stock. Ice-blue eyes regarded Falconer blankly. His close-trimmed hair and beard were both ruddy blond in color. Neither handsome nor welcoming, Henning inspected Falconer's outstretched hand cautiously before taking hold. His grip was as solid as old oak.

Falconer asked, "May I ask what is your standard salary?"

"Three dollars a day," Grobbe replied for the man. "He likes his pay in gold, does Theo."

"Gold it is," Falconer agreed. "And I will make it four." He looked straight at Theo.

"Three dollars is already double the normal fee," Grobbe protested, only half joking. "He may press me for more pay also."

"Four dollars," Falconer repeated. "I'm a stranger, and the work may prove dangerous. Before we start, though, I need to ask you one thing. What are your beliefs about slavery?"

"I have not killed man." Henning paused between each word, measuring each carefully. "But them slavers, they tempt me. They tempt me bad."

Falconer nodded his approval. "There's a freed slave by the name of Joseph who's settling his family into Bethabara. I'd be grateful if you'd find him and tell him we leave at dawn."

CHAPTER 21

Ada Hart indeed had created a haven for her son while continuing the thriving enterprise her husband had founded. Falconer sat surrounded by other weary travelers at the inn's main table stretching nearly the length of the dining room. Five smaller tables were set in the room's corners and within the bay window alcove. The nine guests were joined for the meal by Ada Hart, her son, and another woman who was introduced simply as Miss Goody.

After dinner Falconer attempted to excuse himself, though he was loath to leave the warmth of the room and the conversation. Ada Hart reappeared from the kitchen, wiping her hands on a towel. Falconer watched her walk over and pull out the chair next to his.

"You might as well say it," Ada said after a moment of silence, speaking softly enough that her words would not be heard above the others' conversation. "I can see something upon your features, John Falconer, but I cannot read its message. Until I do, I cannot help you further."

Then Matt popped through the kitchen door bearing a serving plate. "Would you like a sugar cookie, Mr. Falconer?"

Falconer reached over and touched the boy's beaming face. "You are such a helpful lad."

Matt rewarded him with a smile that captured Falconer's heart. "Miss Goody makes the best cookies in the whole wide world."

Ada said gently, "Please serve the guests, son. Mr. Falconer and I need a word."

Falconer watched the boy make his way around the table, then turned back to Ada Hart. She bore the same goodness as her son, aged and enriched by her experiences.

Falconer knew then what he needed to say. Reasoning told him there was no need to speak of such intimate matters with a woman he scarcely knew. Nevertheless, he told her about Serafina.

The telling lasted a good deal longer than Falconer had intended. Gradually the other guests departed, and later Ada Hart guided him into the almost-empty parlor. Her son sat near the fire, far enough away for their words to be private, close enough for Falconer to be aware of the boy as he stroked the fur on his dog and talked of the next day's adventures.

Later Ada Hart excused herself to escort her son upstairs to bed. Before Matt departed, the boy walked over and wrapped his arms around Falconer's neck.

Falconer spent the time the woman was away staring into the fire, his emotions as much in turmoil as the flames flickering before his eyes.

When Ada returned to the parlor, Miss Goody already had emerged from the kitchen and taken a seat in a rocker on the room's far side. She knitted and said not a word, the faint click of her needles melding with the crackling fire and the candlelight's soft intimacy.

Falconer ended his telling with, "I stood like a madman, staring into a future that was not mine to claim."

Ada gave him enough time to be certain he was not saying more. "And then you departed on your mission."

"Not quite." He wiped his palms down the length of his thighs. "I felt God put something on my heart. In my thickheaded distress, though —"

"It was not thickheaded, John Falconer,"

she quietly interrupted. "You do yourself a disservice by discounting the matters of your own heart. God has made us creatures of emotions, and along with other characteristics, He uses them to impart His direction to His own."

He digested that for a long moment. "I still do not know if it was my distress or God who set these things upon my heart and mind," he said carefully.

"How did you interpret it at the time?"

"That it was God. The certainty is a memory now, however. Nothing more."

Ada rose to sweep an ash from the hearth back into the fireplace. "There is little in life that can pain a body more, or cause one more ill, than to be burdened by an unrequited love."

Miss Goody lifted her focus from her yarn and gave Ada Hart a long look. Ada returned to her chair and added, "Be it from the loss of a loved one or the lack of response, I would imagine it is very much the same."

"With respect, ma'am, to spend years in the presence of love and then lose it would to me be a far worse ordeal," he argued.

"My Matt was a very good man, and I loved him with all my heart. The three years since his passage have been as a single winter for my spirit. But we were not discussing my situation, Mr. Falconer."

"No, ma'am."

"You feel God spoke to you."

"Three times, or so it seemed then." He found it easiest to speak if he kept his eyes on the fire. "The first time the message was simply to wait upon Him."

Her own gaze turned toward the flames. "What a difficult challenge that can be at times."

"The second time was the day I bid the Gavis farewell. I felt the need to imply that Serafina and the other young man I mentioned . . ."

The knitting needles stopped. He could feel both women staring at him.

"Nathan Baring is his name. As fine a gentleman as ever I have met. Godly and sincere, strong in his convictions. He holds to his duties, serving family and nation and cause. He comes from a good background. A merchant family. As are the Gavis." Falconer took a long breath, then finished, "I as much as suggested to the Gavis that they should allow Nathan to pay court to Serafina."

Miss Goody spoke for the first time since entering the room. "Well, I never."

Ada glanced at her, then addressed Falconer. "You said there was a third message?"

"That night I had a mental image. For the first years after meeting my Savior, I was beset almost nightly by a most horrific dream. Just before I departed on this quest, the image returned to me. Only I was not asleep. And the image itself was different. The sense of dread was gone. I was seated at my table with the Good Book open before me." Falconer felt his memory empowered by the women's intense attention. "I saw how I had grown, and . . ."

"Yes?"

"I felt that God was pleased with me. It sounds a boastful thing to say, I know."

"No, John Falconer. Think of a father's pride in his son."

Falconer nodded his gratitude. "There was a sense of being given an invitation. To begin on something that both served Him and would draw me closer to Him."

"As do all worthy causes," Ada commented. "This was the beginning of your quest to free the slaves?"

"Four hundred and nineteen," he affirmed. "The same number as were chained in the holds of my slaver."

The clock softly clanged yet another passing hour. "It is late," Ada declared, rising to her feet.

Falconer rose with her. "I apologize for keeping you ladies so long."

"We were honored with your presence. Let me walk you to the door."

"Good night, Miss Goody," he said as he passed.

"I like your tales and the look of you, John Falconer." She busied herself rolling up her work. "I look forward to the next time we meet."

At the front door, Ada Hart leaned against the doorjamb. "I stand ready to help you, John Falconer."

He saw the warmth of a good and open heart in her expression. "Mrs. Hart, your words are a blessing."

She dropped her gaze and said, "I hope you will find your way back here to our table before too long."

Nathan had returned to work, and Serafina and Eleanor Baring were alone. The atmosphere between them had become very comfortable. Serafina was pleased with how the portrait was developing. The woman's formality called out for a more definite and meticulous likeness than she had employed with her parents' portrait. Serafina remained indifferent toward attempting the classical structure required by oils, full of details and dress and background. Instead she kept the surroundings vague, sharpening into focus only about the face, as she had done previously.

The two women halted for tea at midafternoon. The sole housekeeper was away, so Serafina prepared the tray while the kettle boiled. She sat in the chair formerly occupied by Nathan Baring. A clock ticked comfortably on the mantel. A horse clopped by outside, the footfalls almost in time to the clock. Otherwise the house was silent. Serafina drank her tea and worked through in her mind the next mixing of colors that would be required. She would be able to complete the canvas today, she was sure. She found herself already missing the times here, although Eleanor Baring had scarcely spoken to her at all that day.

Abruptly the older woman said, "May I ask if God has ever spoken directly to you, young lady?"

Serafina set her cup down in its saucer, not sure why the words, uttered as they were by a relative stranger, did not disturb her. Instead, they seemed in harmony with the room's atmosphere. "A friend asked me the very same thing recently, ma'am."

"And how did you answer?"

"I told him that to my knowledge, God had never spoken with me in words. In many other ways, however, I have felt Him close enough to trust that my sentiments were indeed based upon communion with my Lord."

"You are indeed wise beyond your years," Eleanor Baring murmured. "My husband felt God spoke to him about the profession my sons should choose. I have long wondered if it was truly God or simply my husband's desire to command the directions his sons would take, invoking an authority they would not question."

"Perhaps . . ."

"Yes? Do go on, Miss Gavi."

"Perhaps it was indeed your husband's desire, but granted God's blessing."

The older woman inspected her carefully. "How remarkable."

"I have often felt that the difficulty with me is not that God is silent. Rather it's that I am not able to hear Him. He speaks, but my ears and my mind and my heart are too clouded by my own ideas, even waywardness."

"That I very much doubt." The woman did not give Serafina an opportunity to disagree. She turned her face to the front window and said, "The hours in your company have been most reflective. Nathan is taking my approaching homegoing very hard. Along with that, he feels his life is wasted. He wanted to be a minister, and my husband objected. Nathan has spent years waiting for fulfillment in a vocation that does not rest easy."

"Your son is a good man, Mrs. Baring."

"Yes. Yes, he is." She pointed at the easel. "May I see the work?"

Serafina usually was reluctant to reveal an unfinished painting, yet there was a sense of harmony with her subject strong enough to overcome her objections. She rose and turned the easel around. Then she moved her seat in order to view it along with the woman. Sharing this moment granted her a distance from the work that was more than mere space away from the easel. She immediately could see that the emotion she had intended was truly captured, the mystery revealed.

She heard the older woman swallow. Then, "You are not painting . . . This is not the Eleanor Baring I see in the mirror."

"Yes, madam. I must differ. It is."

"Nathan will be very pleased." Her sigh was unsteady. "Young lady, I have two requests to make of you."

"Of course, ma'am."

"My housekeeper's name is Sally Long. She has been with us for almost twelve years. More than just a friend, she was my strength during the days following my husband's illness." Eleanor Baring spoke to the canvas upon the easel. "This week her youngest child died of the croup."

"I'm very sorry to hear it, ma'am."

"Sally is taking it very hard. The bairn was her favorite. A little angel. Called Sally as well. She was just eleven months." She set her tea down. "The funeral is in two hours. Please, if you would, accompany my son to the service."

"Of course, madam."

"Take your drawing pad. If you find yourself inspired, perhaps . . ." She shook her head. "No, it is asking too much. You never even knew the child."

"I will see what I can do, madam. You said there were two matters?"

She studied Serafina a long moment. "My end is near. No, please spare us both the unnecessary words. We both know it is so. I lie here watching you work, and I have felt God's hand upon the moment."

"As have I, madam."

"Have you indeed? That makes what I am about to say much easier. Young lady, I sense a deep sadness about you. My son

330

carries a similar sorrow, but he has borne it for so long he manages to hide it better. Yet it is there, and in our time together, I have found myself sensing that perhaps you would be able —"

"Oh, no, Mrs. Baring. Please. I must ask —"

"Ask what, that I not speak words I feel God has set upon my heart?"

Serafina wished to protest, but her power of speech seemed stolen away. It was all she could do to shake her head, just a tiny fraction of movement.

"Perhaps, just perhaps, the Lord has spoken of a time beyond us all," Mrs. Baring said comfortably. "Beyond you, because you see only your wound. Beyond Nathan, because he sees only what the immediate future will bring. Beyond me . . ." She smiled, and in so doing she showed to Serafina the same affection and openness that she granted her son. "Here, then, is my request. If sometime you and my son find yourselves drawing together, I ask that you tell him I give you both my blessing."

The funeral was a most tragic event. The Long family was there in great numbers. Aunts and uncles and Sally Long's own parents. Six other children, all clustered in various stages of distress about a distraught father. The mother was scarcely there at all, which only caused her other children additional anguish.

The coffin stood at the center of the church's front aisle, a tiny thing the size of a narrow wooden crib. Serafina set her sketchpad in the cloakroom and took a firm hold of Nathan Baring's arm. The closer they drew to the front of the church, the tighter her grip became.

Sally Long was seated at the end of the first pew. People stopped to embrace her and spoke words she did not hear. Her only response was to reposition her head so nothing came between her and her child's tiny face resting against a lace pillow.

Serafina gripped Nathan's arm with both hands as she leaned forward and peered inside the coffin. The figure of the baby embodied all the sorrow an earthly existence could hold. She stopped, halting the procession behind her. She forced herself to look long and hard, imprinting the features on her mind and heart.

She was sure there was no way her canvas and paints would be able to give life back to this baby. It was impossible. The emotions and the loss and the absence of life were simply too strong.

She allowed Nathan to draw her away. She was led to a pew. She seated herself, shut her eyes, and prayed. She begged God for some way to overcome the impossibility. But before her closed eyes she saw only the infant's features, lifeless and waxlike.

She opened her eyes. And there before her was the answer.

A child of perhaps three years sat in her father's lap, unquestionably the baby's older sister. Her face held an almost identical oval structure as the infant and the mother. The child whimpered softly and pulled on her father's sleeve. She was frightened and unsettled by all that was happening that she could not understand.

Serafina released Nathan and stepped forward. She leaned down to whisper to the father that she was a friend of Mrs. Baring and she would be happy to care for the little one during the service. When he did not object, she held out her arms and whispered, "Would you like to come outside with me, little one?"

The father looked uncomprehendingly at Serafina. The child must have sensed something warm and inviting, for she responded by reaching up toward Serafina.

The father stirred himself and lifted his daughter into Serafina's arms. She whispered her intentions to Nathan and carried her charge over to the side aisle and out to the back of the sanctuary. The child was dressed in softest wool and smelled of soap and warm baby scents. The child wrapped her arms tightly around Serafina's neck.

In the rear foyer Serafina moved into the cloakroom to collect her sketchpad and charcoals.

She put the child down, and they walked hand-in-hand back into the sunlight. The day was warm, a rare gift in a rain-swept season. Serafina walked slowly, sketchpad and charcoals at her side, gently talking to the child. She learned that the little girl's name was Ella. She let the child direct them until they came to the carriage decked out in black. Ella did not understand the significance of the dark feathers perched upon the horse's head. Nor the black crepe wrapped about the reins, nor the black cloth that cradled the rear portion of the open carriage. Instead, she peered up at the horse, then began talking to it, the animal bobbing its head in response.

Serafina looked a question to the carriage driver, who nodded. She moved closer to the horse, who sniffed the child's hand, then snorted softly. Ella laughed delightedly.

The driver spoke, "Here, little one. Offer

him this sugar and you'll make a friend for life."

"Hold out your hand," Serafina told Ella, "flat like this." She demonstrated and then placed the sugar cube on the tiny palm.

"Now hold it up to the horse like this," and Serafina lifted the little hand to the horse's mouth.

The child squealed with delight as the horse delicately ate from her fingers. Serafina took three steps back, leaning in close to the driver's station so she could see the happy little face clearly. She sketched as fast as she possibly could, drawing the face she had seen inside the coffin, but making the eyes those of the laughing child before her. She incorporated the life, the sunlight, and the joy. She struggled hard to keep her vision clear, wiping impatiently at the sudden tears. Serafina drew and shaded and darkened, promising herself she would have a good cry when she had completed the task.

CHAPTER 22

The three riders covered the distance to Charlotte in two very hard days. Up with the sun, into the saddle, riding until the road was all they could taste and smell. Two brief halts to blow the horses. Cold coffee and apples and good Salem soda bread for breakfast. Apples and cheese and well water for lunch, while the horses munched two handfuls of grain from their nose bags. The day's only hot meal was at sunset — beans and smoked beef and more soda bread. Ada Hart had packed what she referred to as her road bags, and Falconer was certain he could catch a hint of her fragrance whenever he opened the satchels. The last task before they unfurled their bedrolls was to set a pot of coffee by the banked coals to brew all night long. They did not take time for a fire at dawn.

The weather was neither for nor against them. The sky remained mostly sullen and the road muddy. Springtime seemed lost, a word for some other world. But no more rain fell. Twice they passed wagons mired to their wheel rims in boggy pits, lowing cattle straining against the mud. Like other travelers on horseback, Falconer held to narrow tracks that paralleled the main road, such as it was. The North-South Turnpike was somewhere off to the east, running from Richmond to Raleigh to Atlanta. The Salem-Charlotte road was adequate in some spots but mostly rough. The people who traveled it were cautious and well armed.

The wind blew a damp warning of further storms to come. The men cut wide circles through the surrounding forests as they approached the two main towns along the road, Salisbury and Davidson. They spoke to no one the entire journey.

Theo Henning gave no sign he thought anything untoward about their pace or their solitary ways. Nor did he give any notice to how Joseph stayed to one side, both on the road and off.

Their most difficult challenge was lighting a fire for their evening meal. All three men scavenged for dry wood and a place to refill their canteens whenever they stopped. By nightfall they had enough moss and branches lashed to their saddles to cook, but the last glowing embers soon faded, and by morning their muscles were tight with cold and damp.

So it was that three road-weary men entered Charlotte late in the afternoon of the second day.

To Falconer's mind, Charlotte was an odd sort of place. The outer rim was rather wild in nature. Weary as he was, there was no mistaking the tension and threat. The two women he spotted on the road were both running. One held a basket of groceries while the other gripped two children by their upper arms. They all sprinted across the muddy road. The women's faces were shadowed by large sunbonnets, but their fear was clear enough. A group of men outside a saloon watched the women with speculative eyes. The men's hats hung on their backs, slung on woven leather cords. The upper halves of their faces were white, while arms and necks and hands were almost black from sun and hard toil. Theo Henning spoke one word of explanation. Miners.

A sharp crack from farther down the street drew their attention. Theo started to unholster his gun but eased it back into his belt when he spotted a mule skinner plying his forty-foot whip. The train was twenty-two

and fire a shot in the air."

Joseph wheeled his horse around and raced away.

"Let's go," Falconer said. Theo slid off his horse and tied the two to the hitching post before hurrying to catch up with Falconer.

The broad redbrick building occupied the better portion of a city block. The downstairs was given over to an emporium, with lace gowns sharing the front window alongside an assortment of fancy household implements. The two used a side entrance that led upstairs to the offices. The foyer and stairs and upstairs hall were floored in unvarnished slat boards, sanded smooth by years of miners' boots. A half-dozen green doors lined either wall. Falconer passed a doctor and a tooth-puller and a land surveyor. He knew because their professions were stated upon brass plaques. The door belonging to Emmett Reeves, attorney-at-law, was open. The front office was empty. Falconer marched through and opened the inner door without knocking. "Emmett Reeves?"

"Y-you must be Mr. Gavi."

"Near enough. My name is John Falconer."

The man might have been worried about the sight of two tough and road-worn strangers looming over his desk. But he was also a lawyer. "Can I . . . may I see some form of authorization?"

Falconer pulled out the oilskin pouch and handed over the notarized document stating that one John Falconer acted on behalf of Alessandro Gavi in respect to all matters related to a certain gold mine and its ownership.

"This appears all in order, sir." The lawyer had a remarkably deep voice for such a slender form. He wore a coat of blue serge and a stiff-collared shirt. His fingers were long and nervous. "Please, won't you sit down?"

Falconer remained standing before his desk. "I'm here to tell you that the time-wasting has come to an end."

The lawyer responded without hesitation. "In that case, sir, you are an answer to a prayer."

Falconer refused the lawyer's invitation to begin work over dinner that evening. Falconer wanted a clear head to go through the documents and make his judgment on whether the man was trustworthy. The trail had been too wearing for pages of *whereas* and *wherefore*s. Tired as he was, Falconer made two further stops. He went by the bank, presented the documents drawn up by the banker Grobbe, and extracted funds. He then took his two men into the dry-goods store. Ignoring the storekeeper's hostile glances at Joseph, Falconer purchased three sets of clothes — dark suit, waistcoat, white stock shirt. He had the storekeeper wrap them in brown packing paper and paid in gold.

They slept in the bunkhouse connected to the Moravian church, the only place in town that offered shelter regardless of color. Falconer had no intention of separating himself from Joseph.

They joined the lawyer for an early breakfast. When Joseph halted at the doorway, refusing to enter the man's house, Theo Henning declared he preferred to eat outside in the open air. Falconer said nothing but was pleased to his bones over the sight of these two becoming friends.

The lawyer's wife was a soft dumpling of a lady with a warming smile and an excellent hand at the cooking stove. After an enormous breakfast, the attorney covered his dining room table with papers, both Falconer's documents and his own. Within half an hour Falconer was convinced the man was sincere. Everything he said fit with what Alessandro Gavi had described.

"What you're telling me," Falconer finally said, "is this man Joyner doesn't want to seal the bargain."

Emmett Reeves possessed a voice far too large for his frame. "Prevarication is a word that fits this miner like a well-tailored suit."

"Tell me this. Which one is your client — this man Joyner or Gavi?"

"In strictest terms, it would be neither. I was hired by the New York bankers who owed Gavi a large share of money. They bought a share of Joyner's land and mine soon after gold was discovered."

"I know all that. I'm talking about the here and now."

"Well." The attorney blew out his cheeks. "I suppose you could say I stand on the side of Mr. Gavi, who has been steadfast since the very beginning."

"That's what I hoped to hear." Falconer rose from the table. "I want you to travel with us, please."

"I beg your pardon? Now?"

"If you don't have anything pressing." But Falconer's intent was clear. He knocked on the window to alert Joseph and Theo Henning, who were lounging on the back stoop. "I'd like to get this settled and be on my way."

344

■ ■ ■ ■

They left Charlotte by the Cabarrus Trail, each man leading a pair of packhorses. When Emmett Reeves asked the purpose of trailing empty packhorses into the hills, Falconer simply responded, "A hunch." Falconer was alive this day because he had learned to trust his instincts. And they told him to go prepared for trouble.

Around midmorning the hills gradually closed in around them, rising and falling in sweeping waves of green. By lunchtime the sun emerged from the clouds. Dogwoods nestled among the lowland pines. The day warmed a full twenty degrees. The river running alongside the road sparkled and glinted. Theo and Joseph lifted their heads and squinted at the sky, as though the sun were a stranger.

That night they sheltered in an outpost beyond the village of Shelby. The place was not a tavern since no alcohol was served and none permitted. A sign by the owner's cabin warned visitors they would be ejected "if any likker is found." The landlord was a taciturn man who made do with a series of grunts and rattling keys. He pointed them to a kettle boiling on an open fire, with a metal sheet of biscuits warming alongside. Nine men were seated on logs around the fire's edge, spooning up their supper and watching the four men with tight eyes. No one returned Falconer's greeting. Another thumb jerked them toward the stable; clearly they were expected to care for their own horses.

Their shelter was a Cherokee-style tent of woven branches and wattle with a dirt floor. They dumped their bedrolls, tended the horses, then returned to the fire. Emmett Reeves sniffed the steaming pot and announced, "Goober soup."

Falconer saw Theo and Joseph both grimace. "What's that?"

Emmett reached for a tin plate and wiped it with the edge of his shirt. "Best not ask."

Theo Henning explained, "Boiled peanuts and collards. Around these parts, it's called miners' stew."

To Falconer the meal tasted as bad as it sounded. He dined mostly on biscuits. One of the miners pulled out a harmonica and played a few plaintive tunes. Eventually the group around the fire drifted away to sleep. No one said a word to Falconer or his companions.

When they were headed back to their dwelling, Falconer asked, "Are they always that friendly?"

"It's the gold," Emmett Reeves explained. "Don't pay them any mind."

"They wasn't bad," Theo Henning agreed. "Didn't see no guns nor knives."

Joseph stretched his bedroll out on the tent's far side. "I done heard tales of what the mines do to a body."

Theo Henning moved his bedroll to stretch out alongside Joseph. "Them stories are true," Theo said, settling his slouch hat over his eyes. "You'll see."

Falconer was drawn from slumber by the sound of wolves. At first he thought it was another nightmare. But waking only sharpened the howls. He sat up to find Emmett Reeves standing in the doorway. Falconer tucked in his shirttail and slipped on his boots. He followed Reeves to where the same kettle boiled next to the same biscuit sheet. Only the kettle now held gruel. They filled mugs with black coffee and walked out to where the compound joined the road. Sullen men and a few women already traveled the road. No one spoke a greeting in the gray-misted dawn. The hills seemed even closer now, hemming them in on all sides. From high overhead came the howl of the hunting wolf pack.

Falconer watched the silent slit-eyed travelers for a time, then walked back to the tent and fetched his Bible. He knew Emmett Reeves observed him, but the compound's silence infected him as well. He took a breakfast of gruel and buried himself in the pages of the Book.

Footsteps came and paused beside him, moved to the fire, and returned. Theo Henning settled to one side and said in greeting, "Joseph told me of your reading."

Falconer thumbed his place. "It does my heart good to see you making friends with him."

Theo waved for Joseph to join them. "He is a fine man."

"Yes," Falconer agreed. "He is."

Theo made room on the log for Joseph. "Read to us, John Falconer. Drive away the wolves."

They were an hour into their journey when Emmett Reeves reined his horse in close to Falconer and observed, "Hearing you read from the Good Book was an uncanny sensation, if you don't mind me saying."

The morning mist was gradually burning off. Final tendrils stirred about the ground, making the horses stumble upon a road they could not see. Falconer's back already ached. These constant days in the saddle were an ordeal for a seagoing man. "The good Lord has room in heaven for us all, sir."

"Indeed so," Reeves agreed. "But you and your men carry a fierce air. To see you gathered together, the Bible open in those battle-scarred hands of yours . . . well, it warmed my heart, I don't mind telling you."

Falconer nodded his thanks, then used one hand to ease a crimp from his neck. "I have the sensation of being surrounded by danger."

"As to danger, I can't say. I can assure you, however, that we are being watched." Emmett Reeves cut an unlikely figure in the saddle. He wore a string tie and a rumpled suit. Stringy hair peeked from beneath a citified hat of black felt with a satin crown. But he rode well and handled his horse with practiced ease. "We entered gold country not long back."

Falconer nodded in comprehension. "Tell me what I'm seeing."

"The waters we're riding along now are the Cabarrus River. It was once known as Bear Creek, though there haven't been many bear sightings for years now. All the trappers left Carolina for Kentucky long ago." He pointed down at the swift-running stream. "Up here the miners know it by another name, Tallow Creek, called such after the color of the silt. Look up ahead, you'll see the reason why."

The road jinked back on itself and began a steep climb up the hillside. The original road was blocked by a wall of boulders. Falconer eased his horse over to the road's edge and looked down. Below him, eight men and three women worked knee-deep in sludge, shoveling river-bottom mud into a long wooden trawl, through which ran the river itself.

"That device there is called a sluice. It's used to filter out the gold from auriferous river sand. A few years back, all the miners would be panning. The practice got its name from how the first gold seekers used frying pans for the work. They'd slosh the sand about with a bit of water, letting the water and the lighter sand slip over the edge. Gold is far heavier and holds to the bottom. With the sluice machine there, a good team can work through a ton of river mud a day."

The only way Falconer could tell the men from the women was by their headgear. Every one of them was sodden from head to toe with yellow muck.

A lone figure stepped from the pines bordering the river and watched them with a stern look and a cocked musket. He said nothing, just stood and noted their passing. Falconer said, "You know a great deal about this work?"

"I've made a study of it since becoming involved in this mine of Mr. Gavi's. The river folk you see here are a dying breed. They've been panning and sluicing for twelve years now, and most of the gold is cropped. Back when they started, they could pick up the gold with their hands. The largest piece is on display at the Charlotte Mint and weighed in at twenty-eight pounds."

They passed three more sluices in the space of half a mile. Between each were fences and warning signs. Armed guards stood watch over each group. "They need all those guns?"

"What you see down there is the only law in gold country. The guards are there as much to keep the workers honest as they are to watch the yield."

Theo Henning rode up on Falconer's other side. "Them guards, they bury the sacks soon as they're filled. You hear stories down Charlotte way about guards dying or going missing and the sacks they buried never being found."

Joseph spoke up for the first time that morning. "Slaves tell stories too. 'Bout how

351

workin' that gold will break your back. Yes-suh. First your back, then your soul."

The valley through which they passed opened into a wide pasture. The farmland looked rich enough, yet the farm cabins held an unkempt air. The surrounding fields were all given over to weeds. A few cows, horses, and donkeys grazed in the lush undergrowth, but otherwise there was no sign whatsoever of cultivation. "It looks like a blight has struck here."

"A calamity called gold," Emmett Reeves agreed. "A few years back, when the river stopped giving up so much gold, three groups started digging. McComb was the first, then the Rudisill Mine, and the Saint Catherine. The sluice miners laughed at them for a time. The cost was huge and the initial take minimal. Now all three are recovering gold and making money. These days it comes down to who can raise the money to go underground."

"Which is why your New York bankers became involved," Falconer guessed.

"The Joyner place is half a mile from the river," the lawyer agreed. "Without sluice gold, no simple farmer could come up with the capital to dig deep — not even when the farm between him and the river struck gold. So Joyner sold off half his ownership.

Then a quarter more. Then another portion, until he was left with just a one-tenth share."

"He must've come up with something to keep those bankers interested."

"He did. Not enough to cover his costs, though. Then word came that he hit it big. That was last summer. Back in the early fall, Joyner brought in a wagonload of gold and started talking about how he should be able to buy back his holdings. The bankers stuck to their guns. Since then there's been nothing. The last time I came out here, he threatened to fill me full of lead if I showed up again without the ownership papers. Not long after, the bankers offered their share to your Mr. Gavi."

Falconer noticed that Emmett Reeves' voice was showing a trace of nerves. "How far are we from the place?"

"Another two miles along the river road, perhaps three. Then the turning leads through a hollow and up to the farm." The prospect caused the lawyer's features to tighten. "Are you certain he will welcome us?"

"If we gave him a chance, probably not." Falconer dismounted. "We'll stop here."

The river was clearer up this high, the water running fast. They sat on rocks around the steep bank and ate a cold lunch. A pair of guards appeared on the opposite bank. Falconer paid them no mind and eventually they slipped back into the pines and disappeared.

It was the moment Falconer had been waiting for. "Theo, Joseph, I want you to bring out those clothes we bought in Charlotte."

"What clothes are these?" Emmett Reeves asked nervously.

"You just sit tight, sir," Falconer ordered. "We're not after lawyering right now. We're after getting the job done."

CHAPTER 23

Jeb Saunders looked to be in a reflective mood. "You mean to tell me he offered to buy the Moss place in gold?"

Brother Cody confirmed, "Did the deal, left the down payment, scooped up the slaves, and left. Bang and gone."

"How you know Moss wasn't just blowing smoke? Man always did like to brag, even when he was sitting at the table holding nothing but scrap paper instead of proper cards."

"I heard it from the overseer, not Moss. Already told you that."

"So you did, little brother. So you did."

They were riding south, heading for South Carolina and their next buy. North Carolina hadn't outlawed slavery, but they weren't exactly welcoming of the practice either. The only regular auction in the whole state was by the Wilmington harbor, eight days' ride east. And even that was active only when a slaver chose to unload stock. Otherwise the state had a surly attitude about the whole business, far as Jeb could tell.

The previous night, after giving Salem and the Wachau valley a wide berth, they had slept in proper beds at a tippling inn outside Salisbury. Over a dinner of traveler's stew, Jeb had made his brother recount everything he had discovered. For the fourth time. Today, as they continued south, Jeb repeated his questions once more. Cody didn't mind. He was very comfortable letting Jeb do the thinking for the both of them. And one thing was certain. When Jeb finished his cogitating, somebody was going to be in for a world of hurt.

"You're telling me Moss hasn't started preparing for the spring planting."

"Place was such a mess, even Pa would've complained." Which was an exaggeration. Their father had been the laziest man to ever avoid setting hand to plow. "So much fruit rotting on the ground I could smell it from two pastures away. Hadn't even turned over the earth from the last harvest."

"So what we got here is a man who buys a farm but doesn't tell the owner to make ready for the planting season," Jeb mused. "He carts off all the slaves fit enough to travel. Leaves Moss holding a handful of gold. More of the same gold he used to overpay that feller up at Burroughs Crossing, and then us. Now, what does that tell you?"

"That he's up to no good?" Cody offered hopefully.

"You got that right." Jeb punched his hat down tighter on his head. "You know what I think?"

"Nope." Here it came.

"I think we got us a man aiming on going against the proper way of things."

Knowing Jeb, that could only mean one thing. "The feller's an anti-slaver."

"That's what some folks call 'em." Jeb offered his brother an evil smile. "Me, I just call 'em fair game."

Emmett Reeves reined in his horse and pointed down a dusty side trail that wound through a sunlit hollow. "This is it."

Falconer handed the lawyer the reins to his pack animals. "Theo, Joseph, let the lawyer take your packhorses. Mr. Reeves, you follow on behind."

Emmett Reeves twisted the leather straps apprehensively. "Most likely he already knows we're here."

"I'm sure he does." Falconer motioned his two men forward. "But he won't know who we are yet. And hopefully he won't expect what I aim on doing."

They took to the forest trail and soon were lost to shadows and flickering lances of sunlight. A breeze suggested that spring might actually have arrived. But the farther they traversed the weedy track, the more pungent became the smell, a putrid mixture of charcoal and animals and unwashed men and sulfur.

When a stretch of brilliant sunshine up ahead announced the woodland's end, Falconer ordered, "Take off your hats and stow your weapons. You remember what I told you?"

"We do," Theo replied with a firm nod.

Falconer told them again anyway. "I go first. If I go down, you retreat and call this a loss. No matter what happens, you will not open fire. Even if I meet my end, do not take another life."

Joseph shifted uncomfortably in his saddle. He was dressed as the other men, in a brand-new suit of navy broadcloth. Falconer had helped him with the neck, for the man had never buttoned a collared shirt before. "I don't take so well to such comin' from your mouth, suh."

"I appreciate the sentiments. Nonetheless you will do as I say." To halt further discussion, Falconer spurred his horse forward.

The instant they cleared the woodland came the hail. "Who goes there?"

Two guards had been caught lounging on a woodpile. One hefted his musket and walked toward the three. The other took his time, knocking his corncob pipe on a log.

"A good morning to you!" Falconer trotted up, waving an empty hand. "I've just come from Grobbe's bank in Charlotte!"

"That supposed to mean something to me?" A trio of well-dressed men appearing unarmed and riding easy was not enough to raise their alarm. The closer man held his musket with the barrel aimed at the sky. The other stowed his pipe in a pocket and came slowly to his feet.

Falconer dropped from his saddle and started forward. He brushed by the first man, heading for the one by the woodpile. "Do you think the foul weather is finally behind us?"

The second man squinted at the broad-shouldered stranger's approach and finally went for his musket. But too late.

Falconer planted one fist straight into the center of the man's forehead, the sort of blow that would have felled an ox. The man's eyes swam and he dropped to his knees. Falconer swung about just as the first man started to take aim. He gripped the barrel before it could be brought into position and jerked hard, pulling the man off balance. The guard realized the gun was useless and let go, reaching for a long-bladed knife strapped to his waist.

Falconer gripped the man's wrist and squeezed. "You won't be needing that."

The guard's eyes widened as his bones cracked. He started to shout, but Falconer's other hand took hold of his throat. The man's eyes rounded further and began to bulge.

"Joseph!"

The black man was already sliding from his saddle. He drew a length from his rope, cut it free, and knotted it about the guard's neck. Joseph then sent it down the man's back and looped it around the man's waist. He quickly grabbed the hand trying to free Falconer's grip on his neck and tied that behind his back. Falconer drew the second hand back for Joseph to tie as well. "How many guards are there?"

"I ain't telling you a thing," he croaked.

"That's your choice, friend." He lowered the man to the ground and held him as Joseph tied the man's ankles and then drew them up behind him. A final loop was fitted into the man's mouth, silencing him. Joseph had evidently seen his share of hog-tying, both animal and man.

Theo gathered up the guards' weapons as Joseph tied the second guard. They stowed the weapons in the woodpile, then saddled up and headed across the meadow.

The field was shaped like a saddle. The grass was springtime green, a mint shade that flickered almost silver under the sunlight and the wind. Falconer crested the rise and there ahead of him stood a central cabin with a pair of outbuildings to either side. A former barn clearly served as a bunkhouse. The stables framed the entry to the mine.

The ridge rose steep and sharp behind the trio of buildings. In an earlier era the cliff might have sheltered a farmer and his wife from all northbound storms. But now the cliff had been assaulted, and the face held a great looming mouth of a cavern. Just outside this was a steam-driven mill of some sort, a clanking monster that belched great clouds and was serviced by half a dozen men. A sullen stream poured from the mill's side, staining the meadow to Falconer's right with a foul yellow runoff.

Falconer threaded his way around the derelict fence. He was almost to the main cabin before two men leading horses hauling logs spotted him and shouted a warning.

A bulldog of a man clumped steel-toed boots across the cabin porch. "Where's my guards?"

"I was wondering the very same thing." Falconer slipped easily from the saddle, then took his time straightening his back. "Nice to see the sun again, isn't it?"

The man was huge and utterly bald, his head as big as a flesh-covered kettle. Below his ears sprouted a ferocious beard that spilled down his chest. "I'll have their guts for garters! Who might you be, stranger?"

"Well you should ask that, sir." This one matched Falconer for size and had fists like rock hammers. Falconer heard the horses trotting up behind him and hoped Theo had spotted the man bearing down from the mill. Falconer started up the cabin steps. "You must be Mr. Joyner."

"You just hold on there!"

"Any chance of a cup of coffee, sir? My throat is awful parched."

"Get yourself down off my porch! Jem! Bring me my —"

Falconer's punch should have taken the man down, but Joyner moved swiftly for such a huge man, ducking under Falconer's fist and coming up with a haymaker of his own. Falconer stepped back, deflecting the swing with his elbow. His forearm went completely numb. Falconer realized with dismay that what he had taken for a blanket of fat was solid muscle.

Joyner's beard split in a bellow of rage. He punched Falconer solid in the chest, or tried to, but Falconer bulled down and caught the blow on his shoulder. Joyner showed surprise that Falconer did not go down. Falconer, however, was rocked by the man's power.

Joyner opened his arms with another roar, intending to envelop Falconer while he was still recovering. Falconer did not avoid the man. Instead, he used Joyner's forward motion against him, taking a full-fisted grip upon Joyner's beard and lunging backward, scrabbling across the porch's plank flooring. Faster he moved, pulling the off-balance man along with him. By the time Joyner realized what was happening, it was too late. Falconer aimed the man's shiny bald head straight for the corner post.

The post gave way with a crack that sounded like gunfire. Falconer flung the man through the railing and out into the dust. Overhead there was a wrenching splinter as the porch roof sagged under its own weight. Falconer leaped down, tumbling into the dust beside Joyner, and came up with his fists at the ready. But Joyner did not move.

The porch roof tore free and smashed down in a rain of dust beside the miner. Two men came stumbling from inside the cabin, both holding muskets, just as the porch's remaining support beam collapsed. The men raised their hands to protect themselves from falling debris. Before they could re-aim their weapons, Falconer had one disarmed and Joseph the other.

"Theo!"

"All clear!" The big German stood over a pair of men. One groaned and held his head. The other did not move at all. Theo was grinning hugely. "It's not enough to take the man, you got to fight his house too?"

Falconer stood guard while Joseph roped and tied the men. He rubbed feeling back into his bruised shoulder and said, "Gather up the miners."

"My name is John Falconer." There were two cooks and fourteen miners — five from the mill and the woodhouse, the rest from underground. All of them cast astounded eyes at the men who had formerly been their bosses.

Falconer took his time and let them look. Joyner and his six guard lieutenants were roped back to back, all seated in the rear of a mine wagon. Two horses had been set into the traces. Emmett Reeves sat on the driver's bench, the reins loose in his hands.

"I represent the rightful owners of this mine," Falconer continued.

Joyner shouted hoarsely, "Ain't no fancy-pants New York banker gonna come in here and take away what's mine!"

"Joseph."

"Suh."

"Help the gentleman understand the need for silence."

"You get your thievin' hands . . ." The voice went muffled as Joseph fitted the rope across the man's mouth.

"As I was saying, my name is John Falconer, and I represent the owners of this mine. Joyner signed away all but a ten percent share to get the money for that hole you're digging and that mill you're feeding." Falconer studied the men carefully. "I've never worked underground. But I've known men like Joyner. And my guess is, if he's holding back from his partners, he's doing the same with the men who work for him."

Falconer had hit the proper nerve, for a

365

man in the group yelled, "We ain't been paid in two months."

"But you're bringing out gold?"

"Sure we are!" He pointed to the men whom Theo had bested. "They don't want us seeing it, but we know. That's good ore we're digging! And they been hiding it away!"

"Do you know where?"

None of the men responded.

"All right. My guess is it won't be far. More than likely they've kept it close, planning to make for the hills when they had a big enough haul." That was not Falconer's immediate concern, however. "You don't know me, but if any of you can read, I'll show you the documents that make me the legal boss of this outfit. If you can't read, this man's a lawyer from Charlotte, and he'll read it to you. I want you men to stay on, and I'll pay you well. And on time. And I'll give you a share of the profits."

One of the man retorted, "Words are cheap, mister."

"I'm doing away with the guards at the mill's end. You'll work the ore from beginning to end, and you'll see what gold comes out. If the gold is there, you will all have a take. I can't make it clearer than that." Falconer turned away, giving the men a chance to talk among themselves. He said to Emmett, "You'll take these men to Charlotte and hand them over to the sheriff as we discussed?"

"I'll file charges against them just like you said," Emmett agreed. "I'm telling you, though, unless you come back and offer testimony, they'll be out in a matter of days."

"That's long enough. Give us time to sort things out here, find men we can trust as guards, and they can do what they like." Falconer acknowledged Joyner's furious glare by saying, "Whatever we find, we'll pass along your ten percent to Mr. Reeves here. Same for everything we recover from the mine from now on. Mr. Reeves will be the only connection you will ever have to this mine or this land. Show your face around here again and it won't go so easy on you."

Emmett reached over from the wagon and offered Falconer his hand. "Sir, you are one remarkable man. Mr. Gavi is lucky to have you on his team."

"Sorry to have entangled you in this," Falconer replied.

"Wouldn't have missed it for the world." Emmett Reeves flicked the reins. "Giddap there!"

■ ■ ■ ■

They found the cache of gold just after midnight.

By that point the cabin was reduced to dust and scrap. The miners had all taken a jubilant hand in its destruction. Clearly it had been despised as a symbol of Joyner and his guards.

The miners' story came out in bits and pieces. Their willingness to talk at all was fueled by how Falconer and Theo and Joseph labored alongside the miners. There were no weapons. The trust Falconer offered was silent but real.

The miners spoke in turns. Mostly the story came from the ones resting, as they sat on the side of the worksite and drank coffee that grew stronger with the night. They spoke of how all the land in the Cabarras Valley area had been settled and farmed long before gold had been discovered. Those who answered the lure of gold had found themselves with no chance of real wealth. But good jobs were hard to find, and miners' wages were better than farmhands. Most stayed on, meaning there were more workers than jobs. Which meant men like Joyner could promise much and give little. Even the food, they said, had been doled out in meager portions.

When Falconer heard that part of their tale, he ordered the cooking fires relit and the rations store opened. The cooks remained at their oven for hours, doling out flapjacks and smoked bacon and sweet molasses until every man groaned his satisfaction. Falconer let them linger there beneath the stars, savoring the signs of change. He did not ask them to return to work. Instead, he and Joseph and Theo started prying up the floorboards themselves. One by one the miners came over and joined in. Though their faces were wearied by the full day behind them and the next sunrise only hours away, none complained. From time to time they would glance Falconer's way, as though making certain this man was truly different from the one he had just had carted off. Falconer did not speak because there was nothing to be said. Only time would tell.

The cellar was full of more stores, but no gold. Even so, the men watched hungrily as Falconer drew out sacks of fine white flour and salt beef and jars of sweet pears and syrupy plums and all the things they had dreamed of yet not seen in months. Falconer ordered the goods taken to the rations store for the miners. Even with all the miners helping, it took over an hour to clear out the cellar. By that point, the men were smiling. But the grim weariness turned even their good humor into a dark tragedy.

It was Joseph who discovered the false wall. What they all thought had been the cellar's outer rim proved to have a loose brick. Joseph pried it out and another gave way, revealing an opening through which an arm could reach. Torches were brought as Joseph reached through and brought out leather sacks the size of a bread loaf. Another and another and more still. Falconer hefted several and concluded they had all been measured out at about fifteen pounds each. He opened the neck of one, turned to the closest miner, and said, "Cup your hands, please."

The miner's right hand was scratched and bloody from tearing down the cabin. Falconer poured out a stream of dust and pellets, some as large as musket balls. In the firelight their color was so ruddy as to appear almost red.

The miners crowded in on all sides. The only sound was that of Joseph scrabbling deeper into the secret hold, passing sack after sack into Theo's hands, and the crackling hiss from their torches.

Falconer asked the miner holding the gold, "I don't believe I've caught your name, sir."

The miner stared dumbly at Falconer.

The miner to his left nudged him. "Go on, Evault. The man done asked how you're called."

"E-Evault, sir."

"Is that your first or last name, sir?"

"Evault G-Graves, sir."

"Well, Evault Graves," Falconer said. "What you hold is yours to keep."

The man looked from Falconer to the double fist of gold. He dropped to his knees, gripped his hands to his chest, and began sobbing.

The closest miner patted Evault on the shoulder. "His wife ain't well, sir," he said to Falconer. "This gold, it means a lot."

Falconer glanced over to where Joseph was leaning against the wall, staring at the pile of sacks. "How many are there?"

"Thirty-nine have come out," Theo replied. "I can see more but not reach them."

"All right." Falconer lifted his voice so the others could hear him. "Four sacks are Joyner's. Keep four more here for the miners. Come first light, dole them out evenly among the men."

When Falconer clambered up from the

cellar, Theo scrambled to his feet. "What are you planning?"

Falconer rubbed his shoulder where Joyner had caught him. A massive bruise was forming. Bone weary and filthy from the work, he said, "Bring up the packhorses. I'm leaving now."

Joseph rose wearily to his feet. "Not alone, you ain't."

"Joseph, Theo can't manage this mine alone."

"Now, don't you even start with your arguing, 'cause it won't do you a bit of good." Joseph's chin lifted in determination. "Theo's got himself a dozen and more good men."

"I need to get the rest of this gold back and under lock and key before Joyner has a chance to make mischief."

Joseph crossed his arms and took station over the gold. "All I'm saying is, you just pack up your notion of ridin' alone and stow it back in your saddlebag, 'cause you're just wasting time."

CHAPTER 24

For several nights now, Serafina had been awakened by faint tendrils of a dream. Half-formed images came and went with bitter swiftness, drawing her awake with gasps of fear. Tonight was the first time Falconer had actually spoken. She crept from her bed and entered the kitchen to light a taper from the stove's dying coals. Her hands shook as she transferred the light to a candle. She poured herself a cup of well water and drank it slowly. She could not remember what Falconer had said in the dream. Nor could she describe the manner of his speech, if he had been calm or worried or afraid. All she knew for certain was that her friend was very far away and very alone.

She knew she would sleep no more that night. She carried the candle into the dining room, where she lit several more. Quietly she took down the painting on which she had been working, the portrait of the smiling infant, and replaced it with fresh paper.

The candlelight would normally have been an irritation when drawing. Tonight, however, she welcomed it. The light was soft and golden, a comforting enclosure to her chamber. She felt isolated from the rest of the world, and closer to God.

She decided she did not merely wish to sketch John Falconer. She wished to see him take shape beneath her hand, and with every stroke of her pencil she would pray for his safety and his success. And for his swift return.

She drew from memory the first sketch she had done of him. Once again he bowed his head over hands which clenched the pew back. Once more his scar was invisible. Several times she had to stop in her work to breathe away her deep concern. Nevertheless, she continued drawing. And she prayed as she drew.

She felt no need to unravel a mystery for this portrait. Falconer was her friend, and a brother in Christ, and the man who had pointed her toward her Savior. Serafina worked for a while, then took two steps back from the portrait and drew a candle in closer. The image was taking strong form. She could see how she would paint it now. A gentle light would shine down from above. She wiped bittersweet tears from her eyes and reached for her brushes.

Falconer was weary in a manner that no single night's sleep could ease. He had arrived back in Charlotte with the previous day's final light. Both his horse and Joseph's had stumbled as they made their way down the residential street to Emmett Reeves' home. The lawyer arrived soon after. As he helped Falconer and Joseph stow the heavy sacks in his root cellar, he reported that the sheriff had reluctantly agreed to hold Joyner over, but as the circuit court judge would be in town the next morning, Joyner and his men would no doubt be free by midday. They tucked into his wife's hearty meal, then fell asleep like dead men.

After a night's sleep, the three men rode to the Charlotte Mint, the first such establishment outside of Washington. The mint accepted Falconer's deposits and in return issued a document that could be presented to the Washington Mint in exchange for new American eagle gold dollars.

Falconer took his own share in gold coin.

There was no chance for further rest, for the weekly slave auctions began the very next day in both Rock Mound and Hayesfield. The auctions were across the border in South Carolina, since North Carolina showed a largely hostile attitude to the trade. North Carolina permitted slaves, though they were outlawed by some communities such as Salem. Few North Carolina families actually held slaves, and many churches roundly condemned the practice. To spend as much gold as Falconer intended, he would have to travel south.

He settled three heavy sacks of coin into Emmett Reeves' hands. Five wagons and foodstuff and two additional drivers were hastily procured. They left Charlotte while the city still slumbered, crossed the state line an hour later, and split up soon after. Falconer and Joseph and one of the hired wagoners headed for Rock Mound, while Emmett Reeves and the other driver took the road toward Hayesfield.

The sun rose over a dismal scene. The morning was already hot, the field dry enough to generate a cloud of red-clay dust. Bare feet shuffled and chains clanked as more slaves arrived for sale. Those already corralled slumped around a water barrel or nestled whimpering infants or ate from communal pots with their fingers for spoons.

Falconer fought down an urge to take the

auctioneer barehanded and asked, "How many have any experience at farming?"

The slave auctioneer must have sensed he was dealing with an experienced buyer. "Why, sir, you have come to the right place! What you see here before you is the finest collection of field hands in all of South Carolina!"

Falconer's voice sounded strangled to his own ears. "I asked how many you had for sale."

The auctioneer was too excited over a major buyer to notice. He called to his overseer, "You there! Count off the field hands."

"And their families," Falconer ordered. "If I take one, I take them all."

"A wise investment, sir. Very wise." The auctioneer mopped his brow where eagerness and rising heat drew a sweat. "A happy slave is a hard-working one."

His overseer spat a long stream of tobacco and flicked his leather quirt at a fly. Now and then he looked back to where Joseph sat upon the second wagon. A lockbox had been hastily bolted beneath the seat. Joseph nestled a double-barreled shotgun in his lap and propped a second beside him. He gave the dusty field a tightly squinted inspection and paid the overseer no mind.

"I reckon on twenty-one," the overseer said.

Falconer called over, "And household staff?"

"Eight, mebbe nine."

"I've just bought a derelict plantation up Danville way. Two hundred forty acres. Half tobacco, half corn."

"You don't mean to tell me you don't have a single hand!"

"The place is empty save for a handful of folks too old to sell off."

The handkerchief tracked another course across the auctioneer's brow. "Well, sir, as I said, you've come to the right place! There's no finer auction point north of Atlanta!"

"What about special skills? Cooks, nanny, blacksmith, leatherworkers."

"The likes of them won't come cheap," the auctioneer warned. He was a wizened spark of a man, shrunk down to a husk of leathery skin and hollowed features. His black overcoat flapped about his frame like the wings of a crow. But his voice boomed richly, as though all his remaining energy had gone into fueling his cry. "Do you know, I believe I've seen on our manifest that we can supply all your needs. Why, we even have a woman trained in healing."

"Add her to the list." Falconer turned his

back on the human corral. The sight was just too wrenching. "Give me your best price."

"What, for them all?" The handkerchief dangled limply from the auctioneer's hand like a wet and dusty flag.

Falconer signaled for Joseph to open the strong box. "I pay in gold."

They found the clearing just as Emmett Reeves had said they would, three hours north of Charlotte along the Salem Trail. The track leading off the road was easy to miss, covered as it was by chest-high weeds and debris. But the slashed pines marked a line through the trees, there for those who knew what to look for. A ruined farmhouse rose in the midday light. Falconer did not need to tell Joseph what to do. They had come to a point where a gesture was as good as a word, with each man trusting the other implicitly.

The slaves were ordered down from the three wagons. Their chains were slipped off ankles and tossed away. At Emmett Reeves' insistence, both of the wagon drivers they had hired were slaves belonging to the stable owner. The one with Falconer watched through hooded eyes as the slaves were unchained, saying nothing. A fire was lit and children sent to forage for firewood. The kettles were brought out, and the food. Thankfully the old well still had a bucket, or perhaps some other traveler had thoughtfully left one behind, for it was one thing Falconer had forgotten to bring. Silently he rebuked himself for carrying these charges across the state without a single means of drawing water. He loosened the horses' restraints and wondered what else he had forgotten or neglected or just plain gotten wrong.

He ate with the others, using his tin mug first for beans and then for water. He could feel nervous eyes upon him. He knew he needed to speak with them, but weariness seeped through him, weighing down his body until he could scarcely drag his frame over to the nearest wagon. He rolled underneath, laid his head on a likely clump of weeds, and was instantly asleep.

He awoke to the sound of Emmett Reeves demanding, "You didn't bring coffee?"

Falconer slowly emerged from his makeshift shelter. His body had locked up tight as he had slept. He rose to full height in a series of careful jinks and twists.

Emmett Reeves stood before him, his hair wild from the day's exertions, his eyes red with road dust. His jaunty energy, on the other hand, was unabated. He reminded Falconer of a bantam rooster cloaked in black broadcloth. "You can't possibly expect me to make it clear across the state without a single cup!"

Falconer scanned the clearing. Their wagons were pulled up to one side, angled so that each pair of horses had its own area to crop. The rest of the clearing was dotted with figures. "Well, I guess I plain forgot." He rubbed his hands over his face. "Don't you have a law practice to run?"

"That can wait another few days. I doubt my absence will be noticed." Emmett Reeves took a pleased look around. "And I don't mind telling you I'm rather enjoying this."

Falconer walked to the well and drew a fresh bucket, which he poured over his head. He swiped his face clean, then combed his hair with his fingers and secured it in the leather catch. He drew a second bucket and drank deeply. He sighed away the last vestiges of slumber and turned to address the lawyer, his tone sober. "Everything you've done up to now you can excuse away. You were hired to act as my agent. You exercised your duties. But if word ever gets out that you helped me cart slaves to freedom, there could be serious trouble."

Emmett Reeves was impossibly cheerful

for such a weary man. "There comes a day to each and every one of God's servants," he declared, "when they are asked to stand up and be counted."

"I don't reckon I can argue with that," Falconer said, almost embarrassed by the little lawyer's level of commitment. "Your company will be most welcome, sir. And if the mine proves a valid source of gold —"

"I beg you, Falconer," Reeves interrupted. "Don't sully this moment with talk of payment. It's rare enough that a man in my position is given the chance to act selflessly. Let me feel the Savior's closeness for a while longer yet."

Falconer hid his emotions by turning to the clearing. He could feel all eyes on him as he asked Joseph, "How many are we?"

"Don't know, suh. I ain't learned to count that high."

"No matter." Falconer raised his voice and announced, "As of this moment, you are all free. If you care to stay with me, you will be taken to Salem village. There you will —"

"Praise be to God above!" a woman's voice called into the endless blue overhead. "Is it true?"

"I was once a slaver." Falconer knew he should do a better job with his words. He knew also many would not believe him until they were long gone from his care. "Now I am dedicated to freeing as many of you as I possibly can."

"Oh, Lord, Lord above!" The woman healer was so thin her dress made from flour sacks fitted her like a rough-weave sail. Her spindly arms ended in large hands as broad as shovel blades. Her wizened face looked timeless as she approached Falconer. "I'm too old to be fooled with. I'm gonna stare into your face, and you gonna say them words again."

Falconer waited until she was within arm's reach, then said clearly, "I bought you to set you free."

"Oh, praise Jesus!" She lifted her hands to heaven. "What be your name, suh?"

Joseph replied for him. "You can call him the Night Angel. That's the onliest name you need to know."

Falconer waited through another shout to the sky overhead, then went on. "I suggest you all stay with me. We will do our best to get you to safety. If any of you care to leave now, however, I will sign over your papers. I'm sorry that I can't offer you money. I've used all I have to buy you."

The only person who moved was the woman, who continued to shuffle about the clearing, her arms lifted to the sky above.

Falconer raised his voice to be heard over her cries. "Eat and drink your fill. We need as many of you as possible to walk to spare the horses. We leave in one hour, heading north. We travel hard."

The Saunders brothers found Joyner and his men in the fifth tavern they visited. By then they had heard the story three times, each version richer than the last. How a local miner had been run off by an army of mercenaries put together by a group of New York bankers. Jeb Saunders had listened to each telling in silence, not objecting as the number of attackers had grown to ninety strong.

Joyner and his men were digging in to a late breakfast of eggs and potatoes, each man dining from his own skillet. The men watched in sullen wariness as Jeb pulled over a chair and motioned for Cody to do the same. "Name's Saunders," he began.

Joyner ate with one arm curled around his skillet. The other hand spooned up food in a constant steady motion. "Supposed to mean something to me?"

"It appears you and I might have something in common," Jeb replied, speaking as easily as he would to his best friend. "A man solid as an ox and near 'bout as strong. Got long black hair he keeps tied back with a leather string. Like he was some kind of sailor. Or pirate."

Jeb heard a soft click. Cody had lifted his pistol free of his belt and pulled the trigger back from its percussion cap. Across the table, one of Joyner's men was frozen in the act of pulling a knife from his belt. "Easy there, little brother. We're all friends 'round here."

"Yeah, well you just tell that so-called friend over yonder to keep his pigsticker in his belt and his hands where I can see 'em."

"Naw, naw, you got them wrong. The feller's just after picking his teeth. Ain't that right, mister?"

Joyner glanced down the table and said, "Ease up there." When the guard subsided, Joyner turned back to Jeb. "Saunders, sure, I hearda you. Y'all handle slaves. What you want with this feller?"

"First let's find out if we're talking about the same man."

"Dressed like a gent," Joyner said. "Scar running down one side of his face."

"I don't know about his clothes," Jeb said, "but the scar sure sounds right. Say, where'd you get that welt on your forehead?"

Joyner just glowered.

"Yeah, I reckon it must be the same

feller," Jeb said smoothly. "He give you his name?"

"No name. What you want 'im for?"

"He owes me money."

"Yeah, well, get in line," one of the other men muttered.

"How many were there?" Jeb asked.

"Him, the lawyer feller, and two others."

Jeb and Cody exchanged glances. Joyner and his six men all looked like they could handle themselves in a scrap. "Which lawyer might that be?"

"You been asking all sorts of questions here. I got one of my own now. What's in it for me?"

"I got two hundred fifty dollars in gold coming my way," Jeb replied smoothly. "Fifty of it's yours."

"Fifty for me. Ten for each of my men."

"Fifty in gold, mister. How you spread it out is your business."

Joyner reluctantly allowed, "We had gold stored down in the cellar."

"Fixin' to make a run with your takings, were you?"

Joyner ignored the thrust. "Word is, the feller showed up day before yesterday at the Charlotte Mint. Took some in coin, the rest in paper."

Which meant the man was traveling heavy.

Jeb and Cody exchanged a glance. They'd do their best to lighten the man's load. Jeb asked, "Any idea where he might be headed?"

"Far away, if he knows what's good for him."

Jeb motioned his brother up with his chin. "Thank you, Mr. Joyner. You been real help-ful."

"What about my money?"

"First we gotta go find this man."

Joyner was already up and moving. "Not so fast. Long as my gold's in your pocket, you got yourself some riding partners."

Jeb Saunders unleashed his easy smile. "I wouldn't have it no other way."

The healer's name was Hattie, and she praised God until her voice turned ragged though no less fervent. By the time they stopped to blow the horses and drink from a stream, she knew every one of them by name. She looked Falconer in the eye whenever they spoke — the only one besides Joseph and Emmett Reeves to do so. They ate a cold meal of beef jerky and beans scooped by hand from the kettle. The day was hot on the way to unmerciful heat. The sky was pale blue, misted by dust rising off the trail. Falconer knew they needed rest.

But something gnawed at him, more a hunger than a worry, but in truth a good deal of both. Before the group could give in to drowsiness, he had them up and moving again. They responded slowly, yet no one complained.

When they were heading north, he walked up alongside Hattie. "How many are without their families?"

"Don't rightly know, suh. Half, maybe. Could be more." She huffed a hoarse chuckle. " 'Course, being slaves, lots don't have what you might call proper families at all."

"I'm not worried about the law here. I'm worried about their real bonds." He heard her hum a note, which might have meant anything. It sent a faint sensation of pleasure up his spine. "Why do you trust me?"

"Because God's hand is on you." Her voice rose, then broke.

"How can you be certain of that?"

"Don't know, suh. But it's the truth. Ain't I right?"

"I hope so, Hattie. I feel like I'm doing as He has called me."

"Lord, Lord. We praise your holy name." She clapped her hands and hummed again. Her hands were almost as large as Falconer's, with splayed fingers and flat yellow nails. When she clapped them together it sounded like a cracking whip. "Our prayers done been answered."

"Come with me." Falconer steered her over to the wagon being driven by Emmett Reeves. "Mr. Reeves, I'd like you to meet . . . I'm sorry, ma'am, I don't know your last name."

She chuckled again. "Don't know it myself. I was called Stone, after the man what owned the place where I was born."

"Are you married, ma'am?"

"I was, suh. To a good and godly man. He's been gone from me now nigh on twelve years. Yessuh, he's gone to be with the Lord. I miss him, though. Twelve years and my heart still ain't healed up yet."

"Mrs. Stone, I'd like you to please speak with everyone in this group. Find out who has family missing and where they might be located."

She was watching him closely now. As were all those who overheard Falconer's words. "What you want me to do that for?"

"Give the names to Mr. Reeves. I'll authorize him to try and locate these people and buy their —"

"Oh, Lord! Hallelujah!"

Falconer never did manage to finish his instructions.

CHAPTER 25

The sight of nine men riding hard under the midday sun was enough to turn the auctioneer's features into a sheen of terror. Then he spotted a familiar face among the riders and cried with trembling relief, "Why, if it ain't my old pal Jeb Saunders! I ain't seen you in too long, friend. How you been?"

"Boys, this here feller used to be known as Rustlin' Rob." Jeb reined his horse in close enough to force the auctioneer back a step. "Then he went and found himself a better paying occupation. One that don't have him worrying about dangling at the business end of a rope."

"Don't y'all pay Jeb Saunders any mind. He always was a jester." The auctioneer turned to his overseer. "Don't just stand there gawping. Go get a jug out of my cabin."

"That's mighty kind, Rob. But we'll make

do with a drink from your well."

One of Joyner's outriders argued, "I'll have me a pull from that jug of his."

"You do and you won't be riding with me," Jeb said, never taking his eyes off the auctioneer. "Nobody along with me drinks on the job."

"What, you're laying the rules down on all us now?"

"That's right, friend," Jeb's brother Cody drawled. "He most certain is."

Jeb did not need to turn around to know his brother's hand rested on the grip of his pistol. He could always count on Cody to back his play. He said to the auctioneer, "Looks like mighty poor pickings today."

"The auction was yesterday. But that ain't why we're down on stock. And stock ain't what's brought you here, is it?"

"What makes you say that?"

"You know our schedule. You should, you come down here enough." The auctioneer's eyes glittered. "You're after that feller, ain't you?"

"Which feller might that be?"

"The one who come prancing in here and bought up all my field hands in one fell swoop."

Jeb slid from his saddle. "Describe the man."

"That's it, ain't it! I knew that man was up to no good first time I laid eyes on him, sure enough!"

"You just climb on down off your high horse, I'm telling you. I ain't standing out there in the auction yard, and you don't need to be shouting. You just say what the man looked like."

"Big as a mountain and twice as solid. Got a fighter's look to him. Hard as a cocked gun."

"Scar?"

"Down the side of his face."

"That's our man," Joyner cried.

"How'd you trace him here?" the auctioneer demanded.

"Found the feller in Charlotte who supplied his wagons."

The auctioneer tensed. "He's one of them anti-slavers. That's it, ain't it? You're after the five hundred in gold reward."

"Five hundred!" Joyner cried. "You told me two-fifty!"

Jeb ignored the bullish man. "What makes you think he's a meddlin' do-gooder, Rob?"

"He come in here with a strongbox full of fresh-minted gold eagles. Bought up every field hand I had to my name. The hands, their families, two nannies, cooks, a healing woman, five household staff."

"Must've made your day, the man not even bargaining over your asking price."

"How'd you know . . ." The auctioneer grinned. "He bought *your* stock too, didn't he?"

"Where was he headed?"

"Told me he'd come into a plantation up Danville way. Good land but no hands to farm it."

"That's true enough," Cody said from the saddle.

Jeb turned around just enough to shoot his brother a warning glance. Then he asked the auctioneer, "How long ago did he leave?"

"Packed 'em up and headed straight off, couldn't have been more than an hour after yesterday's dawn."

Jeb turned to grip the reins and fitted his boot into the stirrup.

The auctioneer added, "You'll take care of your old buddy Rob, now, won't you?"

"You know it." Jeb eased back into the saddle. "My friends and I are much obliged."

When they were back on the road headed north, Joyner showed his ire. "What're you doing, giving me this tomfoolery about two hundred fifty dollars?"

Jeb took on the patient air of a man dealing with a fussing child. "It's two-fifty for the man dead, five hundred alive. Only I don't imagine this man is the kind who's gonna come easy."

Joyner subsided. "We get him alive, our share's double."

"That's only fair," Jeb solemnly agreed.

Cody waited until they crossed the state border and the men had spread out along the trail before riding up alongside his brother. "What about them slaves he's carting north? At ten dollars a head for returned slaves, that could double our take."

"My guess is the man is hightailing it for Salem town. Once they get inside the Wachau valley, that portion of the game is just plain gone."

Cody mulled that over. "What you figure he wants the Moss farm for?"

"That ain't our concern. All we need to know is that he's gotta head back there to pay Moss the rest of his money."

Cody's face creased in a grin. "You aim on taking that gold for yourself, don't you?"

"Why, little brother. I have no earthly idea what you're going on about."

"And the money Joyner's after. You don't aim on giving him a red cent."

"Wipe that grin off your face," Jeb hissed. "We're riding north and we're riding hard.

You get to the back of the line and worry Joyner's men till their horses start dropping. They know Joyner's not gonna give them more'n he has to. Soon as they start getting saddlesore, we'll see some of them slipping away. Then we'll give Joyner exactly what he's got coming to him."

Cody wheeled his horse around. "That's what I like about you, Jeb. You're always thinking."

Serafina awoke to a dove-gray sky an hour before the sun would appear. The rain had moved south in the night, pushed by a wind strong enough to rattle the panes of her bedroom window. The early dawn was chilly for spring, yet she had no interest in remaining warmly tucked into bed. Her night had been shattered once again. This time, however, her dreams of Falconer had contained vague notions of gunfire and danger. She dressed and went downstairs, chased by fears that made a mockery of the day's invitation.

She worked through the morning, pushed forward by a feverish urge to lose herself in her paintings. But not even this creative fire could ease the fear that threatened to crush her heart. There was no reason for her worry. At least, none that she could name.

Her parents greeted her with subdued voices, now familiar with the intensity she carried to her work. Mary slipped into the room, took one look at Serafina's deep concentration, and departed with the morning Scriptures unread.

Birdsong filled the rear garden, an acclaim to a sunlit day. Serafina heard it but if asked could not have identified the sound. Nor did she acknowledge the doorbell when it rang. All the noises, loud or soft, were mere background clatter. Or they were until her mother knocked upon the dining room door and said, "You have a visitor."

"Not now, Mama."

"Yes, my dear one. This very instant." Her mother's voice held the sort of firmness that brooked no argument. "Stand up and take off your apron. Now let me see you. Wait, you have paint on your forehead."

Bettina motioned her daughter forward and dabbed a corner of Serafina's discarded apron into the pot of clean water and stroked it across her daughter's face. "All right. Now come along."

"Who is it?"

"Mr. Baring."

"Oh no, Mama, he'll want to see the portrait of his mother, and I'm not —"

"Don't bother telling me, daughter."

"But —" Serafina stopped because her mother had already moved through the doorway leading to the hall, and from there into the front parlor. Serafina patted her hair, which she was sure was all awry, and followed.

Nathan stood by the unlit fireplace. "Good morning, Miss Gavi. Madam. I do hope you both are well."

Her mother replied, "Isn't it nice to have sunlight for a change, sir?"

"Indeed, ma'am. I can't ever recall such a wet spring, nor for that matter a worse winter." He spoke without taking his eyes off Serafina. "I was wondering, that is . . . Would it be possible for me to see how you are doing, Miss Gavi? On the painting?"

"It's not nearly finished."

"What a pity," he sighed.

Serafina caught something then, an impression so strong it pulled her from the fog that had been draped about her since picking up her brush that morning. "Something is the matter!"

"No, no." He made a brave face and gave Serafina's mother a small smile. "You must excuse me for having disturbed your morning, madam."

"No, wait. You must tell me." Serafina took a step closer, seeing him clearly now.

"Is it your mother?"

Nathan Baring's ability to mask his inner workings cracked just slightly. "A spell. Nothing more. She has had many of them recently."

"You're very worried about her."

He nodded reluctantly. "She says it will pass. But there is something about her this morning, a pall that no one save me seems to be able to see. The doctor says I am worrying over nothing."

"You are her son. Of course you see what they cannot." Serafina turned and motioned toward the dining room. "Come with me, then."

"May I also?" her mother asked.

"Oh, well, if you wish." Now Serafina felt seized by an urgency that had little or nothing to do with Nathan Baring and everything to do with the sensation of something amiss. But what was she to say? That a nightmare had filled her with foreboding?

Nathan Baring stood in the doorway and looked about the dining room, seemingly fascinated by the impromptu art studio before him. Serafina found herself examining the room through Nathan's eyes.

The dining room table had been pushed to one side and covered with a sheet. Another sheet covered the chairs that were stacked to either side of the table. Only one chair remained by the parlor door, for whichever model might be drawn into use at the moment. More sheets covered the floor about Serafina's work area at the room's far end. Two easels formed a dividing wall that effectively split the room in two, with three more easels folded into the corner.

Serafina observed Nathan's slow entry into the room. The side wall captured him, which was hardly a surprise, since it was almost completely covered with sketches. The wall would have to be completely re-plastered and painted to mask all the tack holes. She apologized to her father almost daily for the damage she was causing. But Alessandro always waved her words aside. Nathan's face held the same intent surprise as her father when he stepped up to the wall. Wordlessly he studied each of the sketches she had done of his mother.

Finally he stepped around to the easel. And stopped once more.

She studied him as well as the painting. She had known it was a good painting for over a week now. She had almost done away with the pencil's darkly embedded lines, softening and softening until the shadings played out a story upon the paper. No longer was Mrs. Baring old. Nor did the painting tell an untruth of a young woman who existed no longer. Instead, the two were melded together, the young woman and the old. Serafina examined it anew and saw that it was a proper and fitting study. The image contained the timeless beauty of an eternal fire. The aged body, with its illness and pain, was also true. Yet it did not dominate the vision. Both the eternal and the earthly came together in the harmony of a faith-filled life.

Nathan caught his breath in what might have been a cough. Serafina was watching with this new sense of awareness, and she understood that he was struggling to hold back, to compress, to keep his emotions all locked tightly away.

She asked, "What is it that causes you this sorrow?"

His features maintained their handsome calm while his eyes revealed the torment within.

"It is not just your mother," she said. "Why are you in such pain?"

His voice was reduced to a whisper by the force required to keep himself under control. "I fear the burden of false visions, wrong choices, and a wasted life."

"You did what your father asked of you,"

she comforted, remembering that she also was doing what her father was asking of her.

"But it is I who will stand before the Master's throne and answer for a life —"

"A life filled with faith and good works," she insisted. "A life filled with devotion to your family and good causes."

He turned his attention fully to Serafina. "How . . . how do you know these things?"

"I speak merely of what I see."

He held her gaze long enough for Bettina Gavi to clear her throat. Nathan turned back to the portrait of his mother and said, "It is truly magnificent. What a wonderful gift."

"Thank you." She understood his intent to bring several meanings to the word *gift,* and she appreciated his gratitude. She also knew that she was only at the beginning of her own exploration into capturing the mystery, the unseen essence, of each painting.

When she looked at the image of Eleanor Baring, she was satisfied.

Falconer and his motley band marched until darkness obscured the road. Falconer directed the first wagon down a narrow track, then hastened back to lead in the others. They carried no lights, and it would have been easy to miss the turning. The small clearing really was too cramped for them all, but the folks were too weary to care. They drank from a trickling stream, crouching like animals in the mud. Falconer had just four canteens, and his only bucket was the one he had taken from the disused farmhouse to water the horses. He eased the wagon traces but did not release the horses entirely, for what reason he did not know. When the horses had their noses deep in their oat bags, he sat on the ground, leaned against a wheel, ate a plate of something Joseph put into his hand, drank his canteen dry, and dozed.

But not for long. He was jerked awake by a sound.

The clearing was packed with wagons and animals and people. The horses shook their heads and jangled their traces, and the group slept wherever they had finished their meal. The adults groaned or snored in their sleep while the children cried and whimpered. From the surrounding trees a hawk complained over having his hunting ground disturbed. It was impossible for Falconer to have heard the night warn him.

Nonetheless he knew he would sleep no more that night. He eased himself up slowly, his body complaining loudly. Intending to make a circuit of the clearing, he stopped when he found two pairs of eyes watching him.

Falconer murmured, "I must have been dreaming."

Both Hattie and Joseph rose from the earth to stand beside him. Hattie asked, "Was it God talkin' or the road?"

"I wish I knew." Now that he was discussing it, he could take the sensation out and study it more carefully. "I have a feeling we're being tracked."

Joseph said, "I done had a creepy crawly feeling under my skin ever since I laid down."

"Why didn't you say something?"

The tall shadow shrugged. "Long as it was just me, it coulda been my tired bones talking."

Hattie was already moving. "Up! Everybody, rise and praise God!" She picked her way over the supine bodies, clapping her hands and calling in her hoarse voice. "We got Glory ahead and the wolves behind!"

Somebody groaned, a child whimpered. But Hattie was prodding them now with her bare feet and clapping louder still. "Y'all been tired before, but never for a reason good as this!" Her clapping and shouting was joined by the horses' whinnying. "We're movin' out now! We can all sleep once we's safe in Glory!"

They marched on through the night into the chill of a dry dawn. Their journey continued through rising heat and thirst. They did not pause for a meal. They marched at a pace that would have made an army proud. Most adults walked to spare the horses, and some carried children. Even the horses seemed to catch wind of something more than dust and sunlight filling the trail ahead. They pulled the wagons with snorting impatience.

And as they marched, they sang.

They sang and they praised God. They sang and they spoke of Glory ahead. They chanted in time to their footsteps. One of them would talk for a while, of how Moses parted the Red Sea. Of how God stilled Abraham's hand before the knife could plunge into his son. Of how God's own Son came down to give them all a reason to keep marching on. On and on and on.

They did stop at every spring and creek and river. They drank along with the horses, then hands patted the horses' flanks to turn them away from the water. Then they rejoined the trail. The endless, dusty, hot, weary trail.

Hattie's voice had long since given out.

But she could clap and walk. She did more than her share of both. Sometimes she would whisper to someone closest to her, and they would start another song for her.

The afternoon stretched out over endless time. Falconer had never known the sun to move so slowly. He had the impression they were drawing close. He could not be certain, for the Salem Trail was little more than a drovers' route and had none of the milestones found on turnpikes. They crested a rise that seemed familiar. The valley descended to a bridge over a chuckling creek, where they all stopped for one more drink. He glanced over at Joseph, hoping the man would agree with him that they weren't far off, but Joseph was walking like the horses, with his head hanging low. Though his arms hung at his sides, a child was clinging limpetlike to his neck. Falconer shifted the boy he carried and decided not to say anything for fear of raising false hopes.

Climbing that next ridge was very hard indeed.

Then they reached the crest. And there before him was the sweetest sight he had seen in many a day. Four valleys stretched out like fingers of a splayed hand. At the center nestled a village. Descending sunlight played over the orderly rooftops like the divine hand. The trails of smoke rising from the chimneys turned into gossamer pillars holding up heaven itself.

Hattie stepped up beside him. She spoke with a voice as low and cracked as an old man's. "Is that it?"

"Salem," Falconer agreed, his voice as dusty and fractured as hers. "We made it."

She eased the child she was carrying down to the ground and clapped her hands over her head. "Y'all come on!" She meant to shout, but there was scarce little volume left. "We're gonna sing now! Yes! We're gonna enter Glory with praise on our lips!"

And so help them, that is exactly what they did. Even Emmett Reeves rose to his feet, standing upon the wagon seat to sing hoarsely with the others. The horses lifted their heads to the clamor.

Doors opened up and down that side of Salem, and villagers began filing out. The community sentries stepped into place like a military escort, and they were soon joined by more and more, all dressed in shades of gray and white and exuding welcome. Falconer sang along with his charges, too tired to feel embarrassed at his lack of musical ability. The afternoon was too fine to be silent.

A familiar form came racing up the trail

toward them. Falconer slipped the child he carried to another pair of hands and bent over to accept the boy's embrace. He lifted him up and breathed in the wonder of this clean slight form whose arms held such an intense comfort as they wrapped around his neck.

CHAPTER 26

They filled the four stables on that side of town and spilled out into the pasture that linked them. Falconer stretched out beneath a pecan tree that had just begun sprouting its leaves. A pair of dogwoods proclaimed in white-clad splendor that spring had arrived and all was well. Falconer dozed and woke to find Matt playing a game of mumblety-peg with three darker-skinned children. Women tended a savory-smelling kettle on a big open fire. Others walked among the still forms, offering mugs of cider and fresh-baked bread. Ada stood to one side, speaking with the pastor and two men Falconer did not recognize. Beyond the fence was gathered what appeared to be the entire village. He dozed off again.

The next time he awoke, it was to find Matt seated beside him eating from a tin plate. "Mama said I could stay as long as I didn't bother you."

"You're not bothering me at all." Falconer reached over and tousled the boy's hair. "I missed you, lad."

Matt's smile outshone the lingering sunset. "Shall I bring you a plate too?"

"Heap it high. I've been hungry for weeks, it feels like."

As the boy raced off, a voice behind him said, "You shouldn't tempt him so, John Falconer. He will pile the food on higher than his head."

"Greetings, Ada." He rose to his feet, then noticed the pastor standing beside her. "Excuse me, I mean, Mrs. Hart."

She made no move toward him, but her eyes were welcoming. "You have been busy, John Falconer."

"They are good folks," he said simply, wishing he could express the tumult that rose in his chest at the sight of her.

"Indeed, they say the same of you," the pastor said, stepping forward and offering his hand. "You are welcome, Mr. Falconer."

"Thank you, sir. That means a great deal to me."

"How many did you bring to us this time?"

"Forty-nine."

The pastor's beard trailed across his dark coat as he shook his head. "That is a larger group than we normally handle in an entire summer."

"We shall manage," Ada said comfortably.

"Yes, well, I suppose we shall have to. We certainly can't turn them away." The pastor's gaze was hesitant. "Do you intend to carry on with more such rescues, Mr. Falconer?"

"If you will permit me."

He blew out his cheeks. "I can scarcely say no, can I now?"

"Indeed not," Ada said, her gaze still warming Falconer's bones.

"I've taken ownership of a farm north of here," Falconer said. "You may use it if you wish."

Ada said archly, "I thought you said you did not care to reside in these parts, John Falconer."

"I said merely that I was a stranger to this green and pleasant land, ma'am." He kept his eyes safely upon the pastor. "But the farm was never intended for my use."

"No?" the pastor asked.

"Not for farming, that is. I wouldn't know the first thing about that profession, honorable as it is. I just hoped it might be of use in freeing more slaves."

"Our own efforts have been hindered since the loss of Ada's husband, may God keep his soul in eternal peace." The pastor looked from one face to the other, then continued in a reflective tone, "There are other ways to help the cause of freedom than driving yourself to exhaustion, Mr. Falconer."

When the pastor had moved away, Ada said quietly, "I-I am glad to see you back, John Falconer. I and my son, as you have noticed." They exchanged smiles, then she continued, "How long will you be able to stay?"

"I must take charge of this farm before the week's end or lose my deposit."

"So when must you leave?" she asked again.

Before he could answer, Joseph came limping over. "Look yonder to the ridgeline."

Falconer squinted to where the westering sun made slanted blades of the forest tree line. There upon the high ridge stood a cluster of riders. Three of them held longbore muskets in the hands not holding the reins.

"I count nine of them," Emmett Reeves said, coming up to his other side.

"They don't seem to be making any move toward us," Falconer said.

"No, they wouldn't. Not if they're who I

think they are."

Ada asked the lawyer, "Who do you suspect them to be, sir?"

Reeves did not answer her directly. Instead he said to Falconer, "It appears you were right in driving us to exhaustion."

Falconer studied the ridge until the silhouettes wheeled about and disappeared. He looked over to see Ada watching him with deep concern.

Falconer said to Ada, "I must leave the day after tomorrow."

"But you need rest —"

"The road calls me," he said, pointing to the men no longer visible and the setting sun, then waving his arm toward his charges, now safe in Glory.

On the morn, Serafina returned to her work at first light. She paused for a Bible study with Mary and Gerald, the three of them lingering long over prayers for Falconer's safekeeping. Then her father appeared in his formal court attire, for he had received an official summons from the Austrian legate. As the invitation had been both public and formal, no one sensed any danger. Even so, her father was rather nervous. He had spent hours during a sleepless night trying to fathom the purpose behind such a summons.

Nathan returned later that morning. Serafina had offered to let him take the portrait of his mother the day before, but Nathan had seen her unease and said he would wait. He did not say that the portrait looked finished to his eye. Nor did he press her in any way. His last words upon departure were the same as those he spoke upon arrival. "I couldn't possibly take the painting until you were satisfied it was ready for outside viewing, Miss Gavi."

Serafina found herself wanting to confess her quandary. About a mystery she could not truly describe. About the challenge she felt to look *beyond* each work and see something else.

Instead, she asked, "Would you like to see my other works?"

Nathan glanced at Bettina Gavi, and they both registered surprise. "I would be most honored."

"One moment, please." Serafina returned to the dining room and began setting up her easels in a curving line that stretched across the entire room. She lifted the paintings one by one from their positions facing the wall before she took a step back and surveyed her work. Finally she called, "You may enter now."

Not even her mother had seen them all at once. Serafina fitted herself into the far corner and saw her two guests move down the line of easels. Yes, the paintings were both good and complete. If only . . .

Mary brought them tea, and they sipped standing before the easels. So it was that Alessandro Gavi found them when he returned, his two ladies and Nathan Baring, cups in hand, viewing the room filled with Serafina's paintings.

"There you are." Alessandro Gavi spoke from the doorway. "My dears, I have someone who wishes a word with our daughter."

"I am still in my day dress, Papa," Serafina said.

"I am sure the gentleman will understand." He nodded a greeting to Nathan. "Mr. Baring, how good to see you, sir."

"Good day to you, Mr. Gavi." Nathan's attention now focused upon the man entering behind Alessandro. "And to you as well, Herr Lockheim."

"Ah. Mr. Baring." Following her father was the legate's principal aide, whom Serafina recognized from her time at the palace. Dressed in full court regalia, his wig was freshly powdered. The polished gold buckles on his heeled shoes matched the brocade woven down both sides of his coat. He attempted to look down at Baring, though the American diplomat stood a full six inches taller. "The legate shall find your choice of company most interesting, Signor Gavi."

"Yes, well." Alessandro gestured to Serafina. "And this is my daughter."

"Ah. The artist in her garret." His patronizing tone was not lost on Serafina. "I shall have a look, if you please."

"But, Papa —"

"Of course you are welcome, Herr Lockheim." Alessandro gave his daughter a warning look.

"Thank you." As he swept by the trio, he fitted a monocle into his right eye. He took his time over the sketches and charcoal drawings arranged on the side wall. "Most interesting. I detect a certain level of experimentation, shall we say, that I would not have expected in one so young."

"Herr Lockheim studied art in Vienna," Alessandro explained. "He is here on behalf —"

"Allow me to complete my inspection before we discuss it further, I beg you."

"Of course, sir." Alessandro gave a slight bow which the prince's aide ignored.

Serafina felt resentment twisting her insides. But her father's unspoken com-

415

mand kept her silent.

Her drawings were displayed by subject. First came the sketches of her parents, both together and then separate. Then was a long row of Nathan's mother. After Serafina had begun work on the painting itself, she had returned to her sketchbook, working from memory, seeking the proper balance between the seen and unseen. The sketches showed a woman regressing in age from someone in the twilight of her life to fresh young maiden.

Drawings of the infant were even more varied, for they began in death and ended in laughter. Serafina had come downstairs several nights after the house was asleep, lured to her sketchpad by half-remembered dream images. Of a child who laughed and lived and gave joy to a family made whole once more. Of a place where no infant died early. Of a realm where she had a family of her own. And children. Where no Venetian liar had stolen her heart. Where all was well. Some of those drawings she had done with a feverish intensity, knowing she could never remake the world no matter how hard she struggled. Yet attempting it in her drawing just the same.

The fourth set of drawings belonged to her latest painting, the one she was just now in the process of completing. Gerald Rivens had asked Mary to wed, and Mary had agreed. Serafina was painting their portrait as a wedding gift. The mystery there had been the simplest thus far to determine. Her sketches showed a couple deeply in love. Their joy was so powerful it shone from the earliest drawings. Serafina watched as the legate's representative spent the most amount of time poring over these. In her second rendition of Gerald and Mary, she had drawn a hand. One appearing from a cloud-flecked sky, reaching down to bless the couple. In later drawings the hand became more ethereal, until it was a mere suggestion, seen and yet nearly invisible.

Herr Lockheim looked thoughtfully at Serafina, then stepped around to the easels and examined the paintings. The only sound in the chamber was birdsong and the ticking mantel clock.

Finally the man demanded, "Why watercolors, Miss Gavi?"

"It is my chosen medium."

"No other reason?"

"I wished to focus upon the faces. Upon the expression."

"And you have left the background utterly empty. Most interesting."

She fumbled with an explanation, for it

was the first time she had sought to express her thinking on this. "I sought to give life to the person, both exterior and interior. The surroundings were unimportant."

"Centuries of painters might disagree, Miss Gavi." For once Herr Lockheim's voice did not carry scorn. "But for an artist of such young years, I confess to seeing some promise in your work."

He glanced at Alessandro, then returned his attention to the easels. "Very well, Signor Gavi. You may proceed."

"My dear, the legate's wife, Princess Margarethe, wishes for you to paint her portrait."

"She has sat for some of Europe's finest artists." The condescension returned to Lockheim's voice. "A commission such as this could mean a great deal to a young student."

Serafina could feel the tension from both her parents. "I should be honored to try and do Her Majesty proper justice."

"Most wise. I shall contact you when the princess is available."

"One moment," Serafina said. "We have not yet discussed the matter of compensation."

Her father stiffened. "My dear, this may not be the appropriate moment."

"Listen to your father, young lady." The nose lifted. "I should think attending Her Highness would be recompense enough for someone in your station."

Serafina remained calm, quiet, respectful. And very determined. "In return for painting her portrait, I wish for Her Highness to help with a matter of crucial importance."

"And that is?"

"The legate, sir, has dispatched someone to pursue John Falconer. His name —"

"Utter nonsense!" The aide struck such a lofty pose his heels left the floor. "Scandalous!"

"His name is . . ." She turned to Nathan. "Mr. Baring, if you please . . . ?"

"Vladimir," Nathan offered immediately.

The aide sniffed. "You have been listening to stable rumors. I assure you, Miss Gavi. No such man exists. The legate does not lower himself to such underhanded —"

"In that case, a letter signed by Her Highness ordering a man who does not exist to return from a task the legate did not order him upon would be no cause for any alarm," Serafina countered.

The legate required a moment to struggle through that reasoning. "This is an outrage."

"These are my terms," Serafina replied. "Good day, Herr Lockheim."

■ ■ ■ ■

A subdued quality marked the household once the aide had departed. Bettina invited Nathan to stay for the midday meal, and he accepted with a similar distracted air. The few attempts to speak of anything mundane passed with little remark. Knives and forks clinked upon the plates. Compliments were paid. Thanks given. Otherwise it was largely a time of silence and introspection.

When coffee was served in the front parlor, Serafina confessed, "I keep having the most horrible dreams about poor Falconer. I carry a growing sense of anxiety through almost every day."

To her surprise and gratitude, Alessandro did not mention the demand she had made of the legate's aide. Instead, he asked Nathan, "Still no word?"

"Nothing whatever. I met with Reginald Langston again yesterday afternoon. His own connections south of Richmond are limited, so he requested the help of other merchants. So far they have heard nothing."

Alessandro Gavi bit fiercely upon his lip. "If anything has happened to the gentleman on my account, I shall never —"

"Please, Papa," Serafina implored. "I can't

bear to think it, much less hear the words."

"No, no, you are quite right." Alessandro struggled to form a smile. "I am certain the gentleman will see his way through."

"Perhaps . . ." Nathan began, then hesitated. He looked at Serafina.

She understood. "Yes, oh yes. Let us pray for him." She rose from her chair. "I will ask Gerald and Mary to join us."

Mary and Gerald Rivens rose from their quiet coffee in the kitchen and returned to the parlor with Serafina. She knew her parents were made uncomfortable by this public prayer outside of a church, but her father's half-spoken concern had fanned her heart's flames.

As Nathan began the prayer, Mary and Serafina clasped hands.

When Nathan finished, Gerald began his own pleading to the Almighty for their friend John Falconer.

When Gerald finished, Serafina could not join the *amens*, much less speak words of her own. Bettina slipped off the sofa to embrace her daughter. The two of them clung together. As Serafina's eyes cleared, she saw the confusion in her father's eyes. Along with the deep concern. She pried herself free and took the seat vacated by her mother. She embraced her father and said,

"It is not your fault, Papa."

"I should never have sent him on such a dangerous mission."

"You did what you thought was best. Falconer wanted this. Remember? He told us all that this was the work he was called to do."

Her father touched her face. "My dear, strong young lady."

"I don't feel strong at all. I feel the weakest person on earth today."

"What a wonderful young woman you are becoming. I wish I could tell you how proud, how delighted I am with you."

"Oh, Papa."

She felt her mother settle into place on her other side. "Falconer is a most amazing man. We can only hope he will soon return to us."

"We must continue to pray," she whispered.

Her father once more touched her face. "It is a remarkable sensation, I confess, to see this faith of yours." He looked beyond her to where Nathan stood by the far wall. "I have knelt in the finest cathedrals on earth. Never have I felt so close to the Divine as here in our little parlor."

CHAPTER 27

Falconer stayed in Salem for two full days. The second night the village held a celebration. The square before the church was turned into an outdoor banquet hall. Ada explained that the gathering marked the beginning of the new planting season. Every family brought a dish, and there was enough food for twice their number. Great pits were dug by the smokehouse, and a side of beef and two whole sheep cooked there on their spits. After dinner a harpsichord was brought from one of the homes, a dulcimer from another. Harmonicas and fiddles and even a reed flute soon joined the instrumentalists. The choirs sang apart from one another, not so much in competition as in distinct and separate harmony. First there was the farmers' choir, then one from the village of Barnstable, then Winston, then the bachelors, and then all the groups together. But the most joyful songs were sung by the visitors, led by Miss Hattie.

Afterward, when the entire congregation was feeling satisfied in every way, the pastor prayed for half an hour, asking the Lord's blessing upon the planting, the new arrivals and their travels north, the community, and on specific members who had ailments or special needs. The last name he mentioned was Falconer, asking first for safe travels and then for his safe return to Salem. When the chorus of amens ended, Falconer found several people watching him, Ada and Matt among them. Only then did he realize the full import of the pastor's final blessing. *Return to Salem* echoed through his mind and heart. He dared not look at Ada again.

Emmett Reeves made preparations to leave with the banker Grobbe and a half-dozen men from the bachelors' choir. The desire to help Theo Henning and the prospect of double wages paid in new gold coin encouraged the village elders to grant the men temporary leave. The sight of this strong band blessed by the pastor before setting off eased Falconer's worry over how Theo would fare at the Gastonia mine.

The next morning Falconer walked the length of the village. Ada joined him, while Joseph rode a dozen paces behind. Falconer was leading as fine a horse as any he had ever seen, much less ridden. Matt was sitting in the saddle and listened to every word his mother and Falconer said while his pup gamboled about the horse's feet. The gelding was on loan from the banker Grobbe, on the promise that Falconer would keep it safe and return it as swiftly as possible. Falconer needed no further reason to come back to Salem.

"How long will you be gone?" Ada asked at his side.

"Let's see," Falconer began, walking with the horse's reins draped over his shoulder. The chestnut mare gleamed like autumn gold in the morning light. "We must reach the Moss Plantation within three days to stay within his time limit. A day to complete the business, perhaps two."

"That could stretch into a week," Ada noted, a wistfulness in her voice that made Falconer want to embrace her on the spot. "And even then you probably will not be able to start back."

Falconer found himself unable to suppress a chuckle.

"You find that humorous?"

"No, Ada. I am laughing because of this tumult I feel in my heart."

Her upturned face was solemn. "You are thinking of the woman in Washington?"

"No again. I wonder at that, I tell you quite honestly." He looked down at her. "But just now I find myself only able to think about the woman walking alongside me."

She flushed and dropped her gaze. For a brief heartbeat of time their hands brushed together. Falconer felt a lingering fire long after she had stepped away to a proper distance.

Ada asked, "And after the farm you must go to Washington?"

"Yes. I have other responsibilities, as you know. The man who sent me on this quest is no doubt concerned by my long absence."

"The woman, Serafina — is it her father?"

"Alessandro Gavi. Yes."

"You will see the young woman again."

"Yes, I will." He wanted to tell Ada that it did not matter. But he could not until he stood before Serafina and knew the truth in her presence.

Ada did not respond as he might have expected. Instead she said, "I sat by my husband's grave yesterday. For a long, long time. I wondered at how I could still love that good man and yet now find my heart expanding, possibly for another."

"Ada —"

She halted him with a slight motion of

one hand. "I beg you to wait and speak when you can do so with an open heart and clear mind."

"Aye," he said softly, marveling at her wisdom. "Aye."

They said nothing more until they reached the village border, and Falconer lifted Matt down. He hugged the boy twice — once for himself and once more for what he wished he could give Ada.

Ada waited until he swung into the saddle. Then she gripped her son before her with both arms across his chest, in a manner that told Falconer she too wished to hold someone else. "Just tell me one thing," she said and could not keep the tremble from her voice.

"Yes, Ada. You don't need to ask. Yes."

She did nonetheless. "Tell me that you shall return, John Falconer."

Matt turned and buried his face against his mother's shoulder. Falconer said, "May the Lord our God keep you safe, Ada Hart." He took a breath to try and still the quake in his own voice. "You and your wonderful son. May He bless you and yours until I am back with you again."

"The only blessing I shall ask for, John Falconer," she said and wiped away a single tear, "is that you return swiftly home."

■ ■ ■ ■

The horses were far more rested than the ones who rode them. Three hours into the journey, Falconer's two days of respite in Salem vanished. The horse's gait jarred his very bones. No doubt Joseph felt the same, but the man made no protest. They left the Wachau Valley behind and soon came upon the stubby Virginia hills. Though the forest closed in and the trail narrowed, they made good progress. By the time they halted at midafternoon to rest their horses, they had covered more than their group had during two full days on the journey south.

The two men rode on until darkness threatened the horses' footing. They halted in a defile carved by floodwaters between the river and the cliff face, and ate a good meal from Ada's larder. Falconer stared into the fire, yearning after more than the woman's food.

Where the road broadened in the approach to Danville, they urged the horses to a trot. They saved half a day, perhaps more, by riding straight on through the town. They spent the night in a drovers' corral, then joined the Richmond Turnpike and pushed harder still, arriving at the Moss farm toward late afternoon.

At the point where the plantation turnoff met the road, Joseph pulled his horse up hard. He slipped from the saddle and stood easing his back and staring at the ground.

"Isn't this our turning?" Falconer asked.

Joseph raised his head to point at a stone milepost beside the plantation path. "For most of my life, that marker shaped the border of my world."

"Then why are we stopping?"

Joseph pointed at the ground by his feet. "Looks like a lot of folks been coming and going down the Moss trail."

Falconer slid from the saddle and studied where Joseph was pointing. He saw just prints of boots and horses' hooves. "Are you certain?"

Joseph squinted at Falconer. "You don't see nothing?"

"Ask me about the feather of wind upon high-topped waves," Falconer replied. "Tell me to read the portent of an approaching squall. But markings in road dust are an alien script to my eyes."

Joseph harrumphed once, then returned his attention to the road at their feet. "I count a whole passel of riders. Can't say for sho' how many, but it weren't that long back."

"How can you tell?"

"See there, the markings in that print?"

Falconer bent closer still and shook his head. "No."

"You can see the maker's mark on that horseshoe, plain as the nose on your face."

Falconer gave up, straightened, and looked up the empty road. "How would our hunters know to find us here?"

"Now you're askin' something I can't answer." Joseph's features tightened. "But I got me that creepy crawly feelin' under my skin."

"As do I," Falconer said slowly.

"What do we do?"

Falconer tightened the belt about his middle, as though it still bore sword and pistol. "We plan."

Falconer approached the Moss plantation with his senses on full alert. At a narrow stream that formed one of the orchard's borders, his horse dropped his head to drink. The fields seemed in far worse shape now, for weeds were the only crop he could see. Falconer looked over his shoulder and tried to spot Joseph back in the woods at the bottom of the hill, but he could see nothing.

They had made their way through the forest on the closest approach to the slave quarters. Joseph had left Falconer minding the horses and crept forward on foot alone. He was back soon enough, shaking his head and announcing the quarters were empty. Twice Joseph had given his one-word judgment over the state of the plantation land. "Evil," he said, shaking his head.

The house simply looked asleep to Falconer. Like the entire hilltop had elected to separate itself from the normal course of farming life and changing seasons. The paint still flaked and scattered. Rotting fruit still added a fermented tint to the air. The crows still cackled from the trees. But there was no other sound. No lowing cattle, no sound of activity from within the house.

After remounting his horse, he rode past the nearest outbuilding and entered the plantation's swept front yard.

"Anyone there?" Falconer's greeting drifted unanswered. He spied a shifting of the outbuilding's shadow. And knew he was not alone.

"Mr. Moss? It's John Falconer. I'm here to —"

"Oh, we know what you're up to." A vaguely familiar figure stepped around the corner of the front porch and stood with gun aimed directly at him. "John Falconer,

431

that what you said your name was?"

Falconer remembered where he had seen the man before. "You're that slaver. Saunders, is it?"

"And you're that man up to no good." Jeb Saunders motioned with his percussion musket. "Drop the reins and lift those hands up where me and my men can see 'em."

Falconer did as he was ordered, glad he had traded mounts with Joseph, leaving Grobbe's horse safely out of harm's way.

Two more men separated themselves from the outbuilding while another four appeared from either side of the house. All aimed weapons at Falconer. "I'm not armed," he told them.

"Dangerous way for an anti-slaver to travel these parts. Alone and unarmed." The musket motioned once more. "Drop out of that saddle. Nice and easy, now. I'll shoot you if I have to. You're worth more to me alive, but not enough to put up with any nonsense."

Falconer kicked free of his stirrups as rough hands pulled him from his horse. He managed to stay on his feet. Two men kept their weapons on him as another jerked his hands behind his back and tied him tightly. Another rope was laced around his ankles. Then a bearish-looking man with a heavy beard stepped out in front of Falconer. "Remember me?"

Falconer ignored Joyner's leer and watched as a man he recalled from his meeting with Saunders went through his saddlebags. The young man called up to the man on the porch, "The gold ain't there, Jeb!"

"Which means he ain't traveling alone after all. Cody, you saddle up and go hunt down this feller's friends."

The man sprinted toward the outbuildings as Joyner demanded of Saunders, "What gold are you goin' on about?"

"Why, the gold he done took from your mine." Jeb Saunders came down the plantation's front steps. "You don't reckon he'd just mosey on up here empty-handed, do you?"

"When were you gonna tell me about that?"

"You got a good-sized head on you, I reckon you oughta have brains enough to figure some things out on your own." Jeb kept his eyes on Falconer as he ambled over. "Yep, you're as big as I remember."

Joyner wheeled about and roared at Falconer, "Where's my gold?"

"Save your breath. I know this kind." Jeb's smile was as empty as his eyes. "He ain't gonna give you a thing but trouble."

"He don't look like much of a nuisance with his hands tied, does he?" Joyner turned back, his breath raspy with rage. "I got something for you, mister."

Falconer ducked the punch, or tried to, but Joyner's fist approached with the speed of a cannonball, connecting on his forehead with a force he felt to his toes. His entire body went numb. He sensed his legs giving way and noticed with mild interest the approach of the earth. He felt nothing, not even as he landed hard. Falconer fell into a pit without a bottom, and darkness was all around.

CHAPTER 28

Nathan Baring had begun stopping by the Gavi home after work. He did so with great deference, never wanting to bother the family and usually declining their invitation to stay and dine. He would come in and seat himself in a corner of Serafina's atelier. That was the one change to their house since the legate's aide had visited; no longer did anyone refer to it as the dining room. The table had even been moved into the parlor for their meals. Nathan would gratefully accept a cup of tea from either Bettina or Mary, then seat himself where he could view Serafina at work. That was his only request — that he might sit for a time and watch her paint. Serafina had been concerned that the man's presence would prove a distraction. Instead, there was comfort in his quiet sharing of the afternoon hours.

That particular afternoon, however, a knock at their front door announced a change to the quiet routine. Mary swiftly entered the room, round-eyed with astonishment. "There's a great fancy carriage as ever I have seen!"

Nathan was instantly on his feet. The knock came louder this time. Serafina followed Nathan into the front room, where Alessandro and Bettina both peered through the drapes. Nathan asked, "Do you recognize it?"

"I fear the worst." Alessandro dropped the curtain. "My dear, you and Serafina retire to the kitchen. Alert Gerald and the other guards." When his two ladies had moved down the hall, he pulled his waistcoat tight over his front and said, "All right, Mary."

But when Mary opened the front door, they all heard the officious voice announce in English, "Her Royal Highness, to see Miss Serafina Gavi."

Her Royal Highness, Princess Margarethe von Hapsburg, was a woman of such majesty that not even her diminutive stature could diminish her authority. She swept into the parlor, all four foot ten of her, her height augmented by a formal wig and shoes heeled in four inches of cork. She wore a brocaded gown with loops of genuine pearls on the bodice. Her powdered cheek was adorned with a painted beauty mark.

She examined the astonished gathering, then announced in heavily accented English, "I wish to see your body of work for myself, Miss Gavi."

"It-it is hardly a body of work, I must clarify, Your Highness." Serafina dropped a curtsy. "I have been laboring on it only for a few weeks."

"Nonetheless I wish to see what you are doing." She nodded to the others. "I request that you show it to me, please."

Once inside the atelier, Princess Margarethe ignored Serafina entirely. Her inspection took longer than that of the legate's aide. She spent a full five minutes in front of the portrait of the infant, then spoke for the first time since entering the room. "The child is dead?"

"Yes, ma'am."

"Who commissioned the painting? The parents?"

"No one, ma'am. That is, Mr. Baring's mother is a friend of the family. She asked me, in a way, that is . . ."

"Do go on."

Serafina took a breath. "She was very concerned about the mother, who is Mrs. Baring's maid. She asked me to attend the funeral and . . . and to do what I could."

The powder nearly masked the woman's features, but her eyes revealed genuine sympathy. "I should say you have done a very great deal, Miss Gavi."

"Thank you, Your Highness."

She moved on to the next painting. Her gaze rose to Mary, then returned to inspecting the watercolor of the couple. "These are servants?"

"And friends, ma'am."

"Yes, your affection for them is most evident."

"Your Highness," Bettina now asked, "would you take tea?"

"Thank you, Mrs. Gavi, but I shall not be staying much longer." She gathered her dress close to her so as not to brush against the easels as she returned to the center of the room. "So, Miss Gavi. I understand you have requested a rather novel form of compensation for your services."

"I meant no offense, madam."

"Is that so?" The princess glanced at Alessandro. "Your family seems rather adept at irritating my husband and his entourage."

Her father gave a formal bow. "Nothing could be further from our intentions, Your Highness."

"Nonetheless, it has happened." Yet the princess did not seem irritated. "Why is it,

438

Miss Gavi, that your parents have not arranged for you a marriage?"

Serafina considered several responses, yet the direct question left her unable to answer.

It was her mother who responded, "We did, at one point, madam. It was a mistake. A most serious one, I'm afraid."

"Then you are as wise a woman as your daughter is talented, Mrs. Gavi. My own marriage was arranged. It was deemed an important union between two rival clans. Everyone has been most satisfied by the results. Everyone, that is . . ."

The princess let the silence hang in the air between them for a moment. Then, "What is the name of the man whom my husband insists does not exist?"

"Vladimir, Your Highness."

She raised her voice. "Johann!"

The attendant stationed by the front door replied, "Your Highness."

"Bring the box with my husband's royal seal."

"At once, Your Highness."

She said to Serafina, "I assume you have proper paper and quill, Miss Gavi?"

Hastily Serafina fetched a sheet of woven paper, her finest quill, and the bottle of India ink. Nathan and her father led her out to the dining table and held the chair for the princess to seat herself. She wrote with a fair hand and signed with a flourish. She leaned back, inviting Alessandro to read the document. "I should think that would resolve any doubts which might arise," she said.

For once, Alessandro's emotions overcame his diplomatic polish. "I-I am speechless, madam."

"A candle, if you please."

Nathan was already bringing a candle over to her. She held a block of red sealing wax over the paper's right bottom corner. When a palm-sized puddle had formed, she accepted the royal seal from her attendant, who had returned from the carriage bearing an embossed rosewood box. She pressed firmly, then affixed a royal ribbon of Hapsburg gold and black and red to its edge. "That will be all, Johann."

"Yes, Your Highness."

When he had retired, she rose and handed the paper to Serafina. "Payment in full, Miss Gavi."

"M-madam, I-I don't know what to say."

"Say tomorrow, at eleven of the clock. As your presence is less than welcome at my residence, I shall return here for the sittings." The princess turned back to the sketches upon the wall. "I am curious, Miss

Gavi. Why have you not released the por-traits? They are clearly finished."

The moment would permit only total honesty. "Their full mystery is not yet revealed, madam."

"What mystery would that be?"

"I-I do not yet know."

She examined the younger woman. "How very interesting." The princess gathered up her skirts. "Until tomorrow."

On the fourth day after Falconer's departure from Salem, the clouds gathered and at dusk the storm struck. The seven travelers overnighting in the Fremdehaus were sub-dued at dinner. Perhaps it was the thunder and the torrential rain, but Ada did not think so. Her own somber demeanor the last few days had permeated the inn, or so it seemed to her. Even her son was less energetic and vivacious. Matt set to his nighttime chores as usual, but the smile was gone. When she came from the kitchen to call him to bed, she found him kneeling on the window bench, staring out at the dark and the rain.

Their private family rooms were on the top floor, directly under the eaves. The rain beat upon the roof like fists pounding a hol-low drum. An hour after Ada had locked the front door and retired, she heard her bedroom door creak open. A figure crept across the floor and hesitated by the side of her bed.

"It's all right, Kinderling," she murmured, calling Matt as she had done when he was very small. She pulled aside the covers. "Come get some rest."

He crawled into bed next to his mother. "Is he safe?"

Ada did not need to ask of whom he spoke. "Falconer is the strongest man I have ever met. If anyone can survive this storm, it is he."

With the comfort of her son beside her, Ada finally slipped into slumber. But the rain followed her, drumming in her dreams and leaving her filled with unsettling images. They came and went as though illuminated by mental lightning bolts, disappearing so fast she was not awakened. Until, that is, Ada found herself looking down upon Falconer crumpled upon a matting of rotten straw. Lightning flickered somewhere far away, creating stripes across his face, which looked horribly pale. And she was filled with a dread that echoed in the great rolling thunder that filled her dream and the room, a booming sound that rolled on and on and on.

"Mama!"

She awoke with a gasping cry.

"Mama!" Matt was standing beside the bed, shaking her by the shoulder. "Somebody is pounding on our door!"

She pushed herself upright and waited for her heart to calm. "Light a candle, please."

He scurried to obey. "Is it Falconer?"

She heard the pounding now. It echoed from far below, louder than the torrential rain still beating upon their roof. She forced herself to be calm for her son. "Let me slip into my dressing gown, and we shall go see."

Most of the doors along the middle floor where their guests lodged were open, revealing vague forms that caught the candlelight as she passed, but she said nothing to them as she continued down the stairs.

Matt was already standing with his hand upon the door's latch when she arrived downstairs. She clutched her robe up tight to her neck, took as great a breath as she could manage, and nodded to her son.

As soon as Matt unlatched the door, it flew open to reveal one of the village's night guards. He touched the rim of his dripping hat. "Forgive me, Mrs. Hart. But a rider came down from the hills with word I thought you should hear."

He stepped to the side so she could see

the dark face looking up at her from the base of the stoop. She clutched the stair railing. "Joseph!"

"They done got him, Miz Ada," Joseph groaned. He was clearly exhausted. "The bad men took him away."

Matt began to cry, and the sound pierced her own despair. She had to be strong. "Matt! Son, go light the fire."

"Mama, he says Falconer —"

"Listen to me!" Her voice was just sharp enough to help the young boy focus on the here and now. She moved forward, ushering the two men into her home. "We must dry these men off and feed them something warm. We will hear Joseph's story and then we will pray. And the good Lord will tell us what to do."

"We're wet right to the bone, Mrs. Hart," the guard protested.

"Which is precisely why you must enter right this instant. Take off your boots and leave them on the stoop. Where is your partner this night?"

"I already sent him for the mayor."

The mayor of Salem served also as the captain of the guard. "Very good. Now both of you, hurry into the pantry. Matt will show you the way." She was already climbing the stairs again. "I must go find something dry for you to put on."

Falconer found the rain to be by far the most difficult aspect of his imprisonment.

He endured the poundings in his skull, from Joyner's fist and from striking a rock upon falling. He accepted what they offered as food. He tolerated the cell's confines. He bore the endless hours. His timepiece was now strapped to the jailer's filthy coveralls, and his cell had no window, so his only means of counting time was the jailer's jangling keys as he made his hourly passage. This he endured as well.

But the rain was indeed a cruel torment.

The Danville prison was housed in a converted stable adjoining the town hall. Brick walls formed three sides, with bars fronting the central aisle. Rain poured through the leaky roof. The air was thick with moisture and mildew and other foul odors.

The jail's only other occupant was a horse thief who had been injured in his capture. After tending the thief's wounds, the doctor stopped in to visit with Falconer. The doc had him turn around to inspect the cut on his head. His touch was far more delicate than his voice. "It true what they're saying, you've been busy freeing slaves?"

"It is."

"Better work on your defense is all I got to say. You speak those words to the circuit judge, he won't have any choice but order you to dance from a noose."

"If that is God's will."

The jailer standing just outside the cell snorted his derision. "I seen all kindsa men go looking for God when it was too late."

Falconer waited as the doctor applied his ointment, then said, "It's never too late, brother."

"I ain't no brother of yourn, you can bet your life on that."

Falconer was not going to argue. "I would count it a great kindness if you would please bring me the Bible from my saddlebags."

"Weren't no bags brought in with you, just the clothes you're wearing and nothing else." To mock him, the jailer drew out Falconer's watch and flicked open the face. "You gonna be much longer, Doc?"

"Why, you got something better to do?"

The jailer grunted and walked away, keys rattling.

"How long have I been in here?" Falconer asked.

"Five days, and it's rained the entire time." The doctor motioned for Falconer to turn back to face him. "You got a fierce

446

lump back there. You say you'd like a Bible?"

"Sir, I would count it as a great boon."

"I don't like the idea of denying a man the Word. I'll see what I can do." The doctor walked to the door. "You strike me as an uncommon man. I haven't seen many in here who'd warrant a second chance. But when it comes your time to stand before the judge, I shall pray that our Lord finds room in His realm for a miracle."

"Thank you, sir." Falconer offered his hand. "Can you tell me when that might be?"

"Hard to say. The regular circuit judge has been taken ill. Word is, his replacement's tied up with a big trial off in Norfolk. I'll see what I can do about your Bible."

An hour or so after the doctor left, the jailer returned with dinner. The salt bacon smelled rancid even when cooked. Nevertheless, he accepted the tin plate and dug in, trying to eat and swallow before the taste hit his mouth. It was a trick he had learned as a child, and it served him well enough now.

The jailer hung about the door, watching Falconer eat. "Don't reckon you'd be chewing any harder if it was a steak."

Falconer finished the pork and washed the taste away with a cup full of water. "I've eaten worse."

"That so?"

Even from the distance of a few feet, Falconer could identify the source of the jailer's pungent breath — it was the sickly sweet odor of applejack, a brandy made from distilling rotten fruit.

The jailer asked, "Seen the inside of lotsa jails, have you?"

"No." The grits and collards he could eat more slowly. "This is the first time."

"Sorta interesting, you asking Doc for a Bible." The jailer used the weeping stone wall to scratch his back. "On account of how you got the look of danger about you."

Falconer set his plate aside and rose to his feet. He approached the jailer, who backed up swiftly. The jailer snapped, "You keep your distance, else you'll find ten kinds of trouble coming down on your head."

Falconer kept his voice calm. "Danger was the code I lived by, and fury my compass setting. But the Lord broke through and called me by name. He would do the same for you."

The jailer's laugh rang through the dripping cellblock. "We got us a preacher man locked up down here!"

"The Lord is calling you," Falconer repeated quietly. "And God is saying, 'Turn,

turn from your wicked ways. Repent and come to me.' "

"Then I reckon God's wasting His breath." The jailer's grin revealed more gaps than yellowed teeth. His breath wheezed a sickly odor of old wickedness. "My pappy always said I was infected with evil at birth."

"As were we all," Falconer replied. "Adam saw to that. Just as Jesus saw to our finally being made clean. Healed of the eternal stain."

"You got an answer to near 'bout everything, don't you?" The jailer was no longer smiling. "Here's one I bet you ain't figured out. How you gonna keep from dancing to the hangman's tune?"

Falconer watched the jailer's jangling departure. When the outer door clanged shut, he returned to his bunk. For the first time since his imprisonment, the rain did not bother him.

CHAPTER 29

Once again, Nathan Baring's mother recovered from her most recent spell of sickness. Nathan began arriving sooner at the Gavi home and staying longer. When Serafina put her brushes aside for the day, they took a turn around the square together. Not even the incessant rain halted their outings. For Serafina, these were the only times she was freed from her atelier. The princess's portrait was taking shape. Serafina had completed the sketches and now moved on to the larger sheet, penciling in the lines that her colors would soon begin to fill. Yet here the mystery was as oblique as it had been transparent with Falconer. The princess was not merely aloof. She presented to the outside world a cold, hard barrier, one built resolutely over years of bitter solitude.

Serafina did not wish to dwell upon the woman's enclosed nature. In her sketches, she had begun examining what *might* have been. Who this woman possibly could have become, given a different role in life. After all, the princess had merely by her coming revealed both a courageous heart and an independent spirit. She sought to remain her own woman despite all the restrictions and unhappiness that surrounded her. In return for the document bearing the royal seal, Serafina offered the princess the only gift she could.

She painted the woman with love. She sought to reveal the heart that might have emerged under different circumstances.

Serafina worked through the midday hour and stopped only when the princess said, "I must depart. I am required to attend a formal dinner for the French ambassador." As the woman spoke the clock sounded five times.

Serafina bounded to her feet. "Your Highness, I am most dreadfully sorry."

The woman actually smiled. "Did you not hear your mother warn you of the time?"

"My mother came into the room?"

"Three times. I signaled her away."

"Highness, I . . ."

"I have been observing you as you worked," the princess said thoughtfully. "It is uncommon extraordinary to see a young lady with such astonishing beauty be so totally given over to a profession that requires selflessness."

Serafina nodded her understanding but could think of no appropriate answer.

"Might I be permitted to see your work?"

"It is not yet finished, Highness."

"Nonetheless, I wish to see what you are doing with such focused intent."

Serafina backed away with a small curtsy. "If you wish, madam."

"Thank you."

As the princess rose and stepped around the easel, Serafina watched the woman study the painting. For long minutes she stood in silence, her expression giving nothing away.

Then the princess whispered, "Oh, to be faced with all the roads not taken."

"You do not care for it? Highness, I could —"

The princess silenced Serafina with an upraised hand. "You, my dear young woman, have a gift. It is not just a gift of the eye and the hand. Artists the world around have that." She faced Serafina, and her visage was unclouded for the very first time. "You have been gifted with a caring heart. And for your sharing of that unique gift, my dear, I am deeply grateful."

The princess swept up her dress and

moved toward the front door, where her attendant stood. She nodded her farewell to Serafina's parents, then stopped in the doorway and asked, "When do you expect to complete this work?"

"A week at most, Highness. Perhaps less."

"I shall count this among my most treasured possessions." She started to turn away, then added, "I only wish it were possible for you and I to become friends."

Night or day meant little inside the jail. The horse thief moaned over his injuries, until the jailer reminded him he was due to hang in three days' time. "You won't be bothering nobody's sleep much longer," he said with a cackle. Gradually the man's cell went silent, until the only sounds in the gloom were the sputtering torches and the constant drip of rain.

There were two jailers. The one who watched over them at night scarcely ever moved from his chair in the front room. The day jailer fed them and made his rounds with a surly sense of responsibility and dark humor.

Late that afternoon, the jailer returned to Falconer's cell. The man's greasy hair fell over his forehead, partly masking the intense gleam in his eyes. Falconer saw how the man had to fight himself to come forward, but said nothing. Falconer rose to stand before the bars.

The jailer's face contorted, and Falconer knew he wanted to joke, to curse, to scorn the prisoner and his faith. But the same force that dragged him forward kept the jailer silent. Instead, he merely handed the Bible through the bars.

Falconer accepted the book with a nod. He pitched his voice low, saying what he had been thinking about since the jailer's last departure. "One of the writers of this holy Book was a man named Paul. Some of what he wrote was sent from a prison just like this one." Falconer turned the pages as he spoke. "You'd think he would complain about being jailed for his beliefs. But Paul felt very different about things. Would you like to hear what he wrote to the church in Philippi?"

The jailer did not respond. Nor did Falconer expect him to. Falconer shifted the Book about until the torchlight falling through the bars illuminated the page, then read, " 'He which hath begun a good work in you will perform it until the day of Jesus Christ: Even as it is meet for me to think this of you all, because I have you in my heart; inasmuch as both in my bonds, and in the defence and confirmation of the gospel, ye all are partakers of my grace. For God is my record, how greatly I long after you all in the bowels of Jesus Christ. And this I pray, that your love may abound yet more and more. . . .' "

Falconer lowered the Bible. "He is imprisoned, yet he writes of *love* and *hope* and *joy.* What makes it possible for him to speak this way? Isn't that a wonder worth examining?"

Falconer came even closer to the bars. He could see the sweat glistening on the stubble covering the man's hollowed cheeks. Close enough to hear the ragged breathing and see the pain in his eyes. And the hunger.

"Every breath has fresh meaning for followers of Christ. Be it a breath drawn in prison or in the open air, it is still a breath of freedom." He lifted the Book into the space between them. "In Paul's earlier days, the Bible tells us that he went about breathing out murderous threats. That defined me as well. You know that is true. One look at my face and you know I've been where you are now, and still further into the pit. Now look at me. Jailed, stripped of everything, yet I still am able to breathe out my love of God."

The jailer's trembling tore his whisper to

shreds. "I done so much wrong."

"Tell God, brother. He wants to hear you and heal you." Falconer paused a moment, then added, "Will you let me pray with you?"

The jailer did not kneel. Instead, he came crashing to his knees. "I done so much wrong!"

Falconer reached through the bars and rested a hand on the man's filthy tunic. "Lord, O Lord, hear the call of this penitent sinner. He confesses his sins before you, and he is sorry."

"Yes, Lord! I'm foul! I'm sorry!"

"Tell me your name, brother."

"Carl."

"Brother Carl, do you confess your sins before God and man?"

The jailer gripped the bars so fiercely the cell door rattled. "Heart, don't fail me!"

"Do you ask the heavenly Father for forgiveness?"

The jailer raised his head a fraction, revealing his terror. "Will He give it to me?"

Only such a man as Falconer could meet that man's gaze. "Ask Him and see."

"Lord, O Lord, take away my awful sin!"

"Do you accept Jesus as your Lord and Savior?"

"If He'll take the likes of me, I do, I do!"

Falconer reached for his cup and extended his hand through the bars. "Then I baptize you in the name of the Father, the Son, and the Holy Ghost. Rise, brother Carl. Rise up. That's it. I embrace you in the faith, my brother. Yes. Now go and sin no more."

Jeb Saunders sat beside his brother Cody on the bench that fronted the tippling inn. Rain fell in a steady colorless sheet off the roof's overhang. Cody leaned back against the wall and snored gently. The man had an animal's ability to store up sleep. He acted when he needed to, and there wasn't anybody Jeb would rather have guarding his back in a scrap. But when there was nothing doing, Cody could ease his mind off the day as easy as a dog curling up in front of a good fire. Jeb had always envied his brother's ability to let the day go. Jeb was too much a thinker to take things so easy. And there weren't many days that had gone down as hard as these last few. Tied to a hardscrabble town like Danville, snared and held fast, they might as well be trapped in the same cage as Falconer.

A man stepped out of the rain. He thumped his boots to clear off the red muck, slipped off his slouch hat, and started down the wooden sidewalk toward Jeb.

Jeb whistled once. It was little more than a quick intake of breath, but enough to draw Cody from sleep. Without moving, his brother tracked Jeb's gaze to the approaching man. Cody remained leaning back, his eyes covered by the brim of his hat. His hand eased around to grip the handle of his pistol. Jeb heard the soft click of the trigger being pulled back.

The stranger approached them, his face giving away nothing. He carried with him a certain aura, of one who enjoyed bringing death.

He was neither tall nor particularly big. Yet his frame held a massive quality, a tension just waiting to uncoil and strike. "You must be the Saunders brothers."

Jeb couldn't place the accent. "That depends on who you might be and why you're interested."

"My name is Vladimir." His boots, trousers, shirt, vest, and hair were all one solid black. His eyes, however, were wintry smoke — almost clear they were so light. Yet they revealed nothing of the man within. Jeb had the impression of looking into windows without a room behind them.

"I seek a man," Vladimir said.

"Yeah, well, ain't nobody here but us." Cody slipped the cocked pistol from his belt and aimed it at the stranger's gut. "You'll be looking elsewhere if you want to see another sunrise."

Vladimir paid the pistol no mind. "I seek the same man as you."

"I'm telling you, that ain't of any interest to us, so you best —"

"Hold on, now, Cody. Hold on." Jeb smiled at his brother. His empty, dangerous smile. "This feller ain't done nothing to rile us. Not yet."

"I ain't sharing my take with nobody." Cody's response to the stranger was as visceral as that of an angry dog. "Especially the likes of him."

The stranger spoke with a raspy voice. "I have no interest in your reward money."

"There, you hear that?" Jeb nudged his brother. "Pack that shooter back where it belongs."

Reluctantly Cody slipped the pistol back into his belt. "He riles me, is all."

"Even so, let's hear him out."

"I will pay you," the stranger said. "In gold."

"That so." Jeb eased himself to his feet. He disliked looking up to anybody, especially when they were talking business. "Well, you know who we are and you know the man is holed up in the jail down by the town hall. Soon as the judge declares him guilty of freeing slaves and hangs him, we get paid. The problem is, the regular judge is laid up with something awful, and the new judge is busy at the other end of the state."

"The sheriff won't pay us until we testify," Cody complained. "So we're left sitting round here, with our gold in someone else's pocket."

"I have no interest," Vladimir said, "in waiting for this judge."

"That so." Jeb grinned once more at his brother. "Out for a little revenge, are we?"

The stranger did not respond.

"Well, maybe you can tell us one thing. Just to show we're dealing from the same deck of cards, you understand. What's the feller's name you're after?"

Vladimir spat out, "He is called John Falconer."

CHAPTER 30

The afternoon following the princess's final portrait sitting, Nathan and Serafina took advantage of a sudden break in the weather and walked for miles. They did not return until dusk was gathering. It seemed only natural for Nathan to let his boots dry by the fire and join the family for a light supper. He was not so much invited as simply included, the sort of gesture one would make to a long-time friend.

Their conversation continued until the candles burned low. Mary and Gerald had long since bid their farewells and retired to their respective chambers. The rest of the family remained in the parlor. The fire was ignored until it almost went out. Nathan went for more firewood and rekindled the flames, taking over the duties as if he had been part of the household all his life. Serafina was the only one who took any notice.

When the fire burned well once more,

Nathan remained on his knees before it. He said to the flames, "Unless we can pinpoint Falconer's location, the document supplied by the princess remains utterly useless."

"Worse than useless," Alessandro Gavi corrected. Clearly the same thought had been running through his own mind. "I feel as though a flame has been lit within me. I wish to go racing off with it."

"But in which direction," Nathan said, still to the fire. "For what purpose?"

Bettina made to rise. "I for one am so weary I can scarcely keep my eyes open."

"I could not hope to sleep," Alessandro said. His gaze was dark and so intent it was hard for Serafina to tell whether he was looking at Nathan's back or the fire or something only he could see. "Daughter, I would ask a favor of you. Before my wife retires, do you think we might pray again together?"

Serafina watched her mother sink back onto the sofa. "Of course, Papa."

"I am so distressed I feel as though I shall never find peace again without . . ."

"Without God," Serafina finished softly.

"Precisely."

"Would you say the words?" he now asked.

Nathan resumed his seat upon the sofa opposite Serafina, next to Alessandro, and nodded to her. "Your father asked you, Serafina."

She bowed her head, but no words came. She sought inside her mind and found the only words she could think of were in Italian. So it was in her mother tongue that she began, "O gentle Jesus, my Lord and Savior, the One who came to me in my darkest hour. O the giver of everything in my life that holds meaning, the maker of heaven and earth. I beg you, great Lord of all. Come to us now."

Her mother began weeping softly. Serafina went on, "We are very helpless, great Lord. You are strong when we are weak. Wise when we are blind. You search in the darkness of earthly pain and worry. You love us when we do not deserve it. You promise peace and wisdom and light. Illuminate our way forward, great Lord. Give us peace."

She heard a strong breath from across the room. She now changed to English. "Most of all, dear Lord, we pray for our friend. Our brother. The man who feels strongest when walking the path of danger. You know his name, great Lord. If I say it, I shall not be able to continue this prayer. So I ask that you speak the name for me. I ask that you find him and protect him."

Her father spoke then. A low sound with

a slight tremor. "John Falconer."

Serafina clenched her hands tightly. Still she prayed. "We ask for a miracle, great Lord. We ask you to reveal where he is. We ask that you keep him safe. We ask that you bring him home. In the name of your Son we pray. Amen."

She was slow to raise her eyes. When she did, she found Nathan looking at her. He spoke very slowly, "I have heard some of the world's greatest orchestras play the music of the ages. Never, though, have I heard a song quite so lovely as that."

Unshed tears created an illumination around his figure. "Are you weary?" she asked him.

"Tired, yes. Sleepy, no."

"Would you mind — would it be possible for me to do a sketch of you?"

Nathan seemed to find nothing out of the ordinary in her request. "If your parents do not mind."

"I have no interest in retiring," Alessandro said to his wife.

"Nor do I any longer," Bettina agreed. "Though I might doze off here upon this sofa."

Serafina rose to her feet. "I shall just go get my pad. No, don't move, Nathan. Don't move."

There was no mystery to this new sketch. Even before she finished outlining his eyes, she knew precisely what she wished to portray.

She sought to capture Nathan's balance between strength and weakness. Pain and peace. Hope and worry. Wisdom and human frailty. Earthly responsibility and child-like trust. Hidden and revealed. This equilibrium defined him.

Serafina finished the first sketch, dropped the page to the floor, and started anew. She rose to her feet, crossed the room, and retrieved the Bible she used for her studies with Mary. She handed it to Nathan and asked, "Would you please begin reading?"

"Aloud or to myself?"

Her father retrieved her sketch from the floor and said, "Aloud, if you please."

"Certainly."

Her father lifted his gaze. "Daughter, this is truly wonderful."

"Thank you, Papa. No, Nathan, you can look later. Just please remain as you are and read."

But as he began reading, she did not resume her sketching, rather stared at the empty page before her. Her hand was poised, but she was listening now to two different voices. One was Nathan reading the Word. The other was somewhere deep inside herself.

Falconer had asked her once if God ever spoke to her. She had considered it from the standpoint of her Lord imparting a message, not of God presenting a challenge.

She finally began sketching again. As she worked, in the drawing she saw her answer revealed.

The mystery was in herself. Not in her subjects, the people she studied and drew and brought to life upon the page. She was called to begin living *beyond* her past, its mistakes and pain. To accept that she *could* fulfill God's destiny for her life. In truth, she carefully looked within and realized even the wound was gone.

There was no reason she could not love anew.

She looked up at Nathan Baring across the room.

He stopped reading to ask, "What is it?"

She only smiled and shook her head, turning back to the sketch.

He asked, "May I see what you have done?"

She took the page from her father's hands

and offered it.

Nathan rose and came to stand beside her, looking at it a very long while. Finally he said, "Is this how I look to you?"

"It is most certainly a remarkable likeness," her father said. "She has captured you."

Serafina turned to look up into Nathan's face. The light in his eyes connected to a new light she felt growing within herself.

The process of farewells took a good deal longer than necessary, yet neither of her parents, still seated in the parlor, seemed to mind. Serafina stood in the front hall with Nathan near the front door.

She asked, "Would you care to take the portrait of your mother with you?"

"I could." He paused, as though the matter required deep deliberation, then said in a low voice, "But if I were to leave it, I would have an excuse to return tomorrow."

"You do not need an excuse, Mr. Baring."

His smile required no further words.

"Would you like to take the sketch of you?" Serafina wondered.

"My mother would be utterly delighted to see it. I would very much like to show it to her."

"I should be grateful if you would take

the infant's portrait with you as well."

"Do you not care to offer it yourself to the child's family?"

"I do not know them, nor they me. I should think it may mean more coming from your mother, the family friend who cared enough to suggest it in the first place."

He nodded thoughtfully. "You are as wise as you are lovely."

"Thank you. I must —"

A faint sound came through the open front door. Only then did she realize she had been hearing it for some time. A carriage of some kind . . .

Nathan stepped outside. Serafina followed and saw the flicker of torchlight. Across the square, a small two-wheeled carriage had pulled up in front of the church, led by horsemen bearing torches. The church's night watchman stood with his lantern hung from a long pole and addressed the leading horseman. Serafina saw the watchman point across the square to where they stood.

The horseman saw them then, spun his horse about, and shouted a command that carried across the square.

Serafina gathered her skirts and rushed down the stairs and across the night-dampened cobblestones as the horse pounded toward her. *Falconer!*

The horseman called out, "You are Miss Gavi?"

"Yes! Where is Falconer?"

In response the man turned and waved the carriage on. Instantly the driver cracked his whip and urged his two horses forward. The other horseman followed close behind.

Serafina and Nathan ran to meet them. Behind her she heard her father's voice calling from their front door.

The carriage drew up alongside her. Beside the driver sat a woman in a road-stained cloak. The driver was a burly man in a round-brimmed hat and a beard that spilled down over his chest. The woman was lovely despite the fatigue that strained her face. She looked at Serafina for a moment, then simply nodded her head.

Falconer awoke from his fitful slumber wondering what had changed. The absence of constantly dripping rain was as unexpected as it was welcome. Falconer dipped his hands into the water bucket and washed his face. He looked up, and sunlight speared the roof through the same holes where rain had fallen. Dozens of brilliant miniature pillars transformed the jail cell. Falconer stepped to the center of the room, standing in a puddle he had avoided up to now, and lifted his face to the light. He reveled in the blinding light and warmth.

He remained there until the jailer's keys announced his arrival. "Done turned nice for a change."

Falconer lowered his head and reached for the Book on his ledge. "I am a man born for waves and wind and infinite horizons. I have wondered if Paul himself ever yearned for earthly freedom while still praising God."

Carl had taken to stopping by when his shift was over, and again before he started. He came into the cell, dragged over a three-legged stool, and seated himself. "I reckon if a man ain't tempted, he ain't strong."

Falconer found himself chuckling as he sat on the corner of the bunk closest to the cell door.

"I say something funny?"

"No, brother." Falconer opened the Book to continue their reading from Philippians. "You said something wise."

Falconer's greatest sense of freedom came during these times of study. He had no idea how long they had been seated there when the other jailer clanked his way across the brick floor. The other jailer demanded, "Carl, what you still doing here?"

Carl was bent over with his forehead

against the cell bars so he could read the Bible that Falconer held toward him. He replied without turning around, "What I do with my free time ain't nobody's business but my own."

The other jailer had a girth so large it spilled across his belt in back as well as in front. Usually loath to shift his bulk from the chair in the front room, he now said, "Folks is talking, is all."

"What folks might that be?"

"Folks who got a mind to take away your meal ticket if'n you don't let the prisoners be." The jailer wheeled about and started back. "You know what's good for you, you'll mosey on home and forget this here nonsense. You got a hankering for religion, there's churches all over town."

Carl waited until the stout door leading out of the jail had slammed shut. He then lifted his head and said softly, "Something ain't right. I better go see what's doing."

"Carl," Falconer called, "don't put yourself in harm's way."

The jailer rose from his stool. "Ain't nobody ever done nothing for me my whole life long. Long as I can remember, I been classed as no 'count. Then here you come, talking to me like I was somebody *good*."

"Which you are. And I don't want to see

you in danger."

The jailer turned and left without another word.

Jeb stood in the shadows by the corner porch of the courthouse. The front steps descended into an unpaved sunlit square. This porch was used by court officials out for a breath of air, and it opened onto an alley. The jail blocked the far end. A wooden structure housing lawyers and land agents was tucked up close to the opposite side. The alley was shaded from the sun, but the heat was still fierce.

Jeb was studying the slat of empty sky overhead when the courthouse door opened. The large jailer announced, "Carl's finally letting your man be and coming out."

"That's good, Fred. You delivered just like you said."

The jailer tugged at his broad belt, clanking his keys. "You think mebbe I could get paid now?"

"You get paid the same as the last time you asked me," Jeb said, still talking to the sky. "You ever seen the like of this weather? One week it's winter. The next it's raining like Noah's flood. Now it's so hot we done jumped from April to August."

The keys jangled again. "I been taking an

awful risk on your account."

"And I'm paying you in good solid gold for your troubles." Jeb dropped his gaze and gave the jailer his empty grin. The one that showed anyone who looked that he wasn't going to be moved unless it was feet first. "You got twenty of my dollars clanking in your pocket already. So here's what you gotta do. Same as last time. Nothing's changed. You clear out the other jailer. You let my man slip into the back. In and out. Two minutes. When that happens, you get your fifty in gold. And not before."

"Th-there ain't gone be no gunfire," the jailer stammered. His jowls trembled below his face with worry. "Your man shoots off a gun, we gonna have ten kinds of trouble."

"No gun," Jeb agreed, though in truth he had no idea how this Vladimir was going to handle his little chore. "Now you get yourself back on inside and make sure the other jailer's done gone home."

He waited until Fred jangled his way back down the alley and disappeared into the jail before heading out into the sunlight. Jeb patted his hat down more firmly on his head.

The black-clad stranger was where Jeb had left him, leaning against the wall next to the hotel entrance, with Cody for company. Jeb didn't like the man any more now than he did when they had first met, but he had two hundred fifty of the man's gold dollars in his pocket, and the pledge of twice that amount again. Vladimir had promised to take care of both the jailer and the miner, agreeing to Jeb's demands with the languid ease of a man who had no intention of paying. Which was why Cody remained on guard beside him. Just keeping the man honest. And because Cody was there, so was Joyner. The enormous miner and his two remaining men stood farther down the porch, watching with sullen glares. Vladimir paid his watchers no more mind than he did the heat.

Vladimir did not turn from his inspection of the sunlight and the empty street as he asked Jeb, "What did you find?"

"Our man says the other jailer is finally getting fixed to leave."

Cody observed, "It was me, I'd be out of that place ten minutes before my shift was done. What's he doing in there anyway?"

Jeb was reluctant to say it, the words sounded that strange inside his brain. "He's reading the Bible."

The words brought both Vladimir and Cody around. Cody demanded, "Say that again?"

Joyner's nail-studded boots thudded across the porch. He was hot and impatient and ready for a fight. "You best not be trying any more of your tricks, Jeb Saunders."

Jeb ignored the miner entirely. He said to his brother, "The jailer's been in there with Falconer all this time. The two of them just sitting and reading from the Book." Jeb shrugged. "That's what our man's saying, anyway."

"This thing is growing crazier by the hour." Cody pushed his hat back and scratched his head. "Whoever thought it'd be this tough to kill just one man, in jail at that?"

"You better not be trying any tricks with my gold," Joyner warned again. "I got my eye on the whole lot of you."

Vladimir turned back to inspecting the sunlight and the dust. "We have company."

When Carl came back inside the jail, his face gleamed with more than perspiration. "There's something funny going on."

Falconer had faced danger so often he could not even count the times. Now, though, his highly tuned senses gave off none of the usual signals. Instead, he felt strangely calm. He looked around the cell. Blocked in on all sides, defenseless — as good as having his hands tied behind his back. Yet he felt no fear. Was this the day?

"They's a group of men down by the hotel. One of them had words with old Fred. I didn't see money change hands, but I can't think of any other reason why Fred would mosey down the alley in this heat."

Falconer only half heard the words. He realized with an idle curiosity that Fred was the other jailer's name. But his entire being seemed focused on something else. Another voice. A feeling of peace, an impression that someone else would do whatever was required.

"Last night I followed a stranger down to the hotel. Man all in black. He talked to others. They's trouble. I may not know much, but I know trouble when I see it, and I'm pretty sure they's out to get you."

Falconer took a deep breath, swallowed, looked down at the Bible he held in his lap. Power poured through the closed cover. He could feel it burning into him, clean as the sunlight streaming through the holes in the roof.

"When I started back, I spotted some other fellers. That is, they spied me."

"Others? Which others?"

"They spoke with a funny twang. Like foreigners or something. Got beards and

skin burned farmer brown. Wearing homespun and black coats. Ain't never seen the
likes of them 'round here before. They asked
did I know you. They asked for you by
name. John Falconer."

Falconer looked over at the wall. The
sense of rightness was overwhelming. "I
want you to go back out there. Tell the men
with beards there's to be no bloodshed on
my account."

"You listen to me now." Carl pushed his
face in tight between the bars. "Them fellers
down by the hotel, I don't know them by
name. But I know their kind. I spent my
whole life 'round the likes of them. They's
killers. They's guns for hire. They'll shoot
you fulla lead and not give it a second
thought. They're as dead inside as this metal
I'm holding." When Falconer did not respond, the jailer's voice rose. "I ain't gonna
let them do that to you!"

"If you're my friend," Falconer said quietly, "you'll go back and tell these newcomers that I am grateful for their being here in
my hour of need. If my time has come,
however, I don't want to meet my Maker
with more blood on my hands."

Carl stood there, his breath rasping in the
sunlit gloom. "You can't ask me to do this."

"I must." Falconer rose to his feet. "Speak

on my behalf. For the sake of a man who cares for you like a brother. For the sake of my eternal soul."

CHAPTER 31

Vladimir no longer showed his normal languid ease. Instead, he frowned and squinted and kept one hand hidden within the folds of his cloak as he watched the small group approach. Jeb reckoned anything that managed to break this killer's calm threatened his own chances of more gold. This time, when Cody stepped to the porch's railing and cocked his pistol, Jeb did the exact same thing.

There were four of them. Jeb did not know them by sight, for he had never been to their valley. But he had heard of them. And the fact that they had emerged was as weird as everything else about this strange hot day.

The lead man was a graybeard and carried a musket that probably dated back to the Revolutionary War. But he held it like he knew which end meant business. And the determination in his pale blue eyes was as harsh as any Jeb had ever seen.

The man looked at Vladimir and demanded, "I am here to ask only one thing. Whom do you serve?"

Vladimir found that humorous. "And what makes you think I should answer you at all?"

"Your words tell me all I need to know," the graybeard replied. "You name your master by the death in your eyes."

"If you see death, old man, you see the reason why you should run while you still can."

"You think I speak of the gun in your hand?" The man smiled, as did two of his fellows. "I do not fear you, servant of death."

Vladimir frowned in confusion. Jeb could see the man's mind scrambling, trying to work through words that did not translate into whatever tongue he had been born to.

"Don't pay them no mind," Jeb told him. "They's from Salem. Ain't that right, old man? What brought you out of your valley?"

The older man kept his eyes on Vladimir. "Go back to your world of darkness and shadows, servant of death. The one inside is a brother and a friend."

Vladimir turned to Jeb. "You know these people?"

"Know of 'em. They's anti-slavers, every one of 'em. Think they can hide away in their valleys like they're a law all them-

480

selves." Jeb aimed his ire at the one who seemed like the leader. Just looking at that old man left him feeling that the gold was slipping away. "There's change coming, old man. The lawmakers down Raleigh way are about to class you anti-slavers as renegades. Same as Virginia. You know what that means?"

"The future is the Lord's," the man responded. "There is evil enough for us to battle in this one day."

They stood on the porch and watched the four men turn away and proceed toward the courthouse. Joyner pointed across the street and said, "There's two more of 'em up on the roof there."

Cody added, "And another on the roof opposite the courthouse. And three more in a wagon on the square."

"I saw them." Jeb kicked at a cornerpost. "What are we gonna do now?"

"Falconer's still locked up," Joyner replied. "He's still up on anti-slaver charges. He's still gonna swing."

"I am not accustomed to letting others do the killing for me," Vladimir stated carefully. "There is risk that his allies will grow and he will be set free. This I cannot allow."

Jeb kept his eye on the square. "Who's telling you what can or can't happen, stranger?"

Vladimir ignored the question. "I have seen men like them before. Back in the old country."

"Where might that be, then?"

Vladimir ignored this question as well. "They cannot be bought, they fear little, and they fight hard." He turned to Jeb. "Can you find more men?"

"What, you gonna start a private little war in Danville's central square?"

Vladimir's gaze was as empty as the sky overhead. "If I must."

"Sure, I can get you more hired guns. But it'll cost."

Vladimir slipped a dark felt pouch from his inner pocket. He passed it over with the ease of a man who cared nothing for the contents. "The more men, the less risk these newcomers will oppose us."

Cody straightened. "Y'all just look over yonder there."

They looked out at the square, where a slight man hurried out of the alley that led to the prison. He headed straight for the graybeard.

"Ain't that the other jailer?" Jeb asked.

"Go to find your men," Vladimir said to Jeb. "And fast."

Carl came back to the cell as if he were going to a funeral. "I done told 'em what you said."

Falconer breathed a sigh of relief. "Thank you."

He dragged over his stool and settled it outside the cell. "Still say I shouldn't have done it."

"No. You did right. Who did you speak with?"

"Some old man. Got a gray beard near 'bout long as my forearm."

That could have been any number of the Wachau men. But Falconer guessed it was Joshua, the farmer he had met that first morning. The old farmer had remained concerned over Falconer's growing closeness to his niece. Ada Hart needed stability. Not some stranger with a scar and the fierce looks of a man who had carried such a past as Falconer.

And yet the old man had come.

Falconer passed his hand across his face. "Were there others?"

"A whole passel. All decked out in homespun and black." Carl lowered himself onto his little stool. "Won't do you any good.

They put their weapons down."

"Carl, look at me." When the jailer did so, Falconer went on, "What if my entire life has been leading me to this hour? What if my last task on earth was to talk about God's forgiveness with you?"

"Don't say them words," the jailer begged. "I ain't nobody worth dying for."

"What if Jesus wanted me here because I have been where you were and could reach you through our common past?" Falconer reveled in a freedom he had never known before. The freedom of laying down his arms, of letting go. "You are a brother in Christ. Who better than you should I give my life for?"

The man's features crumpled, and he put his face in his hands. "What do we do now?"

Falconer settled his elbows upon his knees. "We give thanks."

Vladimir surveyed the cluster of filthy men. "Where did you find these?"

"What difference does that make?" Jeb was pleased with his haul. "They're scallywags and gutter trash, the whole lot of 'em. But they got their own weapons. I checked. And they'll aim and shoot where you say, on account of I promised you'd pay each man another five dollars when the day was done."

Added to the two dollars in gold Jeb had already levied out, this was a staggering sum. More than most of this lot of herders and haulers and no-accounts had earned in a year. By Jeb's reckoning, he'd earned the other fifty in cash he'd pocket for the afternoon's efforts. "You wanted 'em," Jeb finished. "They're here. Now let's go finish the job."

Vladimir ducked his hands under his cloak and came up with more weapons. "Tell them to line up across the street."

"I'll play your captain, but I expect to get paid for it." Jeb gave little strength to the retort, though. Because his attention was captured by Vladimir's secret arsenal. In his left hand the man held a pistol whose entire length appeared chased in solid silver. At second glance, he noted two barrels side by side, like a hunter's gun. With two percussion caps and two triggers.

But the gun was nothing compared to the weapon in Vladimir's right hand. The blade was far too long to be called a knife, yet too short for a proper saber. What was more, the blade was crooked. Like an arm with the elbow bent. It grew broader as it approached the tip. And the edge was sharpened on both sides, the inner and the outer.

"What you got there?"

Vladimir smiled. It was the first time Jeb had seen the man show any expression at all. Jeb knew he had met his match when it came to a menacing grin. "Line up the men, captain."

The gang formed enough of a threat that before they rounded the block and entered the square, the area was deserted. Jeb heard somebody behind them shouting for the sheriff, but he paid it no mind. Unless they deputized the rest of the town's male population, the sheriff would be best off hiding away himself.

Vladimir marched before them. They were nineteen strong. The dusty, silent men laced out behind the man in black.

When they arrived at the entrance to the alley, there was one man blocking their way.

"Out of my way, old man," Vladimir ordered.

The graybeard was stalwart and stern. And unarmed. "I came with vengeance in my heart. But a better man than myself has ordered me to put my weapons down. A man I disliked and feared, if truth be known. I have been afraid he would steal away my niece and her lad I love like my own children. So I refused to speak with him. Though everything others said of him was good and godly."

Vladimir took another step forward. "You will not receive another warning."

The older man only raised his voice. "The one inside that prison cell is better than I. In his darkest hour, John Falconer has thought only of others and of God. He has brought one man to salvation and asked only that we go and save ourselves. How could I not do as he asked?"

"I'll take care of this loudmouth," Jeb said. But he did not step forward.

"I cannot face my niece if I fail her now. I will do as Falconer has asked. I have sent my men away so that they will not be sacrificed on your earthly altar to false gods and wrongful deeds. But I stand here to defend this good man with my final breath." He pointed a shaking finger at Vladimir and shouted, "You shall not pass!"

Cody nudged his brother. "Look behind."

Jeb hated taking his aim off the old man. But he glanced back and found himself being watched by a dozen men, perhaps more. They ringed the square, except for three men still perched on the roofs. "Where are their weapons?"

"Weirdest thing I ever did see," Cody muttered.

"Enough," Vladimir snarled. He spun the

blade so that it flickered like a deadly mirror in the sunlight. "You wish to die, old man? So be it."

But a shout halted the black-clad stranger in his tracks. The nineteen men wheeled about at the sound of a whip cracking like gunfire. They watched as the bearded men in homespun moved to either side of the road.

Into the square rode the strangest apparition in what Jeb had already called the strangest day in his very strange life.

The carriage was drawn by six black steeds, so lathered they looked mottled. Even so, it was clear these were the finest horses he had ever seen. But the horses were nothing compared to the carriage.

Dusty as the vehicle was, it glistened in the sunlight. Every surface was gilded, right down to the wheel spokes. A royal crest and a golden crown adorned both doors. The three drivers were uniformed with double rows of buttons shining brighter than the carriage. Out of the nearside window leaned a young woman whose beauty outshone even the carriage. Her blond hair looked white in the sun. Her headscarf was blown back across her shoulders. Her hair billowed about her. Her mouth was open, and she spoke with an accent that made her shouted words into a song, one of fear and outrage. And courage.

Behind the carriage galloped four men in dark official-looking suits, bearing the stern expressions of professionals. Long before the lathered horses were reined in, the men Jeb had gathered were already drifting away. It was one thing to play hired gun against an untrained, overmatched foe. It was another thing entirely to face an enemy not only trained but armed with authority.

The carriage door opened and the blond woman scrambled out. A man appeared behind her and shouted, "Serafina! No!"

"Where is Falconer? What have you done to him?"

The first man leaped from the carriage, then a second man, this one younger and bearing the same authority of the men still on horseback. "Serafina!"

This time she halted.

"You must come back!"

She returned to the carriage, where a fourth and final person emerged. Another woman, this one in a feminine version of the clothes worn by the men now crossing the square toward them. The remainder of Jeb's posse faded away into the dust and the heat as the young man sheltered Serafina behind him and declared, "These men are federal marshals! I have a warrant to take custody of one John Falconer."

The first man to have emerged from the carriage walked toward the man in black and declared, "You must be the one known as Vladimir."

"And if I am?"

The man was well padded and better groomed. A man used to fancy front parlors and sending others off to do his bidding. But he now trembled with fear and the trip's exertion, though he stood his ground. "I bring you a document bearing the seal of the legate Prince Fritz-Heinrich von Hapsburg. Ordering you to return to Washington and cause John Falconer no harm. In fact, it orders you to *protect* him."

Vladimir made his weapons disappear, then held out his hand. He unfolded the document, read it, then carefully inspected the seal. "It appears genuine."

"More than appears. It is."

"In that case, my business is done." Vladimir refolded the document and started across the square.

Joyner shouted after him, "What about my gold?"

Vladimir gave a careless wave at the carriage and the entourage. "Ask them."

The gray-clad woman spoke for the first

time. She looked ill with fatigue, yet her voice was the clearest sound Jeb had heard all day. "Where is John Falconer?"

"In the jail."

"Take us to him!"

Jeb let the homespun army shoulder him aside. They bore no arms, but he wasn't about to make trouble while federal marshals glared at him. "Come on, Cody. Let's hit the trail."

"But what about our gold?" he whined.

"There ain't none." Jeb found himself too worn out to pay Joyner's answering snarl any mind. "Don't ask me how, but that feller in there bested us. He's been locked up and a hair's breadth away from the noose, and still he took us down."

Joyner growled, "We shoulda shot him when we had the chance."

"Woulda, coulda, shoulda." Jeb was suddenly so tired he could hardly place one foot in front of the other. "We done lost. We got to fold our cards and get out while we still can. That's all there is to the telling."

CHAPTER 32

Falconer stumbled as he crossed the jail's threshold, but there were hands at the ready to steady him. His jailer Carl. Ada Hart. Serafina Gavi. Ada's uncle. Alessandro Gavi. Nathan Baring. "Please, you're not going to want to touch me" was all he could think to say. "I need a bath."

"You're alive," Ada said. "God be thanked. Are you all right?"

"Fine." He blinked in the overharsh light. "I'm going to be fine."

"God be thanked," she repeated, reaching a hand toward him but stopping herself.

Falconer saw the look Ada gave. First to Serafina. Then to him. And understood it was not his filthy state that forced her to hold back.

He smiled slightly, then said to Ada, "You look awfully weary."

"As she should," Alessandro Gavi said. "She came all the way to Washington and then refused to remain there until we knew that you were safe."

"Your man Joseph would have come as well had we not all ordered him to stay," Nathan told him. "And he only agreed when I insisted that he would endanger us and our mission if we were accompanied back into Virginia by a freed slave."

Serafina said, "Nathan Baring woke up a federal judge in the middle of the night to obtain the warrant for your release."

Her father added, "And Serafina obtained an order from the legate's wife, stamped with the prince's own seal, ordering Vladimir to leave you alone."

Falconer's head spun with the confusion of so many details at once. He had no idea what they were talking about. And it did not matter.

"Well, my deep gratitude to you all. What now?"

"You must go to Washington," Alessandro replied. "Where the judge will decide if the case against you has merit."

"It does not and he will immediately dismiss all charges," Nathan said with confidence.

"And after that?"

"You're free to do as you please."

He looked at Ada. "Where is Matt?"

"With his grandmother on the farm."

"You must go back to him. He will be sick with worry."

She searched his face with eyes that held words her mouth would not shape. "And what of you?"

Falconer looked at Serafina. He saw a beauty that could not be denied. But that one look was enough for him to know she was not his to claim. Nor, in truth, did he any longer wish to do so.

He turned back to Ada. "Soon as I am able, I will come home."

ABOUT THE AUTHORS

T. Davis Bunn is an award-winning author whose growing list of novels demonstrates the scope and diversity of his writing talent.

Isabella Bunn has been a vital part of his writing success; her research and attention to detail have left their imprint on nearly every story. Their life abroad has provided much inspiration and information for plots and settings. They live near Oxford, England.

1/16/09
Noted pgs. 57-58 wrinkled